GHOSTS

Also by G X Todd

Defender
Hunted
Survivors

GHOSTS

GX TODD

First published in Great Britain in 2021 by
HEADLINE PUBLISHING GROUP

2

Cataloguing in Publication Data is available from the British Library

Hardback ISBN 978 1 4722 3320 2

Typeset in Bembo by Avon DataSet Ltd, Arden Court, Alcester, Warwickshire

Printed and bound in Great Britain by Clays Ltd, Elcograf S.p.A.

Headline's policy is to use papers that are natural, renewable and recyclable
products and made from wood grown in well-managed forests and other
controlled sources. The logging and manufacturing processes are expected to
conform to the environmental regulations of the country of origin.

HEADLINE PUBLISHING GROUP
An Hachette UK Company
Carmelite House
50 Victoria Embankment
London EC4Y 0DZ

www.headline.co.uk
www.hachette.co.uk

For Cath.

I hope we're friends until we die.

And then I hope we become ghost-friends
and walk through walls and scare the shit out of people.
It's gonna be *great.*

STIRRINGS

Seven years ago

Matilde

This would be the last time Matilde visited town before the killings broke out in earnest. The parking lot, which accommodated a run of five stores and a laundromat, held a handful of cars at 10.47 that morning.

She pulled into the handicapped space nearest Pets-U-Like, cranked her window down three inches and shut off the car's engine. She sat for a moment, arthritic hands loosely hooked over the steering wheel. To any casual observer, she would've simply been an old woman fortifying herself before braving the cold. To anyone who truly knew her – which maxed out at a total of two people besides herself – Matilde wasn't fortifying herself, she was listening intently to something only she could hear. She nodded a time or two, grunted, and turned in her seat to her companions. It was an awkward half-turn because she was bundled up in thermal underwear, sweater, cardigan, a scarf-and-hat combo and a winter coat that reached all the way to her knees. The old woman knew deaths were coming – she'd been told so many times over the past few days – but she had no intention of dying of pneumonia.

'Sit nice and quiet for me now, my darlings,' she said to the dogs in the back seat. Her voice held the faint trace of an accent. Austrian, maybe, or German to a discerning ear (or a Nazi-inflection to the more bigoted ones).

The two Dobermans silently regarded her, one panting, tongue lolling out of its mouth, the other with its head cocked as if perfectly understanding its mistress and planning on being the best boy ever.

'I will be five minutes. You will be good for *five* minutes.' Puffs of mist accompanied her words.

The climb out of the car was done with more sprightliness than might've been expected from a woman of her advanced age. She was aware of one particular car parked right at the back of the lot – a brown Chevrolet sedan, nine years old – its driver sitting motionless behind the wheel and staring at the pet store's frontage, but she didn't spare the car or its occupant a glance. He was a stranger to her and would always be a stranger to her. Instead, she trooped to Pet-U-Like's entrance, boots crunching on the salt-sprinkled asphalt, waited for the automated *beep-whoosh* of the door to open out of her way and stepped into the temperature-controlled warmth of the interior. She wiped her feet on the welcome mat (it had pawprints of all shapes and sizes marching over it), stomping them twice for good measure.

The store was an assault on the senses: the smell of dried pet food and sawdust, and the squawk and chatter of parrots, budgerigars, cockatiels, parrakeets and finches in their *clink*ing wire-framed cages along the back wall.

The young man behind the counter wore a name-badge pinned to his red polo shirt, too far away to read, but Matilde was a recognised if infrequent visitor, well known to the staff, and they to her.

'Morning, Miss Matilde,' Jacob said.

As soon as her name was spoken aloud, the twittering birds fell silent, eerily and completely. If you were to wander to the back to check on them, each might have had its shiny dark eyes turned all as one, directed towards where the newcomer stood.

'How do you *do* that?' Jacob asked and, as with all the other times, his bewildered awe never failed to raise a smile in the old woman.

'Magic, my boy. Do you have my order?' She clomped over to the counter on thick-soled boots, unwinding her scarf as she went. Her clomps were substantial and heavy, her features lined but lean. The bulk of her multilayered wardrobe disguised the fact that she was a slender but well-built woman, seemingly well into her late seventies. The fact she was one hundred and six years old would have had many claiming her to be a bald-faced liar.

Jacob gestured to the platform trolley off to the side stacked high with sacks of dog kibble. At eighteen, he was oily-haired and oily-skinned, with an unfortunate combination of acne and shaving rash blotching his throat and neck; the hair condition would dog him through to his mid-twenties, the skin condition less so.

'Ready to rock 'n' roll,' he said, and began ringing up the purchase. 'You're taking a lot with you this time. Almost cleaned our stock out.'

'I won't be coming down off the mountain for a while,' Matilde told him as she counted out a wad of bills.

He cast her a curious glance but didn't ask any questions. Being the sole progeny of the town's Baptist minister, Jacob's politeness for his elders had been cultivated from a young age. Besides, Matilde was a quasi-recluse and kept largely to herself. Most people were happy to exchange pleasantries with her, but conversation of any depth rarely passed between her or her fellow townsfolk. The old woman was adept at playing the crazy-old-lady card, enough to keep most people at bay.

Today, however, she broke tradition.

'What time does your shift finish, dear?' Her arthritic fingers were unusually deft as she accepted her change, tucked it into her overstuffed billfold and shoved it back into her coat pocket.

'My shift?' Jacob asked, the only sign of his surprise a slight widening of his eyes.

'*Ja*. What time?'

He blinked. 'It . . . It's a half-day today, so I close up at one.'

'Very well.' The old woman gave a decisive nod. 'You will go straight home, yes? No loitering about, as you young people are wont to do.'

'Er, sure?' He gave her an odd glance as he shrugged into the fleece jacket that hung from the back of his chair, locked the cash register and came around the counter. He grabbed hold of the trolley's handles, ready to follow her out.

The old woman didn't move, blocking his way. She would never tell the young man that she liked the way he chatted to the birds as he put out their food and mopped the floor in front of their cages, and Jacob would never tell the old woman how much he liked her dogs – not because they were cute or well behaved but because they seemed to love her so much, their adoring eyes following her without deviation whenever she was in sight.

'You must promise me you will go directly home,' she insisted, not budging, even when Jacob leaned into the trolley's weight and glided it a few inches towards her.

For the first time, a faint smirk curled the young man's lips. It died a quick death when she scowled at him.

'You *will* go home, Jacob,' she snapped. 'Do you hear me?'

'Y–yes, ma'am.' She so rarely called him by his name that her use of it now set his heart pounding in his chest. It wouldn't be until later, when he was sitting at the kitchen table, a bowl of cereal for lunch before him and the TV on, that he would see the local and national news reports start to roll in; they would continue to roll in throughout the rest of the day. And the day after. And the day after that. A school shooting over on Sycamore. A runaway bus barrelling through the fast-food joint near the town's only gym. The massive explosion in the electrical store adjacent to Pets-U-Like. By two that afternoon, all the birds would be dead, burned alive by the fire that would sweep through the pet store. (If there had been a police investigation – which there wasn't and never would be – officials would have discovered that the explosion had been caused by something man-made and viciously inventive.)

'I swear,' Jacob repeated, when the old woman still didn't move out of the trolley's way. 'I'll go straight home.'

With a final nod, Matilde went ahead of the young man to open her car's tailgate. He lifted sack after sack of dog food into the back. The dogs didn't watch him, they watched their mistress, and their mistress watched the sedan parked at the rear of the lot. It hadn't moved.

'Jacob, there isn't much time left.'

He hefted the eighth bag. 'I'm moving as fast as I can,' he grunted.

'No. I do not speak of dog food. I speak of the voices. They are, Lord help us, beginning to wake up.' She said it softly, never taking her eyes from the stranger in his car. 'And more will start their whisperings. You won't understand what that means yet, but you will. Perhaps you will even hear one yourself, and you must try to not be afraid, my boy. To be afraid is to fear death, and fearing death is a pointless thing. It comes for us all and, at least, this time, it serves the greatest of purposes.'

The young man had transferred the last but one bag of dog food and had straightened up. He mirrored the dogs, staring at the old woman, and she in turn stared at the man, who was now exiting his car. He didn't approach them but began pacing back and forth in front of it. His head was turned, his dark, unblinking gaze fixed on Jacob and Matilde.

Without saying a word, Matilde opened the rear door to the car and both dogs immediately jumped out. They came to stand guard on either side of their mistress, ears pricked, hackles raised, their attention now firmly on the man, who had stopped his pacing and was facing their way. The Doberman nearest Jacob growled deep in its chest.

'Easy now,' Matilde murmured. 'Let him make his choice.'

'Who *is* that?' Jacob asked.

'I have no clue. And I suspect he doesn't know himself at the moment.' Her voice dropped lower. 'Yes, yes, I see it. I see he is listening . . .' Frozen in her staring match with the strange man, the old woman could have been speaking directly to him, or even to the young man beside her, but in reality she was speaking to herself and to the unseen part of her that listened back. 'Such a long life I've had. Far too long for such a simple woman as me, but we must hang on a little longer, mustn't we? We must decide on what to do for the best. To help or to hide. *Ja*, I know, a little of both might work, but it will be so hard for them at the start. So very, very hard.' She sighed, a sound so sad and resigned it puffed a long stream of fog from her mouth. 'You will talk to Jonah, won't you? You made a promise to each other.'

The young man was confused and didn't try to hide it. The chill that scurried across the nape of his neck had little to do with the frigid air. 'Jonah? Is that the man over there? You said you didn't know him.'

Matilde smiled faintly. '*Nein*, dear boy. Jonah isn't someone you can see. The same as who I was talking to just now isn't someone *you* can see. But they are real, regardless. The voices in the dark, whether visible or not, will be more real than any of you are ready for, I warrant – as they are for that poor gentleman over there.' All smiles had faded from her lips. 'Oh, dear me, this is not going to end well.'

The man in question had taken up his pacing again, his strides quick and agitated. His mouth was moving, angry words spitting out as he raged, his head shaking back and forth.

Both dogs were growling now, steam rising from their muzzles.

'What's wrong with him?' Jacob whispered, his voice quavering. 'Should I call the cops?'

'No. I suspect he is one of many by now. The police will be too preoccupied to be much help to us.'

The old woman moved a single step forward, both dogs shadowing her, their heads lowering, growls getting louder. The stranger stopped in his tracks, sending a nervous glance their way. Two seconds passed. Five. Then he jerked into motion, hurrying back to the driver's-side door and clambering inside, slamming it shut behind him. He didn't drive off, but he didn't reappear either. He sat motionless again: a dark, still shadow in the interior of his car.

'Finish packing for me, *Sonnenblume*,' the old woman said quietly, her attention never wavering from the sedan. 'You need to lock up soon and go home. Yes?'

Jacob hastily murmured his agreement and finished packing the last bag into the car in record time.

Jonah

Frank was eighty-three years old and ready to die. Since moving into Sunny Grove, he had been diagnosed with early-stage dementia. Frank didn't have dementia – he had no serious medical conditions outside of angina (and a particularly painful case of gout in his right big toe). He wasn't depressed beyond what any octogenarian would be who'd outlived a spouse and two children and was stuck in a retirement home, and he wasn't an overly religious man who was eager to meet them on the other side. Frank was simply tired of living. He was eighty-three years old and ready to die, but not before he'd won one last game of backgammon.

Sunny Grove's common room was a tableau of the advanced stage of ageing, which was to say it was occupied by predominantly slow-moving, slow-talking, slow-thinking senior citizens whose families had dumped them there for fear of their own lives becoming tragically burdened. Ninety-five per cent of the room's occupants were seated in comfy tall-backed chairs and were in varying stages of lethargy and sleep (some merely napping, others enthusiastically sawing away at logs). At a tortoise speed painful for any observer to watch, a tiny old lady, frail as a baby bird, shuffled her way across the room with the aid of a walking frame. She paused by Frank's backgammon table, wheezing through her mouth. He had picked this table because it sat alone in the bay window, affording him a little privacy and a truly lovely view of the outside gardens in the late-afternoon sun.

Beatrice's rheumy eyes were owlish behind her spectacles. She dropped them to the games board he'd set up. 'Want me to whup your ass again?' she asked him.

Frank's smile was polite but stiff. A mild antagonism had grown between the two after he had repeatedly caught her cheating at gin rummy. 'Thank you, no. I'm waiting on someone.'

'On *Jonah*?' She said it snarkily, because she knew it would rile him and in her old age she had discovered that annoying others was a fun way to pass the time. She guffawed at her own joke, almost losing her top denture in the process.

Everyone in the retirement home knew about Jonah. Frank spoke to him all the time – it had always been easiest to speak to him out loud. Which was a problem when Jonah couldn't be heard by anyone but Frank. With Frank's diagnosis, Jonah had become a figment of Frank's dementia, a long-lost relative conjured from Frank's past who appeared only to him. What none of them understood was that Jonah was as real as any of the snoring old coots lounging around the common room or pottering in the garden, and that Jonah had lived inside Frank's head for nigh on four decades.

For Jonah, Frank wasn't (and wouldn't be) his first or final home. Jonah had lived an unfathomable number of lifetimes, had shared history with men and women, princes and politicians, spent time with the rich and the poor alike, but revealing such information at Frank's next doctor's visit, or to any of the carers, would result only in an increase in medication and both Frank and Jonah wandering the corridors as a drooling, mindless zombie for their remaining days. And now was *not* the time for Frank to be anything less than clear-headed.

Jonah was as ready to die as Frank. More so, in fact, for he had seen every form of kindness and brutality the human race was capable of. He had lost more loved ones than had been written about in the epic poems and was more tired than every single elderly person in every care and retirement home in the world. But the world was about to change in new and terrible ways, the people in it brought to a brink that no one but a handful could foresee. And Jonah was one of them. He sensed the coming change like a dog sensed a storm.

But, first, backgammon.

'What's all this, then? You teaming up on me, Frank?'

The cheerful-sounding woman standing behind Frank's chair was slim, young and disarmingly attractive. Her buoyant youthfulness was like a beacon in a place filled with such infirmity and illness. She brought a blazing light that spread a revitalising energy throughout the common room. At the sound of her voice, a number of residents woke from their naps and offered the woman friendly greetings and waves.

'Beatrice was just leaving,' Frank said pointedly, staring stone-faced at the little bird-like woman bent over her walker.

Beatrice gave him a toothy smile. 'He's a sore loser is what he is. Doesn't like being bested by a woman, that's what I think. You be sure to give him what-for, Ruby dear.'

'Will do, Mrs P.' Ruby gave the older woman a jaunty salute and placed a turquoise-coloured teacup on the table by

Frank's elbow. The aroma of strong black coffee wafted up.

Beatrice shuffled away from them and Ruby removed her jacket and placed her handbag on the floor. 'You're always so awful to her,' she said as she took the seat opposite.

'She's a bitch, that's why,' Frank muttered, keeping his voice low. Beatrice had bad eyes but her ears were bat-sharp.

'Frank!' Ruby laughed. The smile lingered on her lips, but her eyes grew serious too quickly.

They silently went about making their first dice throws and moves. Three moves in, Frank spoke under his breath.

'Did you bring it?'

She didn't look up from the board. 'Hm. In my purse.'

Frank took a sip of coffee while he considered his checkers. They both knew he wasn't allowed coffee, but neither said a word as he enjoyed a second, longer sip, smacked his lips and sighed in contentment.

Ruby's smile reached her eyes again. 'Good?'

'Yes, ma'am.'

'It's my mom's favourite blend.'

'I can understand why.'

Ten more minutes went by. Frank and Jonah watched the girl. She was quiet today, far quieter than usual. Friday through Sunday evenings were Ruby's set work shifts at the home, but she had come in early today, purely to indulge Frank in a game. For eight months and three days she had worked at Sunny Grove and it was on her third evening that she stumbled across Frank at 2.34 a.m. in the kitchen, illuminated by the glow of the open refrigerator. He'd been halfway through removing the makings of a cheese sandwich. (He didn't sleep much these days – a side-effect of having Jonah – and had almost as much energy as Ruby did, despite his years.) After a good-natured argument about the recommended fat intake for people with known heart conditions, he had spent the rest of her shift accompanying her on her rounds while eating said sandwich, and they had chatted like two old comrades. It had become their routine during those hushed, sleeping nights – although he had graduated from a cheese sandwich to turkey. Healthier for him, she claimed. They were similar in a lot of ways, not least in their shared love of board games, ghost stories and sandwich fillings.

'I'm not sure about this, Frank,' Ruby said, her hand hovering over one of her checkers.

'You're winning. Don't take mercy to an old man now. Go in for the kill.'

She paled and grimaced, drawing back her hand. 'Is that your attempt at a joke?'

On the table her hand had curled into a fist, and Frank covered it with his larger one. His was strong and tanned, with a sprinkling of grey hairs on the back. Where his fingers were callused and cracked (overused and under-loved), her hands were pale and slim. Unmarred. Like the rest of her. But not for much longer.

There was regret etched in Frank's face, but there was determination, too. 'No, love,' he told her softly. 'Of course not. Everything will be fine. You must trust me.'

She wouldn't look at him. 'I do, but there's no going back from this, and I just—'

A squeeze to her hand silenced her. 'It's a miracle you're here – that you and your brother found your way to me. To Jonah. You realise that, don't you?'

She finally met his eyes. Searched them.

'Without you and Albus,' Frank said, 'Jonah would have chosen to die with me here. I'm not someone who believes in Fate, Ruby, but I don't think it was by chance that you and I met when we did.'

Ruby turned her hand over and gripped on to his palm.

Frank cocked his head, listening intently to something, and then glanced around the room. Following his example, Ruby did the same. Most of those who'd awakened at Ruby's arrival had dozed back off, blankets tucked over their laps. At some point, a carer had entered and turned on the large TV set in the far corner. It blared a cooking show at high volume. Huddled in the double-wide doorway, two female staff members were whispering to each other, their heads close together. One appeared as though she'd been crying.

Frank lowered his voice anyway, leaning over the table. Ruby mirrored him, moving closer.

'Jonah will explain better than me when it's time, but right now all you need to understand is that a ripple effect has been started. The way I see it is the whole world has been holding its breath since the very first day we stepped foot on this land. Such a long while it's been holding its breath, waiting to see what we'd do with the life we'd been given, and it's been holding it for so long it began to suffocate, wanting nothing more than to let it all go. Instead it built and built and built, and we . . . We wouldn't ever let it just *breathe*. We did the exact opposite, in fact. We smothered it.

'Jonah has played witness to so much of what's happened. Him and Matilde – another old-timer like me who hears a voice as I do. And a third. One that remains nameless to them, though he's gone by many: Trickster, Meddler, Deceiver. They have survived to bear witness to all our victories and shortcomings, have played their parts time and again, enlisting help when needed from people like you, like Albus. And now the three of them are *here*. On the same continent for the first time since the very beginning. And the world has finally – *finally* – released its breath.'

Ruby sat transfixed. 'And the voices?' she whispered.

'They're coming,' Frank said with a finality that made the girl swallow. 'And there's nothing that you or I or Jonah can do to stop them. We *shouldn't* stop them. It's not our place to. But we must prepare for what will happen afterwards. That's what we have to do now.'

Her hand had remained cold despite the warmth of his encasing it.

Frank nudged his half-empty cup aside and pushed his chair back, releasing her. The game was over.

'Bring your purse,' he told her, and rose.

Ruby followed the old man from the common room, his gait hitching, his limp pronounced. His head cocked for a second time and he nodded, murmured a thank-you, and in two more steps his limp eased out and disappeared. He walked tall, as a man half his age. He went directly to room number forty-two, opened the door and went inside. The room was light and spacious, tidy, with the bed neatly made and countertops cleared of clutter except for a cluster of family photographs on a bedside table. But those details were unimportant now.

Frank turned and held out a hand. 'I'll take it now.'

For the count of five, Ruby stood motionless, frozen in place, then she reached inside her bag and brought out a cloth-covered package. It was heavy and bulky enough to overhang her hand. Frank accepted it from her.

'Thank you,' he said, and reached up to give her hair an affectionate muss. 'Thank you for all those turkey sandwiches and for giving this old man your time and companionship. Go on now. But don't go too far.'

'I remember,' she whispered, but didn't leave. First, she spent a long moment committing his face to memory, exactly as it was – the crinkles at his eyes, his smile, everything. She didn't want to forget. Then she left the room and went to the cleaner's closet that backed against Frank's room, nothing separating them but a single wall made up of timber, plasterboard and a modest layer of mineral fibre for insulation.

Six minutes later, a single gunshot rent the air and, despite expecting it, Ruby jumped where she sat and began to cry.

Hari

Seven years before he would earn the name the *Flitting Man*, the small boy watched the two sisters from across the street. They had a nice set-up. On their hands and knees outside their single-storey house, a case of sidewalk chalk passed back and forth between them as they created a masterpiece of art in pastel pinks, purples, blues and whites on the end of their driveway.

They sported identical stone-washed-denim jeans and collared white T-shirts. The slightly bigger girl wore her blonde hair in a ponytail and the other – a darker blonde – wore hers in pigtails. Some days, their father would fondly call them Ponytail and Pigtails, accompanied by playful tugs on said -tails. The girls had been disrupted in their sidewalk art only once, when their father had returned in the family car and pulled on to the drive. The girls had squealed happily at the car's honk, skipped out of its way and scurried back into place once it had passed, like disturbed ants returning to a piece of abandoned fruit. The dark-haired man who had climbed from the vehicle had offered a brief, preoccupied greeting to his daughters, thrown to them from over his shoulder as he'd banged his way indoors.

'Can I have the purple chalk already?' Ponytail was complaining. 'You've had it for *ages*.'

Neither girl noticed when the boy crossed the street, slipping from in between parked cars, and sidled closer.

'I'm not done yet,' Pigtails said. 'Can't you use the pink?'

'I don't *want* the pink, I want the purple. I'm trying to draw the unicorn's horn and it *needs* to be purple or else it won't look right.'

Pigtails huffed and passed the purple over. 'Here. Be quick.'

Ponytail snatched the chalk, bent, her tongue tucked into the corner of her mouth, and got to work.

'Hello.'

Both girls' heads popped up, and they stared at the boy as if he'd jumped out of the sewer grate.

'May I draw with you?' he asked.

The sisters exchanged a look. Ponytail, the bolder of the two, was used to being the designated spokesperson. 'Who're you?' she asked.

The small boy, brown-haired and brown-eyed and slender as a blade, placed a hand over his heart. 'I'm Hari. I live not far away.' He nodded up the street to nowhere in particular.

'How old are you?' the older girl asked suspiciously.

'Seven. How old are you?'

'I'm nine,' she said self-importantly before jabbing a thumb at her sister. 'My sister is seven.'

'Seven and a half,' Pigtails corrected.

'Can I draw with you?' he asked again. 'Please?'

Another look between the girls, and Pigtails shrugged. The bigger girl gave Hari the up-down, her eyes roaming over his button-up shirt and freshly pressed slacks. She didn't appear impressed by what she saw.

'OK. But you can only do yours over there.' She gestured to the sidewalk off the end of their driveway. 'And you can't use any of the pinks or purples.'

'OK,' Hari agreed, walking over to the girls and crouching down. 'Can I have the . . . red, white and yellow?'

Pigtails carefully handed him his chosen colours and Hari accepted them with a thank-you. He studied their chalk pictures before standing up. The girls had drawn a smorgasbord of misproportioned animals – unicorns, a zebra, pink and pastel blue ponies wearing bonnets with flowers in them, and a puppy with a big purple bow on its head. There was no scaling to the animals' sizes. The puppy was twice the size of the zebra.

'They are good,' Hari lied.

Pigtails smiled brightly at him. The older girl showed him her teeth. There was a marked difference in their expressions.

Hari carried his chalks to his designated spot and got to work.

'You talk funny,' Ponytail said after a few moments, not looking up.

'Hm,' Hari said, distracted by a tricky part that he wanted to get just right. 'I am not from America.'

'Where you from?' Pigtails asked, eyeing him with the pure, uncensored curiosity that only children possessed. 'Kansas?' She had recently become obsessed with *The Wizard of Oz* and now believed everybody she had never met before hailed from Kansas and had seen a hurricane up close. That would be her next question if he answered in the affirmative.

'I was born in Yireh Shalem.'

Pigtails' button nose screwed up. 'Where's that?'

'In Asia.' Hari added more red in a hard, enthusiastic scrub.

'Huh,' Ponytail said, unconvinced. She focused closely on adding wings to her unicorn. 'Why'd you move here, then? Did your parents make you?'

'I have no parents.' Hari sat up, head tilting as he perused his drawing. 'There. I have finished.'

'*Already?*' Ponytail said, scowling as she straightened. 'I don't believe you. Lemme see.'

Both girls came over to him and stared mutely down at Hari and his picture. He explained what they were looking at. 'Here is you,' he said to Pigtails. 'And you . . . I am sorry, what is your name?'

In a faint voice, the bigger girl told him her name.

'This here is you,' he said to her. 'Your mother is over here by the front window. And this man, standing above you, is your father. See? I have used the brown chalk to colour his hair in dark, like the man who returned in the car.'

'How'd you know our sofa was yellow?' Ponytail asked.

'What . . . what's all the red for?' Pigtails asked, as if not entirely sure she wanted to know the answer. Her older sister had grabbed her hand and had pulled her protectively back, away from Hari and his chalk drawing.

'That is blood,' Hari said, and smiled up at them. He had a nice smile. Friendly, he would be told on many an occasion.

A resounding crash sounded from inside the single-storey house, as if something heavy had been thrown against the wall. What could have started out as a scream was abruptly cut off, so quickly there might never have been a scream at all.

Hari got to his feet, tutting at all the chalk smudges on his pants.

'*Girls!*' Their father bellowed, out of sight but very much heard. '*Girls, get in here right now!*'

Both girls flinched, heads swivelling to face their home. Through an open window, the drapes in the front sitting room waved lazily in the breeze; their deep forest green would be a nice match for the summery yellow fabric of the sofa and armchairs inside.

'*Girls, don't make me say it again! COME HERE.*'

'Your father is calling you,' Hari told them. 'You should go before he gets angry.'

The sisters, clasping hands, started up the drive. Their sneakers scuffed over their chalk drawings, Ponytail's right foot smudging through the head of her unicorn, turning its horn into more of a purple-bruised lump than a spiked protuberance.

A minute later, after the girls had vanished inside, more muffled crashes came from the house, the shattering of crockery or glass, and something more piercing, more human. Hari didn't look back as he strolled away down the street. His hands were stained red with chalk-dust, but he didn't bother to wipe them clean.

The Last Letter of Ruby Mae Hartridge

August 31st, Sunday (Seven years post-voices)

Dear Albus,

Forgive the hurried scrawl – Jonah and I have composed many letters over the past eight years, but this is by far the hardest (and also the one I have the least amount of time to write). It is a goodbye when I don't want to say goodbye. It is a wish in words when I would speak it to you with my lips. But we often can't have what we want, Albus, so we work with what we have. And I have pen and paper.

Oh, Al, forgive us. We have willingly sent something terrible your way. I wish we could come to you, explain everything to you, but we are both far beyond that now. You are on your path, and Jonah and I are set on ours. The world is spinning out and we are all spinning with it. When it stops and scatters us to the dirt, I fear where each of us will land. Some things are unknown even to me. Especially to me. For too long, too many of us have looked only to ourselves. We tread on others to reach for our own selfish wants and needs. So much greed and cruelty. So much entitlement and indifference to the suffering of others. It is past time for it to end.

Jonah and I have also come to an end, Al. We knew this day would come. I go with love in my heart. Such a powerful, all-consuming love. For you, for the friends we've met along the way, for the friends I'd yet to meet. I think that's all that matters in the end. That we love and be loved, even though we've suffered so. It will be what binds us. Not hate or envy or fear. But there are more sacrifices to come, brother. Dreadful, heart-breaking sacrifices. And betrayal. Such betrayal my heart breaks for it. But first we must hold fast to what we love, because that is what he seeks to tear from us.

Did I ever tell you why he is called the Flitting Man? It's not, like he thinks, because he seeks to be so prevailing as to be a part of all minds, all eyes, all ears, all hearts. No, he is called the Flitting Man because he is but the flitting of a shadow, brief and passing. He will not be remembered as anything more than a frightening bedtime story, lost to dreams of a happier place.

All these years and all these letters I have spent wishing for a future that is brighter than the past we made. We're all allowed to fail, Albus – there is no shame in it – but in failing, we must pick ourselves up and strive to do better. In any and every way we can. I hope you understand that and can one day forgive me for my failings.

Never forget how much I love you.

Your sister, always. And your friend,
Ruby and Jonah

THE LOST PART

Arrows

Amber

Two days ago

By the age of fourteen, Amber considered herself a veteran of death. It had visited her in all its many forms. She honestly wondered if there was anyone left alive in the world who wasn't a veteran, like her.

The old deaths were the most common, of course. The ones who'd died in the early days, when those creeping, whispering voices had tickled into ears, invading homes as well as minds. These corpses were now rotted and desiccated, shrunken down into something sad and lonely and forgotten. They littered the world, accumulated in gutters, heaped at the sides of roads after the cleaning crews ceased their work. They piled around the bases of the highest tenement blocks and office buildings. In rivers and along coasts, floating like the spilled contents of sunken container ships, their journeys given over to the whims of the tides. They lay like discarded children's toys in yards and driveways. And when they couldn't be seen, Amber knew they were there, lying mouldering in their beds, turning to soup in their bathtubs, hanging from the beams in attics and garages, or laid out side by side on the concrete floors of basements. Father, child, mother. Parents bracketing their little ones in a last effort to comfort and protect. Over time, Amber had started to marvel at the infinite variations in which death had visited these places. The dark imaginations of people hadn't failed, even when everything else had.

Old, stale death didn't scare her so much any more. It was toothless and impotent. It was the new kind, with its wetness and foul smells, that brought fear. Violence lingered. Trailed its invisible fingers down her skin and breathed a chilled whisper down her neck. *Soon, girl,* it said. *Soon it'll be your turn.*

That kind of violence only ever came at the hands of the living.

Amber shouldn't be scared. From where she stood, statue-still, in the Inn's front parlour, she could hear the clatter of crockery from the back of the building, the *chop-chop-chop* of vegetables and the distant buzz of Bianca's and Cloris's conversation as the two women prepared dinner in the kitchen. They were homely sounds. Comforting. This place was safe. Had been for all of the six weeks Amber had been staying here. Yet her heart beat a dull, rapid thud in the hollow of her throat and the material of her sundress plastered itself hot and sweaty to her skin.

She stared at the man standing at the far end of the Inn's yellow-bricked driveway. He'd been there for almost four minutes now. Amber knew this because she'd counted the seconds off in her head – one Mrs Sippy, two Mrs Sippy, three Mrs Sippy, four.

He hadn't done anything. Hadn't raised a hand in greeting, hadn't even shifted his weight from one foot to the other. In all appearances, he posed no threat. But it was his motionlessness that didn't sit right with her. Normal people don't just stand there and do nothing. Normal people fidget, or scratch their butts, or rub their noses.

Amber's toes clenched. She desperately wanted to go get Bianca but was afraid that, if she took her eyes off the man, when she returned, he would be gone. And losing sight of him seemed somehow worse than not raising the alarm. Losing sight of him would be *bad*. She was sure he couldn't see her; she stood to one side of the large picture window, behind the heavy drape, peering around so that only one of her eyes showed.

She could hear Jasper's distant gurgling from the kitchen, too, now, doing his baby-best to join in with Cloris's and Bianca's discussion. A call would bring the two women hurrying to see what was wrong, Amber knew this, and yet when she opened her mouth her vocal cords were as motionless as the man outside.

'What're you staring at?' said a voice in her ear.

Amber startled away, one hand swatting at the space next to her head, finding and slapping a bony shoulder. Mica frowned quizzically at her, one hand rubbing at the spot she'd hit. He was a little older than her, but they stood head to head, height-wise. Bianca had once laughingly asked Amber if she had been putting horse muck in her shoes to make herself grow faster. Amber had been confused by the comment (they didn't have any horses at the Inn), and her confusion had made Bianca laugh all the more.

'You've been staring out the window for *ages*,' Mica said, peering over her shoulder.

Amber immediately looked back at the driveway, fear tightening through her stomach when she found it empty, just like she'd feared. She searched the trees, the hedgerows, eyes moving with a quiet panic, but the man had slipped between the invisible folds of the world and vanished.

'No,' she whispered miserably.

From the corner of her eye, she felt Mica's suspicious gaze turn on her. She could tell from the sudden faint curling of his lip that he probably thought she was pulling a prank on him, even though she'd never once pranked him *or* his stupid brother.

'There's nothing out there,' Mica said, and what could she

say to that? It was true; there was nothing but the unmarked bricks of the driveway, the deep emerald of the grass and the softly swaying trees and hedgerows that lined the property. She should tell Mica what she'd seen, but Mica thought she was crazy. She knew this because she'd overheard him say so to his brother. Deep down, she knew they didn't mean to be cruel – they were just boys who thought they understood everything yet understood nothing much at all. She wasn't crazy or crackers or cuckoo.

She left Mica where he was and went to the kitchen. She walked fast, her shoes *click*ing on the bare wooden flooring. After a pause, louder clomps came from behind as Mica quickly followed.

The smell of baking bread made her traitorous stomach clench on a pang of hunger. Bianca stood at a chopping board with a large paring knife, dicing bell peppers. Cloris was at the centre island, carefully cutting slices from a freshly baked loaf. The bangles on the older woman's wrist jangled as she sawed. Jasper sat in his high-chair, a toy car in one chubby fist and a whole host of plastic toys strewn on the floor around him where they had been tossed. Amber instinctively moved to him, placing her hand on the warm, silken hair of his head. He blinked up at her, lips pursing and blowing a spitty raspberry in welcome.

'Hey, you two.' Bianca greeted her with a warm smile, teeth beautifully white in her dark-skinned face. From the first time she'd seen it up until now, Amber felt something infinitesimal relax in her insides. 'Just in time to set the table.'

Amber's mouth had half opened, ready to spill the words she urgently needed to say, but Bianca's words forestalled her. Amber closed her mouth, swallowed dryly, glanced at the bare table where they usually ate and stepped out of Mica's way as he came past, grumbling under his breath, to collect the place mats and cutlery from the drawers.

Amber couldn't do it. She couldn't tell them. They would think she'd been imagining it, was being silly and—

'You OK, hon?' Bianca asked, knife no longer chopping but hovering over half a waxy green pepper.

'*There's-a-man-out-front*,' Amber blurted, saying it in a single breath, rushing it out so she couldn't call it back halfway through.

There was a beat of surprised silence. None of them was accustomed to Amber saying much more than a 'yes, please' or a 'no, thank you' or a 'hello' or a 'goodbye'. Unless she was talking to Jasper, who was her little buddy.

'Out front,' Amber repeated. 'A man. I saw him. Standing at the bottom of the driveway.'

'Just now?' Bianca asked, the question as sharp as the knife she held.

Amber nodded.

'Cloris, take Jasper.' With that, Bianca left the peppers on the chopping board and came across the kitchen, knife in hand. She swept past Amber, going out through the kitchen door, calling back over her shoulder. 'Mica, go get your brother. Be quick now. And bring the bows!'

Amber shared a look with Cloris – the woman's painted eyebrows were higher than ever, almost disappearing into her greying hairline – then Amber was hurrying after Bianca.

She hadn't gone to the picture window but walked straight out through the front door. Amber found her at the top of the porch steps, knife held down at her side, in full view of anyone who was looking.

They were in the habit of leaving doors and windows unlocked during the day – the Inn was so far off any main thoroughfare that passing traffic wasn't a concern. You had to know this place existed to find it. Now, all those unlocked doors and windows felt like an invitation, a calling card to anyone who wanted to wander inside, to take whatever they wanted, *do* whatever they wanted. Why hadn't they prepared better, put up some defences, locked down the ground floor? Why had Amber thought she'd be safe here? She wasn't safe. Nowhere was safe.

Fear, like a winter wind, blew through her.

In less than a minute the boys had returned with their bows – not children's playthings but fibreglass constructions with precision sights – and Bianca was directing them to split up and perform a perimeter sweep of the Inn. She had already ordered Cloris to take the baby upstairs and barricade themselves in Jasper's room.

'Is that necessary?' Cloris asked.

'I am *not* debating this with you, Cloris. Please just do as I say – go on upstairs and barricade yourselves in until we holler the all-clear.'

Cloris nodded to her, said, 'Be careful,' and headed back inside.

Bianca waved Arun to come along with her to the right, but it was Cloris who Amber watched. A swift stab of protectiveness jabbed into Amber's gut as she watched the older woman climb the wide, carpeted staircase with Jasper in her arms. The boy gazed back at Amber over the woman's shoulder, burbling something around the little fist he had stuffed in his mouth. He was always trying to talk to them. He was getting so big.

Only Mica sharply saying Amber's name brought her attention back to him.

'Let's go,' he told her. 'Stay close to me.'

She followed after him as he tromped defiantly ahead of her, his feet grinding and crunching into the yellow-gravelled pathway. The path wound its way along the southern side of the Norwood Cove Inn, a four-gabled, three-storeyed hotel that boasted thirty-plus rooms with green-slatted shutters on their windows, white-railed balconies supported by impressively large white columns and enclosed verandas front and back.

The Inn's white-wood cladding rose in a huge bleached wall

on Amber's left. It should have felt like a shield, like something solid and protective towering over them, but it didn't. It loomed, shading them in a gloom that made her shiver. Amber glanced up at the windows, expecting to find the stranger she had seen staring down at them, having somehow gotten inside their home, his unblinking gaze tracking them as they passed below him.

The window was empty, of course.

She winced at the gravelled crunch of Mica's stomps. He was making so much noise. She wanted to tell him to stop, to be more careful, this wasn't some boys' game he and his brother were fond of playing, but her voice remained locked up small and tight behind her tonsils. She stepped on to the grass verge, shoes sinking into its lush, green carpet, silencing her footfalls. Mica continued his noisy tromp, holding on to the carbon-fibre bow. It looked too big in his hands. He'd already knocked a yellow-flighted arrow, ready to loose. Amber had watched him and his brother practise firing their bows down on the beach, their wild and heady laughter riding the ocean's breeze as they'd run to collect their arrows. She knew it made him feel brave, that weapon. Too brave.

They passed the covered pile of chopped wood stacked against the Inn's southern wall, ready for fireplaces and wood burners. Her feet *shush*ed on the grass; Mica hiked his pants up one-handed, the weight of a large binoculars case clipped at his waist dragging at his jeans. A warm tickle of air touched the back of Amber's clammy neck and the skin between her shoulder-blades grew taut and squirmy.

Eyes burned into the back of her head, but she couldn't turn to look. She kept her gaze on Mica, considering the slight kink in his hair with more focus than it deserved. If she looked back, she'd see that too-still man, nearer, staring at her. Then, every time she chanced another glance back, he'd have halved the distance again, transported silently closer, though she'd never see him move.

She found herself squeezing her muscles *down there*, her bladder pinched and shivery. She had to clench her teeth to stop them chattering. She ached to say Mica's name, to make him turn around so *he* could be the one to spot the stranger who was so close behind them now. She gripped the sides of her skirt in her clammy palms.

Mica swept his bow over the enclosed vegetable garden (Amber could see the lemons peeking out at them through the chicken-wire fencing), then stepped clear of the path and did a slow circle, panning around to look at her. His eyes widened and Amber whimpered quietly.

'What's the matter?' Mica asked. 'You look like you've seen a ghost.'

He looked straight at her and only at her. His eyes didn't flick over her shoulder, didn't see anyone else. *Turn around, chicken*, she told herself. *Turn around and see for yourself. There's nothing to be afraid of.*

She forced her neck to twist, her eyes to swivel.

The pathway behind them was empty. The expanse of lawn was unoccupied, as was the driveway. She released a pent-up breath, closed her eyes. Maybe the man *had* been an apparition. Maybe he'd never been there at all.

She let go of the sweaty clumps of her skirt and flexed her stiff fingers.

A swift, sharp sting to her shoulder flashed her eyes open. She glimpsed the yellow-tipped arrow fly past, a fleet line that became visible only when the arrow embedded itself in the front lawn's grass.

Upset, she clamped her hand over the cut on her upper arm and turned on Mica, a frown pulling down the corners of her mouth, but Mica was stretched high on his toes, as tall as he could get, and the unmoving man stood half hidden behind him, only one eye visible from behind Mica's head, like Amber's one eye only had been visible from behind the picture window's drape. The way he held Mica, lover-close, had rucked the boy's shirt, a slice of his slim belly on show. His bow dropped soundlessly to the ground, cushioned on the grass.

Amber stared, unable to move, unable to speak as a speck of blood in the middle of Mica's torso rapidly bloomed outward, an unfurling dark-petalled flower that saturated the front of his T-shirt. He had worn the shirt many times since Amber had arrived at the Inn. She'd always avoided looking at it – it had a wolf's-head design on the front that made her think of terrified, bleating sheep and lost girls alone in the woods.

The sting of the cut on her arm, where Mica's loosed arrow had sliced her, faded into the background. She forgot about the bow Mica had dropped. She forgot the Inn and its white clapboard siding on her left, the window above their heads standing blank and empty (no help there), the piled firewood stacked nearby (too far away to reach), forgot the vegetable garden behind the chicken-wire fence, the yellows of the lemons, the greens of its lettuces, beans, spinach and broccoli and the ladders of tomatoes, each deeper red in the falling dusk than ever, but not as richly deep as the red of Mica's blood. Amber couldn't tear her eyes from it.

It was only Mica's whimpering gasp that brought her gaze leaping to his face. His eyes were dark, drowning pools, his mouth loose and soft. She thought he mouthed *help* at her, but how could she help when the grass gripped her feet and death held her in its thrall?

The man behind Mica had strapped an arm across the boy, holding him still for the blade he'd slid into Mica's back. On the back of his hand, a black tattoo, a spiral, was stamped into his skin. A dizzying vortex that made the world tilt and shift in Amber's vision.

The stranger's eye watched her, its centre so black there was no telling where the iris ended and the pupil began. The eye blinked and something unlocked in Amber's throat.

She was a quiet girl – always had been – but quiet girls still know how to scream. The cry tore up and out, erupting from her throat. The grass and earth shook at the power of it and released their grip on her. Light and free, she spun away from Mica – his death so new he was still in the throes of it – and did the only thing she could.

She fled.

Amber may have run, but she couldn't leave. She dashed back the way she and Mica had come, sprinting for the Inn's front stoop and entrance. Far away, on the other side of the Inn, she heard Bianca calling her and Mica's names.

Amber shouted back, her voice cracking, unpractised at being used so much or so loudly. '*He's here, Bianca!*' Thank God Cloris and Jasper were already inside, locked in an upstairs bedroom.

Pebbles skittered under Amber's running feet, spitting out as she took the corner at full speed. She didn't look back, didn't want to see if death was chasing her down, its knife wet from Mica's blood, its hand reaching for her shoulder to clamp down, spin her around and shove that hot blade under her ribs. Her limbs felt hollow and boneless. She was so light she flew.

Far to the north-west, tiny as fine-grain sand, a flock of birds flew and wheeled in tight formation. Her eyes flicked to them for the barest instant, the murmuration billowing outwards, flattening; to Amber it resembled an outstretched hand that beckoned to her. The birds understood. They knew death was coming for her and Amber fervently wished in that moment that she were one of them, with wings that could take her away from this place and the violence being unleashed on it.

The Inn's long driveway, leading up past the front lawns and out to the road, called to her. *Fly away*, it said. *Leave now. Don't go back.*

But that was fear talking, and she wouldn't listen. She could feel death closing in, yes, but she also felt the silky softness of

Jasper's hair tickling her palm. Felt his baby weight in her arms, sturdy and warm, as she lifted him from his cot, and the vibrations of his happy gurgles buzzing under her hand while she sang nonsense tunes into his ear to make him laugh. She turned from the driveway and the free-flying birds and leapt up the front porch's steps and dashed inside. She threw herself against the heavy door, slamming it shut and throwing the deadbolts home.

Trembling, breathing hard, she backed up, knowing it wouldn't stop the man for long. There were too many ways to get inside. Numerous ground-floor windows. Two more entrances on this level alone. She was only buying time. She realised she was crying, her cheeks wet and dripping, and she wiped her face dry in the crook of her elbow.

Running feet thudded the porch and the door rattled in its frame. Amber gasped. Couldn't help it. The rattling stopped. More booted thuds and the man appeared at the large picture window. His hand cupped his brow against the glass as he peered in. It was getting darker, the daylight outside dimming with the setting sun and backlighting him, his features masked in shadows, but she felt his gaze as it passed over her, his head's panning stopping and settling on her. His breath steamed up the window. He moved back, used the knife's tip to draw a wavering, screeching spiral on the fogged-up glass. The blade left spots and smears of Mica's blood in its wake. Done with his artwork, the man went right, striding past the window and out of sight, his drumming footsteps quickly dropping away.

Amber didn't wait – she scampered across the foyer, shoes clacking on bare wooden floors, heading for the wide staircase up which Cloris had disappeared with Jasper. From the rear of the Inn, she heard Bianca and Arun storm into the rear reception in a clamour of crashes and curses.

'*Mica! Amber!*' Bianca sounded panicked, scared. It added an extra-thick layer of anxiety to Amber's bubbling fear because

Bianca didn't *get* scared. She was smart and tough and didn't take crap from nobody.

Bianca called out again, more than panic in it this time. Desperation.

Amber froze with one toe pressed to the staircase's bottom riser and whispered Jasper's name, torn, her hands gripping the sides of her dress and squeezing. Cloris had Jasper in his room, but Cloris was in her sixties. She wouldn't be able to run fast or far, not with a baby to carry.

From the back of the Inn, glass shattered, a horrendous sound that resounded through the ground floor. Shouts came next, angry and confrontational. Whoever had come for them had gotten in.

'No, no, no,' Amber sobbed, low and miserable, the material of her dress clumped hot and damp in her fists. Her forearms burned from holding on so tightly. She couldn't draw air in fast enough to catch her breath.

Arun was yelling, but it was lost in a series of thuds. Bianca screamed and it sounded so much like '*Go!*' that Amber flinched. She snatched her hands away from her dress and leapt up the stairs two at a time. She hit the first landing, grabbed the newel post and propelled herself up the next flight, not realising she was gasping, 'I'm sorry, I'm sorry, I'm sorry,' over and over again until she'd reached the top and was panting in big, ragged gulps. The carpeting up here was plush, thick, it stifled her footfalls as she ran the length of the hallway to the nursery. It was locked, and she knocked furtively.

She heard movement behind the door.

'It's me,' Amber whispered, breathless, brushing shaky hands over her tear-stained cheeks.

A scrape as something heavy was slid out of the way. The lock disengaged and Cloris's watery eye and painted eyebrow appeared in the gap. Seeing Amber alone, she opened the door wider.

'Quickly, dear, in, in.'

Cloris relocked the door and moved to shunt the antique dresser back in place, but Amber stopped her with a hand flat to the varnished wood.

Cloris glanced up, surprise evident in the high hike of her brows at Amber's forwardness. The older woman left the dresser where it was, the door unbarricaded. Her fluffy grey hair was flattened on one side. Her mascara had run and her powdered brow and temples were chalky and streaked with perspiration. She had bitten all her lipstick off.

'We have to go,' Amber told her. 'Now.'

'I heard . . .' Cloris began, and swallowed. 'I thought I heard screaming.'

Jasper was standing up in the makeshift crib they had made for him, his chubby hands holding on to the blanket-covered siding of the crate. He cooed at Amber, and the tightness in her chest, the crushing fear, eased back a fraction as affection surged up to take its place. She hurried to him, his arms already up, fists clasping and opening, wanting to be picked up. She took a precious moment to lean down to him, his little hand snagging hold of her dress. She stroked his hair, kissed his head. He whined in complaint as she backed away, working his grip loose to do so. He lost his balance and dropped on to his butt.

'They . . . they hurt Mica,' Amber admitted quietly, not looking at Cloris. The words were difficult to get out, not because she'd uttered more words in the last fifteen minutes than she had to anybody other than Jasper since arriving at the Inn, but because she was speaking of death and she was afraid that if she spoke of it too loudly, it might find them again.

'*They* who?'

'I don't know. The man I saw. Maybe more.'

Cloris stared at her, speechless.

'We have to go,' Amber said again. A bulky shawl was folded neatly on the armchair next to the crib and she snatched it up, shook it out. It smelled of Bianca – of the lavender oil she used to help her sleep, of fresh air and turned soil – and something caught in Amber's throat, sharp as a fish-hook. She swallowed it away, something tearing inside her as it went down, and made quick work of wrapping the shawl around her front.

'We can't just *go*,' Cloris argued. 'What about Bianca and the boys?'

Amber watched the door as she worked on hastily folding the shawl into a papoose, expecting it to any second burst inwards in a spray of splinters and flying wood. The wood was solid, the lock weighty, but it wouldn't stop anyone from getting in, not even if the dresser was pulled in front.

'I don't understand.' Cloris was wringing her hands. The multitude of rings on her fingers glinted and flashed. 'What do they *want*? Food? Surely they'd take it and leave if that was the case. Do they somehow know Albus? Is that what this is about?' She stopped the wringing to plump at her hair, working the flattened side back into shape.

The Inn belonged to Albus's uncle, but Albus lived here now with the family he'd collected and brought with him: eleven of them, including Amber and Jasper. No one knew the Inn existed unless they'd been told about it. Albus himself had felt confident enough to leave with the others on a rescue mission, believing Amber and the rest would come to no harm if left alone. How wrong they'd been.

'What are you doing?'

Amber had watched Bianca do this many times whenever she took Jasper out into the vegetable garden with her. The boy had worked his way back on to his feet, and Amber reached over to pick him up. He was heavy – he enjoyed his food: eating it, playing with it, smearing it over his face and in his hair. It took a little manoeuvring to get him secured in the shawl's front sling. Catching on, Cloris moved to tighten the knotted ends at Amber's back, talking the whole while she did, a low, fast murmur about sneaking to the kitchen for knives, about being quiet so they could maybe take any intruders by surprise.

Amber didn't tell Cloris that Mica was beyond their help now, and that she suspected Arun and Bianca were, too. She didn't say a word about Cloris being unable to walk far without complaining about her sore hips. Hitching Jasper closer to her chest, adjusting to his weight, Amber reached a hand out without raising her eyes and laid it on Cloris's forearm. She had never willingly touched the woman before, and it was enough to stop Cloris's sentence mid-flow.

'I have to take Jasper now.'

She could feel Cloris watching her, could almost feel her thoughts whirling around them like little desperate moths bumping and searching for escape. A hand patted over Amber's and squeezed it gently.

'Yes, dear. Yes, I understand.'

The three of them made it all the way down the narrow, unlit service stairs to the kitchen. Cloris paused to glance out of a window, rising up on her toes and leaning far over the sink to do it. She abruptly whirled away from the view and scurried over to Amber. She no longer resembled the woman Amber had come to know: prim, refined, a bit snobby. She was a pale imitation of herself. Haunted. Amber expected her hand to be cold when Cloris clasped hers and urgently tugged at her to follow, but it burned on her skin. Amber was ushered through the utility room, the smell of old fabric softener closing around them.

At the door leading outside, Cloris paused to face them, her lips trembling. She touched delicate fingers to Jasper's fine, wispy hair and then brought the same hand up to close over Amber's chin, cupping her in a palm so soft and so warm that Amber made a quiet, involuntary noise.

'You're a good girl,' Cloris whispered to her. 'I should have told you that before.' With a final squeeze and a shaky smile that softened all her smudged and painted edges into something surprisingly lovely, Cloris released her, opened the exterior door just wide enough for Amber and Jasper to slip through and bustled them out.

Before Amber had time to even think about saying anything, the door was shut again and Cloris was gone.

The land fell away in steps at the rear of the Inn's grounds, from high-grassed lawns to rock and shale and, finally, to the dark, wet sands of the beach and the never-ending ocean. The ruffled white breakers rolled in with the tide, their rushing swells greeting Amber's ears. The salt air, still warm from the setting sun, cleared her nose of the Inn's shut-in mustiness of ageing furniture and varnished wood. A set of steep exterior steps led down from the raised decking to more gravel, which ran east to the front driveway and west to the gardens and beach.

Indistinct voices drifted into earshot. She heard the scrape of a chair leg on decking. The rear porch was dotted with furniture – rocking chairs and spindle-backed seats where guests could come to relax and stare out to sea. It was where Amber always knew to look for Albus, sitting silently and rocking himself, like an old man trapped inside the body of a twenty-something-year-old.

A screen door creaked, springs squawking in protest. The reception door. It had needed oiling since Amber had arrived, but no one had gotten round to it. The screen banged shut. There was a bump, a vicious curse, an urgent scuffing of feet, and then, so suddenly that Amber flinched, a howl of emotion that lifted so high she felt sure it would push back the tides and send the gulls scattering to the skies.

Cloris's wail didn't last long; it fell into short, raspy shouts, the same demand over and over. 'Let them go! Let them go, damn you!'

'*Cloris.*' Bianca's voice was slurred, muffled, as if she had a mouthful of marshmallows. She fell into a smothered sob and any further words were washed away by the crashing of the waves and distance.

Jasper's heavy head had settled on Amber's collarbone and his sleepy breaths puffed warm against her throat, close and rhythmic. The shouts hadn't disturbed him, but the furious thundering of her heart soon would. Amber dashed to the steps, placing her feet carefully on each one as she hurriedly descended.

At the bottom, she hesitated, exactly as she'd hesitated at the staircase when Bianca had called out to her.

Don't look, a small voice whispered to her. *You'll regret it if you look.*

But Amber had to. She couldn't leave them without seeing.

She went to the white latticed panel that fenced in the space under the Inn; they ran the entire length of the raised veranda's underbelly. She unlatched the gate and opened it to darkness. She didn't want to go under there. Wild animals made their nests in that dank, fetid space. Creepy-crawlies built webbed kingdoms and made cocoons of their victims. Injured cats dragged themselves in there to die.

But it was the only way to get closer without being seen.

She murmured comforting words to Jasper (and to herself) and ducked to fit through. Above her head, an endless tunnel of wooden slats, seamed with light, stretched away, the last bits of daylight slicing the floorboards into lines. To her left, maple-leaf-shaped holes punched through the latticed sidings, allowing her a dot-to-dot view of the lawns, the ocean. She crept closer, the spongey soil like walking on foam bedding. The rich, pungent smell of earth tickled her nose. Fine, gossamer webs brushed her face and arms.

Jasper moved fitfully against her, and she stopped breathing. A warm sigh snuffled from him and the boy settled down. She glanced over her shoulder, back to the gate's access, its frame haloed with muted light. She should take the boy and leave. Run, and run now. But something larger than fear had control of her; she felt like one of those thousands of birds on the distant horizon, joined to its wheeling, feathery mass whether she wanted to be or not. She turned when those nearest to her turned and banked when her neighbours banked.

She stayed low and duck-walked awkwardly with Jasper. A few more yards and she would be able to see. She crouched next to the panelling, placed her eye to a hole and looked.

That man. That rat-bastard man with his black eyes was on the lawn. His knife had been replaced with a bow. It wasn't a child's plaything he held but a weapon made of fibreglass and fitted with calibrated sights.

The grass brushed his shins. A black nylon quiver leaned against his leg, a bushel of yellow-flighted arrows bristling from the top. He pulled an arrow free and notched it but didn't draw.

He called over to the veranda, who to, Amber didn't know. His words were stolen from her, the wind picking them up and tossing them aside.

Jasper wriggled again, reminding her how foolish she was being for staying.

She was distracted from her thoughts when the man drew the bowstring back in a swift, smooth pull, releasing it as soon as it touched his cheek.

The arrow shot away so fast Amber's eyes lost track of it. It thudded home somewhere above her head and Cloris let out an agonised cry. A wailing howl, a sound so torn with grief, shivered through the floorboards over Amber's head. Dust and dirt misted down and she lifted a protective hand to cover Jasper's head, even as flecks caught in her eyelashes. She blinked and blinked again, tears spilling free.

A second arrow was loosed and *thunk*ed into its target, but no cry came – only a weary expelled grunt. Bianca's wail dropped down into a hoarse, wallowing moan, as if she knew there were no ears to hear it and no one left to care even if they did.

Amber bit so hard at her lip she tasted blood. The birds were inside her now, flapping through her chest and amassing around her heart, a tumult of motion that made breathing difficult. She stood up fast and retreated, almost tripping on her wobbling legs. She hurried through the striped light and fell back through the gate, the door almost tearing loose from her hold as a stampeding gust of wind blasted down the side of the Inn. She hooked the gate closed to prevent it from banging, her jittery fingers barely able to latch it.

She darted across the gravel path to the grass, phantom cries chasing after her, not knowing if they were the tormented cries of her friends or the strident calls of the seagulls gliding in from the sea and riding the building winds. Her foot slid in mud and she tensed, unbalanced for a moment, clumsily regaining her footing as another forceful blast of wind shoved her roughly, urging her onward. A deafening blanket accompanied the gust, a tin-whistle that assaulted her ears from the inside and blared its insistence. Her hair whipped around her head, and Jasper, now awake, whimpered into her chest. Amber broke into a run, fleeing her home, her new family, and made it all of ten yards before she stumbled to a halt.

Another stranger, one she hadn't yet seen, stepped out from behind a long line of hedgerows and into her path. Had this man been stationed here the entire time to keep watch? To catch anyone attempting to sneak away? It seemed likely, and Amber felt like a fool for not thinking of it.

He was younger than the other man, his cheeks blemished with old acne scars, his hair greasy as the wind flicked it into his squinting eyes. Amber might have still considered making a run for it – he might have been young, but he looked somehow soft and a bit doughy around his middle – but he stood facing her with his feet planted wide and a deadly-looking black gun pointed at her chest, where Jasper lay cradled against her.

Burning, impotent tears prickled at Amber's eyes. They had been so close. *So close.*

Like a wild animal, Amber instantly settled into complete stillness, as she had done when she'd seen the first stranger standing at the end of their driveway. She only blinked and breathed as she watched. But Jasper could feel the frantic knocking of her heart against her breastbone and he shifted in his sling, his head bumping her chin as he whined in unhappiness.

The young man unclipped something palm-sized and boxy from his belt and lifted it to his mouth. Despite the wind and the tinny whistling in her ears, Amber heard his words.

'She came out with the kid. I have her.'

PART ONE

A Dawning

CHAPTER 1

Pilgrim

The diner's chrome-handled door didn't make a peep as Pilgrim pulled it open; it glided smooth and silent on its rust-free pneumatic swing-arm.

Pilgrim gazed up at it thoughtfully.

Remarkable the things that keep on working while everything else falls to shit, a quiet voice murmured in his head. *No rhyme nor reason to it.*

'Hm,' Pilgrim said.

The welcome mat was covered with leaves and dirt. Signs on the walls that were once a vibrant blue, yellow, green had faded to washed-out pastels. Pilgrim moved further into the ruined diner, treading carefully over the red tiled floor, his gun drawn as he approached the staff access to the diner's long counter; tall swivel stools dotted its length, leaving odd gaps where a handful of seats had been ripped out like pulled teeth. It reminded him of a young woman he'd known, of her bloodied and empty gums, where a cruel and hateful bastard had yanked out her teeth, one by one. Ruby had been beautiful once, her smile bright with intelligence. This memory of her was a recently examined grave for Pilgrim, and he backed away from it, not wanting or needing to excavate any further.

He slipped into the space behind the counter, gun leading,

but the area was clear. No one waited to jump him or attack.

On the far wall, through the serving hatch, was the kitchen (where the grill cook had once stood in his chef's whites and flipped beef patties and scrambled eggs to order). It was gloomy, no natural light reaching back there. Pilgrim cocked his head to listen while he counted booths. Twelve. He counted stools. Ten, with four missing.

While he counted, nothing stirred.

Not even a mouse, that solitary voice whispered in his ear. Its name was Voice, because Pilgrim had refused to give him a name that was personal or even mildly affectionate. For a long time, Pilgrim hadn't looked upon Voice affectionately at all.

Pilgrim's feet cracked over glass and smashed tableware, over crunching leaves and grit that had swept in through a broken window or two. He didn't attempt to quieten his footfalls. He was thankful for his boots. There was a bell next to the cash register and he rang it with the butt of his handgun. It chimed into the stillness, clear and true.

No reply came. No sounds at all.

'This isn't getting us to the Inn any quicker,' he muttered, tapping an impatient finger against the gun's trigger guard.

We won't be getting anywhere with no gas in our tanks. You need to eat, and they *need to eat.*

Pilgrim glanced out past the front windows to the diner's burnt-out neon sign and the empty stretch of highway where he'd left his travelling companions. Four women of varying heights and ages. He still wasn't entirely sure how he'd found himself outnumbered one to four by so many females.

Four to two, if you wanted to count me, Voice said.

Pilgrim didn't want to count him.

The tallest woman, Sunny, had resorted to cupping both hands over her mouth, her cheeks puffing out as she blew into them. She acted like they were in the dead of winter, yet, judging by the morning's warmth, the temperatures would climb close to ninety by lunchtime.

Look at her, Voice said, and Pilgrim felt a vague, ghostly nodding sensation inside his own head, trying to direct his attention back to Sunny. *A walking corpse has more meat on it than her.*

Pilgrim had already moved on to the two women standing closest to Sunny. Pilgrim knew Lacey and Abernathy better than he knew the other two women combined, but they were from completely different eras of his life. Old friend and new. There was a clear decade of age between them, Lacey being the younger at around eighteen. They were engaged in somewhat awkward conversation, Lacey's eyebrows scrunched in a scowl as she listened to whatever Abernathy was saying. He couldn't see Abernathy's expression – her back was to him – but her hands gesticulated animatedly as she talked. He eyed them warily.

Scared Abernathy is spilling some of your secrets? Voice asked in a wily tone.

Pilgrim's scowl no doubt mirrored Lacey's. It was true that Abernathy knew things about Pilgrim that no one else did. Dark, painful things that he'd left far behind, where no roads travelled and nothing grew. But, more than that, he wasn't entirely sure how he felt about Abernathy and Lacey getting along on any sort of friendly terms.

Because she's a psycho, you mean, Voice said.

Pilgrim sighed, holding on to his temper. Abernathy wasn't a psycho. Her morals were perhaps a little more flexible than might be comfortable for some, but whose weren't these days? He trusted her, and that wasn't something he did lightly or often.

Voice dropped his voice to a barely discernible grumble. *If you ask me, it's Tyler you should be keeping your eye on.*

Standing a little to the side from the others, staring back towards Pilgrim and the diner with a contemplative expression on her face, Tyler was the smallest of the four women. From this distance she was almost child-sized next to Sunny. Her arms were folded loosely, her right arm tucked inside her left elbow so the stump of her wrist was out of sight. A casual viewer would never know she was missing the entirety of her right hand.

Keeping his voice low, Voice said, *She's probably killed more people than either you or Abernathy. And that's saying something.*

Pilgrim didn't want to think about it and certainly wasn't about to bring it up anywhere near where Abernathy could overhear.

Wonder what she's mulling over . . . Voice mused, staring towards Tyler, along with Pilgrim.

'You're not hearing anything from her?' Pilgrim asked him, his lips making only the slightest of movements. Pilgrim wasn't the only person here who heard a voice in his head. Tyler had her own version of a voice, one that Voice was still trying to get a grasp on.

Nothing right now, no. Tommy hasn't said a word to me all morning.

Suspicion sat heavily in the space between Pilgrim and Tyler, so dense he could practically see the lazy shimmer of it hovering like a heat haze above the parking lot's asphalt. It sat heavily between *all* the women, passing back and forth in the weighted looks they shared, landing like rocks in each word they batted back and forth. There hadn't been much conversation on the trek down from the hill they'd camped out on the night before.

As if suddenly aware of Pilgrim's gaze, Lacey looked over at him. He didn't miss the slight narrowing of her eyes or the flash of impatience on her face. He also couldn't miss the dark smudges of her bruises or the swollen knot of her cheekbone. Something hot and dangerous twisted inside him at the sight.

He turned away from the window (before she got the bright idea to come in here after him) and went back to his search. He hadn't spent more than maybe a minute studying his companions, but that minute already burned away at him, hot and insistent, lost to a level of introspection he didn't have time for.

I really want a milkshake, Voice said as Pilgrim slipped behind the counter again. *You think they served milkshakes here? I bet they made them with ice-cream. Too thick to suck up through a straw and cold enough to make your teeth ache.*

Pilgrim's stomach gurgled emptily at the description as he headed directly for the hotplate on the back worktop, the heaviest, sturdiest item in sight. He ripped the cord out of the electrical outlet and hefted the hotplate's weight. Perfect.

Strawberry. Not vanilla or banana. It has to be strawberry. Or mint chocolate chip.

Pilgrim slung the hotplate through the serving hatch and listened to it crash and clang in there as if an overzealous cymbal performer had been woken into life. He waited for the echoes to fade. Listened some more, the seconds passing by painfully, like jabs to the back of his head. He heard nothing.

Pushing through the kitchen's swinging doors, he was blocked by a large preparation station: it was all countertop griddles and stainless-steel surfaces. To his left were more stainless-steel cabinets, covered in dust and cobwebs, and racks of pots and pans. The hotplate he'd tossed lay broken on the floor (there were no cymbal players in sight). To his right, past a double-wide sink and drain board, the maw of a walk-in freezer drew his gaze as only the impenetrable darkness beneath a bed could draw a child's. Monsters lived in such places.

Or old, rotted meat, Voice said.

Pilgrim sniffed the air but could detect only cold metal and mustiness.

A flickering orange glow ignited within the freezer's dark interior, a soft-flamed illumination that warmed and licked at the shadows. Pilgrim knew the light wasn't real, but he couldn't look away. He'd taken two steps nearer before Voice pulled him up.

What're you doing? he asked sharply, and the light from inside the freezer blinked out and it was a small boxroom crowded with darkness once more. *I thought we were done with these little ghostly apparitions of yours.*

'I did, too,' Pilgrim muttered. He turned away from the freezer. Spotted the dim alcove of a pantry in the opposite corner and made his way towards it, kicking the dented hotplate out of his way.

'*Pilgrim?*'

Lacey's call came from the front of the diner. He hadn't heard her enter; she'd come in through the same silent door mechanism he had.

Abernathy's voice came with her. 'You aren't doing your counting thing on all the pots and pans in there, are you?'

When Abernathy first knew him, Past-Pilgrim had a fascination with counting objects. It helped bring structure and order to a place where chaos and madness ruled. He didn't rely on such methods often any more, but she liked to remind him of their shared history whenever the mood suited her.

'I told you all to wait outside,' Pilgrim said, ignoring her question. If Abernathy and Lacey were in here, it meant they were all in here.

Women are awful at taking orders.

A second later, Tyler said, quiet but discernible, 'Tommy heard that.'

Pilgrim felt mild satisfaction at Voice being caught out. Voice couldn't get away with such comments any more. His audience was no longer limited to Pilgrim.

'The restrooms need checking,' Pilgrim called through to them, figuring they might as well be useful now that they'd ignored his instructions. There had been two closed doors at the far end of the diner counter. Didn't look like they'd been opened in years.

'I'm on it,' Abernathy said loudly, her voice moving away as her boots crunched across the tiles. 'I need to check for tampons anyway. My Aunt Flo's about to visit.'

Ugh, why does she have to share stuff like that? Voice complained.

'Because it's Abernathy,' Pilgrim said.

The kitchen's double-hinged door swung inward and Lacey appeared. The pinch of her frown eased when she saw him. She was limping. It was hard to miss. Pilgrim dropped his eyes to her feet, which were encased in too-large boots. Boots they'd taken from a dead man. A man who'd been very much alive before Pilgrim had shot him through the chest, but there wasn't any point dwelling on such things – that man was dead and they were alive, and they needed food. It was the only reason they had stopped here. To find food. Nothing more. There were farmhouses dotted along the highway but searching each one would take time they didn't have. Still, letting Lacey rest her battered feet for a short while wouldn't be a bad thing. Previous to finding her, she'd been without footwear long enough to slice the soles of her feet to ribbons.

But not for long.

No, not for long.

'Go sit down,' Pilgrim told her. 'Take Tyler and Sunny with you.' He could see them loitering outside the swinging door. 'I'll be through in a minute.'

Lacey's frown returned, and he didn't think it was from concern for his well-being this time. She looked pissed. Something tightened at the corners of her mouth and he waited for her to voice a complaint, mildly surprised when she turned around without a word and let the door swing shut behind her. Maybe her feet were bothering her more than he thought.

You know it's not her feet, Pilgrim, Voice said tiredly, as if talking to a particularly obtuse child. *She won't rest properly until she finds her niece. Same as you couldn't rest easy until you found Lacey.*

Pilgrim stared at the closed door where Lacey had been,

silently chewing on his words, before turning back to his task. He made quick work of his search and within three minutes was carrying everything he'd found back through to the diner.

The four women occupied a booth nearest the main door, Tyler and Sunny with their backs to him (with a sizeable gap beside Sunny and nearest the intact window, which she'd left empty), and Abernathy and Lacey on the bench seat opposite them. There were no menus to peruse, only the dirt and dust of the tabletop.

Abernathy whistled and raised a hand as if he were a waitress and she were beckoning him over. He had a mind to ignore her, but the box was cumbersome, needing two hands to hold it, and he wanted free of it. He dumped it on the table in front of her so that it made a nice solid *thump*.

Unperturbed, Abernathy smirked a little and said, 'I'll take the burger, extra Cheddar, pulled pork, pickles. The works . . . What, I'm sorry, what was that?' She cocked her head to him, making out he'd said something when, in fact, all he was doing was eyeing her in silence. '*Yes*, I want fries.' She gave the others a look as if to say, *Who wouldn't want fries?* 'And a large Coke. Just find a bucket and fill that sucker up. I'm parched.' She licked her lips for effect.

'I'll take the French toast,' Lacey told him.

These two could be a real problem for us if they ever did get buddy-buddy.

Pilgrim's expression must have changed from unamused to outright disappointed, because Lacey attempted a smile. 'I'm sorry. What you got in there?' She straightened up, craning her head to get a look inside the box.

He shoved it into the centre of the table where they could all reach it. Lacey pulled a face at the smaller boxes of porridge oats and a one-pound bag of sugar.

'Breakfast,' he answered.

'I guess cold gruel was my second option,' Lacey said.

'Sugar!' Sunny said brightly, reaching in to pick the bag up. Her wrist was painfully narrow. If anyone here needed a truck-load of sugar dumped into her diet, it was her. 'I haven't had sugar in an age.'

'Eat up,' Pilgrim told them. 'Ten minutes and we're moving.'

There wasn't a great deal of talk as they went about mixing oats with the water they carried; they were hungry, their stomachs hollowed out and grumbling, although no one had complained. Each took their turn scooping out sugar, watching almost reverently as they transferred the white heaps to their cold porridge and stirred it in. Lacey held the bag for Tyler as she used her one hand to dip her spoon inside.

It tasted pretty good, and Pilgrim ate fast, sitting one booth over, alone but facing their table so he could keep an eye on them. He finished before they were even halfway through. It might not have been a cheeseburger and shake, but it filled a hole and would keep it filled for a while. They would take the rest of the packets when they left.

Wanna practise real quick while we wait for them to finish? Voice asked him.

Pilgrim hesitated only a moment before placing his left hand flat on the table and leaning back in his seat. He felt jittery and impatient to get moving, but he knew this was important.

Through the smashed and missing windows, he listened to the insects, the birds, the wind, the susurration of leaves on the trees, relaxing his neck and shoulders in degrees, breathing calmly. His heartbeat ran slow – slower than normal, its rhythmic thump meditative and countable, which he liked (literally the only part of this he did) – and warm, mellow tingles worked their way through his body. The fingers of his left hand twitched and stretched as if they were trying the fit of a new glove. On the tabletop, they fluttered in a jerky tap-dance before settling into an ordered tapping, going from pinkie to thumb and back again, the uncoordinated movements smoothing out as they repeated themselves over and over.

Pilgrim left Voice and his hand to their practice – feeling the odd pull and tug of ligaments working independently of him – and idly worried at his group's progress. Their pace, their speed, the miles left to cover before they reached the East Coast, where Albus's Inn was located. He – *they* – were going too slow. Walking speed wouldn't be enough.

He silently watched as Tyler rose from her seat, carried her bowl over to his table and slipped on to the bench opposite him. He let his troubled thoughts settle so that they skimmed like colourful fish, gliding silently below the surface of a lake, and waited for Tyler to speak.

For a while she simply watched his fingers, Voice so engrossed in what he was doing that he didn't notice her attention straight away. When he did, Pilgrim's fingers stalled in their cadence and stopped.

Tyler's gaze lifted to Pilgrim's. It was so clear and direct it was like being sliced clean open. 'We need to move faster,' she said and, as usual, her words were straight to the point and without dressing.

'I know,' Pilgrim said.

'We can't delay. Jay may have already arrived. He and Clancy may have already . . .' She shook her head and dropped her eyes, which was very much *not* like Tyler.

'I know. I'll get us there.' He didn't promise her they'd get there in time, because he didn't believe in giving false hope. That kind of thinking helped no one. But he knew this was his fault; he'd sent Jay and Clancy ahead to a place he thought would be safe, and now he had to fix his mistake. He would do whatever needed to be done.

It's not your fault, Voice said quietly. *You didn't know the danger. None of us could have known the Inn's location had been compromised. None of us could have ever guessed the Flitting Man would be searching for it.*

As true as that was, it didn't change anything. He remembered the last image he had of Clancy and Jay, the two of them standing side by side at the roadside, distance and the fine mist of rain blurring their features. Jay had cupped his hands around his mouth and the thin thread of his shout had reached Pilgrim's ears, dampened by the drizzle.

'*Good luck!*'

Pilgrim recalled having to clutch Tyler's wrist tighter, preventing her from breaking away and rushing to the young man. She'd lifted her free arm in a wave and Jay had waved back. Clancy had stood motionless, the rain slowly drenching her, plastering her greying hair to her head. For some reason, Pilgrim had found himself staring at her, not wanting to forget this image of them, of her, not wanting to forget how Clancy reached out to Jay to place her hand on his shoulder. They both understood Pilgrim was leaving them behind. He'd had no other choice, but that hadn't made the decision any easier.

'Voice is getting better,' Tyler said, lifting her chin to indicate Pilgrim's unmoving hand. 'He's progressed from moving just your pinky. Tommy is impressed.'

Pilgrim made a small sound of acknowledgement, uncomfortable under Tyler's scrutiny as she chewed on a mouthful of porridge, aware that behind the interested sheen of her eyes she wasn't the only one watching him.

He doesn't like giving up control to me when he doesn't need to, Voice said, and Pilgrim knew he wasn't addressing him.

A second later Tyler was nodding. She daintily swallowed her bite before speaking. 'It isn't like lending someone your car, is it? It's a whole different level of trust. I'd say it's not something many people would be comfortable with.'

'He's lucky I let him practise at all,' Pilgrim said.

You won't even let me use your dominant hand, Voice complained. *What do you think I'll do? Impede your ability to jack o—*

'Stop,' Pilgrim cut him off. 'Or practise stops. Your choice.'

Voice mumbled something too low to make out.

Again, Tyler shifted topics before Pilgrim had gained full traction on the last one. He wondered if she did it deliberately, to keep him unbalanced, or if she were simply moving along with her rapid thought processes.

'I dreamed again last night,' she said, stirring the remains of her porridge, her eyes never leaving his. 'Did you?'

Admittedly, Pilgrim hadn't slept much, despite his body's need to – the days preceding Lacey's rescue had been fraught, to say the least – but he'd been unable to settle for long. Due in large part to having Lacey back at his side after a long separation and being afraid to let her out of his sight, even if it was to close his eyes and rest. Another part of it was down to his sleep being plagued by unwanted dreams.

'Yes,' he admitted. 'The same ones we spoke about already.' That wasn't entirely true. These dreams had been slightly different. The same red skies had dominated, of course, filling his ears and head with an awful, crackling static that scratched his nerve endings as effectively as nails against rusty metal. The oppressive power from that boiling red sky was ever-present in these dreamscapes, bearing down as if a great storm was building. The pressure became heavy enough to swell his head in sickly, dense waves until it felt like his skull was a huge, infected boil in need of being popped. Except this time he hadn't been alone in his dream. He had stood beside others like him, many hundreds of people, perhaps more, standing shoulder to shoulder, heads tilted back, eyes fixed on that monstrous red sky. Some of those faces held rapturous expressions; others seemed dumbstruck by what they were experiencing. More still appeared terrified. But they all, without a doubt, were experiencing the same thing.

'I saw you,' Tyler said, her eyes very serious. She licked at her lips as if they were suddenly bone-dry. 'In my dream. I looked over to my right and saw you, standing maybe fifty feet away, staring upwards, like all the others.'

A shiver passed down Pilgrim's back. 'How do you know it was me?'

'It was you.' She said it calmly, with conviction.

'What . . . what did I look like?' He didn't know why he asked that, but the words were out and he wouldn't call them back. 'My expression, I mean. What did I look like?'

'You looked . . .' Tyler slowly tilted her head, wetting her lips again, as if struggling to find the right word. 'You looked . . . relieved.'

It took a few seconds for Pilgrim to realise the lengthening silence wasn't reserved to his and Tyler's table. No more clinking spoons in bowls or sounds of eating or talking came from the table next to theirs. When he looked over, he found Lacey looking back at him, empty spoon in her hand. Beside her, Abernathy glanced from her to Pilgrim and back again (she was the only one among them who heard no voice of her own). Sunny had swivelled in her seat so that her head was turned in Tyler's and Pilgrim's direction.

'I dreamed the same thing,' Lacey said quietly. 'What you said, about others being there. I saw that, too.'

'Me, too,' Sunny murmured, meeting Pilgrim's eyes fleetingly before shrugging her narrow shoulders and turning back to Lacey. 'And Beck.' She tilted her head to the empty space beside her.

'This is, like, the third time you've gestured to this "Beck",' Abernathy said, using fingers to add inverted commas around the name. 'And I for one feel the need to point out the invisible elephant in the r— *Ow!*' She threw Lacey a murderous glare before ducking down to rub at her leg. 'What the fuck.'

Pilgrim didn't need to have seen Lacey kick Abernathy to know what had happened. He wasn't totally up to date on the whole 'Sunny and Beck' situation, other than Lacey telling him it was complicated and for him not to draw too much attention to Sunny talking to someone who wasn't there. But, you know,

Pilgrim had spent some time in a psychiatric care ward and talking to invisible people wasn't anything new to him. Wasn't really new to anybody any more if you got right down to it. Everyone found their own way to cope.

'Jesus Christ,' Abernathy muttered, straightening up from her rubbing. 'Am I the only person around here whose brain hasn't shit the bed?' She glanced angrily around at them all, making sure to include everyone. 'Dreaming about some red sky that speaks to you or some other crazy shit? Having invisible friends to hang out with? If this is what it means to hear a voice, you all can well and truly keep them to yourselves. And kick me in the leg again, little girl,' she said, turning on Lacey, 'and I'll break your foot clean off and feed it to you.'

Before Pilgrim could warn Abernathy to cool off, Lacey beat him to it.

'Well, start thinking before opening your big mouth and I won't have to kick you.' She held Abernathy's gaze, looking close to bored in the face of the older woman's wrath.

Voice laughed, a mix of delight and pride in the sound. *My my, our girl's gone grown up.*

Pilgrim was noticing. There had been very little opportunity to get into details about what had happened to each of them on their separate journeys before reuniting, but he could see the changes in Lacey. The sharpening around the edges. The wary alertness. Her softness, the naïvety that had swaddled her like her grammy's hand-knitted blanket when he'd first met her outside their farmhouse, had been shaved off her with each violent altercation, each close call, each vicious act witnessed, until all that softness had been whittled down to hard lines and defined features. A deep sadness welled up in Pilgrim at what she'd had to lose in order to survive. The lines around her mouth were no longer from smiling but from hunger and pain. Her eyes' wattage had dimmed, their lustre darkening to a harder focus. It had been a necessary transformation,

Pilgrim knew, but it made him grieve for her all the same.

Tyler broke Pilgrim from his thoughts and Lacey and Abernathy from their stand-off, although Pilgrim thought he spied a traitorous twitch to Abernathy's lips (though whether from amusement at Lacey's gall or from pure irritation, you could never say for sure with her). Either way, Lacey turned back to Tyler before it fully formed.

'More of us are having them now, the dreams,' Tyler was saying, sitting straight-backed and eager. 'That has to be what this means. Why we're seeing so many others in them, all in the same place. We're waking up. Our voices are getting stronger. I *told* you this would happen, that it *had* to happen.' The guilelessness on her face ignited a slow-burning anger in Pilgrim, his booted toe beginning to tap with it beneath the table, but he didn't say anything. 'They'll be becoming more and more aware of each other. Like ours can hear each other now. It's an inevitable progression.' The more she spoke, the more excited she seemed to get. 'Everything has been leading to this point. Don't you feel it? It had to happen this way to bring us all together.'

'We're not some big happy family,' By the tightness in Lacey's jaw, Pilgrim knew she was getting as angry as he was. 'You were in that cornfield. You *saw* what a group of voice-hearers and their so-called leader did to me. They tried to set me *on fire*, for God's sake. You heard what Sunny said about the horrific things they did. You even read some of it.' Sunny had a whole journal full of the evil experiments they'd inflicted on other voice-hearers, all described in minute detail.

It's not bedtime reading, that's for sure.

But Tyler wasn't listening. Not really. She was getting too drawn in by her own narrative to get derailed so easily. 'But that's in the past! This has to change things. It *has* to.'

'And what about people like me?' Abernathy asked, picking at a bit of oat stuck between her teeth. 'How're we gonna fit into this new world order of yours?'

'And Jay,' Pilgrim added, knowing his name would hit its mark with her. 'He's not like us, either.'

Tyler's excitement waned as quickly as it had burst into life. Her chin lowered and she gazed into her nearly empty bowl of gruel. If it had looked unappetising before, now it looked like regurgitated wallpaper paste. She pushed the bowl away and quietly said, 'I'm done.'

'We're all done,' Pilgrim said, getting to his feet. 'We're leaving. Get packed up.' He began gathering up the scattered packages of oatmeal on the girls' table and stuffing half of them into the side pockets of Abernathy's pack, the rest into his. The sugar went into his, too, along with one of the bottles of water.

Pilgrim, Voice murmured. *I think something's happening outside.*

As if hearing him, Tyler's head came up and turned towards the windows.

Perfectly on cue, Lacey's head swivelled to the windows, too.

For Pilgrim, it was a gradual realisation, like a dawn's seeping light creeping into a drape-darkened bedroom. He had stopped his packing, slowly becoming aware of the complete absence of sound from beyond the diner. Outside, all birdsong had ceased. There were no insects buzzing, no rustling leaves or breeze combing through the grass. No skittering of litter along the pavement, and certainly no road traffic. It was almost like falling deaf.

Abernathy grumbled around a last mouthful of porridge as Lacey nudged at her and told her to move.

'Jesus, hold on,' Abernathy mumbled, bringing her bowl with her as she scooted out of the way.

A second later Pilgrim was heading for the diner's door, striding past Lacey as she made it past Abernathy.

Outside, the highway was deserted, no broken-down cars for as far as he could see (if you didn't count the solitary rusted heap of a station wagon parked out front of the diner's entrance).

It was a lonely length of road, with long stretches of nothing between farmhouse, diner and the next set of farmhouses. The wind had dropped. Everything was still.

The others had followed him out, the door soundlessly shutting behind them.

Pilgrim walked to the roadside, his head swivelling left to right, looking for something he knew couldn't be seen. He wasn't capable of hearing like Voice did, but he felt *something*. A prickling power in the atmosphere, brewing up electricity, as though the dreams that had haunted their sleep – of red, static-filled skies awash with bursting, crackling sound – had stalked them from their blankets. He looked up, but the skies were a crisp forever-blue moving to cloudy white; to the west, at the farthest ends of the road, a hazy band of dusty yellow billowed up in the distance like a miniature dust storm.

'What are you hearing?' Pilgrim asked.

Something, Voice whispered. *It's something. I'm not sure.*

'Be specific,' Pilgrim demanded, knowing he was being curt but unable to soften it. His nerves buzzed. A crawling sensation pricked the back of his neck. The small hairs on his arms stood on end.

There's always a kind of low-level droning now, Voice began hesitantly. *It's everywhere, all the time. Doesn't matter where we are. Bits of it crackle and tune in clearer if I get closer to it – like with Lacey and Tyler, except not really, because when I turn an ear to them, they're like the clearest crystal to me now, no matter the distance. They're just quieter or louder, a difference in volume but with no interference.* As an aside, Voice adds: *Tommy thinks that has more to do with us spending time listening and talking to each other than anything else, though.*

Pilgrim's teeth ground together. 'OK, I get it. What's your point?'

So, generally, it's like having highways of traffic constantly running on all sides of us. But now . . . a section of that traffic just got a lot louder. Voice paused, as if gathering his thoughts. *North-east of us. Something's happening over there. I don't know what.*

Pilgrim looked to Lacey and Tyler and registered the same awareness on their faces.

'You're getting this, too?' he asked them.

Lacey nodded.

'Yes,' Tyler said.

'How far north?' he asked Voice.

I'm not sure. Maybe Tommy—

'Tommy says perhaps ten miles out,' Tyler said. 'But she's not sure if it's a group or even a fewer number of voices who are . . . stronger. We're not close enough to hear what's going on.'

Pilgrim turned his gaze north-east. Would others be sensing the same thing? Were they standing to attention right now, heads lifted, eyes attentive, listening to something only they could hear, exactly like he'd dreamed them all doing last night? Maybe they, too, had risen from where they sat or lay or stood to move out to where the sky was uncovered, or were climbing to higher ground and seeking out open spaces, like people did in the old days when they needed better signals for their cellphones.

As if hearing his thoughts, Tyler said, 'If our voices can hear them, chances are there'll be others that can, too. Especially if they're nearer to them than we are.'

Abernathy was still holding her bowl with its cold slop, but she'd given up on eating. She frowned around at them. 'What the hell's going on?'

'Voice-hearers, we think.' Pilgrim pointed. 'That way. Maybe a large group of them, we're not sure.'

That shut her up. Abernathy didn't hear a voice; hadn't when the voices came and didn't now. She and many others never would. The deaths, the killings, the murder-suicides, all were carried out by those who heard whisperings in their heads, listened to the murmurings in their ears. They had been told to hurt those around them, hurt themselves. Self-destruction was the voices' sole weapon, and they had wielded it with great success.

After those first few weeks, when the deaths finally died down, people like Abernathy had turned their grief and hatred on to those they considered responsible. Anyone suspected of hearing a voice had been hunted down, dragged out in front of baying crowds and executed. The voices had ushered in a world-wide genocide that humankind had never seen before, and for those who'd survived it the overriding emotions were hatred and rabid paranoia. Who could be trusted? Who would be next to die? Those who still heard a voice went to ground, figuratively and literally; many hid from themselves as well as others, shutting out the murmurings as best they could. They lived a lie, afraid of what they were and reviled for what those like them had done. For seven long years, they'd stayed there, in the dark, alone, their shame slowly curdling to bitterness, their bitterness ripening into resentment. A fertile soil into which the Flitting Man had sown his seeds of dissension. He'd always been here, of course, in one guise or another, but he'd bided his time, waiting and watching. An insidious and poisonous little bug.

Tyler's right – we're getting stronger, Voice said, and Pilgrim could feel the drop in his words, the opening pit that yawned into nothingness beneath them. *We're hearing each other more and more. Ruby said this would happen, too.*

That deepening sense of awe in Voice became something terrifyingly infinite to Pilgrim; he felt horribly exposed as he stared back at it. The thousands of faded, invisible stars in the bright dawn sky opened into unblinking, intrusive eyes as they all looked down on him, pinpointing him, *seeing* him. Hanging above his head, the diner's unlit neon sign loomed, its name mocking them.

Happy Campers Diner.

A flare of light, as bright as sheet lightning, flashed at the edge of his vision.

'Oh my God.' The soft syllables of Sunny's Southern accent dripped in astonishment, and a look of dumbfounded shock painted her face.

Eyes had widened all around him.

Far in the north-east, lifting above the gentle rolling swells and dips of long-grassed fields, rising over treetops and the distant jutting roofs of buildings, a huge billowing mushroom of churning, black smoke rose into the sky. Lit from inside, it roiled with hungry red fire.

A second detonation ignited, flashing nuclear bright and whiting out the world for an instant. When Pilgrim could see again, the flame-filled smoke had doubled in size. He felt fingers wrap his wrist, holding on so tightly it hurt. Lacey. He hadn't seen her move to stand next to him. From his other side, he was vaguely aware of Abernathy dropping her porridge bowl and spoon to the ground to cover her ears with both hands.

A rapidly expanding wave of air had already washed past the far-away treeline, bending the tops flat and compressing grass in the fields as it rippled outward from the explosion. It covered that ten miles of distance from blast to diner too fast for Pilgrim to react and the first shockwave hit them in a hot blast of wind that shoved at him and rifled through his shirt. The second followed on its heels, much stronger, pushing him back a full step. Lacey's hold tightened on his wrist as the double explosion smacked their ears, an angry titan's booming two-clap that Pilgrim felt right down to his soul. Behind them, the remaining glass in the diner's windows and door shattered. The rusted station wagon shook and groaned on its axles. Under his boots, the repercussive blasts rumbled through the ground, echoing back and back as if the earth's core were rumbling from a terrible, insatiable hunger.

'Holy crap,' Lacey breathed. 'What *was* it?'

'It can't be a nuke,' Abernathy said. 'It can't be.'

'Do you hear anything over there?' Pilgrim asked Voice.

A moment of silence, then: *I hear* something. *So I guess it's not nuclear, otherwise everyone would have been vaporised, right? But that louder burst of static is gone now.*

He passed on what Voice had said.

'It's happening,' Tyler said, and her eyes were as bright as the explosion, lit from within with a fervour Pilgrim liked less than the excitement he'd seen in her inside the diner. She pressed her fist to her chest, her words quiet but said with an intensity that made them shake. 'It's what he's been waiting for. What he told *me* to wait for. He's been here, all this time, getting us ready for this moment – the Flitting Man. The *Flitting Man*,' she said again. No one had mentioned that name since the night before, when Tyler's admission of meeting the Flitting Man (and the revelation of him being a teenage boy called Hari) had struck Pilgrim largely mute on the subject and rendered the others a confused mess of fearful, shocked and disbelieving. The fact that Hari had been walking among them for a while, perfectly disguised as a child, had unsettled Pilgrim deeply. It was as though all the bedroom closets of their collective adolescence had been ripped open and the Boogeyman set free. Now every creak and bump in the darkness meant that, soon, the monster could be standing right behind them, its fetid breath blowing hot on their necks.

'He's not just a boy,' Tyler said, and Pilgrim saw that the bright fervour in her eyes wasn't purely excitement as he'd thought at first; there was fear there, too. 'He's everywhere. He can see everything. None of us can hide now. Not any more. He must know what we did in St Louis – one match sparked and burst into life, and now others are igniting, too.'

'Quite fucking literally,' Abernathy muttered, kicking her dropped spoon as if the utensil had somehow offended her.

'News will spread as fast as the fires. All his waiting is over. *Their* waiting' – Tyler pointed to the north-east – 'is over.'

Whether it was the truth or not, this kind of talk didn't sit well with Pilgrim. Didn't sit well with Lacey or Abernathy, either, judging from their expressions, but it didn't stop Tyler from saying it. Last night, when she'd revealed the Flitting Man's identity, she'd sworn to him (and Abernathy, though Abernathy clearly didn't want to hear it) that she wouldn't keep anything from them again. She was done with lies and secrets.

All at once, the world started anew; the animals that had hunkered down, hackles raised and ears flat, were now giving themselves an invigorating shake and scampering out of cover. Insects chirruped, birds sang, the wind blew – it kicked up the dirt around their feet, bringing with it a heavy smell of smoke – and through it all Pilgrim imagined he heard the endless whispering of countless voices, rustling like leaves in the trees all around.

He checked the highway again, east to west, and when he scanned the far distance, he paused. The hazy, yellow dust cloud he'd seen had grown larger. What had at first been a miniature dust storm on the horizon had expanded into something entirely more real. He couldn't hear it yet, but he knew he would, and soon. Vehicles.

Chapter 2

Lacey

The world had shifted under their feet. A seismic realignment as though Lacey had lifted one boot to take a step and her foot had landed in a place she had *not* been expecting. A stumbling misstep, and now the direction she was walking in was totally off. Her bearings had already been wonky, her world off-kilter after losing Addison, her true north shifted clean off the map and into some other plane of existence where Lacey couldn't go. Only her continued glances over at Pilgrim saved her from careening off course. He was a solid land mass in these rough seas, the sight of him the only thing that could steady her.

When she wasn't looking at him, she would check the distant sky, tracking the explosion's dispersing smoke, frozen black and hazy like a dark raincloud. Where they stood at the roadside, the air was humid and heavy, the light filtered sandy-beige through a desert smog of clouds. Pilgrim called it storm weather. The way he said it made Lacey think he wasn't talking about everyday weather storms.

Tyler's Flitting Man talk had made Lacey want to punch her in the throat. It was fear-mongering in Lacey's view, no matter if it was based in truth or not, and she was done with being scared of intangible, unknowable dangers. In fact, she was failing to feel much besides a disordered amalgamation of resentment, anger and a bone-gnawing worry. Her feet hurt like a bitch, too, but her physical pain paled in comparison to the never-ending reel of images flipping through her head: of Alex, her best friend's dead and lifeless body lying on the floor of a desecrated church; of seeing her niece's tear-stained face as Lacey shoved her into an under-stairs closet and shut her in the dark, alone, to hide from a pack of feral hunters who wanted to rip them apart. Lacey had to believe Addison had gotten away safely – she'd heard rumours that a library bus of rescuers, of all things, had whisked the girl up and vanished her away. But believing Addison was safe and *knowing* it were two very different things, and without having her niece in front of her where she could visibly affirm the girl's health and physical condition, faith wasn't doing Lacey a whole lot of good. If not for Pilgrim and his steadfastness, Lacey feared she might have run off towards that smoking explosion in the distance and begun digging through the mountains of ash until every body had been accounted for and identified as not belonging to her niece.

All this trauma and despair, and here Tyler was, preaching the gospel of the Flitting Man. The changes Tyler was crowing about accounted for everything bad that had happened to Lacey. Voices starting to get stronger. Voices becoming aware of other voices and being able to locate each other. Wasn't it the Flitting Man's fault that Lacey didn't have her niece with her right now? Wasn't it *his* fault Alex was dead and Lacey was as beat up and screwed over as she'd ever been in her life? *Fuck* him. They'd been tracked and run down like dogs because of what Lacey had locked inside her head. Whether Tyler wanted to believe the Flitting Man was uniting people under a banner of brother- and sisterhood for good or not, violence and bloodshed rode with him, and Lacey and her family had suffered for it.

Violence and bloodshed have come from both sides, her Voice said.

It was funny how Voice didn't really sound like Pilgrim, even though that was where he'd originated from. Lacey had been a waiting receptacle, and Pilgrim shot and left for dead at the roadside, neither of them aware of the perfect alignment of variables needed to make a miracle of transference into a reality.

On occasion, her Voice would say a specific word or statement that reminded her of Pilgrim – in the way his intonation pronounced a syllable, maybe, or in a particular vocab choice – but that was as far as comparisons went. It had endlessly fascinated her at the beginning, thinking about it. Was her Voice a direct product of Pilgrim, like a child to his father? Or was he an opposite, a mirror for everything Pilgrim wasn't? Was he now becoming more a product of Lacey because of being solely inside her? Would that change now that her Voice could hear Pilgrim's Voice, and would potentially hear even more, like Tyler's Tommy? Everything evolved and adapted to its surroundings, right? That was nature. Which meant her Voice was now intrinsically different to Pilgrim's Voice. He was uniquely her own.

Or maybe none of that mattered and Voice was his own thing, separate and singular.

It was all kinds of a mindfuck and didn't really matter in the end. She'd gotten into trouble with voice-hearers and non-voice-hearers alike. Her Voice was right when he said violence and bloodshed came from both sides. People could be endlessly cruel and it had little to do with what they heard in the dark recesses of their minds. Pilgrim had shown her the folder he'd obtained from a hospital in St Louis. The photographic evidence of what scientists and doctors had done to voice-hearers had imprinted itself in Lacey's mind, the images swimming up out of the darkroom of her memory, often when she least expected them. Charred, flaking flesh. Shaven skulls sutured with ugly spider-leg stitches. Raw, weeping wounds singed into scalps. Mouths gaffer-taped shut.

That hospital wasn't the only place such experiments were being conducted. There were other laboratories, facilities, warehouses. In fact, Pilgrim had learned of the largest one of all, out on the East Coast, exactly in the direction they were heading. Its name was Elysian Fields. It sounded like an old folks' retirement home, but somehow Lacey didn't think they ran old-timey movie evenings or handed out pots of Jell-O with their patients' arthritis and blood-pressure meds.

Maybe Lacey should care about what was being done in those places. Maybe she and the others had an obligation to stop what was happening now that they knew they existed (the same way Pilgrim, Abernathy and Tyler had stopped what the doctors had been doing in St Louis). But Lacey found it difficult to latch on to any ideas of rescue or retribution. Those people were strangers to her. Each photo of sutured skin or bound eyelids, though terrible, was sewed or taped on to the face of someone she didn't know, when all she could see when she closed her eyes were the superimposed faces of her loved ones. Her grams, Addison, Alex, Pilgrim – even Sunny. Her indifference to everything and everyone else left her hollow. Cold.

She glanced at Pilgrim, needing the anchor of him to keep her from spinning off into her resentments. He was scanning their surroundings, his face furrowed in its usual grim expression as he stopped to stare into the distance. Lacey had been lost in her thoughts, but little time had passed between the blast rocking through them and shattering the diner's windows and now. Sunny was a few steps away but Lacey saw her lips moving as she talked quietly to herself, looking to her right and up, as if to a taller man standing beside her. Sunny paused to listen. Nodded.

Unaware of Lacey's slow descent into bitterness, Voice was a near-constant buzz in the inner depths of her ear, too low for her to make out. He wasn't talking to her.

'*Shhhhh*,' Tyler said, although no one was speaking aloud or in need of any shushing.

Pilgrim's eyes found Lacey's. He looked even grimmer, if it

were possible. She shrugged at him, frowning, wondering what she'd missed.

Tyler was a wisp of a woman in her sundress, her bare arms hanging at her sides and the sleeves of her hoodie tied around her waist in deference to the morning's building heat. The stump of her right wrist was clearly on show. She never tried to intentionally hide it. If it had been Lacey, she'd have tucked it into her sleeve or slipped it into her pocket.

Next to her, Sunny murmured something, but it wasn't for Lacey's ears. Lacey tightened her jaw on a sigh when she noticed Abernathy directing a scowl at the taller woman. Sunny's talking to herself was going to be a problem if the woman wasn't careful, and Lacey wasn't sure she had the energy to come to her defence if it did.

Lacey bit at the inside of her cheek, keeping silent, and turned back round. She'd spent little more than a day in Abernathy's company and was already getting tired of her bitchiness. She didn't know how Pilgrim put up with it. She'd feel bad for him, except he didn't seem to let it bother him.

'What're you all staring at?' Abernathy asked, looking past Lacey.

Dust cloud, Voice answered.

Sure enough, Pilgrim and Tyler (and now Lacey, Abernathy and Sunny) all stared along the broken and overgrown highway towards the dusty yellow cloud that lazily drifted above the road.

'What's causing it?' Sunny mulled aloud. At some point that morning, the woman had torn off a sleeve of a shirt to tie around her head to hold back her hair; it made the lean angles of her nose and jaw seem sharp and hungry.

When no one immediately answered, Abernathy said, 'Wile E. Coyote?'

Cars, Voice said. *Heading this way.*

Lacey's breath stopped. Actual *cars*? How many?

More than one, I'd say.

'Wait, I see them.' Abernathy was catching on.

'We need one,' was all Pilgrim said.

'Yes,' Tyler agreed.

'Hold up now,' Abernathy said, dividing her ire between the two of them. 'We don't even know who they are. They could have something to do with that explosion.'

'Doesn't matter,' Pilgrim said. 'We need a car.'

'I think it's more likely the explosion and whoever was over there is drawing them out,' Tyler pointed out. 'Same way it did us.'

'Even more reason to avoid them,' Abernathy said, dead-eyeing Tyler.

'We're not really prepared for a confrontation,' Sunny said, brow creased with worry.

She wasn't wrong. No one was in good health. Between them, they sported a truly impressive array of scrapes, cuts and bumps. When they'd briefly paused to rest before hitting the diner and to consult the map, a collection of moans and hisses had chorused as they'd moved stiffly back into a walking rhythm again. The lacerated, swollen soles of Lacey's feet hurt more than the rest of her combined. Standing *hurt*. Hurt more than walking or sitting did. Her jaw ached from gritting her teeth. Her hips were sore from how she'd adjusted her stride to alleviate the pain, yet each step stung sharper, bit deeper. She hoped the dampness she felt in her bandages and socks was sweat and not blood.

At some point you need let me try and help with that, Voice said, chastising her.

She couldn't. She hadn't wanted to slow them down. She was desperate to potentially lessen any miles between her and Addison. If Voice got within a certain distance of her, there was every chance he would be able to hear Addison again. He'd done so before; he could do so again. It was their only lead and Lacey clung to it like a barnacle to a ship's sinking hull.

She also hadn't wanted to slow them down because Pilgrim and Tyler – and Abernathy, too, to a far, far smaller degree – were rightfully concerned about the friends they'd sent on ahead to the Inn, and Pilgrim wasn't the sort to make attachments. It made Lacey awfully curious – jealous, too, if she were being truthful with herself – that he had befriended these people in her absence, and seemingly so easily. She'd asked a strategic question or two about them, digging away at his short answers, pushing for more than his offered age, appearance and banal personality descriptors. The most interesting thing she'd learned was that Jay had been obsessed with finding her ever since he'd read her personalised note scribbled inside Pilgrim's copy of *Something Wicked This Way Comes*. It was also pretty embarrassing. She'd scrawled a boatload of kisses at the bottom of that message. She'd never in a thousand years expected anyone to see them. But that book had led Pilgrim back to her, so she was glad she'd written in it, sickening number of kisses or not.

They always came back to each other, she and Pilgrim. It was like they were somehow magnetised, one to the other. If she believed in any kind of mushy shit, she might even think they were destined to. Everything had started on that dusty Texas road with Red (or Ruby, as Pilgrim called her) and now, heading to this Inn on the coast, everything was leading back to her. Or at least back to her brother, Albus. And Albus was part of that looping path, too, wasn't he? All of them on the same pre-joined chain, going round and round and round, as if the St Christopher necklace Lacey had taken from Red now symbolised the circular pathway she found herself on. Red was its connector – the mechanism that joined them up in this never-ending cycle – and the rest of them were the links along the way.

Don't you think Pilgrim is like the silver St Christopher medallion strung at the centre of our chain? Voice asked, eavesdropping on her idle thoughts. *Carrying us across deep and treacherous waters?* He shut up suddenly and hunkered down small behind her ear.

'Shhhh,' Tyler said, and Lacey got the feeling she was repeating what Tommy had already told Voice. The shorter woman was standing up on her toes, as if the added couple of inches would help with Tommy's reception. 'We're trying to listen . . .' Her head tilted, then her gaze locked on to Pilgrim. 'Yes. We think there's at least four.'

Pilgrim's sharp eyes had been tracking the fence running on their right past the diner's parking lot, its white, flaking paint and chipped wood beams in some disrepair. Now Lacey followed the same route to a narrow dirt road and towards a sparse grouping of trees. Through trunks and branches a large two-storey brick-built house poked out, a separate barn-styled garage next to it. She caught glimpses of the garage's deep red wooden slats and off-white beams. Broken windows stared back at her from the house's first storey.

Pilgrim cocked his ear upward and Lacey found herself doing the same.

Hear them? Voice whispered.

A skitter of fear tightened through her stomach. The low drone of engines was steadily getting louder. She twisted around, but the long stretch of highway was empty but for that rising dust cloud. Seeing her do it, Abernathy twisted to look, too, her hand going to the holstered gun at her hip.

'We need to get off the road,' Pilgrim ordered, sharp enough to make her jump. 'Now.' He pointed to the dirt road heading for the house.

No one argued. Tyler and Sunny hurried ahead, and Lacey limped after them, her feet flaring hot as molten metal. She bit her lip to hold back her moan, tears pricking her eyes.

She heard Abernathy come up behind her, and an arm wrapped her waist. A portion of her weight lifted blessedly off her feet.

'I'm fine,' Lacey muttered, annoyed at needing the help, especially from her.

Abernathy snorted. 'Sure you are.'

Pilgrim appeared on Lacey's other side, his arm joining Abernathy's at her waist. All the weight lifted from her feet and, between the two of them, they carried her, her oversized boots dangling as they rushed her up the path. The prick of tears burned hotter; Addison had only recently learned how to tie her own shoes, and even then she got it wrong half the time. Who was helping her with her laces while Lacey wasn't with her?

A sob built in her chest and she viciously bit it down, teeth catching on that soft inner flesh of her cheek. She tasted blood. Coolness descended as they moved into the shaded tunnel of trees.

It doesn't hurt to ask for help sometimes, Voice whisper-said, and he could have been speaking of her feet or of Addison, but it didn't really matter. Either way, it fired her annoyance because he was shining a spotlight on something she didn't want seen. It was so easy to forget Voice had an audience besides her now, and that he didn't think twice about being a snitch.

'You should have said you were suffering,' Pilgrim told her.

'I wasn't. I—' But Lacey didn't finish because Voice had already given her away. Besides, she'd rather Pilgrim think Voice had meant her feet and nothing more. He had enough to worry about.

I'm sorry, Voice said, in what, to her ears, sounded like the most insincere apology she'd ever heard from him. *I'm just looking out for you.*

Behind them on the highway, the dull, distant roar of engines rolled towards them.

Lacey gripped on tighter as Pilgrim and Abernathy ran.

Chapter 3

Pilgrim

Lacey weighed barely more than a sack of rocks; she was all bones and lean muscle. She jostled against him as he ran, her hipbone jabbing on every stride.

The double-wide wood-built garage was a yawning hole. Along the back wall ran a long workbench with a rack of rusting and cobwebbed tools hanging above it. The bench itself sheltered mounds of decomposing leaves, twigs and dirt, washed in by years' worth of winds and storms. Pilgrim took all this in and then dismissed it.

Tyler and Sunny waited for them by the house's side entrance, not wanting to enter unarmed. He wasn't inclined to trust either woman with a weapon just yet. Maybe never.

The door stood ajar.

'It was unlocked,' Tyler told him. Her eyes were big, with nerves and uncertainty and because they were just plain large; they were the eyes of an innocent, if you didn't know any better.

The odds were good that the house was long abandoned, but Pilgrim didn't trade in odds.

We should've gone back to the diner, Voice said low in his ear. *You'd already cleared that.*

'No, I need the second floor,' Pilgrim muttered distractedly.

'And more places to hide.' The last thing he needed was four women getting in the way of gunfire if shooting broke out.

He handed Lacey off to Abernathy and drew his gun. It felt good and heavy in his hand. Still, he hesitated. Not because he didn't have a plan forming in his head – he did – but because this time he wasn't alone. He had others besides himself to think about, and that was new for him. New and a little scary.

What're you waiting for? Voice asked, whispering, urgent. *They'll be here any minute.*

There had to be four vehicles, at least, possibly more, going by the size of the dust cloud their wheels were kicking up. And that was three too many. The only people travelling in convoy were people organized under a common purpose (and in Pilgrim's experience, those kinds of purposes rarely accounted for folk who didn't share in them).

Still, he hesitated, not knowing if this house was any safer than having them hide in the open somewhere. He stared at the door, at the cracked windowpane, at the warped wood at its base, where it curled away from its lower hinge. The handle was brass and too shiny. As if recent hands had been polishing it with use.

'Christopher,' Abernathy said to him, and he hated that she used his birth name. 'Are you moving your ass or what?'

Pilgrim had gone by many names in his lifetime, each one an attempt to forget the last. Christopher, Sol, Hoyt, Pilgrim. He barely remembered who Christopher was any more, doubted he'd recognise the man if he came up and rapped his knuckles off his head.

Abernathy was the only one who called him it, and Pilgrim wished she wouldn't.

He shoved through the door, shouldering it open, going in fast and low, gun ready. His eyes darted, scanned. His nostrils flared. The hallway reeked of mould and rot. The carpeting squished under his boots. Wallpaper peeled from the walls, brushing his shoulders as he passed. He checked the room to his left. A kitchen. Dank and filthy. Breakfast stools overturned. Dirt-streaked sideboards. The light murky through grimed-up windows and ratty net curtains. The room was unlived in and empty.

Next door along, on the right. A den. A dusty black leather two-seater. An entertainment cabinet as wide as the wall. Chunks lost from the plasterwork where spreading damp had pulled large-framed posters from their fittings. Glass lay in broken, glittery piles. The dead and silent flat-screen TV showed their shadowy figures as everyone piled inside. There was a large window slatted with a closed aluminium blind. Near the bottom, slats were bent and hanging, their gaps affording a view of the front of the property and, more importantly, the road. He ducked to glance through but could see nothing but the patch of road directly out front.

'Abernathy, stay with them. You' – he pointed at Sunny and the woman blinked – 'not one word from Beck. Understand?'

Beck was trouble not only for Sunny but for all of them. There was a tough conversation coming Sunny's way in her near future, whether Lacey wanted to protect her from it or not.

A confused crease bisected Sunny's brow, but she ventured an uncertain 'Sure, okay.' Which would have to do.

'Where're you going?' Lacey asked him. There was some concern in how she said it, but touchiness, too. Probably not happy to have him out of her sight again. He understood; he didn't want her out of his sight, either.

'I need to get a better view of what we're dealing with. I won't be long. Stay out of sight,' Pilgrim told them, and returned to the hall. Unsurprisingly, they started talking as soon as he was gone.

There was no time to finish his sweep of the ground floor. But he heard nothing, and he'd learned to trust his instincts. He ran for the staircase and went up two at a time, boots clomping and echoing through the house. A number of alarmed creaks and cracks climbed with him, but the stairs didn't cave in and send him crashing through their floorboards.

They're voice-hearers, for sure, Voice said, almost too quiet to hear. *They're coming through the closer they get. I'd guess at around ten of them altogether.*

'Be quiet,' Pilgrim growled. Their voices' ability to remain quiet during times like these was fast becoming crucial. If Voice could hear them, they could potentially hear Voice.

Pilgrim headed for the north-west corner and entered what had evidently once been a child's playroom. Plastic tubs filled with colourful plastic toys. A waist-high doll's house. A play mat with a faded schematic of roads and roundabouts, junctions and traffic lights, where a child could navigate their Matchbox cars along the network of streets. A wooden-framed chalkboard stood on its stand in the corner. Spidery white lettering in big bubble writing read 'Miss Mattys English Clas'. Miss Matty had been teaching her imaginary students the Alphabet. A for Apple. B for Bus. C for Cat.

Matty was most likely dead somewhere in this house or in the surrounding area. A pile of chalky bones and desiccated skin laid out next to her parents.

Pilgrim jogged across the road-system play mat to the window. From here, he had a far better view along the two-lane highway and of the four vehicles driving carefully along it. He watched as the short line of vehicles avoided first a downed tree and then a cracked fissure that had opened up asphalt from verge to centre line. A quad bike, a UPS-type delivery van, and two cars. Where the hell they'd gotten fuel for them from, he didn't know. The stuff was scarcer than popsicles on a hot day.

He wanted one of the cars. The one at the back would do. It was smaller than the others, but that mattered less than the fact that it was lagging a little behind the rest of the cavalcade.

Clearing the fissure, the quad bike pulled out in front and, even through the pane of glass and the packing insulation of the wall, Pilgrim heard it, felt the dull vibration through the floorboards, saw it in the faint blurriness of the shaking window. Two people sat astride the bike. No helmets. Hair streaming. They came up fast to the diner's parking lot, decelerating to a slow cruise, both heads turning to check the restaurant out, then the throttle opened up again and their speed increased. Good. They would be going too fast to take the turn towards the house. Pilgrim felt a slight ease in the tension across his shoulders.

'That's right,' he murmured. 'Keep going.'

He'd have time to take up position in the copse of trees next to the roadside – grab Abernathy on his way out for extra firepower – and wait for the smaller car to draw level. An ambush would work. It had to. His need outweighed the risk, as long as the risk was his to bear.

He was about to step back from the window when the quad bike skidded, braking so hard the back tyres left snaking skid marks on the asphalt. Gravel sprayed in an arc.

The rider sitting pillion was staring towards the house, and Pilgrim sensed Voice roil in anger, a frustration that thickened to a knot, and Pilgrim knew someone had broken their silence. And by someone he meant a voice. And by a voice, he could guess who. Beck.

He swore under his breath as the pillion rider tapped their buddy on the shoulder and pointed up the dirt road and watched as the quad bike made its turn on to the track. There it waited, and Pilgrim waited, too, sweating, his pulse beating in his temples.

He muttered a small prayer to himself: 'Don't all of you come up here. Don't all of you come up here.' The two on the quad, he could handle. In fact, they might make his plan easier in the long run. Dividing and conquering had served Pilgrim well in the past.

The UPS van came next, the last two cars in the convoy

slowing in its wake as the speed of the van slowed, slowed, slowed as it neared the farmhouse's turning and the idling quad bike. Pilgrim's fingers tightened around the butt of his handgun as the pillion rider waved the van onward, and the remaining vehicles coasted past the turn-off without stopping. As the three vehicles continued on their way, the quad's rear wheels spun in a spit of dirt, the bike skidding in its tracks as it accelerated in a burst of speed up the farmhouse's dirt road and disappeared beneath the canopy of trees.

A call came up to him – Abernathy shouting his name – but he spent three precious seconds waiting to see if any of the vehicles broke rank to turn back and follow after the quad.

No one did. The two riders approached alone.

Pilgrim may have smiled as he ran for the stairs.

CHAPTER 4

Abernathy

Abernathy hated babysitting, and she especially hated it when it entailed looking after grown-ass women.

'Don't you even have a knife I could borrow?' Lacey said.

Abernathy had already informed her that, no, she did not have a weapon for her. That wasn't to say she *didn't* have a knife, just that she wasn't about to hand it over to some teenager she didn't know squat about except for what Christopher had told her. Sure, he treated her like a long-lost baby sister, but that didn't mean Abernathy had to.

Thinking of people not to trust, Abernathy checked on Tyler, but all the woman was doing was kneeling at the window, nose to the windowsill, focused on what was going on outside. Which was a wise thing to be doing, if you asked Abernathy, except she couldn't join her because Lacey was still talking at her.

'I don't want to keep it. I'll give it back.'

'You should have grabbed a knife from the diner when you had the chance,' Abernathy said, considering moving to the window anyway and screw Lacey and whatever she wanted to do.

'I didn't *think* to grab one because we left in a hurry to watch a freaking *bomb* explode. I was distracted. You know what?

Forget it. I'll get my own blade.' Lacey turned to leave, presumably for the kitchen.

Abernathy caught her wrist. 'No, you don't. Stay where you are.'

Lacey jerked her arm away, breaking Abernathy's grip with an ease that surprised her. The teen was pissy, and Abernathy thought that maybe she needed to reassess a few things about this girl. First being, she wasn't a girl. Eighteen was plenty old enough to be a problem to her.

'I know you have one,' Lacey said, more quietly than Abernathy expected. 'I just wanna be able to defend myself.'

Abernathy opened her mouth, but Lacey's eyes widened, her head swinging towards the tall streak of piss who liked talking to the air. 'Sunny, no!'

Sunny had her hands up, long fingers spread wide in a cease-and-desist gesture. Her eyes were directed left of where Abernathy was standing and up half a foot. Abernathy frowned from the woman to the space next to her.

Sunny was obviously upset. 'Beck, you said you wouldn't,' she said, mouth downturned.

Beck again. Of course it was.

'*Sunny, shut him up*,' Lacey hissed, obviously tipping into panic.

'Oh no,' Tyler murmured. She hadn't moved from her position at the window and Abernathy didn't need to look to hear the rev of an engine out on the highway, hear it gun louder as it failed to pass the track that led to their farmhouse. She wasn't entirely sure if this was part of Christopher's plan or not, but if she had to guess . . .

It seemed like no time at all passed before Tyler's back zapped straight as if she'd been shocked with a Taser (Abernathy knew this from first-hand experience) and she whispered, 'They're *coming*.'

'Who is?' Abernathy demanded.

'I don't know,' Tyler whispered again, as if whispering would help them now. 'A bike, I think.'

'Shit. *Christopher!*' Abernathy yelled it towards the doorway he'd disappeared through. '*Company!*' She snapped her fingers to get Tyler's attention. 'Get away from the window, little rabbit, before they see you.' And wonder of wonders, Tyler did as she was told.

Abernathy reached under her pack to the back of her waistband and pulled the bowie knife sheathed there. She flipped it around and offered it handle first to Lacey. The girl readily gripped it without a word of thanks. Typical.

Abernathy was about to shoo all three women out of the man-cave they'd been dumped in, but Lacey was already doing it, ushering Sunny and Tyler towards a connecting door leading to an adjoining room. Abernathy followed. It was furnished with plush sofas, low coffee tables, ornaments draped in cobwebs and a grand fireplace packed with old, grey logs. Everything was filthy with dust. The door to the hallway was shut. Opposite the connecting door, a third door opened on to the cracked black-and-white-tiled flooring of what had to be the house's main foyer.

The engine stopped right outside the side entrance and revved a number of times. Showy and aggressive. A motorbike, for sure. A big one, by the sounds.

'Brazen fuckers,' Abernathy muttered. She drew her Sig Sauer from the holster at her hip, in two minds about it; she was low on ammo and didn't want to waste it. Tyler had chugged to a stop and Abernathy snagged her wrist, pulling her around the nearest coffee table and towards the open doorway.

Silence descended as the engine cut off, and a cold needle of expectation pricked her bowels. She wanted to yell out for Christopher and his gun again but instead checked over her shoulder to make sure Sunny and Lacey were coming with her. The taller woman, with her slim frame and her stupid multicoloured hemp knapsack, had stayed at the limping girl's side. Had even moved to cup Lacey's elbow to support her.

'Move it,' Abernathy hissed, hurrying past them, and almost accidentally shot Christopher in his stupid face when she came out in the foyer and found him descending the stairs in a mad rush.

The side entrance crashed open, door slamming the wall. Glass shattered.

'*Yoohoo! Anyone home?*'

Pilgrim froze on the steps and Abernathy froze with him, her hand hot and sweaty around Tyler's forearm. She could hear the small woman's short, panting breaths.

The broken tiles beneath their feet clinked. Behind her, Lacey and Sunny became statuettes.

Abernathy eyed the tiles between them and the room across the foyer. The majority were cracked or splintered. It would be like trying to walk across smashed pottery.

A second man, different from the first, yelled, '*Girl Scout Cookies! Get three boxes for two!*'

Sniggers and guffaws. They had a couple of fucking comedians on their hands here.

Glass crunched as the men's feet stamped inside. Abernathy was extremely aware that the hallway the men were entering was the same hallway that ran the length of the house, all the way to the open, airy foyer and the staircase where she and the others were playing musical statues. Walk twenty-five yards and here they'd be.

A door squeaked and a resounding crash erupted from the kitchen.

Tyler flinched, bumping into Abernathy's shoulder.

More crockery smashed, joining the rest on the kitchen floor. Laughter drifted down the hall as a heavier clatter sounded. What in hell were they doing in there? Throwing furniture?

Christopher was patting the air at them, and Abernathy knew

what he wanted. Not to come any further. Back up. And he was reversing, too, ascending the stairs in careful steps.

Another quiet *clink* of feet and Lacey appeared on Abernathy's right. She was shaking her head vehemently and gesticulating for him to come down, but Christopher wasn't paying her any mind. He pointed to the doorway at their backs and the instruction was clear. Get off the tiles and out of sight.

'He's going to draw them upstairs,' Lacey muttered.

What kind of batshit plan was *that*? Last thing Abernathy would want was to trap herself up there alone and outnumbered. But Christopher was a big boy. And they had themselves to worry about.

She nodded for Lacey to do as she'd been told and back up, but the girl was scowling and not budging.

'We're not *leaving* him,' Abernathy mouthed almost silently, trying to keep the annoyance off her face. 'Just do as he says.'

'Lacey.' Sunny had retreated, her skinny butt already partway through the sitting room's doorway, her feet safely back on carpet, her hand on Lacey's shoulder.

Tyler tugged for her arm to be released (Abernathy had forgotten she was holding on to her), and she let her go, relieved to have her hand back. Abernathy swiped her sweaty palm on her jeans.

Lacey went reluctantly and Abernathy herded everyone quietly back into the room. Sunny went for the closed door leading to the hallway and stayed there as if readying herself to barricade it closed if necessary. Tyler ducked behind the nearest sofa, out of sight, which suited Abernathy just fine. She wasn't any use to anyone anyhow.

The two men exited the kitchen and stomped their way across the hallway into the man-cave. They whooped their way inside, plastic cracking as they kicked games controllers tethered to consoles, the metal blinds rattling as they knocked into them.

Abernathy faced the doorway connecting the man-cave to

their sitting room, all that separated them a thin panel of door, half closed. Through the crack between door and doorframe, shadowy forms flitted by.

Abernathy's heart hammered in her chest, pulsed down to her gut where her muscles tensed tight. She couldn't pretend her arms weren't trembling as she held her gun two-handed and aimed. Its grips were slick. Adrenaline fizzed through her veins. A primal excitement curled in the pit of her stomach, a wildness that was exhilarating. Her finger tightened around the gun's trigger.

She was aware of Lacey at her side. Lacey hadn't ducked behind the nearest piece of furniture but stood shoulder to shoulder with her, bowie knife in hand. That was interesting.

From the floor above, a loud thumping, of someone running across floorboards. To Abernathy it sounded obvious it was a fabricated noise designed to draw attention. Who ran that noisily? No one, that's who. But the two idiots in the other room weren't too bright. No more whoops came from in there, no more trashing the place. A silence that didn't last more than two seconds, when Abernathy figured they were exchanging glances and maybe a super-short game of Charades. And then a sudden thud of footfalls.

There was a moment when she was convinced they would burst into the sitting room with them and gunfire would explode, triggered like landmines – hot-jacketed shrapnel flying everywhere – but the two men stuck to familiar territory and pounded back into the hallway and ran for the foyer, bypassing their sitting room altogether.

Feet *chink*ed and skated across broken tiles and then found the staircase. They went up – *thump-thump-thump-thump* – but they hadn't reached the top when Abernathy's boot cracked a black tile underfoot, right down its centre. The guy in the rear, his rat-tailed hair hanging down his back, was halfway up the staircase, but he was turning around to look. She shot him in that sweet spot between his shoulder-blades. *Bam*. One bullet.

No one could call that a waste.

The guy went sprawling, bumping down the stairs on his belly. It would've been funny if not for his friend, who'd whirled round to see what had happened. His Neanderthal gaze fell on her, and she was smirking, figuring it was easy enough to shoot him, too, but his hand was flashing up and what the hell was *that*? A fucking *Uzi*?

A line of bullets spat out, tearing into the wall at her shoulder, and she was sure she'd have been cut in two if Christopher hadn't appeared at the top of the stairs and swung what looked like a kiddies' wooden chalkboard. It smacked Uzi-guy in his head, and he stumbled sideways, colliding with the bannister. Bullets ripped into the tiles at Abernathy's feet and someone grabbed her pack from behind and hauled her out of range.

A second splintering crack and the gunfire ceased and the man folded over, holding on to his head.

Abernathy's ears were ringing – nothing ever prepared you for gunshots, especially not indoors – and her body thrilled at the smell of gunpowder, muscles light and loose with the release of adrenaline. Over her ear-ringing she heard the guy's moans. He sounded like a baby calf missing its mama's teat.

'You almost got us killed,' Lacey snapped, releasing her hold on Abernathy's bag and shoving past her.

Abernathy caught herself on the doorjamb. 'What?' she said. A minute ago, Lacey was being a brat about leaving Christopher to fend for himself. Now she was mad that she'd stepped in and helped? Someone needed to make up their mind.

Lacey stalked away, limping through a sea of clinking ceramics and up the steps to where Christopher had disarmed the Uzi-toting guy and was patting him down for more weapons. The moaning had stopped but he sat slumped on the steps with a grimace on his face, blood dripping off an eyebrow, hair matted wet and dark to his scalp.

Abernathy followed after Lacey, gun hanging from her hand, not wanting to put it away yet because it would make her feel like a guilty kid hiding the marker she'd used to scrawl across the wallpaper, and that pissed her off, so she re-holstered it anyway, sliding the gun in hard enough to tug at the waistband of her jeans.

'Gary?' the Uzi-guy said, throat full of gravel. He was stretching his leg out to try to nudge his friend where he lay spread-eagled like a starfish. 'Gary, you all right?'

'Pretty sure he's not,' Abernathy told him.

'Sit still,' Christopher instructed the man. Done with his pat-down, he gripped the guy under his arm and half dragged, half lifted him to sit two steps higher, out of reach of his dead buddy. Christopher wasn't overly rough with his treatment, but the guy winced all the same.

'Why'd you shoot him?' Uzi-guy demanded, squinting at her through an eyeful of blood. 'We didn't do nothing to you.'

There was recrimination in his narrow-eyed glare, and that pissed Abernathy off even more. She looked at the others, but all she got from Christopher was a blank-faced stare and from Lacey an annoyance so loud she might as well have been screaming it. She didn't bother looking at Tyler or Sunny, loitering at the foot of the stairs. She didn't give a shit what they thought.

Abernathy shrugged. 'You came in here, hollering and wrecking the joint. Was that supposed to make me think you were being friendly?'

Uzi-guy shot her a venomous look. 'We weren't sneaking. Gary joked about selling Girl Scout Cookies. We made sure you heard us.'

'You were armed.' Tyler said it in her measured way, which Abernathy usually found condescending as fuck. Right now, not so much.

Sniffing, the man wiped a rough hand over his face, smearing his blood. 'Gary wasn't.'

'First-aid kit?' Christopher asked, directing his question at Abernathy.

He wanted to use their supplies on this piece of garbage? She shook her head at him and returned his stare. She gave up pretty quickly, though. She recognised that look. He'd continue to stare at her until she did as he asked. It wasn't even a battle of wills with him; he would just wait her out until she got fed up. Sighing, she shucked off her pack and unfastened the top, digging her arm in deep and rooting for her kit.

Lacey had climbed up to the dead man, wasting her time by feeling at his neck, checking for a pulse. She straightened up. 'Shooting someone in the back wasn't exactly our plan.'

Speak for yourself, Abernathy wanted to say but didn't. She found the plastic container and pulled it out. She threw it, a little too hard, at Christopher, but he caught it smartly. He set about staunching the flow of blood leaking from the guy's head. Uzi-guy gasped and gritted his teeth as Christopher worked.

'Will the others come back for you?' Christopher asked him.

The man said nothing for a long moment, then fidgeted and gave a sullen shrug. 'Maybe?'

Christopher's eyes sharpened on him. 'They'll be back,' he said with confidence.

'What made you come in here?' Tyler asked. 'Did you hear one of us?' She'd come near enough to place her hand on the bannister. Abernathy was beginning to feel like they were chess pieces on a board, each manoeuvring for a better position. She saw Sunny was keeping well out of it and, honestly, Abernathy thought she was the wisest of all of them.

Uzi-guy's frown was heavy and unfriendly, but he answered her question. 'Gary does that. Hears stuff. Better than the rest of us do. He said there was *one* of you. Not five.' He cast his dark, hostile gaze over them.

'Nothing to hear in me,' Abernathy said, smiling with her teeth.

'Me, neither,' Sunny said.

Abernathy blinked, swinging a confused look on her.

'Where are you heading?' Christopher asked him.

Uzi-guy's mouth twisted into an ugly sneer. 'What's it to you?'

'You're heading further east,' Lacey answered for him. 'Same as us.'

'Is that so? Did you like the fireworks show some friends of ours put on just now?' The guy looked at each of them, letting his words sink in. 'Lit up the sky like a calling card, didn't it? Better believe that shit's just the beginning. It's all gonna be moving fast now. You mark my words.'

Abernathy's suspicion spiked at the looks Christopher, Lacey and Tyler exchanged with each other. 'What's he mean?' she asked.

'You have your zip ties?' Christopher asked her.

She did, but that wasn't answering her question.

'It's our time now,' Uzi-guy said, staring dead at her. 'If me 'n' Gary knew two of you in here weren't with voices, we wouldn't have spent time fooling around. I'd have come right in and shot you in your dirty faces.'

Abernathy felt the burn of anger flush her cheeks. 'Now I'm extra sorry I didn't shoot you in the back, like I did your buddy.'

Fury lit up his eyes, and Tyler yelled, 'Be careful!'

Christopher grabbed for the guy as he lunged off his step, teeth bared. Lacey skipped away, hopping down a step and stumbling on her gimpy feet, crying out in pain.

Abernathy didn't move. Wouldn't give him the satisfaction. She could have shot him before he'd made it within three steps of her and they both knew it.

'Abernathy,' Christopher demanded, voice gruff with the effort of forcing the man back on to his butt. 'Zip ties.'

'The tide is changing, sweetheart.' Uzi-guy grimaced a smile as Pilgrim roughly pinned his arms back. 'It's *your* turn to feel what it's like to be hunted. I watched my wife burn because of people like you. A gang of you, standing around a pit filled with our bodies, heaped so high I was waiting for it to come tumbling down. You could smell it burn for miles. See the smoke from even further. It filled up the sky like a furnace. Like a cook pit.' His voice faltered. 'The biggest barbecue you ever saw. Made my mouth water, smelling it. Can you believe that?' Tears welled but didn't spill over. 'My burning wife smelled so good it made my stomach growl. *You* did that to me, you murderous fucks. We'd done nothing and you *did* that to us.'

'So what? It's your turn to burn everything down now? That's your grand plan?'

'Something like that,' he said, his lip lifting to bare his teeth. 'He's in the east now. Did you know that? Flitting Man's gonna find you fuckers and burn every one of you out. Ain't gonna be no kind of fancy facility for you to escape to any more. Just a graveyard of ash and bone. Same as you gave to us.'

There were two simple words in his little speech that landed like mini-explosions, rocking Abernathy's world for a second time that morning. A 'fancy facility', he'd said. Had this idiot heard of Elysian Fields?

'You know about a facility out there?' Tyler asked him carefully.

'Look, I'm not saying shit with *her* here,' Uzi-guy said, refusing to drop his eyes from Abernathy's. It was only Christopher saying her name that made Abernathy finally look away from him. No one else spoke.

'The ties,' Christopher said quietly. 'Now.'

She passed the zip ties up to Lacey, who passed them to Christopher. He zippered the man's wrists to the bannister and left him there, descending to the dead man and checking his pockets. He didn't seem to find anything useful. She didn't think he would say anything more, but as he came down past her, he said, 'I would've dealt with them.'

'Maybe,' she said, eyes following him. 'But you're not on your own any more, remember?'

He stopped with his back to her, head partway turned in her direction. 'And neither are you. Next time, think about who's standing next to you before shooting.' She knew he meant his precious Lacey but wouldn't give him the satisfaction of acknowledging it.

'Best be quick,' Uzi-guy said, his tears all dried up. 'Another ten minutes and it won't be just me you'll need to deal with. Best be long gone before then.'

Christopher didn't bother turning to address him, either. 'No one's going anywhere,' he said. 'Your friends still have something I want.'

Chapter 5

Lacey

Lacey was the new owner of an Uzi, and she didn't like it one bit. There was no precision to the weapon. It was a thing that killed indiscriminately with no finesse and no conscience.

Stop complaining, Voice said. *It's better than nothing*.

The injured man, his head wrapped in one of Abernathy's bandages, watched silently from his perch on the stairs. He outwardly kept his peace, but Voice said the inside of the man's head was anything but silent. After briefly outlining his plan with her, Tyler and Sunny, Pilgrim had taken the keys to the quad bike from their captive and enlisted Abernathy's help, both of them disappearing outside. Lacey was getting pretty tired of being left out.

She'd been tasked with watching the injured guy, although he wasn't capable of doing anything, tethered like he was. She and Sunny had already dragged his dead friend off the stairs and left his body in the dining room off the foyer. Done with their first order of business, Sunny had leaned herself against the bannister's newel cap, arms folded over the top, and Lacey and Tyler sat on the bottom steps, using the opportunity to rest for a minute. Lacey's feet throbbed abominably. It made her want to chew on the Uzi until her teeth cracked. It didn't stop her leg from jigging up and down, though, or the pit in her stomach from cinching tighter and tighter with every second that ticked by.

You know, I believed him when this fella said they didn't want to hurt us, Voice said quietly. *I think they got excited when they heard people like themselves in here.*

'Excited for us to join them in killing us some non-hearers?' Lacey muttered. 'Sounds great.'

The bannister creaked as Sunny shifted against it. Her eyes caught on Lacey's, but she didn't say anything.

No, it's more than that. Tommy told me—

'Tommy is on mute,' Tyler said from her seat two steps above Lacey's. 'They need to stay quiet as much as possible for now. There's trouble in them being overheard at the wrong times.'

'Like this, you mean?' Lacey nodded at the man with his bandaged head and the spilled blood on the stairs.

Tyler's mouth was an unhappy line. 'We're not alone with ourselves any more. We can't pretend we are. The dreams we've been having, what this man and his friends have done, that explosion out there. A small part of what's happening, I'm sure. People will be eager to cast aside the humiliations they've suffered these past seven years and will be swept up in their fervour to retaliate. For bad or good, he's giving them that.'

Sunny's expression was troubled. 'The Flitting Man.'

'Yes, of course the Flitting Man. He's been feeding on what's inside of us for a while now. And not just the animosities but the need to find a place where we belong, to be accepted for what we are now. I should know. He got to me, too . . .' she trailed off, her gaze shifting away.

'What did you do, Tyler?' Lacey asked. She hadn't realised she was going to ask the question until it was out of her mouth. 'I see how Abernathy treats you. How Pilgrim doesn't trust you. Why?'

Tyler didn't answer straight away. 'I hurt some people,' she said softly, still not looking at anybody. 'People who were trying to cure us of what we are. What we hear. They were doing despicable things to us. So I . . . I chose to stop them.'

She killed them, she means, Voice murmured.

'I stopped them, but I hurt Abernathy in the process and I betrayed Pilgrim. I regret that very much.'

'But not the stopping part?'

'Not— I . . .' Her conflicted expression warred with itself before easing back into calmness. Her eyes lifted to Lacey's. 'No. Despite the guilt I carry, I don't regret that.'

Lacey glanced down at the stump of Tyler's arm, at how dainty she was, in stature, in strength.

Dainty and dangerous aren't mutually exclusive things.

The injured guy broke into their conversation. 'What're you doing with that bitch?' He nodded along the hallway to where Pilgrim and Abernathy had disappeared. 'She's not one of us. She's got no loyalty to anyone but herself.'

No one spoke up to defend Abernathy. It wasn't the fact that Abernathy had killed this man's friend that bothered Lacey so much, it was how she'd made Lacey back down from saving Pilgrim from his lone-wolf save-the-day heroics, and then the woman had immediately done exactly as she pleased (and almost got herself and Lacey shot up in the process). Why was it one rule for Abernathy and another for her?

Abernathy lives by her own rules. Voice said it in a disgustingly dreamy way, as though he understood Abernathy on some soul-deep level Lacey never would.

'This fancy facility you mentioned,' Tyler said, her laser-focus disconcerting. 'How do you know about it?'

The injured guy became cagey under the scrutiny, his eyes skittish. 'Just stuff we've heard. Word gets passed on, if you know where to listen, like Gary did. You know what I think, though? I think the Flitting Man already found it. I think he found that place and he burned it to the ground. We're gonna go and find out for ourselves. Hey, you should come with us,' he said suddenly. 'There's nothing to say you can't tag along. It's only *her* who wouldn't be welcome.' He sent a dirty look over Sunny's shoulder and down the hall.

'Hate to break it to you, but we're not going anywhere with you,' Lacey told him.

'All this back and forth is pointless,' he said, his tone going hard, his eyes shining. 'Can't you feel it? Feel *us*? I woke up last night from a dead sleep, and it was like waking up to a new world. Like it was breathing again, free and easy. *Alive*. I know you feel it, too.'

From the corner of her eye, Lacey gauged Sunny's and Tyler's reactions. In truth, Lacey *had* been feeling it. For days now. A hunted, terrorized awareness of everything and everyone around her. She had felt watched. Spied on. Violated. It was only with Pilgrim finding his way back to her that those feelings had morphed into something more. Something that could be useful to her. If she ever wanted to find her way back to Addison, she knew she would need to embrace this new awakening – in Voice and in all voices – and let it guide her to where she needed to be.

'We're finding each other now,' the injured man said, and Lacey envisaged a widening door, battered and worn, opening in his head; a welcoming light glowed from within, beckoning her nearer. 'That's why me and Gary came in here. We're all in this together, every one of us. And no one will ever get to hurt us again. We won't let them.'

Sunny shifted uncomfortably, glancing to her side, where Lacey imagined Beck might be standing. 'This is dangerous talk. You should stop.'

She's right, Lacey. Let's stop this.

The injured man shuffled to the edge of his step, his tied hands preventing him moving more than that. His eyes flicked up the hallway and his voice lowered. 'All you'd have to do is get her gun off her. Or untie me and I'll do it. We won't harm the man. We don't hurt our own.'

Pilgrim will hurt you, *though*, Voice said, more loudly, and with more bravado than Lacey knew he was feeling. She could sense his unease, perhaps because Lacey had been listening a little too intently to this man's words. But she had her reasons – every one of them beginning with the letter A.

At the end of the hallway, a crunch of footsteps on glass made Lacey's heart leap into her throat. As if Voice had conjured him by name, Pilgrim stood in the open doorway. He waved Lacey to him.

'Sunny, keep an eye on things here?' Lacey asked, taking a deep breath to steady herself as she stood. Sunny nodded. 'Shout if he tries anything.'

'I will.' Sunny hovered for a second as Lacey limped past, and Lacey almost laughed at the protective gesture. A small trip was the least of Lacey's concerns right now.

She wanted to lean a hand on the wall as she hurried along the hallway but didn't want to touch the mouldering stuff, and she didn't want Pilgrim to see her needing the support. He stepped outside with her, leaving the door open so he could see back to the foyer, where they'd left Sunny and Tyler in charge of their captive.

'Sit,' he said, pointing to the steps.

She gave him a look. 'I'm not a dog.'

'I know. Humour me anyway.'

Despite the knot in her stomach, she sat and was relieved to do it.

'We've found a fuel canister and a hose to syphon the bike's fuel. Abernathy is carrying everything behind the garage. Which is where you, Sunny and Tyler will wait while—'

'*No*. No way.' Lacey was well on her way to steaming angry, a welcome heat to douse her nerves. 'I'm not some kid you can shove behind the nearest bit of cover and tell to sit on her hands.'

'I wasn't finished,' Pilgrim said. He didn't raise his voice, but Lacey found her teeth *click*ing shut. 'You'll wait there with this.' He reached past her to what she'd failed to notice leaning against the wall.

Her eyes widened. Her pleasure at seeing the hunting rifle should have set off alarm bells. Like a kid wanting candy, she opened her hands for it. Pilgrim almost cracked a smile as he handed the weapon over.

'They left it strapped to their bike,' he said. 'Anyone could have circled round and taken it.' He shook his head, unimpressed. 'I'm amazed they've stayed alive this long.'

She ran her palm along the laminate wood of its stock. It wasn't as cared for as she'd have liked – it needed cleaning and oiling – but the bolt slid smoothly enough and it felt wonderful in her hands. It was loaded, too. 'Was there any—' She didn't need to finish; Pilgrim was reaching into his pocket and bringing out a handful of brass cartridges.

'Sweet,' she said, accepting them from him.

'Do you trust Sunny?'

She paused. His mouth was bracketed with unsmiling lines, his eyes serious and steady. She shoved the cartridges into her pockets while she thought it over. Her gaze moved past him to the garage that resembled a barn. She didn't know what she was looking for in there – there was nothing but useless old tools and a rotting workbench; an old life left to decay and rot. Barns weren't really her favourite things these days.

'I'd like to,' she said.

'And Beck? He's careful to be quiet around me and Voice.'

She wasn't so sure of her answer this time. 'Not so much,' she replied, honestly. 'I'm pretty sure he tries to talk her into stuff she doesn't want to do.'

'You need to have a conversation with her. No more putting it off.'

'I can't, Pilgrim. You've seen how she is. Beck's as real to her as you are to me. It would destroy her to know she'd been lying to herself all these years, that she'd rather make him up than accept the truth about herself. Who are we to tell her what to believe?'

'You need to figure it out. I wouldn't ask if it wasn't important.'

Her mouth was as unsmiling as his.

'Lacey, I mean it. If you can't do it, then I will.'

She sighed. 'Fine. I'll do it.'

'Good. If you're happy with how it goes, give her the Uzi.'

That surprised her. Surprised Voice, too, judging by the small *huh* sound he made. A second later a grumble of irritation came from him.

2.0 says good luck, Voice said, keeping his volume low. *He thinks we'll need it.*

That's what he called Pilgrim's Voice sometimes. Version 2.0. He reasoned he'd been around longer. There was no pretence of affection to the nickname. She didn't think her Voice was all that pleased that Pilgrim had moved on without him, and she doubted Pilgrim's Voice was happy that hers was being such a dick about it. That was one difference about them, at least. Hers seemed to be more immature. Lucky her.

Abernathy was coming around the side of the garage, hands empty, her walk unhurried, as if she didn't have a care in the world. Most people would call it arrogant.

I like how she walks.

Voice liked Abernathy full stop. He gave her a pass for ninety-nine per cent of her questionable behaviour, and Lacey wasn't sure what to make of it. He wasn't in the habit of taking to people as fast as he had with Abernathy. As far as Lacey was concerned, the jury was still out.

She struggled to stand up, not wanting to be sat on her butt when Abernathy arrived. Pilgrim offered her a hand and, after a second, Lacey took it. 'You're being very trusting, letting me make all these big decisions,' she said to him.

'If we all end up with Uzi-sized bullets in our hides, I'll be sure to rethink letting you make any more.'

Lacey smirked and shoved his helping hand away.

'Talk to Sunny – do it now, while there's time,' he said, all joking aside.

'Sir, yes sir.' Lacey saluted smartly, and this time his smile cracked free, just a little, before he turned away and left her on the step, alone but for her rifle.

Chapter 6

Pilgrim

A high, strident whistle reached Pilgrim's ears. He couldn't hear the sounds of engines yet, but that didn't matter.

Good luck, compadre, Voice whispered, then fell silent.

The staircase was empty. Abernathy had taken their prisoner outside, tasked with putting distance between him and the farmhouse. Pilgrim wasn't about to risk having any more warnings go out to the rest of his group of what waited for them here. Tyler had calculated that a hundred yards from the house should be a safe amount, or at least far enough away to make any form of communication difficult; Abernathy was to tie him to a tree out there. Pilgrim had heard no gunshots, which meant she'd either left him gagged and alive or she'd found a quieter way to permanently silence him.

The people approaching would know something wasn't right, of course. Both of their friends were missing and that would be warning enough.

Lacey had whistled only once, which meant there was one car. Which was good. It meant they were being cautious. Not planning on overrunning the place or bursting in under a hail of gunfire.

A second later, he heard the solitary engine approaching. It rumbled to a stop somewhere on the road, not coming any closer, and Pilgrim slipped into the den, kicking through the cracked bits of plastic and wiring on the floor and to the metal drapes. He went to one knee.

A compact car, small and bug-like. He smiled. It idled at the turn-off to the dirt track.

'What're they waiting for?' he murmured. But he knew. They were listening.

Inside his head, Voice was soundless. He might have been gone altogether if Pilgrim hadn't known any better.

He rested his hand on the windowsill. The coolness of the glossed wood under his fingertips. He listened to his heart beat, regular and solid. Concentrated on his breaths. Counted them going in and going out. A sensation of stillness dropped over him, a glass-perfect lake with no ripples and no currents.

'How many?' he asked.

On the windowsill, his index finger tapped. One, two, three, four times. He waited for a fifth. None came.

Four people.

The car's rear door opened and someone climbed out. They were too far away to determine age or sex, but they held something in their hands. No one would be sent back here unarmed. They jogged away from the vehicle into the copse of trees, cutting through, heading away from the side entrance Pilgrim and the others had entered through. They were either aiming straight for the front door or planning on circling round to the rear of the property from the other side.

The car edged forward, taking the turn and starting up the dirt track. Pilgrim didn't wait for them. He left the den and ran for the foyer. Behind the staircase, towards the back of the house, a ground-floor extension opened up into a large breakfast and seating area. Ceiling-to-floor panes of glass gave an expansive scenic view of the backyard with its Olympic-sized swimming pool, rolling fields and treelines.

Ten rounds remained in Pilgrim's handgun and four people

were heading their way. Still, he didn't plan on drawing his gun if he could help it. Any noise made would be what he wanted them to hear and nothing more.

His boots crunched across the foyer tiles, then thudded up the stairs. Hitting the top, he paused to breathe and listen. The car had pulled up outside. The quad bike was gone but its tyre tracks were there, printed into the dirt for all to see. Pilgrim had considered covering them, but there hadn't been enough time and, in truth, this worked in his favour. The missing bike and the silence would be unsettling for them. They would be on edge. Confused. If the bike wasn't here, had their friends left with it? If so, why hadn't they returned to the convoy?

An opening of car doors. Pilgrim heard a low murmur of discussion. No doubt visually assessing everything Pilgrim had just gone over.

It was important they didn't get it into their heads to start their search outside. He didn't want them anywhere near the garage.

'Voice,' Pilgrim murmured.

Just be quiet until they leave, Voice said, hushed and furtive. *They won't think to look for us up here.*

Almost as one, the talking outside fell silent.

It was your bright idea to stick around and wait for them to come, Voice continued. *We could have just ridden off.* A pause, as if he were listening to Pilgrim speak, then glee in his voice. *I know! I can't believe they made it so easy. Who leaves the key hanging in the ignition like that? The idiots.* Voice went deathly quiet after that last word and Pilgrim could feel the intensity in how hard he listened. Pilgrim expected Lacey's Voice and Tyler's were doing the same.

Pilgrim listened, too.

More murmurs from outside, followed by someone louder, this person accusing. Car doors clunked shut and Pilgrim heard a single *boop* of an alarm activating.

A second later Voice whispered, *Got it. Go.*

Pilgrim ghosted left along the upstairs mezzanine and carefully lifted the bedside table he'd retrieved from a bedroom. He heaved it over the railing, leaning over to watch it fall. It hit the floor with a booming *crash.* Wood splintered, cracking as loud as gunshots. Its drawers popped out and skittered across the tiles.

Three more paces and Pilgrim had cleared the mezzanine. The front door burst open and a mad rush of feet ran inside. Tiles cracked and split. More footsteps pounded in from the side entrance. Men's voices called to each other. It was difficult to separate them, but he guessed at three. Which left one outside?

'At least one upstairs,' someone said, the man's voice floating up from the foyer below.

'There's blood. Look,' a second man said.

A second piece of furniture waited for Pilgrim outside the master bedroom. The kiddie's blackboard. Except Miss Matty's lesson was now A for Ambush, B for Betrayal and C for Chaos. The grain of its wood was stained dark with blood. He grabbed it, took aim and slung it under-armed, fast and powerful. It sailed through the bathroom's open doorway at the end of the landing. Aim true, it clattered noisily into the wall and dropped into the bathtub. He sidestepped into the master bedroom and silently closed the door. He didn't wait around as more shouts went up and running feet stampeded up the stairs – he crossed to the open window and climbed out on to the first-storey roof of the ground floor's extension. He stepped left, out of sight, his back to the wall.

The roofing sheets were moss-covered and treacherous, and he stayed where he was for a moment, eyes closed. He heard thumps and shouts from the floor behind him, but he didn't let it worry him. From memory muscle, he drew his hunting knife with his right hand and raised his left, holding it flat. He fully relaxed his fingers. Felt the whole appendage wash cold, tingling clean through to his fingertips. His hand numbed quickly and he felt a single, indirect pull, a puppet's string of ligaments. His pinkie finger twitched and wiggled.

He opened his eyes and turned left. He didn't hurry (staying undetected for this was more important than speed). His middle finger gave a twitch and he stopped. He stepped cautiously to the edge of the roof and peered down.

Beneath him, the fourth man had one hand cupped around is brow as he peered through the back window of what was the farmhouse's kitchen. He held a snub-nosed revolver. He hadn't wandered far from the car; it was around the south-east corner of the house, little more than fifteen yards away. Pilgrim glanced towards the garage. Lacey was watching him, only the left side of her head, left arm and the barrel of her rifle in view. She had the man below Pilgrim sighted for shooting. Pilgrim hadn't known she could handle her rifle ambidextrously. He shouldn't be surprised.

Only twenty seconds had passed since he'd climbed out on to the roof, and he didn't wait for the man below him to look up and spot him, or for the others to glance outside and see him there. He crouched, placed his now warm hand (his again and in full control of it) on the roof beside his boot, didn't bother counting to three – numbers were of no use for this – and vaulted to the ground.

From that height it was impossible to land silently, and the man startled and spun around. Pilgrim grabbed his gun-hand, locking it down, and thrust forward with his knife. The blade slid tip first into the man's throat. It silenced any noise of surprise, but Pilgrim knew it wouldn't silence any voice in his head. He followed after the man as he tipped backwards, falling, and slid the knife free. A gush of blood came with it.

In his thirties, face prematurely lined and grizzled with grey-flecked stubble, the man gurgled and babbled, blood spilling from his mouth, and a distant part of Pilgrim was regretful it had come to this.

'This him?' Pilgrim pulled the revolver from the dying man's limp grip and shoved it behind his belt.

Voice responded in the affirmative, more sensation than sound, and Pilgrim dug his hand into the man's pockets, avoiding the blood that was seeping through the front of his shirt. The car keys were in his right front pocket.

Lacey had put up her rifle. Pilgrim wasted no time in tossing her the keys in a high, graceful arc. She caught them against her chest and retreated safely behind the garage. He drew the man's revolver and backed away from him.

The stranger gasped in wet, bloody pants, his mouth opening and closing as red frothed between his lips. His skin was pallid. He would be dead in less than a minute. Despite this, the man held out a blood-covered, beseeching hand as Pilgrim lifted the gun. It was a useless gesture and they both knew it.

'I'm sorry,' Pilgrim said, and mostly he meant it, because he hadn't woken up this morning with the desire to kill anyone for a set of car keys, and this guy hadn't expected to be bleeding to death on the back decking of this farmhouse. Yet they'd both come here armed and willing to shoot at strangers, and that couldn't end well for everybody.

Gary getting popped in the back was just a bonus death, I guess, Voice said darkly, making no effort to lower his voice any more.

To eliminate any last doubts about detection, Pilgrim shot the man in the heart, killing him, and ran for the far corner of the farmhouse, away from the garage and away from Lacey, counting six steps by the time he was passing the tall picture windows. He glanced inside and saw the remaining three men in the foyer finish their race down the stairs and skate across the tiles. They froze when they saw him. Eyes locked. Pilgrim fired a further two shots, windows shattering in a waterfall of glass, and the men dived for the floor.

Pilgrim left them there, tucked his head down and ran.

CHAPTER 7

Abernathy

'You've well and truly screwed up the terms of warfare,' Abernathy said.

Uzi-guy was slumped against an oak, his butt in the dirt and sandwiched between thick, gnarly tree roots. His arms were tied behind his back, his head shrouded in a dark blue sweater she had found and tied around it to blindfold him.

He didn't respond to Abernathy's observation, but then she didn't expect him to.

'How is anyone supposed to get the jump on you now that you all have internal radio transmitters built into your heads?' She squatted down and dug in the earth, picking through bits of twigs and grass. She didn't like being this far away. If things went to shit, she'd be next to useless out here.

A thought occurred to her. 'Is that the whole point of it? So that no one can hide themselves away any more? You all can track and trace each other? No one gets left behind? Seems like a pretty vulnerable position to put yourselves in, if you ask me. Survival is based on being able to go to ground if you need to. You've all gone and fucked yourselves over.'

She found a rock, not too small and not too big, and threw it at him. It hit the top of his head but, still, she got nothing. He was still as a corpse.

'I don't even know why I'm talking to you,' she muttered. 'You can't answer me.'

The report of a gunshot echoed through the trees and Abernathy's head came up. She waited, then two more came.

'There's my cue,' she said, and stood.

That finally got a reaction, and Uzi-guy's head lifted. His nose and mouth made bumps under the sweater's material. The shape of his lips moved and churned and a muffled mumble came through the gag she'd stuffed into his mouth. Bringing him out here wouldn't do them much good if he went yelling his head off now, would it? Besides, she had little interest in anything he had to say.

She'd used a good twenty zip ties getting him out here and securing him. She had maybe ten left. She paused momentarily, standing over him. He couldn't see her, of course, but he stilled, as if sensing her. Maybe he heard the slide of her gun coming out of its holster. Maybe he felt her considering it. She stood poised, gun aimed at his sweater-enshrouded face, not much thought going on inside her head other than that yes/no pendulum swinging back and forth.

Her finger curled around the trigger.

He had stopped his mumbling.

'You know, don't you?' she murmured. 'Yeah, you do. You know.'

She thought of what Christopher would say if he discovered she'd shot an unarmed man, tied and helpless, his eyes and mouth covered. But the trigger felt good under her finger; all it would take was one smooth pull. Five pounds of pressure to release the gun's sear and drop the hammer. Such a satisfying amount of resistance. As if its trigger-pull had been made specifically for her. She wondered what Uzi-guy's voice was saying to him. Was it offering comfort? Was it telling him to be brave? She'd bet it was calling her a fucking whore and a bitch and wishing she would contract some horrendous disease that would make her tits rot off and her cooch fester. She didn't see how his thought processes would be different to any other man's, whether he heard a voice or not.

She holstered the Sig and turned from him, leaving him there without another word. The only two reasons she didn't shoot was because it would give away their position and, if she were lucky, his friends would never find him and the bastard would die of starvation. It was a horrible way to go, she'd heard.

Abernathy climbed on to the quad bike, fired it up, revved it as loudly and brazenly as this fucker and his dead buddy had done on arriving, and accelerated away in a spray of dirt.

Breaking from the cover of trees, she spotted Christopher easily, cutting through the field, sprinting. He was bearing down on the treeline fast, following the snaking tracks in the tall grass the bike had made on her drive out here. On seeing her emerge twenty feet north of where she'd entered, he immediately adjusted course.

Two men were in pursuit and a third man trailed further back. When Christopher altered direction, all three trampled their way off the bike's tracks and into the tall grass. The stems fought them, probably grabbed at ankles and legs, but no one was giving up. Christopher had a good head start, but they were almost as fast as him.

The man in front lifted an arm and, while running, fired off a wild shot.

Christopher ducked down but didn't stop.

'Come on!' Abernathy shouted, and stood up on the bike's footboards, drawing her gun, holding it steady in both hands. She aimed carefully. They were too far away, but she fired off two shots anyway. They went wide, but the two faster men stumbled and zig-zagged, losing ground. The one in front tripped and went down, lost in the tall grass. The guy behind him stopped and tried to help him up but got waved on. '*Get him!*'

Christopher kept going.

She didn't worry about the third guy. He'd already fallen back. Wheezing his lungs up, by the looks, the unfit fuck.

Christopher was almost on her, and she sat back down, readying herself.

He arrived in a storm of gasping breaths and pounding footfalls. His weight landed on the back of the bike, the suspension sinking. His too-hot body jostled against her. As soon as she felt him grab on to her, she hit the gas and they shot off.

'This was a stupid fucking idea!' she yelled at him, and the wind whipped the words from her mouth. Her eyes teared up. She steered the bike back into the trees, erratically dodging trunks, going faster and turning sharper than she'd previously dared now that Christopher's weight anchored the bike down. 'They could have shot you!'

He didn't reply, but he wasn't arguing with her, either. They could have taken these people out. They had the numbers and enough weapons, if not the spare ammunition. But she'd seen how Lacey had baulked at the idea, how Sunny had frowned and Tyler looked away. Pilgrim had argued that damaging the car in the ensuing crossfire would have negated all their efforts in getting it, and Abernathy could give him that, but you had to take risks to get what you wanted. Pussyfooting about didn't do anybody any favours.

Christopher had forestalled further debate by saying that they could choose to conserve ammo and keep the damage and bloodshed to a minimum, if they played it smart. Which Abernathy knew was a backhanded comment on her not being smart, but she'd been outvoted and she knew when a fight was a losing one. She'd been promptly tasked with driving the bike out here, far away from the action, and don't think she hadn't noticed.

Bullets *ping*ed and *thunk*ed the tree trunks around them. Not many. Four or five. Seemed their pursuers were as loath to waste their bullets as they were.

Abernathy opened up the throttle and was increasing the distance between them with every passing second. Those shots had been a last desperate attempt to stop them. She also knew that at some point soon they would abandon the chase altogether to go salvage what remained of their bedraggled group. These people had taken a loss, yes, but it wouldn't be deemed an outright catastrophe. More of them lived than were dead. Minimal bloodshed, indeed.

She aimed the bike at a gap in the trees and they flew into the open. Gravel spat out from under the tyres as they hit the road's shoulder. She stomped the rear brake. The bike skidded and Christopher leaned into her with the sudden drop in speed. She turned them east on to the highway. Up ahead, past the diner and its dead neon signpost, she saw the tail end of a small car speeding away from them. Christopher's arm appeared.

'There,' he said, pointing, breath hot and fast on the side of her face. 'They're out.'

She opened up the gas, wanting to catch up to the others before anyone else decided to come back and check in on them. The quad surged forward, its powerful torque biting tyre tread into the blacktop. She whooped with the exhilaration of it all. They were on their way!

PART TWO

The Inn

Chapter 1

Addison

Sometimes mischief danced in Hari's eyes, like a little fluttering fly trapped in lantern light. Addison saw it. She was good at seeing stuff. Good at sitting or standing or squatting down, real still. People forgot she was there she was so small and so quiet.

Only person who didn't forget was Hari.

His eyes, they saw as much as hers did. Maybe more. He knew how to be quiet, like she did. The quietest, littlest mouse. It was very . . . Addison struggled for a word to describe what it was.

Impressive, Fender murmured inside her head.

Yes. Impressive. She'd never met anyone as quiet and still as her. Not that she'd met many people, and none her own age. He must've learned it from someone, though, like she'd learned it from Chief and Fender.

Hari was lying a few feet from her on the parlour floor, curled on his side, head on a cushion taken from one of the fancy curly-wooden-armed chairs. He was supposed to be sleeping, like she was, but his eyes weren't sleeping. They were open and staring at her. He smiled when he saw her looking, and that mischief danced again. Addison's mouth smiled in return, because that's what you did when someone smiled at you. You smiled back. Even when you didn't feel like it.

'Why are you not sleeping?' Hari asked in a whisper.

'Not tired,' she said, not planning on saying anything else. Her curiosity got the better of her, though. (Lacey said it would get a cat killed someday, which made Addison feel bad. She liked cats. She didn't want any of them dying just 'cause she got nosy sometimes.) 'Why do you speak so funny?' she asked him.

Hari's teeth were a pale blur in the darkness when he smiled. 'I was born very far away from here.'

'How far?' she asked, trying to not sound suspicious.

'You see the ocean outside?' he said, and she nodded – no one could miss it. The sea was as big as the sky. It filled her eyes up to the brim. 'I am from far on the other side of such an ocean.'

Well, that was a claim. It was interesting, too, because she used to like to think about boats, about how they floated and bobbed and didn't tip over. But since seeing how much water they were plopped into she'd had a change of heart about whether she wanted to go in one. 'You came here on a boat?'

'A ship, yes. It took many weeks.'

'Why didn't you fly on a plane? Lacey told me 'bout how they'd mark the blue in the sky with tail smoke. White smoke. Long, wispy lines of it.'

Hari shook his head once. 'A ship is easier to hide away on.'

'Why was you hiding?'

'Because I should not have been there.'

'On the boat?'

'Yes.'

'But why?'

Another smile, another pale blur of white teeth. 'No. It is my turn for a question.'

Addison frowned. She didn't know they were taking turns. Maybe she wouldn't have asked so many if she'd known.

'If you had to choose, would you be a cautious but curious little bird, or a bold little snake?'

She was still frowning. Felt it up there, a small fist crumpled between her eyebrows. 'I don't know. That's a weird question.'

'You should think on it for a bit and let me know.' With that, Hari's eyes closed and he went back to pretending to sleep.

Close by, Albus was a tree log, laid out on his back. Addison knew he was real sleeping and hadn't heard a word of their conversation. His breathing was smooth and deep, same as the ocean outside breathed smooth and deep, waves washing in and waves washing out, for ever and onward. It was a nice sound. Peaceful. She was glad he was sleeping – it had been a long day. A difficult day. Filled with a lot more digging than Addison had planned on.

Gwen's breathing was awake breathing, same as Addison's. It came a tiny bit quicker, was interspersed with weary sighs and the occasional soft throat-clear. The chair she sat on creaked when she shifted her weight. It was positioned in the parlour's big picture window so Gwen could watch outside. She'd been doing that a lot. Watching outside. And her rifle never left her side. It made Addison nervous. *Gwen* as a whole made her nervous. She'd never been Addison's biggest fan. (She kinda blamed her for some Bad Stuff that had happened, and though no part of it was *technically* Addison's fault, nothing would have gone bad in the first place if Albus and everyone had stayed put at the Inn.)

Chief had come to sit beside Addison, an unbreathing shape of shadows: head bowed, shoulders hunched, haunches folded up tight to his body. Oil black from his large, shiny eyes and smooth head to the soles of his black animal feet. No one could see him and no one could hear him besides Addison. He was her friend and nobody else's. Not even Fender's, really. They didn't get along too good.

She sniffed a hint of mud and grass with his arrival and breathed it in deep through her nose. She wondered if he'd been wandering outside, where they'd dug treasure holes, the leftover earth piled nearby. She pictured the row of low mounds in her mind, the humped soil taking on the shape of the sleeping humans laid out beneath them: resting heads, curved shoulders, the dips at stomach and waist, the flare of a chest or a foot. Bianca, Cloris, Mica, Arun, Rufus. The adults' bodies were slightly larger compared to those of the two brothers. Teenagers, they'd been, Bruno said. Earlier, Chief had wanted to get a closer look, but Addison hadn't allowed him. It wasn't their place to go snooping. They hadn't known these people. Not like Albus, Bruno, Gwen and Hari had. They had been their family, and now they were buried like treasure, except not the kind of treasure that can ever be dug back up.

They got turned into porky-pines, Chief whispered, head leaning low over hers.

Porcupines, Fender corrected.

They *had* looked like porcupines, four of them sitting in their rocking chairs, facing out to sea, their bodies bristling with yellow-tipped arrows, as if someone had stood on the back lawn and fired shot after shot at them. Five of Albus's family were now gone, and two more missing. Amber and Jasper. So many names, but Addison made a real hard effort to remember them because they were important to Albus. Important to Bruno, Gwen and Hari, as well.

Addison and Chief had helped the others comb through the Inn from the roots of its head in the attic down to its pretty underskirts beneath the porches, but Amber and baby Jasper were nowhere to be found. It had been decided, through arguments and tears and flaring emotions, that tomorrow, at first light, they would leave the Inn and start their search for them. Albus would try to track them – he was a scent-hound that sniffed out colours rather than smells, but his methods worked just as good.

Addison needed to sleep. Her head was a boulder resting on her cushion and her limbs were lead pipes. But still her dry, aching eyes wouldn't close. She turned on to her other side, putting her back to Hari and facing Chief beside her in the dark.

He hummed quietly to himself as he played with a silver coin, rolling it over the backs of his ink-black knuckles. It was attached to a long silver chain that glinted and shimmered as the coin flipped and rolled. The coin had a man marked into it, holding a walking stick and carrying a baby on his back.

Addison smoothed her fingers over the top of her thigh, felt the rigid circle of the St Christopher medallion in her jeans pocket, knew Chief didn't really have the necklace – that he was just fooling with her – but needed to check on it anyway. For good measure, she traced along the wedge of the small sketchbook she kept in her seat pocket, too. Her treasures.

Chief's hands were empty when she looked back at them. He smiled at her, teeth sharp and white, his wide mouth curled with his own mischief, a different kind to Hari's, and when she smiled back she felt the natural lift of muscles in her face. No faking it this time. His smile dropped and his smooth, hairless head swung away towards the large picture window where Gwen sat alone and on watch.

'What is it?' she whispered to him.

Stranger, Fender whispered, instead of Chief.

A shout, deep and booming. Bruno's. Outside. He'd been walking the perimeter.

Gwen was on her feet. Albus and Hari awoke, too. Alertness crackled. Addison sat up, her eyes following Gwen's moon-bright hair as she hurried over to the bolted and secured front door, her shoes knocking drumbeats on the thin carpeting. Addison's heart knocked along with it, thudding hard under her breastbone.

The door was big enough to admit an ogre (or a troll with his legs lopped), but Gwen flung it open as if it were half the size and stepped out into the sound of *whooshing* ocean waves and a tinkling ring of the windchime, rifle tucked into her shoulder and ready to shoot. Addison remembered what Gwen had said earlier that afternoon, her grief growing wicked black spikes that ripped into anyone standing too close. '*If* one *stranger steps foot on this land . . . I'll blow their goddamn heads off.*'

Gwen appeared on the other side of the glass, framed in the window like a storybook picture. The beam of a flashlight bounced off her, hitting her face. She squinted her eyes, head turning away. Her mouth moved as she spoke, and she didn't look afraid, so it must be Bruno. She didn't lower her gun, though.

'She's not gonna *shoot* him, is she?' Addison whispered, fearful. Bruno wasn't a stranger, and she *liked* him. A lot.

Chief scampered over to the window and pressed his face to the glass, hands splayed flat to it in a pose of outright nosiness. He shrugged back at her as if to say, *Maybe?*

'Have they come back for us?' Hari asked. He was sitting cross-legged, eyes lambent in the darkness. Despite his words, he didn't look particularly scared by the thought. He probably figured his calm expression was masked by the dimness, but Addison could see it all the same. Alex had called her *eagle-eyed*, which she guessed meant eagles had really, really good eyesight.

Albus was up, too. He made a noise in the back of his throat as if to say, *No*, and made a gentle patting motion with one palm that made Addison want to scoot under it so it patted directly on her head and soothed all her Bruno-getting-shot worries. He stepped over Addison's outstretched legs and she craned her neck to look up at him. Albus wasn't troll tall, just normal tall, but he towered over her, swallowed her up in his shadow, and she felt a shiver of ants crawl up her back and across the nape of her neck. She shoved her blanket aside and popped up behind him and followed his footsteps, close enough to feel her toes brush his heels.

Outside, Bruno and Gwen were arguing in quiet voices.

Addison guessed they were arguing about the stranger-man standing with them.

'I wouldn't have seen him if his radio hadn't gone off,' Bruno was saying. Bruno was the biggest man Addison had ever seen close up. Big through the shoulders and chest and arms, but not through his middle. He was as thin as everyone else through his middle. He moved graceful and slow, the kind of slow she imagined big ships made when they steered into dock. He had skin as dark as soil, but not black like Chief's. It was soft, too. He'd let her stroke his arm once and it had been nice.

Beside him, the stranger-man was a dwarf. His head stayed down, eyes on the ground as if he didn't want to look at any of them. His arms were locked behind his back, Bruno's big hand wrapped around his bicep, roping the two of them together. Had Bruno tied him?

Chief sidled around the group and ducked behind Bruno's back to check. He popped back into view to give her a thumbs-up.

Yep. Tied. Did that mean he was their prisoner now? She'd never had a prisoner before. What was he even doing here?

He was left behind to keep watch on the Inn, Fender said.

'How d'you know that?' she whispered.

Because that's what Bruno just said, if you'd been listening.

Oh.

'Is he the bastard who killed them?' Gwen took a menacing step towards the stranger and the man seemed to sink down into himself, shoulders hunching up around his neck like he was a turtle trying to get back inside his shell. Was it turtle or tortoise? She could never remember, and Alex wasn't around to ask any more. Without conscious thought, her hand went to her back pocket where she kept Alex's sketchbook.

Bruno held up his free hand, stopping Gwen before she could poke her rifle's muzzle into the man's stomach and maybe shoot a second belly button into him. 'Let's get him inside first, okay?' Bruno said. 'We don't want to question him out in the open like this.'

As Gwen hovered between doing some belly-button shooting and backing down, Albus stepped into the pause. He rested a hand on her shoulder – his smooth palm and missing fingers holding Addison's attention for a long second – and the touch seemed to settle the woman. A breath left Gwen in a long sigh that Addison felt sure could fill up half the world, but she lowered the rifle and gestured for Bruno and the stranger to go ahead of her, and they all filed back inside.

It was then, as Addison followed Albus, and the huge door locked shut behind them, that she saw Hari. He hadn't moved from his cross-legged position on the parlour-room floor, pillows and blankets mussed around him. He had sat the entire time, letting the scene play out, viewing it like a movie-show acted on one of those huge screens people used to sit in front of in row after row of chairs in long lines. In the dark. Sometimes with food. (*Movie theatre*, Fender provided, hushed.)

('Thanks,' Addison replied, equally as hushed, because manners were important, according to her aunt.)

But Hari had been watching, all right. His dark eyes told her so. Like Addison had already worked out – Hari saw most everything.

Gwen and Bruno had tied the man to a dining-room chair, and Addison had no problem with that if it meant Gwen would put her gun down. They'd set him up in front of the massive stone fireplace; it was so big it looked like a giant's mouth getting ready to swallow the stranger, chair and all. Without even chewing. Eat him right up. A single lantern was lit, burning low on the hearth. It threw long, creepy shadows across the wooden floors and elongated shadow-puppets climbed the walls.

'Who are you?' Gwen asked.

That seemed like a great question to start with. Addison

wanted to know who he was, too. He was maybe around Albus's and Gwen's age, twenty or thirty or whatever they were (years and time remained a murky subject for her). Being just eight years old made it difficult to judge things by the passing time. But this guy wasn't old. He wasn't a teenager, either. His hair was oily and black and his eyes were dark and darting – he couldn't seem to settle on where or who to look at. He was biting his lip hard enough to hurt. Addison wanted to tell him to quit biting it, but being with Lacey and Alex had taught her when it was a good time to interrupt Adult Talk and when it wasn't, and this was most definitely *not* a good time. Without meaning to, she had swapped places with Hari, taking a seat on her blanket a safe distance from the adults, while he'd risen to his feet and moved a little closer to them.

'I said, *who are you*?' Gwen accompanied her question with a kick to the chair's leg. And maybe the man's leg, too, going by his flinch of pain and squinty-eyed wince.

It also made his lip pop out from between his teeth, which Addison was happy about. She didn't want to watch him chew through it like a sausage.

Chief crouched on his haunches next to her and leaned into her side. She drew comfort from his presence, even though there was no heat to it.

'J–Jake!' the man stuttered out. 'My name's Jake.'

Gwen had grown scarily still since kicking his chair. She stared down at him for a long count of ten. It made Addison nervous, all that silence and staring.

'Jake,' Gwen repeated. 'Were you the one who tied up our friends, Jake? Was it you who shot them full of arrows?'

Jake's eyes darted again, as if searching for help. Albus, of course, remained quiet as Gwen took the lead, and Bruno did his scary best by standing as tall as he could (which was *tall*) with his strong arms folded over his chest (which were *strong*). Addison wasn't fooled. She knew Bruno was a big, softie bear.

But Jake didn't know that. His eyes slid away from stern Bruno-Bear and flicked to Hari.

'You should answer,' Hari said quietly, and it was like listening to music spoken aloud. Far too pretty for a setting like this. But it seemed to help the trembling man, because he straightened a little in his seat and opened his mouth.

'I was here, *but*' – he blurted when something dangerous flashed across Gwen's face – 'but it wasn't me! I didn't hurt them, I *swear*. I was just here for reconnaissance. To keep watch. Report in. That's it.'

'You had a weapon,' Bruno said. He had a black pistol shoved under the back of his belt. Addison had noted it while he had been helping lash Jake to the dining chair.

'Yes. Yes, you're right, I did. But it was for protection only. I wasn't here to *kill* anybody.'

'There are five graves outside that say otherwise.' At the coldness of Gwen's voice, Addison's hands squeezed into fists, her bloodless icicle-fingers curling into the warmth of her palms.

'You're a murderer whether you nocked an arrow or not,' Gwen said.

'Look, I–I was here but I wasn't alone. *They're* the ones who went inside – i–in here, I mean.' He nodded around at the parlour. 'I waited outside while they came in. That was it. You have to believe me.'

'I don't have to believe a thing,' Gwen said. 'My friends are dead and in the ground, that's all I know.'

'Why're you still here?' Bruno asked. 'Why didn't you leave with the others?'

Jake dared to look away from Gwen to mutely shake his head at Bruno.

'You knew there were more of us?' Bruno asked him. 'You thought we might come back? Is that it?'

Silence.

Addison looked to Albus. His long hair was messily tucked

behind his ears, his jaw so tight it could've been made of rock. He looked furious and frustrated all at once, but distressed, too. His eyes spoke for his mouth sometimes, and now they transmitted such a deep, aching wretchedness that Addison felt it punch her in the heart.

'Why did you wait?' Bruno demanded. 'What do you want from us?'

But Jake had clammed up and was saying nothing. Bruno and Albus shared a look. It spoke a lot more than what Addison could decipher just from using her eyeballs, but Albus had turned pale as chalk-dust. And that said enough. Nervous, Addison shifted off her butt and on to her knees – not quite standing but not quite sitting, either.

Gwen snatched up Jake's collar. 'Did you already radio in that we're here?'

Again, Jake said nothing. He was shaking in his seat, though. A fine trembling that Addison could see even from across the room. Her eyes went to the black-and-yellow bumble-bee walkie-talkie clipped to Bruno's waistband, not far from his new gun. If it had been Jake's job to hang around here with a walkie-talkie, surely he'd have reported in to whoever was on the other end by now, right? Did that mean others were coming back to finish what they started? Why did they even *want* to come back, if that was their plan?

'He will not easily give details,' Hari said, his soft voice sliding like a shadow through the dimly lit room. 'Look at him. He is too scared.'

Gwen said nothing, merely glared down into Jake's face. He licked his lips. Licked them again, leaving them glossy and wet. His eyes darted, darted, darted.

Gwen suddenly straightened and stepped back. She nodded at Bruno to take over and retreated past where Addison knelt and headed for the back of the room, where the wide staircase led to the upper floors. She and her shadow slipped behind the stairs and into the dark passage that led to the reception foyer.

'We need to know why you're here,' Bruno told the man in the chair. 'And *not* talking isn't an option here, Jake. Because *not* talking would mean I'd have to *make* you talk, and that won't be pretty. Not pretty at all.' Bruno-Bear had moved up to loom over Jake, and his bulk, along with Gwen's abrupt disappearance, seemed to do the trick because Jake's mouth flapped open and closed in his rush to answer.

'Look, I'd like to tell you, okay? I'd really like to tell you, but I can't. If I talk, they'll *know* and they won't take me back. I'll be worse than dead to them. And I have to go back, man. My girlfriend is there. I love her and . . . I love her so much, I—' Jake's voice cracked on a sob. Addison had to look away when more sobs quickly followed, along with a string of snot that dripped to his lip. 'I can't . . . have you people going over there . . . and hurting anyone, okay? I can't do that. I just can't.'

'Going over *where*?' Bruno asked.

Jake looked stricken. 'No place, okay? It's no place.'

Bruno curled his hand around Jake's throat, and his hand was so brutishly large, his fingers so long, that they completely covered him from jaw to collar. Addison swallowed and imagined she felt the constricted bob of it bump up against Bruno's squeezing palm.

'What place?'

Jake's face slowly darkened as Bruno's grip tensed. His eyes got big. His mouth popped open, but no sound emerged.

'*What* place?'

Jake squeaked, his words breathy and high-pitched. 'Elysian Fields! It's' – flappy mouth movements – 'called Elysian Fields!' He sucked in a breath when Bruno eased his chokehold.

Albus caught Bruno's attention and mimed rocking in his arms. Baby.

Jasper, Fender whispered, though Addison hadn't forgotten the name.

Bruno jerked Jake's chin up and the man flinched so hard the chair's legs stuttered on the floor. 'What about a girl?' Bruno asked. 'Thirteen years old, gangly. And a baby, maybe twelve months. You see them? You know where they're at?'

Jake sniffed, wet and snot-filled, his watery eyes flicking from Albus to Bruno. 'If . . . if I tell you, will you let me go?'

And, with that, Bruno-Bear wasn't soft or cuddly any more, not even a little bit. He appeared to grow a foot in height, his shadow growing huge behind him as he stepped in so close he practically straddled Jake's legs. He dropped his other big hand around Jake's throat, one over the other, as if getting ready to twist Jake's head clean off with a *Pop*!

Addison rocked back on to the balls of her feet, afraid but ready, and Chief leaned away from her, his head cocked and hyper-vigilant, small body vibrating with tension.

Bruno didn't raise his voice, but Addison winced all the same. It was somehow worse than if he'd chosen to shout. 'You'd best be telling us what you know, son. Before I do something I regret.'

Addison watched Jake's eyebrows twitch and quiver, and his words twitched and quivered along with them. 'Th–they're safe, okay? I can tell you that much – they're safe. No one's hurt them. They tried to get away, but we caught them. They're not hurt, but that's all I can say, okay? You can do what you want to me, but that's *all* I can say.' He teeth clicked shut on that last word and something closed in his expression. His lips pressed into a thin line, his jaw clenched so hard Addison didn't think anything could pry them back open. Not Bruno, not a crowbar, not nothing. His cheeks were still wet from his tears, but his eyes were dry.

It was Hari's head turn that brought Addison's attention to the back of the room. The shadows parted, darkest within dark, as if a doorway had opened, and Gwen walked out. She was holding something down by her side. Not her rifle – she'd finally let that go. It leaned up against the side of the fireplace next to a brass tool-set that Addison had investigated earlier that evening (tongs, little brush, pokey-metal-stick thing, a miniature shovel). No, Gwen was holding something long and twig-thin. With a yellow-feathered tail.

Addison suddenly wished Gwen had held on to her rifle.

Albus must have seen the arrow at the same time because he stepped into Gwen's path, holding an arm out to block her. He shook his head at her. *No*. And Addison wanted to add her own *No* because Bruno was doing just great without using anything pointy.

Gwen tried to step around Albus, but Albus stepped with her. 'It's fine, Albus,' she told him, and Addison knew she was trying to sound convincing, but her tight smile said the exact opposite. 'Everything's just fine.'

Bruno had stepped back from Jake, his hold on the man's neck falling away. 'I've got this, Gwen. We don't have time to get distracted. They have Amber and Jasper. We need to pack this guy up and get out of here.'

'We will,' Gwen said. 'We will – just give me one minute. *One* minute.' When she stepped around Albus this time, he hesitated long enough to let her pass, and when she shouldered Bruno aside, not ungently, Bruno didn't stop her, either. She centred herself in front of Jake.

No one else had noticed that Hari had angled himself a foot nearer, but Addison had (he could go as unnoticed as Addison did when he wanted to). And she'd bet Chief's left ear he'd done it to get a better view.

'I'm only going to ask this once, Jake.' Gwen twirled the arrow and Jake's eyes followed it, riveted to that pretty yellow flight. 'Tell me why you came here? Why did you murder our friends?'

Jake's lips were white and trembling. 'I . . . I can't,' he whispered.

The twirling had stopped; Gwen had the arrow clamped so tightly at her side that the feathered end quivered. Addison couldn't help but notice that she held it like you would a dagger. 'Say that again.'

'I— Please. It – it wasn't personal, okay?'

'*No.*' Unlike Bruno, it seemed to take a real effort for Gwen to lower her voice. 'No, you don't get to say please to me. You'll get the exact same amount of mercy you gave to my friends.'

Albus moved in near to Gwen, as if his physical closeness could penetrate the tightly clenched fury and grief that pulsated around her. He made a soft, fearful noise in the back of his throat and it distracted Addison for a second. Was he afraid of what Gwen might do, or was he afraid of the man's answer?

'Why come here?' Gwen asked again. '*Why?*'

'Look at him – he will not tell you,' Hari murmured, and there was something close to a challenge in the quiet words, whether he meant there to be one or not.

Addison gasped at how fast the arrow moved, at how it flashed down like a comet in the sky and embedded itself in the top of Jake's shoulder.

The man squealed.

Addison clapped her hands over her ears and Chief scampered away in a crawling scramble and was gone before the squeal ended and a second erupted, louder than the first, as Gwen wrenched the arrowhead out.

'Answer me!' Gwen screamed in the man's face.

Albus had stumbled back a step as if shocked by the sounds erupting from in front of him, his eyes wide and his own hands pressed over his ears to block out the shock of noise.

Jake was crying and sputtering, shaking his head too hard to reply.

'*Why?*' Down went the bloody arrow, same spot, deep into the meat. Addison's hands clamped tighter to her ears, but nothing could block out the awful squeals.

Bruno had grabbed Gwen's wrist and yanked her away, his other arm wound tight around her waist. The arrowhead, left skewered in place, got knocked by Gwen's fist as she fought Bruno's hold.

'Enough!' Bruno yelled at the same time as Jake screamed: '*We knew about the Inn! We knew it was here!*' He whined through his sobs, his cries falling into frantic, unfiltered speech. 'I was told to keep watch – to be a lookout, so no one gets out – we were here for Albus, that was it – that was all I was told, but this girl came running out with a kid because, because, you weren't *here*, Albus, and I didn't know if this girl knew you or if she was somebody else. You should have *been* here, but no one would tell us where you were, so they took the girl with them because we couldn't *not* take somebody back. But she wouldn't let go of the baby, she wouldn't, so they took that, too. They want you to understand – it's why they killed your friends. You don't fuck with these people, all right? You don't *fuck* with them.' Spittle flew from his lips. The yellow-tailed tip of the arrow trembled as he quietly wept. 'Please don't hurt me. Please don't hurt me. I'll help you, all right? I'll help you get them back, I swear.'

Bruno held Gwen at a safe distance, both of them winded and panting for breath, but Gwen wasn't fighting to be free any more. She appeared drained, smaller, a younger sister to her bigger, tougher sibling.

'Why Albus?' Bruno asked. He could have been asking Jake the question, or Albus himself. The big man's eyes went back and forth between the two.

A herd of gazelles was galloping through Addison's chest and, from the expression on Albus's face, his own herd was galloping through his, too. Albus shook his head, a quick left-right-left, eyes wide.

'What do you want with him?' Bruno took one step nearer to Jake, and the man moaned miserably.

The man's face was a mess of tears and snot. 'I don't know,

okay? I don't ask questions, I just know that his sister and him are important. I do what I'm told, okay? I just do what I'm told.'

A small, involuntary sound had come from Albus at the mention of his sister. His brows had slammed down and he looked all kinds of bewildered and troubled and mad that Addison couldn't decide which emotion he was feeling most. She watched in fascination as a muscle in his jaw flexed and bulged. A strangely threatening growl rumbled from deep in his chest.

Bruno spoke for his friend. 'You know of his sister, too?'

Jake blinked and two fat tears rolled down his pasty-white face. 'If the Inn gets mentioned, Albus or Ruby get mentioned, that's all I know.'

'And we're supposed to believe you don't know anything else about it?' Bruno demanded.

Weary, defeated, Jake shook his head at him and went to slump in his seat but stilled mid-motion, hissing a breath through his teeth. Addison winced along with him – she couldn't help it. That arrow sticking from his shoulder looked so painful.

'What about Amber and Jasper?' Gwen asked. 'What'll happen to them?' At Jake's blank stare, she snapped: 'The girl with the baby.'

'I don't know,' Jake whined feebly, but this time Addison didn't think he was being entirely truthful. His eyes skittered away, the same way her aunt's would whenever Alex asked where the last of their Tabasco sauce or the final bit of their jerky had gone.

'You'll take us to this Elysian Fields,' Bruno said finally. It wasn't a question. 'You'll take us, or we'll find it ourselves and we'll have absolutely no need for you any more. You know what that'll mean for you, don't you?'

When you didn't need anything, you threw it away. Or you burned it in the campfire. Even Addison knew that.

'Yes,' Jake whispered. 'Yes, I swear I'll take you.'

They might have gotten more out of Jake, but a pale wash of artificial light passed over the window, a ghostly sliding of shadows swinging left to right. The heavy furniture piled up to block the other entrances to the parlour transformed into three awakening, hunch-backed beasts, and Addison cringed away from them before realising what they were. For that illuminated few seconds, the adults in front of her became black silhouettes, made more of darkness and shadow than of flesh and blood. And then the brightness fell away and the window reflected nothing but orange lamplight and the black night beyond.

Chapter 2

Jay

Jay drove slowly, the hearse's dipped headlights turning the grit and dirt of the road into the cratered surface of the moon. The tyres crunched loudly through the open windows, the circulation of warm, muggy air better than no breeze at all. It couldn't prevent the damp trickle of sweat on his neck or the sticky warmth in his armpits. The swamp heat trapped between his back and the driving seat was close to combusting.

They followed the winding coast south. Dark, empty countryside rolled out to their right and patches of moonlit water twinkled on their left. Jay didn't know how an ocean so vast could hide so completely. He caught glimpses of it only when the gently undulating land dipped low enough, or when the trees and vegetation pulled back, creating a window to be viewed through. On occasion, the land opened up entirely and the Atlantic Ocean stretched out as far as the eye could see, the silhouettes of unlit, silent vacation homes and rambling farmhouses lining the coast.

The stars and unfettered moon provided more light than Jay thought possible. He hailed from Memphis, a decayed and abandoned relic of the vibrant, artistic city he remembered as a teenager, where live music had played to the small hours of the night and cigar smoke and the sticky aroma of BBQ briskets and slow-cooked pork flavoured the air like pheromones. He was used to having buildings hem him in, to navigating alleyways and walkways narrow enough to be called rat-runs. These open stretches of land, the vistas that were as wide and long as the sky, made his breath catch. He had to force himself not to stare; Clancy had told him off for it more than once.

'I spy, with my little eye,' he said, head swivelling left to right. 'Something . . . beginning with . . .'

They were passing a hulking, rusted petroleum tanker, driven off-road through a boundary fence and into a field. The grass was so tall it brushed the tanker's sides. The once-white container had tipped on to its left flank, its skin bubbled and scabbed by a patina of rust. Jay could smell the metal as if someone were holding a handful of pennies under his nose. He smelled grass and dry dirt, the melted asphalt after the day's baking heat. He smelled salt in the air and a lush vegetative fragrance that made him think of Amazonian jungles.

'Watch the road,' Clancy told him.

Jay quickly corrected the hearse's drift. They'd been close to joining the tanker in its field. 'Something beginning with T,' he finished.

'You want me to take over?' Clancy asked, ignoring his I-Spy clue. Her eyes roamed his face, her concern as bright as the moon.

'I'm okay,' he said.

'You're sure? We haven't stopped for a while.'

'I'm good. Honest.'

'All right, but let me know if you change your mind.' Clancy was quiet a moment. 'Tanker?'

Jay grinned. 'Nope.'

'Is it inside the car or out?'

'Out,' he said. 'Technically. But that counts as your first clue.'

Clancy's head turned from him, her attention drifting to the scenery outside. The map in her lap crinkled softly as she leaned forward. Reaching behind her, she hooked her greying plaited hair and pulled it over her shoulder. Even in the dimness, Jay could see the darkened patch of sweat along the line of her spine.

'Tree?' she asked, absently fingering the woven length of her braid.

He threw her a mildly offended look. 'We've played this game for hours. You really think I'd pick "tree"?'

She hiked an eyebrow at him. 'You've already used "grass", "sky" and "sun", so yes, I think you'd pick "tree".'

'No, no. This one's clever. I'm being clever.'

She made a humming noise that told him she plainly wasn't convinced by this. 'Right. Let's see. Something *clever*.' She wore a small smile as she went back to looking. She leaned further forward. Her hand dropped her braid and pressed both hands to the dashboard, map crumpling in her lap. 'Signpost,' she said.

Jay frowned. 'Huh? How does that start with a T?'

'No. *Signpost*.' Clancy pointed, and the metallic jingle of her charm bracelet added its own sound of discovery.

Jay found himself leaning with her, holding the steering wheel tighter as he strained to read the sign in the dark. He pressed the accelerator, speeding up a little, wanting the headlights to reach it. When they did, he braked to a halt.

The sign's lettering was white on a dark background. Green, he thought.

But for the quiet grumble of the engine and the *tinks* coming from under the hood, everything was quiet.

A shifting squeak came from Clancy's seat. 'What does it say?' she asked, a hint of impatience in her voice. 'Your eyes are younger than mine.'

'*Welcome to the Norwood Cove Inn*,' he read. '*Dining and Lodging since 1856*.' He turned to her, knew his mouth was hanging open a bit. 'We found it,' he whispered.

'We did,' Clancy murmured, her head giving a faint nod, gaze glued to the sign. 'I didn't quite believe him, you know.'

'You thought he lied about this place?'

'It's not that I thought he lied, exactly. I just wasn't entirely convinced by his motives for sending us here.'

'He didn't have any motives,' Jay argued, feeling defensive and a little bit angry. 'You couldn't keep up with the pace Pilgrim had to set, so he left us behind.'

Clancy's eyes came back to him. Their sclerae were a dull bluish-white in the muted luminance of the lit console. 'I know you wanted to go with him. I'm sorry for that. Truly.'

Now he felt bad. She'd already apologised for Jay's need to chaperone her here, but he couldn't seem to let it go. He was bitter, he guessed. He knew what Clancy thought of him: he was this young, naïve guy who hero-worshipped Pilgrim because the dude could face down a .44 with nothing but a nail-gun and could persuade a bunch of strangers to crash a van travelling at 40mph, just because he needed them to. But that wasn't why Jay respected him. He admired Pilgrim for the simple fact that the word 'quit' didn't exist in his vocabulary.

'It's fine,' Jay said. 'We made it. Besides, you needed me.'

A brief smile. Her teeth were bluish-white, too. 'Oh, I did, did I?'

'Yep. It's not like you can play I-Spy by yourself.'

'I might as well have. I'd have won every game, same as I did with you.'

'Har har,' he said.

She gave a soft laugh and reached over to pat his knee, and any remaining tension between them lifted away. Jay returned his attention to the sign. The Inn's pebbled driveway was so pale it seemed to reflect the moonlight. It made him think of the yellow-bricked road from *The Wizard of Oz*, which, in turn, made him think of a young woman who was lost in a scary land and needed to get home.

'You think he got to her in time? Lacey?' Jay asked. It was the reason he and Clancy were here alone while Pilgrim was someplace else. Not quitting. Not stopping until he found the young woman he'd been searching for.

'I think God help anyone who tried to get in his way.' Clancy wasn't thrown by the change of subject; it was a conversation neither of them was ever far away from. She sat back and began folding the map. They wouldn't need it any more.

Jay put the hearse in gear. 'Ready?' he asked her.

Clancy popped the glove box and stowed the map away inside. It clicked closed with a finality that Jay felt inside his chest.

'Ready as I'll ever be.' She drew in a deep breath. 'If this Albus fellow is in residence, like Pilgrim claimed, he'll be two for two in my book.'

Jay took his time turning into the driveway, not wanting the overgrown bushes at the entrance to scratch the hearse's paintwork. The tyres bit into gravel, the pale bricks grinding together as they started towards the Inn.

It was a grand building decked out in white clapboard and dark window shutters. A white-railed veranda ran the entire length of the porch, the floor laid with dark wood that was glossed to a sheen that streaked silver moonlight. Four high columns supported a first-floor balcony. All the windows' shutters were open and the interior unlit. The front door, tall and wide enough to accommodate two basketball players side by side, was closed and unwelcoming.

'Is that a *library* bus?' Clancy said, voice soft with astonishment.

Parked at an angle, the bus sat silent and empty. The faded decals on its side showed a stack of books and an arc of words that read *Feed the mind, Free the imagination*. It was a library bus, all right, and it looked like it was in no rush to be moved. In fact, *nothing* moved.

Jay felt a leak of disappointment drip into his stomach. 'Nobody's here,' he muttered.

As if to refute his statement, the huge front door swung open on a silent inward sweep. A woman stepped out, appearing from the darkness, a mirage that carried a rifle, handling it with an ease that Jay imagined the made-up Lacey of his mind would. He knew *all* about Lacey and her rifle from Pilgrim. But this woman was too old to be her, her hair too light, but his reaction was so strong he couldn't help but say her name aloud.

'Lacey?'

It was the only word he got out before the light-haired woman, a ferocious look on her face, swung the rifle up and aimed it directly at them.

CHAPTER 3

Addison

Addison jumped to her feet when she heard the car engine. A soft rumble, like that of a contented cat, big as a panther. She hadn't heard a big cat purr before, but her friend Alex had mimicked one for her once. It had made Addison laugh.

'Gwen, wait!'

Gwen didn't wait. She'd squirmed out of Bruno's loosened grip and gone to snatch up her rifle from beside the fireplace. The bolt on the gun *clack*ed as she checked it.

'Don't go out there!' Jake warned, his hair a wild, sweaty mess, his eyes grimaced with pain. 'Don't—' The stock of Gwen's rifle slammed the side of his head and he slumped sideways, soundless. He would have fallen, chair along with him, if Albus hadn't leapt forward to steady him. A long line of drool poured from the unconscious man's mouth.

Addison had time to snatch a quick breath before Gwen was at the front door. She unlocked it, deadlocks clunking once, twice.

Thunk.

Thunk.

The big door seemed to intake its own breath as it yawned wide, inhaling in fearful expectation as Gwen stepped through. On the porch, the windchime rang in welcome. Even at eight years old, Addison knew moving out into the open like that was about as silly as you could get.

The car's engine and the ocean waves and the moans and shouts and thudding of Bruno's and Albus's chasing feet all came together in a swell of noise, everything moving so fast Addison found herself dashing after Albus without thinking. Bruno was already through the doorway.

Addison grasped the back of Albus's shirt and let him tow her, a ship and its tugboat, until they, too, were trampling out on to the porch. Gwen had shifted into a shooting stance, shielded partly behind one of the white pillared posts. Albus made a guttural noise, loud and urgent, but he might as well as have made it at the wooden post for all the reaction she gave him.

The crunch of tyres on loose bricks skittered over the pebble-drive. Through a forest of bodies – Albus's, Bruno's, Gwen's – Addison spied the car. It was halfway up the long driveway and heading their way. She wondered if whoever was inside it could feel the brewing violence building like a storm around the Inn, feel the fury and pain and the intent to hurt swirling round and round, close to eruption.

Albus's arm swept Addison back, pushing her behind him, protective but blocking her view.

Maybe the car's occupants *had* felt those broiling emotions because the engine note cut lower, the car's speed slowing. Even the ocean's waves seemed to shush, and Addison wondered if the fish, too, were floating and listening real hard, like she was listening real hard. She also wondered if fish had ears.

She chanced another peek. The windshield was a blanked-out white, moonlight reflecting from it and hiding any passengers from view. The car was dressed all in black. It was a funny shape at the rear, long and boxy.

'Death is here,' Hari said.

Albus tensed up and Addison heard a soft intake of breath

from Gwen. And that's all there was time for before a shot rang out, shockingly loud, and the car's windshield smashed into a trillion-bajillion pieces. Addison dropped into a crouch behind Albus's legs, grabbing on to his calves, the noise of the gunshot ricocheting and ringing. From inside the car, she heard a scream.

'*Shit!*' Bruno cried, a bad word that must've popped out by accident, and he ducked down behind the porch's railings, pulling Albus down with him, jostling Addison so she nearly fell on to her butt.

Gwen cranked the rifle – *click-clack* – and fired another shot, and a third, this one pinging off the metal of the car. Contact sparks flared in the dark.

'*Stop! Stop shooting!*'

The cry was high-pitched, a man's or a woman's, Addison couldn't tell – all she heard was the pain in it, and it made her stomach clench, a painful stab right under her ribs. She released Albus's calves and monkey-dodged him, staying in her crouch as she slipped along the back of Bruno and gripped the material of Gwen's pants at her thigh. Tugged. 'You're gonna *hurt* them.'

'That's the idea,' Gwen snapped, and fired a fourth shot.

Shouts. Definitely a man's. A stranger's voice filled with panic. 'Stop shooting! Please stop shooting!'

The car's engine had died, but its two headlights beamed out, slicing through the dark, so bright it hurt. After the loudness of the gunshots, the night was heavy and stuffed all around them. From inside the car a *clink* of broken glass sounded. A shuffle of movement. A horrible moan.

The man's voice again. 'Oh my God, oh my God.'

'Step out of the car!' Gwen called.

'I can't!' There was a hysterical pitch to it that stabbed the ache deeper into Addison's gut. 'You shot us! There's . . . there's blood everywhere. Oh my God . . .' He trailed off, words too low as he spoke to whoever was inside with him.

Someone pressed closer to Addison, and she expected to see

Chief, scared and searching for comfort, but it was Hari, hunkered down next to her. His head was cocked slightly, an intense look on his face. There was no playfulness or mischief in him now.

Albus made another sound, this one sharp and admonishing, his arm waving her and Hari back.

Gwen's stance was locked rigid against the porch post, gun unmoving as she sighted down the barrel. 'Throw your weapons out! I want to see them!'

There was an edge of something to the man's hysteria now. 'We don't have any! We're not armed! Look, I have to get her out. I can't see properly in here. We need to get out.'

The driver's door was shoved open and two hands appeared, palm out and empty. Empty but shiny. Wet.

Blood, Fender whispered. *They're wet with blood.*

Addison let out a small moan; Gwen's gun went *click-clack*.

Bruno had pulled Jake's handgun out at some point, but he gripped it down near his knee where he was crouched, rather than aiming it at anyone. 'Stand down, Gwen,' he hissed at her. 'We can shoot them just as easily outside the car as in it. Let him get out.'

She didn't acknowledge him, but her curled trigger finger did relax a fraction.

Bruno lifted his head enough to call over the railings: 'We have guns on you. Don't do anything stupid now.'

'I'm just getting out, all right?' the man called. His head came into view and, boy, did he have *a lot* of hair. It wasn't so much long as really, really thick. It curled at the ends, winding around his ears and into his collar. He was slim and slight but not weak-looking, even though he was hunched over slightly, half out of the cab and half in it.

'Take it easy, take it easy.' He stood up, keeping his hands high. He moved out from behind the door in a nervous side-shuffle and, when no more shots rang out, he skirted around the front of the car, limping, his hands held aloft the whole time. He talked as he went, an anxious prattle that was more distracted than directed at anyone in particular.

'We were told to come here. To ask for an Albus. Is there an Albus here? Or maybe his uncle? I think we were told he lived here with his uncle at some point. Hoyt sent us. Do you recognise that name? That's what we were told to say. That Hoyt sent us.' He stumbled a bit at the passenger door, cursing before catching himself on the handle and yanking it open.

Albus didn't make a sound as he rose from his crouch. Addison tipped her head back to peer up at him.

His lips were parted in surprise.

He had a blank look of shock on his face.

He knows that name, Fender whispered.

The next second Albus was moving. Past Bruno, past Gwen. Gwen gasped out his name, swiped for his arm, but Albus was already out of range and taking the porch steps two at a time. Bruno went after him and Addison scooted forward to watch through the porch railings as Bruno caught hold of Albus's elbow, but the slighter man shook himself free. Their feet chomped the drive, gravel eating their boots to the soles.

The stranger was half inside the car now, the top portion of his body out of view as he leaned in through the passenger-side door. He'd been talking the whole while, a low, comforting drone that Addison couldn't make out.

'Can you hear anything?' she whispered to Fender, but all she got was that airy feeling when Fender didn't have anything to share, like a tiny, cool breeze passing through the back of her skull.

She made to sneak off the porch, behind Gwen, but a small hand caught hold of her shoulder. Hari. Getting up in her business again. Did he think he had to protect her? Like a mama bird looking out for its chick? Lacey used to do the same, except Lacey was a cuddly wood pigeon and Hari was a baby hawk.

Addison might be bad with ages, but even she knew he wasn't all that much older than her. A handful of years, tops. She didn't need him looking out for her.

She scowled at his hand and shrugged it away. There was a moment's resistance, when she thought he might latch on to her harder, tighter, and refuse to let go, but his fingers lost their grip and disappeared. She got all the way to the bottom step before Gwen's sharp, do-not-fuck-with-me bark stopped her in her tracks. She'd sounded a lot like her aunt Lacey.

Albus and Bruno had made it to the car and were helping the man lift his companion free. There were a lot of grunts and curses. Addison saw how the wild-haired man's eyes slid to Albus's fingerless hands a time or two as Albus added his strength to lifting the woman clear. The three men shuffled backwards with the slumped weight of what appeared to be a woman held between them and they carried her to the grass. Albus reached out to cradle her head as they lowered her.

In the moonlight, Addison could see the blood. It darkly stained the woman's shirt, her arms, the lap of her pants.

The wild-haired man was moaning again, the same name over and over again as he leaned over his friend, his face close to hers, his hands cupped to her cheeks.

'Clancy, no. Please, no. Clancy? Clancy, do you hear me? Come on, don't do this to me. Please don't do this.'

Addison could see the woman clearly now. She was *old*. Fairy Godmother old. Older than all of them put together. Like maybe even a hundred. Her hair was braided silver like the silver of the St Christopher medallion. Addison had only ever seen that hair colour once before, on the head of the sleeping woman now buried in a treasure hole out back of the Inn. Now this silver-haired woman was sleeping, too. Maybe silver hair was bad luck.

I'd say she's in her forties, Fender said, and there was sadness there. Addison heard it. *Not old at all.*

Albus's head turned, his gaze zeroing in on her where she crouched at the porch's bottom step, huddled against the balustrade. She didn't think she would ever get used to him doing that – locating her so easily. Playing a game of Hide and Go Seek with Albus would be no fun at all. (Not unless she put away his sister's necklace first. He always seemed to know where it was.)

With a hasty hand-wave, Albus beckoned her to him.

Chapter 4

Albus

Albus sat back and stared at the two strangers, one alive and one dead. Found he could do little more than stare because the whole scene was shifting around in ways he couldn't understand. He felt dislocated from it, watching from above, all colour leached away by the hearse's hot white headlights, sounds muted and echoing in his ears, travelling down a long, hollowed-out tunnel.

The man knelt in front of him, hunched over, his shoulders rapidly rising and falling in hyperventilation. His teeth were clenched, face shiny with a grease of sweat. Thick strands of hair were stuck like tentacles to his brow, with more curled over his ears and down his neck. He had more hair than anyone had a right to, dark as night, dark as the blown-out pupils of his pain-wracked eyes. In fact, he looked a great deal like Hari (if Hari were a decade older than his thirteen years), and the comparison served only to further disassociate Albus from his surroundings, made him twist his numbed neck around to glance over his shoulder and check on the boy, needing to see if he was actually there and was, in fact, real and present. Hari was trailing after Gwen as she and Addison hurried their way over.

The woman lying between him and the man didn't move. Her chest remained still, her closed eyelids didn't flutter. She might have looked peaceful if not for the ghastly wound in her throat where the bullet had ripped through her flesh. Too much blood saturated the front of her shirt and pants, the sight of it shaking Albus, a swift dizziness rushing up to say hello. He had to press a palm over his chest, feel the reassuring thud of his own too-fast heartbeat, to steady himself as he swayed.

'You have a lot of blood on you. Are you hurt?'

Bruno's muffled words clicked sound back on to half-volume, its brown, earthen tones settling a grounded weight around Albus's feet and ankles, planting him firm. It was one of the aspects of his chromosthesia that Albus was most thankful for: that visual, almost tactile, comfort of 'seeing' his friends speak.

The stranger gazed down at himself, dumbly silent, then stared up at Bruno as if unable to understand his question.

Shock, Albus thought. This poor man had to be in shock.

Bruno's words came through a layer of muddy water. 'Let me see.' He got down on one knee, his big hands gentle – the opposite of what they'd been inside the Inn, gripped around their prisoner's neck – as he helped the stranger manoeuvre an arm out of his shirt. The man stiffened and whimpered.

Blood. Too much of it. Not all of it the woman's. A gory hole, perhaps the size of a dime, had punctured the guy's abdomen, high on the side and just below his last rib.

'I felt a – a punch, but I . . .' The man, wide-eyed, gazed down at the wound, as if it had appeared out of nowhere. 'I didn't feel anything 'til now. No pain or—' His face winced closed. By the time Bruno finished taking the shirt off his other arm, wadded it up and pressed it over the wound, the stranger was panting for breath.

Albus had his hand on the man's back. Didn't remember placing it there. He patted him very gently, like you would an upset child who had fallen and grazed their knee. He met Bruno's eyes and his friend's were hooded with regret, his mouth set in a dejected line.

'Who are they?' The words were the bright, angry flare of a flashlight to Albus's eyes; a staccato Morse code relaying Gwen's hostility. It brought a cold reality with it, too; a chasing-away of the last of Albus's disconnect. Sound sharpened. He felt the breeze, cool on his damp neck, felt the hard pound of his pulse. He breathed in the hot smells of the hearse's engine and the warm rubber of its tyres, the grass, the brassy blood-soaked cotton of the strangers' clothes. All of it too real.

Albus shook his head in reply – he didn't know who they were – and he didn't miss how Gwen's fingers clamped white around the grips of her gun. Tallulah the rifle (once Rufus's rifle) was slung over her shoulder, but she had her handgun out. She held her arm down at her side, straight and tense. In the wash of the hearse's headlights, a red dot above the gun's trigger guard signified that its safety was off. Hari hung back, not moving to join the group. He was a cautious boy by nature, and Albus couldn't fault him for keeping his distance this time, either.

Gwen addressed the injured man. 'Who *are* you?' she demanded. 'What're you doing here?'

The man's head jerked up, his gaze stalling on Gwen's gun for a moment, a deep wrinkle creasing his brow. 'Jay. I'm Jay, and that' – he directed a short nod at the dead woman, breathing heavily through his words – 'that's Clancy. You . . . you killed her.' Tears swam in his dark eyes. They turned on Albus. 'Are you him?' It came out as a whisper, the man's breathing turning ragged. 'Are you Albus?'

A thousand questions bloomed like a cloud of balloons, bouncing off each other, their strings tangling into knots, each one tugging insistently at him because so many things had happened and he hadn't had a single moment to digest any of it. He wanted to throw his head back and howl at the sky, wanted everyone to stop talking, stop moving, just *stop* for five seconds so he could get his bearings. He imagined his sister, Ruby, coming up to stand behind him, the weight of her hands settling on his shoulders, and it wasn't hard to feel her so close, not since her St Christopher had returned to him with Addison, and a part of Ruby returning along with it.

Focus on the simplest thing first, he thought he heard her say. *Break it down to its smallest, easiest component. What did he ask you?*

He asked if I was Albus.

And are you?

Yes, of course he was.

Then tell him.

Albus patted the man's back once again, very gently, and nodded. Yes, he was Albus.

'Have you been here before?' Gwen asked Jay, cutting off any reply.

'*No.* Never.' Another wince, pain and frustration making Jay fidget under Bruno's tending hands.

'I think you should lie back. Here.' Bruno cupped the back of Jay's neck and guided him down. Albus helped as best he could.

The man lay less than two yards away from his dead friend. His head was turned her way. Albus watched as his tears spilled over, leaving a snail-like track on his skin. He was so young. Younger than Albus. Not yet twenty-two, if he had to guess.

'You shot them,' Addison said to Gwen, her young face scrunching up in accusation. 'You shot them full of holes.'

His legs weak, Albus got unsteadily to his feet and reached for the girl, not wanting her up in Gwen's face and causing more problems. Not wanting her to see any of this but knowing she'd seen far worse in her young life and that he couldn't shelter her from it, not even if he wanted to. He drew her back into the circle of his arm, and she reluctantly came, bumping up against him. Her body pumped out heat, fairly quivering with pent-up energy. Her eyes were waiting for him when he looked down. He squeezed her to him in a half-hug, hoping to calm her, and tapped his other hand to his ear, indicating that he wanted her to listen.

'Albus,' Addison whined softly, lips barely moving. 'Fender can't hear you right when you're thinking so muddled.'

Take a deep breath, little brother. And Albus did as his sister advised, letting it out slowly.

Good. Now quiet your mind.

He nodded to Addison and tried to wipe the strain he knew must be showing from his face. He pushed one thought to the surface and held it there.

— Hoyt. Ask him how he knows this man called Hoyt. The only man I knew who was called that is dead.

Dead for four years, in fact. When Albus had last seen him, Hoyt was being kicked to the ground by a hunting party, the mob's collective blood braying for the need to maim and kill. Albus had had no choice but to leave Hoyt behind. The mob had beaten Hoyt with fists and feet, with bats and pipes, as Albus had steered Ruby away, his sister's body leaden with defeat and tears streaking her face. The last image they'd had of their friend was of Hoyt being hoisted off the ground by a rope around his neck and the exuberant men cheering as they heaved him high, his feet kicking futilely at the air.

Addison turned to the man and said, 'Albus wants to know how you know Hoyt. 'Cause he's pretty sure he's dead.'

The man's – Jay's – damp gaze flicked from her to Albus and back again, and Albus could clearly read the confusion he felt over this girl speaking for him, not knowing that Albus was, essentially, a mute. But Jay went with it, and he earned brownie points for that.

'Don't know anything about him being dead.' Jay's breathing seemed a little easier now that he was prone, but it still came more shallowly than Albus liked. Bruno's grim expression told him he didn't like it, either. 'But Pilgrim likes his names. He's had three, by my last count. Clancy said . . .' He paused to breathe, to swallow. 'Clancy said Hoyt was likely just another name he used. That Pilgrim *was* Hoyt at some point.'

Addison had stiffened under Albus's arm, but now she outright twitched. '*Pilgrim?*'

Hari moved to their left, and Albus only knew this because his silhouette momentarily flickered past the front of the hearse's glowing headlights.

A loud curse burst from Jay, taking them all by surprise and, with more speed than Albus thought the injured man capable of, he snatched his shirt out of Bruno's hands.

Gwen's gun snapped up.

'No!' Addison shouted, lurching away from Albus. But Albus was moving with her, and he knocked Gwen's forearm up, clumsily shoving her hand skyward, the gun looming large as it passed by his face.

Gwen convulsively pulled the trigger, the shot shockingly loud next to Albus's ear, no more than half a foot away. He felt the percussive blast of it hit his cheek, the punch of it, and he yelped as a needle stabbed so deeply into his ear that he felt it slide all the way through to the other side. The hot, ejected cartridge scalded his cheek, and he jerked back, teeth snapping shut and catching his lip. He tasted blood, his ear alive with agony.

Gwen's voice came to him through miles of fog, a fading flashlight on dying batteries. He had to squint at her lips to read them, his hearing deafened by his palmed hand and the squealing drill excavating beneath it. 'Albus, I'm so sorry! Are you okay?'

She'd placed a cupped palm over the top of his, and the added pressure hurt his ear all the more, but he didn't flinch away. That would only upset her more.

He nodded, gestured weakly that he was fine, even though it was a lie and the piercing ringing in his ears told him so. He made what he hoped was a soft, placatory noise and looked pointedly at her weapon, pushing it gently aside and safely away from everyone, wanting her to put the thing away. He was so done with guns and arrows and weapons in general that he wanted to throw every last one of them into the ocean and let them sink to its deepest bed.

Gwen's eyes were pinched, distressed – distressed but angry, too – so angry at everything in the world, including herself, that he wished he could stroke her hair and tell her that everything would be all right. But he couldn't. Not here, not now. So he waited, looking at her steadily and asking in the only way he could, biting down on the gnawing pain so it didn't show. She held his eyes for long seconds, her self-reproach evident, and with a final check in Jay's direction, she holstered her weapon.

Jay was lying frozen, his head up, his hand sunk wrist-deep in his shirt's chest pocket. Dribbles of black blood ran down his belly and side, despite Bruno's pressing hand on his abdomen.

Eyeing Gwen and moving cautiously, Jay pulled a folded piece of paper from the shirt's wrinkled pocket and dropped his head slowly back as if it weighed too much to hold up. Unmindful of Bruno working to replace the reacquired shirt back over his gunshot wound, Jay cursed a second time at seeing the dark stains on the paper. He shakily attempted to wipe it clean, hands jerky with agitation.

Hari hadn't said a word as he'd circled the ground to hover near Bruno's shoulder. But now he held out his hand to Jay, a silent offer of help.

A moment of deliberation came and went, then Jay wordlessly passed the folded paper over to Hari, his agitation calming as the boy blotted the paper dry on his clean shirt, the fabric spotting dark with blood.

With Gwen's gun now safely holstered, Addison went right back to Jay, crouching down on his other side. 'You said *Pilgrim*, I heard you,' she told him, one small hand reaching into her seat pocket and pulling out a slim notebook.

Albus hadn't seen the book before, but she must have had it this whole time. As she fanned its pages, he glimpsed dozens of pencil sketches flip by, flicking too fast for his eyes to catch. She went too far, stopped, flipped back. Opened the book on a picture.

Albus leaned closer to see, ignoring the vicious stab in his inner ear at the movement.

It was a man and a motorbike. The bike was finished in near-perfect scaled accuracy, from hard-case luggage racks to exhaust and side mirrors, the scenery all around pencilled in and shaded: the desert, the low, scraggly bushes, the grass growing into the dust from the sides of the road. Even the man himself, his long legs crossed at his booted ankles as he leaned back against the bike's seat, arms folded, the set of his shoulders defiant yet aloof – all captured minutely. The only part that wasn't was the man's features. The artist had sketched his jaw and his hair ruffling in the breeze but hadn't been able to concentrate their pencil on his eyes, nose or mouth. The aspects that would bring him to life. His face remained a blank. And yet an uncanny familiarity nudged at Albus, an impossible train of thought that he couldn't see through to its end. Wouldn't.

You see it, though, his sister seemed to whisper to him, a smile in her voice. *I know you do.*

'Is this him?' Addison asked, and held the sketchbook up for Jay to see. 'Is this Pilgrim?'

Jay said nothing as he stared at the drawing, but Albus *did* see it, and so did Jay: it was that same inexplicable familiarity being mirrored back to him. How could one man – whether he called himself Pilgrim or Hoyt – connect so many of them? Addison to Albus (and Ruby), and now to these two strangers on the front lawn of his uncle's Inn.

'It's hard to say for sure.' Jay held out a bloody hand for the book.

Addison wrinkled her nose at it. 'Nu-huh. You look with

your eyes, not your hands.' She held the book nearer to his face, out of his reach.

'Yeah, that's him. That's Pilgrim, all right.' Jay said it with such quiet confidence that Albus felt the conviction rather than heard it. A shiver passed through him, hairs standing up all over his body, and he clamped his jaw on the judder. It shot a sizzle of pain up his ear canal and he pressed his palm flat over his ear once more.

'How can that not be him?' Jay was saying, looking around at the others. 'The hair. The boots. Even the posture. Everything's the same. Who *drew* these?' he asked, and made another grab for the sketchbook.

Addison tutted and moved it away. 'Alex did,' she said, and flipped through the pages to find more.

'Albus, do you know this Pilgrim?' Bruno asked, and the usual fuzzy brown-fur of his speech didn't envelop Albus like it usually did; it was a weak, threadbare version, and seeing it brought a new fear crashing down. His hearing was malfunctioning. That gunshot firing so close to his head had damaged something inside him. Maybe something irreparable.

No, no, he thought. It couldn't be permanently damaged. It needed time to recover, that was all. It *had* to recover. How else would he be able to track down Amber and Jasper? They could only trust Jake's information so far. Albus's chromosthesia was the only thing that would lead them the rest of the way. Without it, Albus was useless. No, worse – he'd be a hindrance. No hearing, no working hands, no ability to speak. He'd be good for nothing.

He flexed the palm pressed to his head, his missing fingers giving a ghostly flex along with it, and a nasty needle-point jabbed up to greet it. It made his breath catch.

Remember, what you have is a gift, Albus. Ruby had said it to him not long after Jonah had come to her, and right before their parents had set their family home on fire. His sister's beautiful rose-red tones had unspooled from her mouth like silken ribbons. *A dangerous gift, but a gift all the same. It lets you see people like me, people who don't even realise they're special. Without it, Jonah never would have known I was open to him. Never would have chanced making the jump to me. Don't forget how coveted a gift that might be someday. Don't ever take it for granted, and don't ever leave anyone like me alone and undefended, Al. They'll need you, even if they don't know it. Just like Jonah and I need you.*

'Albus?' Bruno said more loudly, frowning at how Albus was cupping his ear.

Albus hastily dropped his hand back to his side, not wanting to answer any awkward questions.

Addison had paused in her flicking and angled a new drawing towards Jay, holding it there while her head craned around to find Albus. He slowed his racing thoughts, pinned them in place, and formed his words carefully and precisely.

– Yes, I know this Pilgrim. He was a good friend to my sister and me back when we knew him as Hoyt. But I was sure he'd been killed. I saw him hang. He sacrificed himself for us.

Addison passed on what he'd said, popping a shrug at the end of it. 'I shot Pilgrim. *Bang.* Right here.' She pressed a fingertip high to the left side of her chest, then looked down at Jay's torso and winced in sympathy. 'I didn't mean to, not really, but he came outta nowhere and I was scared. He got his own treasure hole digged. But now *he* says he knows him.' She stabbed the finger at Jay, in case Albus didn't know who she meant. 'Maybe he didn't stay killed or sleeping in his hole like we thought?'

'If any man got shot in the chest or hanged, he'd be dead,' Gwen said flatly, and Albus had to agree with her. There was no coming back from such injuries. Not without hospitals, or paramedics, or fast-response units. Gwen's fingers lightly rested on her gun's grips, but the weapon remained holstered, its safety on. A good sign. 'I don't know what you people came here for,' she said, 'but you shouldn't have. The chances of this Pilgrim, or whoever he is, being the same man Albus knew are impossible.'

'We just got done following the voice of Albus's dead sister on a rescue mission to save this child,' Bruno said, his eyes – slightly bulbous under their hooded lids – sliding a look towards Addison. None of his words were mocking or argumentative. He said them with great care, each one making a point that Gwen would find hard to refute. 'There are stranger things at work here than a man surviving a gunshot wound or a hanging. We all have past lives. He might have known Albus in his.'

'Whatever the case,' Gwen said, waving her hand as if to bat away his words, 'we're not about to debate modern-day miracles. I don't want anyone else turning up before we can get out of here.' She threw a glance over her shoulder towards the Inn, and Albus did the same, noticing how she studiously didn't look at the dead woman lying at their feet.

The light from the lantern in the parlour cast a dull orangey glow through the Inn's picture window and the dread that had been curdling Albus's stomach – but had been tamped down by the unexpected diversion of Jay and Clancy's arrival – surged back to life. Nothing moved beyond the glass, but that didn't mean the man they'd captured hadn't regained consciousness. If anything, the stillness made Albus's abdominals contract tighter.

'He's coming.'

The words bit chunks of terror out of Albus's dread, his thoughts immediately turning to the Flitting Man. Had he been the one to find them? Was it him behind the killings of his friends? The question was *how*? Albus and Ruby had always been so careful. Only a finite number of people knew of the Inn's location, all of whom were in Albus's presence right now or dead (or had very recently been resurrected from the grave, if Jay was to be believed). Yet the only reason they'd come looking for him *or* the Inn was because they were looking for Ruby and

Jonah. And they believed Albus would be the only person with news of their whereabouts.

'Pilgrim or Hoyt' – Jay saying that name shocked Albus all over again – 'whatever you want to call him – he's coming. That's why me and Clancy are here. He sent us ahead of him because he thought this place would be safe.' Jay laughed without humour and it quickly transformed into a dry, hacking cough. He wasn't looking good – his dusky skin had paled, his eyes had hollowed; he wasn't gasping for breath but his inhalations seemed lighter and faster, as if his lung capacity was diminishing.

As insane as it was that Hoyt could be alive and on his way here, Albus felt a tiny spark of relief flare bright. Belief was breaking through, the beams in the hull of his ship bending inward under its mounting pressure, water trickling in and hope pouring in with it. It swelled inside the hold of his chest, his heart growing large and full. Even the rancid, piercing pain in his head eased for the briefest of moments before his gaze fell back upon the dead woman in the grass.

'He's really coming?' Addison asked eagerly. 'When?'

Jay squirmed under Bruno's pinning hand, clearly in discomfort. 'A day. Maybe two? He can't be far behind . . .' He trailed off as he blinked and squinted and blinked once more. 'I feel kind of dizzy.'

Albus's full heart began to deflate. Two whole days. A gust of cool ocean air rushed over them, whistling into his broken ear, making it ache like a rotten tooth. It ruffled the grass and mussed their hair, and with it came a chill that Albus felt on the inside as well as the out.

'We can't stay here that long.' Gwen pulled on Albus's arm, tugging him back, and Albus allowed her to do it. Addison stayed crouched over Jay, close to climbing on the poor guy, too intent on their exciting new discoveries to sense the sudden shift in the group.

Hari stood up, the folded paper he had been holding falling from his hands to drift to the grass. He was shaking his head, a slow back and forth. 'I have a bad feeling, Albus,' he said. The boy looked behind him, up the driveway, as if expecting to see another vehicle pull in at any moment.

Albus backed up another step, Gwen's tugging becoming insistent.

Bruno brusquely nudged Addison aside and bent to inspect Jay's injury. He groaned so low that Albus swore he felt it rumble through the soil under his feet.

'We really shouldn't move him,' Bruno said, his head-shaking mimicking Hari's. 'The bleeding will start up again. And with the bullet still inside . . . He's already lost too much.'

'I'm not leaving,' Jay said, face set stubbornly. 'I have to wait for Pilgrim.'

'It's not safe,' Bruno told him.

'I don't care! Just, I don't know – shove me in a bush or something. I'll be fine.'

Addison had picked up the blood-stained paper and was holding it reverently in her hands, head bowed over it as if in prayer.

'If you want,' she said, looking up to meet Albus's eyes, 'I can stay with him.'

Albus's immediate impulse was to refuse her. Oh, how he wanted to gather her up and bustle her along to the library van and drive far, far away from here. The thought of abandoning her went against every single protective instinct in his body. The Inn, once the safest of harbours, was now a glaring, red target – it was a site of murder and abduction, of spilled blood and terror. It was the last place on earth Albus wanted to leave *anyone*, never mind an eight-year-old girl. But where Albus was heading would be even more treacherous. The Flitting Man was all around them now, a spectre that peeped out from the shadows, and he was whittling Albus's family down, one by one.

Anyone connected to Albus, or his sister, would be in danger.

'No. You must stay with us,' Hari said, and Albus felt his eyes go wide, because Hari's golden tones were bright and true. Its honeyed shine had lost some of its lustre, the colour less rich, but it flowed in uninterrupted loop-de-loops.

Addison's expression turned mulish. 'I can do what I want.'

'You cannot.'

'I can, too.'

'Albus, tell her she must come with us,' Hari said, turning to face him.

Albus found himself opening his mouth, words of compliance dancing where his tongue should be. Which was crazy, because, one: Albus wasn't physically capable of saying *anything*, even if he wanted to; and, two: he had already realised that Addison coming with them *was not* a good choice. Didn't think Hari coming along was ideal, either, but leaving the boy behind hadn't worked out so well in the past. Albus had learned that the hard way.

Plus, there's Hoyt, Ruby whispered in his good ear.

Yes. Hoyt was coming. And Hoyt was possibly the only person Albus had ever met who would be capable of handling the storm that was heading their way. There was no doubt in Albus's mind that Hoyt could be trusted to protect Addison.

'Albus, let's *go*,' Gwen insisted, tugging at him again, but this time he twisted away from her, pulling free. She stumbled a bit, surprised by the loss of his weight (surprised by his resistance to her, too, he was sure). Hands raised to quieten them down, Albus fixed his gaze firmly on Addison and relayed instructions in clear, concise thoughts. A second later, the girl repeated them for him.

'Gwen, Albus says to go check on Jake, then get ready to move. Pack the library bus up with whatever you think we'll need. Bruno, you gotta help carry Jay over to the hedge over there. If he won't come with us, we need to hide him good.'

'I'm not coming with you,' Jay stated.

The girl swung to face Hari. 'And Hari, you should get something for Clancy. Digging treasure holes takes too long, but we should cover her with something. Leaving her out feels wrong.'

Albus raised his eyebrows. He hadn't said anything about covering the dead woman. But he was grateful to Addison for including her.

There was a split second when nobody moved, but then Albus swept a hard, uncompromising gaze across each person and it was enough to spur them into action. He went to Addison and bent down to her height. The girl's gaze felt weighty on his. He had to work at keeping eye contact with her.

'Me and Fender know Gwen hurt your ear,' she said, even going so far as to move her lips in exaggerated motions so he could follow them. 'Your superpower is broke.'

Albus glanced over at Bruno, but his friend was busy getting Jay ready to be moved. He gave Addison what he hoped was a convincing *Don't worry, I'm fine* look.

She rolled her eyes. 'I won't tell no one. But you'll need me and Fender extra hard now. To speak for you 'n' stuff. Specially if you can't hear good.' She looked so sad for him.

He shook his head at her. Made a staying motion, palm flat and pressing downward.

She seemed to halfway regret her offer to stay. 'I just think that maybe you need a sidekick more than ever, and I should—'

He pressed his hands down against the tops of her shoulders, cutting her off.

— No. You stay.

She looked so unhappy about it he lifted a hand and gently ran the palm of it over the soft curls of her head. She had never flinched at his touch, despite his hands being a grotesque imitation of what appendages should look like. He'd noticed that about her, right from the start. There was no judgement in anything she did, there simply wasn't room for it in her. She approached everything in the same way – with an innocent acceptance that was inclusive of everyone and everything. It was such a precious thing. *She* was a precious thing.

He stroked her head once more and made sure his thoughts came through strong and firm.

— Don't come out until you see Hoyt – until you see *Pilgrim*. No coming into the open, unless it's completely safe. No matter what happens. Do you promise?

There was a short delay while the message was passed on, a small, thoughtful crease forming while she listened. 'Me, Alex and my aunt would always pinkie promise when we promised each other stuff.' She said it slowly, working on figuring something out. 'But you don't got pinkies.'

Albus smiled. No, he certainly did not have any of those.

'Wanna palm promise instead?' She held her hand up as if waiting on a high-five.

Albus huffed a laugh and bumped her palm with a soft pat of his own.

'Palm promise,' she said, and nodded resolutely. She looked a little happier than she had. 'Let's go help Jay now. Bruno's gonna bust him up good if he tries to do it by himself.'

Chapter 5

Jay

Jay awoke to a stinging smack to his cheek. His eyes sprang open and he found himself staring into a pair of intense eyes. The girl's face was sweaty, framed with dark, springy curls. A pinch of a frown appeared between those grave eyes and she whispered, 'Should I slap him again?'

She looked very familiar, but Jay winced from the thought because he hurt too much. Like, *really* hurt. His head and his chest and his side. Ugh, his *side.* A rolling nausea washed through his stomach and he wanted to upchuck everything he'd ever eaten. He squeezed his eyes shut and concentrated on breathing.

The girl slapped him again.

'*Oww—*' A small hand, hot and clammy, clamped over his mouth. Jay could feel her alertness, hunkered low over him, the warmth of her passing down her arm into the fingers clamped over his cold face.

'Shhhh. You gotta be quiet. We're in our hidey-hole.'

Grass closed him in where he lay, but it was too dark to see anything else. Jay breathed through his nose and lifted his head, swivelled his eyes to look around. He shouldn't have. His skull split down the middle and his ribs cracked apart like a side of beef cleaved open by a butcher. He moaned softly, the sound muffled by her palm. He touched tentative, shaky fingers to the area under his ribs, discovered a rough mesh of wrapped bandages wound tightly around his abdomen.

Gunshot. Dear God, how had he forgotten he'd been *shot*? On the back of that thought came the recollection of Clancy, dead, her braid snaking around her head and her throat ripped open. He thrust the image away before it could fill his head and blind him.

'Was sure Bruno was gonna drag you to the bus to spite you,' the girl whispered to him. 'But you kicked up a storm and opened up your wound. Then you went to sleep.'

His breathing stalled. 'Mmmrrrrwe?'

'Huh?' Her dark eyes gleamed down at him. 'If I move my hand, you can't be noisy,' she warned.

He nodded his understanding, and she lifted it from his mouth. Jay licked his dry lips and tasted the lingering salt of her skin. In a low voice, he said, 'Where are we?'

'Bushes.'

His confusion cleared in stages. First, he breathed in the richness of soil and plant-life. Then he felt things poking at him in places no one should ever be poked. A few quiet cracks and rustles marked the girl moving around to get comfortable. He wanted to move, too, but a numbness had seeped into his middle, collecting like freezing rainwater in his gut, and he was afraid that moving would ignite the grinding pain under his ribs again.

'Why're we in a bush again?' he asked quietly.

''Cause we're *hiding*.' She said it as though it was the most obvious thing in the world and he was being stupid.

A latticework of branches and leaves sheltered them. The brilliant glow of the moon was an indistinct shape that peeked from time to time through his swaying, branching world. It was like being swallowed alive by a forest beast. He felt mildly ridiculous being stuffed in here, but then *he* wouldn't think of looking in a bush if he was doing a search, so maybe it was a better idea than he gave it credit for.

In small degrees, Jay slowly turned his head to the side, the spindly fingers of branches sifting through his hair and trailing fingers down his neck. He couldn't have been passed out for long; thirty yards away across the lawn, the hearse sat still and silent on the driveway. Its headlights were dead. A small, bumpy hillock in the grass confused him for a second before his breath caught. The pain that hit him this time wasn't in his abdomen but in his heart.

Clancy.

They had covered her with a blanket. He'd been covered him with a blanket, too, and something soft and warm was laid under his back, protecting him from the worst of the poking vegetation. His and Clancy's assailants were thoughtful, if nothing else.

Angling his head a little more, he could see parts of the Inn. It was as darkly cloaked as when he and Clancy had driven up to it, but a flickering candlelight moved inside behind the large picture window. They were in there. As a backdrop to the Inn, glimpsed in patchwork through a wall of leaves, a lighter, bluish-grey band stamped itself low across the sky. Dawn wasn't far off.

The tall, broad-shouldered black dude appeared on the porch, guiding a second man with a hand under his arm. He seemed to be supporting a good portion of the second man's weight. This guy was shorter and new; Jay hadn't seen him yet. The shorter guy took the porch steps carefully, his arms locked strangely behind him. When they turned to the side and began tromping over the drive to the parked library bus, Jay realised the man's hands were tied.

With a *whoosh* and a faint rattling *clank*, the library van's door slid open and the two men climbed aboard, Bruno helping the captive along.

Beside Jay, the girl was murmuring to herself.

'But I don't want to.' A pause. 'That's not *fair* . . . No, because it isn't. I *do* care, I just—' The next part dropped into a petulant whisper. 'Pilgrim can find Albus, even if I didn't.'

Jay lifted his head to try to see her better in the darkness and the corner of a branch poked his face near his eye. It scored a hot line past his temple.

'*Ow.*' He awkwardly freed an arm and pushed the offending twig away.

A shadow detached itself from the foliage as the girl leaned over him. 'Don't move so much,' she scolded.

'It's okay for you,' he whispered back. 'You're tiny.'

He got the sense she rolled her eyes at him. The cold numbness in his belly was dissipating, replaced by a gradual burn that would soon have him writhing in discomfort if he didn't find a distraction.

'What's your name?' he asked.

A pause. Stillness. Then: 'I'm Addison. And you're Jay, like the bird.' She pursed her lips and made a soft, blowy whistle, more air than sound.

'Why're you in here with me?'

'Fender doesn't think I should be. He's worried about Albus. He thinks I should go.' She sighed, the gust warm on his face. 'But I saw this.'

A rustle of what he thought was leaves and then something was being held up in front of his face. A piece of paper. *His* piece of paper. Or, more rightly, Pilgrim's.

On the printed-out photograph, Addison pointed to each person in turn. Though Jay could barely make out the figures in the dimness, he'd looked at the photo so often he knew each by heart. Especially the girl on the right.

'That's my mommy, my great-grams, and' – a double-tap of a finger – 'my aunt.'

Jay's mouth went as dry as old leather.

'And, there, in my mommy's tummy—'

The pictured woman had a sizeable baby bump, Jay knew.

'—is me,' Addison finished proudly.

He couldn't believe it. He couldn't. 'You're Lacey's *niece*?' he croaked.

'Yep.' The photo disappeared from sight as Addison folded and slipped it away into one of her pockets. 'This paper's from my house. So I know you're telling the truth about Pilgrim being alive, even if Gwen thinks you're a no-good liar. Huh. Wait.' She sat up straighter, looking like a truckload of confusion had just been dumped over her head. 'You know my aunt's name? Did Pilgrim tell you that?'

'I know her,' he blurted, wincing when a swift wrench of pain cramped through his side. He'd forgotten to keep his voice low, but the girl didn't hush him. 'Well, not really, but kind of. It's why Pilgrim didn't come with us. He had to go find her first. She needed his help and he went to get her.'

More silence.

His vision was pulsing in time with the pain under his ribs, but it had adjusted to the darkness all the same. He could see how Addison's lips had parted, her mouth opening on a breathy sound. She gazed at him, her eyes wide. Her throat rippled as she swallowed. 'Lacey will be coming, too?' she whispered. The way she said it, so hopeful and small, as if speaking it too loudly would take it away from her and make it disappear, brought a hot lump to Jay's throat. 'Coming *here*?'

'Yeah. Pilgrim wouldn't leave her behind. He'll be bringing her, for sure.'

Tears flooded the girl's eyes and white teeth bit down on her bottom lip. She chewed away at it as if it were the only thing preventing her from sobbing. Jay placed a shaky hand on the nearest part of her he could reach, which happened to be her side, not caring about the sharp scratch he got for his trouble. She felt so delicate to him, all rib-bones and fast-pumping lungs.

She mumbled something.

He shifted an inch closer, trying to find a spot in the process that didn't hurt so much. 'What?' he whispered.

'She's coming today?'

'Maybe,' he said, not entirely sure. 'Or tomorrow.'

Addison turned her face away. 'Yeah,' she murmured, not speaking to Jay. 'I know.' She sniffled and shook her head, curls bouncing. She drew into herself, balling up, nose pressed to her upraised knees. 'I don't want to, either, but . . . Why *can't* I—' She cut herself off mid-sentence. Her voice thickened with more tears. 'Albus does, I know . . .'

Jay felt uneasy and helpless, listening to her argue with herself. He lay still, feeling hot and sick, sweating through his bandages. 'Who're you talking to?' he asked nervously.

She sniffed and lifted her face to him. Tears streaked her cheeks, but she wiped her palm across her eyes and released a long, hiccupping breath. 'They're going to Lesion Fields. Albus and Bruno and the others,' she said, ignoring his question.

Jay stiffened, his stomach cramping so hard his right knee jerked and he grunted in pain. '*Where?*' He knew that name. Elysian Fields was a rumoured experimental hospital or facility – or both – that Pilgrim had learned about in St Louis. In Jay's experience, it wasn't a place *anyone* should be paying a visit, not even the people who'd shot at him and Clancy.

'They can't go there,' he said, but it came out garbled and his vision pulsed with darkness. He didn't want to close his eyes again. What if he didn't wake up? Fear clambered up his throat and he said the girl's name, blindly reaching out for her.

Addison scooted nearer, tucking his blanket in around him, swaddling him like a baby. Something hard nudged into his hip (he thought he heard the slosh of water). He tried to grip on to the girl's shirt, but his hand got gently diverted away and tucked into his blanket. She'd curled his fingers into a fist and wrapped her hand around it through the layers. Her grip was strong for such a tiny girl.

‘There, do you see?’ she whispered, leaning low to speak in his ear. She was pointing north out through their bush, away from the hearse and the driveway and the Inn, and he twisted his head as best he could to look. His eyes met leaves, of course, but she grabbed a branch and bent it out of his way. He squinted, following her finger.

‘Far out, to the birds. You see ’em?’ Her whisper was close and intimate, as if imparting some dark, scary secret. ‘The birds, they know something.’

It took him a moment to focus his eyes and, initially, he thought she was pointing out a distant range of storm clouds to him, but they didn’t hang still and heavy like storm clouds should. The dark mass billowed upward as he watched, a bloom of black particles that suddenly collapsed in on itself, plummeting back towards the earth. He lost sight of it for an instant and then it swept into view again, veering north. Tendrils broke free, too slow to keep up, and a paler mist trailed after its denser, darker body.

Birds. Thousands of them. All flying together.

‘They know something we don’t. That’s what Hari said.’ She paused and frowned. ‘Hm. Does that make me a curious little bird?’ It didn’t sound like a question for him, so Jay let it pass him by.

She absently rubbed her fingertips over the branch’s leaves and reached over with the same hand, pressing a single fingertip to the middle of Jay’s forehead. A stronger smell of vegetation came with her.

‘Anyway, that’s where I think Jake will lead Albus. To the curious birds.’

Jay blinked, the change of subject, the new name, the pain gnawing at his side, all a confusion that he was finding difficult to hold on to.

Her eyes glimmered in the darkness. They seemed to grow in size until they were as bright and big as the moon and he had to squint or else burn. She pressed her finger gently into his brow, as if implanting the information directly into his brain, and that single digit was an anvil on his head, pinning his entire body to the ground.

Don't bury me, he wanted to plead with her. *I'm not ready to be buried.*

Something hot and sweaty clamped harder around his hand and he almost screamed before realising it was Addison, holding his hand through his blanket. She'd been holding it this entire time.

'You have to remember the birds,' she whispered, her voice sinking inside his head to join the rushing of blood, the pumping of capillaries, her warm breath and whispering voice like floating in an ocean, waves and waves of it brushing over his skin. She was singing, the lyrics filling him up, but he couldn't swim out to them all, and the melody he was drowning in – one so achingly familiar to him – began to drift away on the tide.

'Do you pinkie promise?' she asked, lifting up to peer down at him.

He let out a long, thin sigh as her shadowed face ghosted into two, side by side. Twins. Pilgrim never mentioned twins.

'Do you?' both versions of her mouth asked.

And he said, 'Yes,' because 'Yes' was a word his dizzy brain didn't need to search for. It was easy and ready in waiting.

'Don't worry,' Addison said, and patted him on the head, like he was a good doggie and she was very fond of him. 'Shh, you rest.' Her fingers curled into his hair, bunching it in a gentle fist, and she breathed out: 'You have *so much* hair,' and her double-set of eyes widened at the discovery. 'I really like it. And I'm really sorry you got shot. Gwen didn't mean it.'

With a final shushing, her touch-points on him – at head and hand – vanished, and Jay became unmoored. The earth under his back tilted and he squeezed his eyes shut as the rustling of undergrowth tipped him sideways. His stomach lurched sickly.

From somewhere outside of him, a delicate tinkling sounded, bells as tiny as acorns, and it was such an incongruous noise he chanced slitting one eye open.

Darkness.

Crinkly leaves.

Talking?

He carefully leaned his head to the opposite side and, through branches and a sea of grass – a lawn? – he was seeing . . . a bus. A *library* bus. *It's been here all along*, a little part of him said.

'Why is there a library here?' he whisper-mumbled, his brain reminding him to be quiet even if he couldn't remember what for.

The talking grew louder, but it was impossible to decipher. Thumps, the sound of feet on wood. A porch decking? Yes, there was a wraparound porch with white railings and white pillars. Thumping feet came down the steps, followed by the crunch of gravel. The driveway. Jay squirmed the slightest bit, one hand fumbling at his side, and the swift jolt of pain was like a splash of cold water to the face.

The lighter blonde woman, the one he'd first mistaken for Lacey, was marching directly for the bus's cab door. She swung up into the driver's seat. Albus and the smaller boy headed to the library's rear sliding door. There, Albus hesitated before ascending the steps, looking over in Jay's direction, even though Jay was sure he couldn't be seen. The boy stopped, too, said something, and the man nodded in reply. Albus's shoulders seemed to slump, his head lowered, but he continued up the stairs.

The boy hung back, nose lifted to the air as if he scented something on the wind. Head swivelling left then right, his feet took him around the back of the bus and towards the far side. Albus couldn't see what the boy was peering towards, but he stood there for long seconds, his head canted attentively. When nothing happened, Jay began to drift, his eyelids drooping as a crushing need to sleep fell over him.

He forced achy, tired eyes to follow as the boy backtracked to the bus's open doorway and skipped inside. Once he was out of sight, Jay's body slowly relaxed, his muscles softening, his limbs turning boneless. His jaw cracked wide on a yawn.

The van swayed with the hollow treads of feet clomping through the interior. In the narrow side windows, the shadowy shapes of Albus, the larger bulk of the black dude and the smaller boy filed through. The engine rumbled to life and a long, sibilant hiss released into the night. An interior light flicked on, illuminating the van's main body and, through the narrow window, Jay sleepily catalogued empty beech shelving and purple bracketing. Colourful posters. Carpeting. A second hiss joined the first, and a rolling mechanism clanked as the sliding door shut itself, closing with a bump of rubberised seals. The bus's headlights punched a hole straight through a line of bushes on the far side of the Inn's property, the same kind of hedgerow Jay was currently cloistered in. The bare beam stripped the hedge back to roots and inner-branch structure, an X-ray of its innards.

'Shit,' Jay mumbled. He hoped no one shone a light like that on his and Addison's hiding spot.

The engine got louder, the parking brake disengaged and the bus rolled forward, swinging around, its tyres grinding pebbles together as it chomped them for breakfast. The van creaked on by, driving up on to the lawn and cutting through the overgrown grass as it bounced its way past the abandoned hearse. At the end of the driveway, its rear lights flared traffic-light red and the bus made its laborious turn on to the road, pointing its nose northward.

On a last long, deep sigh, Jay closed his eyes. He listened to the van's engine note fade and he began to fade, too. The night became so quiet, and his bed of earth and leaves and borrowed blankets became so very, very comfy. His last thoughts before slipping into the waiting darkness were of pinkies and promises and curious, flying birds.

Chapter 6

Albus

Albus observed Jake from across the library bus. He was sitting on the carpeted flooring beside Bruno, secured to a handrail behind him. While Gwen drove (and Bruno shuffled and adjusted his position), Jake hadn't budged an inch. He sat with his back wedged against the shelving, his legs straight out, shoulders set and head facing forward. To shift at all might invite a fresh torrent of pain from his punctured shoulder, or a wave of throbbing soreness from the head wound that had split open his scalp.

Bruno had patched him up as best he could, but Jake looked worse than awful. He kept his eyes closed. His face was pale and sheened with sweat, and, earlier, when he'd given them specific road signs and landmarks to look out for, the concentration needed for him to get the words out in some form of recognisable order had worried Albus greatly. Gwen had hit him *hard* with the butt of her rifle. Maybe she had caused more damage than just the scalp wound.

Gwen had remained quiet as she'd concentrated on navigating the roads, but her attention was overly focused for the task. She'd always been tightly controlled. Her recent volatile, reactive behaviour was in direct opposition to the logical thinker Albus knew her to be. But losing her best friend, followed by the discovery of Cloris, Bianca and the boys on the back porch, had been too much, too traumatic, and now her emotions were ruling her head.

She wouldn't be drawn into conversation whenever Bruno tried, and she hadn't spoken to Albus, either, when he'd made his way up the van to stand beside her. He'd hovered, hanging on to the back of the passenger seat as she steered them down the slip road and on to the north-bound highway. She hadn't uttered a word, even as silent tears tracked their way down her cheeks. She'd swiped angrily at them, ashamed (if Albus knew her at all), at being seen to be upset. He'd pretended to gaze through the windshield.

They hadn't needed to speak for Albus to understand. Gwen had shot and killed people before – it was an unavoidable part of their lives now. But she'd never before killed an innocent. Prior to Jay and Clancy's arrival, she had been more than prepared to enact violence on those who deserved it, but the ones she'd ended up hurting weren't guilty of anything more than being in the wrong place at the wrong time. Now one was dead and the other grievously wounded. How could she reconcile her actions to such an appalling outcome? So Albus had stayed nearby, even as every bump and sway of the van slid a hot, lancing needle deeper into his eardrum. Even as the ringing whine travelled like a drill into his jaw, making him want to tear his face open, rip his ear off and yank his hair out by its roots. He stood patiently and did none of those things, because it wasn't what Gwen needed from him then.

Eventually, her tears had dried and she'd glanced over at him with bloodshot eyes. She didn't thank him in words; she didn't have to. He saw the gratitude in the softness of her gaze, felt her affection in the brief touch she brushed to his arm. And Albus had nodded to her and left her alone, moving back into the library proper.

Their friends' deaths had unbalanced them all. Rational

thought had taken a back seat and they were rushing full tilt towards something none of them really understood. They were acting on instinct and a wild, desperate need to protect the remainder of their family before it was too late. If that meant strangling answers out of unarmed men and stabbing them in the shoulder, then so be it.

What about protecting Pilgrim? Ruby asked, and Albus closed his eyes, because it hurt to hear her voice when his sister was dead, and it hurt to think about Pilgrim, too, when leaving him behind was like being offered the return of his fingers only to have them cruelly ripped away again. He was the last person alive who Ruby and Albus had confided in – about a lot of things, including Jonah's existence and Albus's chromosthesia. With the loss of Ruby, having Pilgrim would have been the next best thing, but to wait for his arrival would have meant not only gambling on a contingent of Jake's pals not turning up at the Inn, but also on letting Amber and Jasper slip further and further away. And Albus had already lost too much. He couldn't lose them, too. He wouldn't dig any more graves.

You must be careful, Al, his sister said, and she sounded so fearful for him. *I advised you to gather these people close to keep them safe. I told you that he would want them, didn't I?*

She had. She'd said the Flitting Man would seek out rare people similar to her, people who didn't hear a voice of their own but had a place for one regardless, like she had with Jonah. But the Flitting Man wasn't a Jonah, nor was he a Matilde. He wouldn't be a guiding, helping voice, one that strived for balance. The Flitting Man would use people for his own selfish needs. He would live off them like a helminth until every speck of goodness had been leached away.

Albus thought of Gwen, of Bruno and Hari. He thought about Amber and Jasper, the two youngest members of their group, and couldn't stomach the idea of their lives being taken over by something so manipulative, something so full of deceit and avarice. He'd rather die than let that happen.

It's better we all die than you let that happen.

It was an effort, but Albus forced his sister's ghostly voice away and opened his eyes. He watched Hari nudge Jake in the leg. Jake didn't stir. The boy had sat himself in the middle of the floor, equidistant between Bruno and Jake on one side and Albus on the other. He faced the front of the van, and Albus realised that Hari had positioned himself so that everyone was in perfect view, as if he were sitting at the head of a table.

Another nudge. 'Do you live there?' Hari asked, and Albus almost allowed his eyelids to drift shut again, the soft golden pulse of Hari's words a balm to the penetrating ache in his ear, somehow bypassing most of the damage.

'It's an eco project,' Bruno's deep rumble said. 'Some government-funded research initiative into green energy, I'm betting.' The directions Jake had given them had included keeping a lookout for signs to Trinity Hills.

'Yes. But what is there?'

Barely a mumble: 'Power.'

Albus had to lean forward and turn his head, angling his good ear towards Jake. The man didn't bother to open his eyes, his head bobbing a little with the rocking of the van. 'The facility . . . has lights, radios, heat. A never-ending supply.' He was slurring his words.

'So you *do* live there?' Bruno asked.

A ghost of a smile was Jake's only response.

Bruno glanced at Albus, his brow crinkled in concern.

Hari tugged at the material of Jake's pants, presumably not wanting the man to fall into another stupor when he had more questions to ask. 'What are you doing there?'

Jake's head bobbed an inch lower, then another, until his chin touched his chest. 'Waiting,' he murmured.

'Waiting for what?'

'Right time.' Jake's head rolled up again, his eyes squinting open to land on Albus. 'So much waiting. Everything had to be . . . in its place. Everything had to be . . . just right. The animals, the birds. You. Us. *We*. The red storm on the horizon. The Flitting Man, of course. And the voices. You know all this. Don't you?' Jake aimed the question at Albus, appearing disoriented for a moment and unsure of himself. He looked at each of them in turn, his confused, heavy-lidded gaze making a slow, drunken journey from Bruno, to Hari, up past the book counter to the driver's seat and back to Albus again. This kind of talk reminded Albus too much of when Ruby and Jonah got down to debating too much, reminded him of when Albus and his sister had paid a visit to an old woman's cabin up in the mountains of Wisconsin. Matilde and Ruby could be as secretive as two conspiring witches hunched over a bubbling cauldron when they wanted to be. Cryptic messages and hidden meanings. At the time, Albus had secretly felt kind of special being included in their collusions, even if only on the periphery. But now all he felt was a building annoyance.

Jake's voice lowered to a careful whisper. 'You know he's here, right? You *know*. Divide and conquer, that's the idea. That's how they always did it back then. Us and Them.' He laughed – a broken, messy chuckle that pulled a grimace from Albus. 'It's how this is all gonna fall down around our ears if we aren't careful.' He laughed again, and a hard gust of wind hit the side of the van in its own cosmic guffaw. Albus felt the yawn in the vehicle as the sudden push lifted the van up on its axles.

Gwen fought the wheel as they wobbled and weaved in place. 'Woah.'

Another gust, much more violent than the first, and the wheels squealed some, the slew of the van shoving them left. Albus pressed both palms into the thin carpeting for balance. Bruno and Hari braced themselves against shelving and floor alike. Jake's jaw had clenched, his back jammed against the handrail behind him. The wheels thumped over something solid, front then rear, a sudden skittering that snaked along the undercarriage. An ear-splitting double-thud slammed the back wing of the van and the floor beneath Albus leapt up. His butt thumped back down and his teeth clacked shut. He stifled a yelp as a flash of pain lit up his inner ear.

'Woah woah woah!' Gwen yelled.

The library van's back end slid out, a muddy, juddering careen that slammed them hind and ass into a solid, unmoveable wall. It screeched with distressed metal. Albus was thrown on to his side, his shoulder connecting with the floor hard enough to make him grunt. Through the narrow side window, the body of a truck blocked Albus's view; their right flank and the truck's left met at a messy angle. He checked their other side and sat up abruptly, eyes widening at the multiple darts of movement from the far side of the highway, most lost behind the rusted husks of cars and concrete median.

'Is everyone all right?' Gwen called back to them, twisting around in the driver's seat. Albus must have had a look of alarm on his face because Gwen's head whipped to her left and she swore loudly. 'Shit! Get away from the window!'

She dived from her seat, landing on the floor behind the hip-high book counter and out of sight. Something smacked off the driver-side window, splintering it with a horrid *crack*, but failed to break through. Whether she'd shut the engine off herself or it had cut itself out, the rumble of the idling motor was gone and in its place the distinct howl of building winds buffeted them as if a great elemental beast was swatting at the van from outside, transforming it from a land vehicle into a flimsy boat on choppy waters. It rocked from side to side.

Albus ducked low into cover as something heavy whacked the van's outer wall next to him. A barrage of thuds and thumps followed – some kind of projectiles – and the library van became a hollow, beating drum. Shouts joined the assault, but their attackers' calls were lost in the maelstrom of sound that resounded through the interior. How many were out there? It sounded like an army.

The van's interior strip-lights were on – those that were working – illuminating the main body of the library. It made the world beyond the windows all the dimmer, the fast-turning weather accelerating the day to a premature dusk. From the outside looking in, Albus and his companions must have looked like tropical fish in a lit-up tank. Perfect targets. Behind the stubby book counter, Gwen popped up into view and slapped a hand on the button panel on the wall and the van fell into gloom. Better.

The pelting strikes halted.

Albus chanced another glance and spotted two, three, four people rush across the blacktop, hopping the concrete median and dodging down behind two rusted heaps that were once 4x4s. He couldn't be sure if they were armed or not, but they were fast and they were purposeful.

He did his best to say 'Four,' and got a nod from Gwen. She had retrieved her rifle from the cubby-hole behind the counter and she used the long muzzle to knock the rear-view mirror to an angle so she could see out of the driver's splintered side-window.

'Crap, I can't really see anything,' she muttered, and left her station to come around the counter, staying low.

Bruno left his side of the van and crawled over to Albus. He had his gun in hand, too.

'We're trapped in here,' Bruno said quietly, not wanting to be overheard. 'The only doors we can exit from are on their side.' He was right – the truck they'd crashed into was blocking the passenger-side door.

'*We have guns on you,*' a call came, rising above the wind. '*Come out or we'll open fire.*'

Gwen scurried across the open space between the counter and where Albus and Bruno huddled, passing in front of the narrow window in a fast dash. She hunkered down with them. Hari stayed close to Jake, mostly spread-eagled on the floor, his head up and dark eyes on Albus as if searching for reassurance. Albus patted a palm at him, instructing him to stay where he was.

'I think they took out our back tyres,' Gwen said, and her words came through the muffled deafness in Albus's ear as a trickle of low-lying white fog, meagre and insubstantial. 'A rumble strip, maybe? Are these bastards with you?' She raised her voice at Jake, and even that did little to ignite the mist of her words before they were snuffed out.

Jake sat askew, his head and torso slumped sideways while his bound wrists kept his lower body centred. He hadn't straightened himself since their collision and needed a nudge from Hari and a repeat of the question before he understood he was being addressed.

He shook his head groggily in reply. 'Shouldn't be. This road . . . should be clear.'

Gwen didn't press the issue. Albus didn't think the guy was capable of lying at this point.

'They can't want the van,' Bruno said. 'They made us crash it.'

'I guess tyres can be replaced?' Gwen said.

'*You've got five seconds to slide open that fancy door of yours and step on out.*'

'We've got guns, too, assholes!' Gwen shouted back. 'You try and come in here and we won't be doing any counting before opening fire.' She shrugged at Albus's raised eyebrows. 'What? I can threaten, too. We don't want them bum-rushing us.'

He was merely thankful she wasn't starting off this exchange with a volley of bullets. The Gwen of earlier that morning would have probably been blasting away before asking any of these questions.

The shouting man didn't reply to her threat and simply started counting. '*One . . . two . . .*'

A sudden delicate pattering tapped across the van's roof and Albus looked up to see raindrops spot the skylights. Above them, the sky was grey and stormy.

'Great,' Gwen whispered, head tilted back and staring at the same view. She lowered her gaze to him, then looked at Bruno. 'So do we have a plan?'

'I say call their bluff,' Bruno said. 'They'd have to be crazy to want to start a gunfight. We could all end up dead.'

'I do not think they are bluffing,' Hari said from the floor. 'I saw guns. Maybe they think we are the bad guys?'

'*Three . . .*'

Albus's heart thundered in his chest and a mini-heartbeat throbbed in tandem in his bad ear. He shrugged his contribution to the dilemma, the movement jerky, and patted the air with his hand again, indicating that they should all probably get down, just in case.

'*Four . . .*'

'We're not coming out!' Gwen yelled, shifting on to her stomach, lowering herself next to Bruno as he did the same. Her face was a foot away from Albus's. When their eyes met, she gave him a shaky smile. 'I *really* hope they're not crazies.'

Albus sincerely hoped the same.

He didn't hear anyone call out the final count of five and he had the briefest moment to feel a slither of relief ease the tension in his shoulders, but then that fifth second was over and his entire world erupted in the thunderous cacophony of gunfire.

PART THREE

Empty Nests

Chapter 1

Lacey

You're not relaxing, Voice complained.

She wanted to yell at him: *How could she* possibly *relax when Abernathy was trying to* kill *them?* The woman was driving like a lunatic. The only thing preventing Lacey from being catapulted across the back seat was the fact that she was wedged so snugly between Sunny and Tyler, with a pack lying across her lap, that it was physically impossible to move. On top of fearing for her life, being cramped and too hot wasn't conducive to a relaxing environment.

The windows were fully wound down, and a strong breeze whipped inside, shoving messy hands into Lacey's hair, but it wouldn't help, not when it came time to climb out. She, Tyler and Sunny would need to peel themselves away from each other wherever their bare skin had touched. A far more intimate scenario than Lacey had envisaged back when they'd stolen the small car at the farmhouse. She fervently wished it were a bigger model.

At least it's fuel efficient, Voice said, returning to his background ministrations.

Pilgrim had syphoned the last of the fuel from the quad bike and emptied it into the car's gas tank.

Sunny hadn't spoken much since their talk at the farmhouse.

Lacey hadn't wanted to outright tell Sunny she was delusional and that Beck was an imaginary person she'd conjured into being in order to shield herself from the knowledge that it was Sunny herself who heard a voice. So she hadn't. Instead, she'd had a candid conversation about Beck being a liability, and if Sunny couldn't keep him in line, Pilgrim was going to lose his shit and cut them loose. It had seemed to work. She got the feeling that the thing Sunny feared most – outside of losing Beck – was being alone.

You have to admit it'd be safer if you'd told her, Voice ventured. *For all of us.*

Maybe. But mostly Lacey was annoyed at being given ultimatums. She stared at the back of Pilgrim's head. Her ire had dampened a little since he'd tried to force her hand, not only with Sunny but with their direction of travel, but moving was good. Moving was *going* somewhere, and going at this fast speed was far superior than being stuck walking. (But there was still a perverse side to her that was secretly enjoying Pilgrim suffering within the cramped confines of their stolen car.)

He was a tall guy and looked like he'd scrunched himself up inside a kid's pedal car, his knees jammed against the glove box, the top of his head touching the roof. He held on to the handle up there, his elbow sticking out of the open window, but it didn't prevent him from white-knuckling the dashboard every time Abernathy steered aggressively, dodging tyre-killing craters or felled telephone poles in the road. Lacey had lost count of the number of times he'd bashed his skull off the roof and a gruff curse popped out.

They had left the multi-lane highway a while back and were now barrelling down a single-lane road. Dirt blew up as the tyres sped too close to the shoulder. Grit pinged and cracked off the undercarriage. The violent wind swirling through the cranked-down windows smelled of dust and grass and long-lost summers.

Abernathy took a corner at speed, almost skidding them off

the road, and Pilgrim snapped out a particularly inventive expletive as his head cracked off the doorframe this time. Lacey leaned heavily into Tyler, any embarrassment she felt about squashing the woman's boob and their slick arms sliding against each other having died a death about twenty miles back.

'You said you wanted to get there,' Abernathy snapped at Pilgrim.

He grunted. 'Yes. Without further head injuries, preferably.'

Everyone's nerves were frayed. They'd been trapped inside the tiny car for hours. At first, Lacey and Pilgrim had argued over whether or not they should detour over to the explosion site; Lacey had wanted to see if anyone else had been attracted to all the smoke and fire (and by 'anyone else', she meant anyone who might have potentially spotted a library van tootling around or an eight-year-old with a curling mop of hair). But Pilgrim had vetoed the idea – it was too risky; the Inn was of higher importance, and it was actually guaranteed to be there.

Lacey had demanded a vote.

She should have known better.

They'd tied 3–3, because Lacey had insisted on including Beck (the other vote being Sunny's), so Pilgrim had opened the floor to *everyone* and, in the end, Lacey had lost by five votes to four. So here they were.

They spotted more smoke plumes dotting the horizon on the drive, though their origin fires were far smaller in nature. They'd even watched a bunch of people fighting in a parking lot outside what used to be a tavern. Not many, perhaps eight or nine. But the battle had been brutal. Bloody. The kind of violence that dragged fighters to the floor, where they bit and tore at each other with teeth and nails. Abernathy had sped up to get past them and hadn't slowed the car since.

Lacey shot a glance at the speedo when she noticed their road was barrelling towards the brow of an incline. She clenched her teeth and braced her hand flat to the roof – some good it would do her. Her stomach flipped as the car crested the hill and she could've sworn the tyres left the ground.

Tyler gasped.

Sunny made a gurgling noise in the back of her throat that was likely a throttled scream.

The suspension sank as the car touched down and they all bounced in their seats, elbows knocking into each other.

'Jesus effing Christ,' Lacey muttered.

'Stop,' Pilgrim said, and pointed to a patch of dirt at the junction they were fast approaching. 'Stop there.'

It was mainly farmland they'd been passing through, dotted with copses of trees and lush bursts of vegetation, and this was no exception. To their right was a large swathe of golden-brown wheat or dead grass (Lacey had difficulty telling the difference), and on their left were rolling green fields lined with trees.

As Abernathy pulled over, Lacey could see why Pilgrim had asked her to stop. Tunnelled into the waist-high wheat-grass, a huge tanker had ploughed off the road. It had rolled on to its side, belly exposed, skin bloated and bubbling. Faded red lettering was stamped on to its flank, unreadable from this angle.

Pilgrim threw his door open and unfolded his body from the seat. He left the door swung wide as he waded into the field, stalks swaying out of his way.

Abernathy popped her door open, too, and got out, shoving fists into the small of her back and arching her spine. She groaned and rolled her shoulders.

Tyler's elbow and shoulder jostled Lacey as she worked a mechanism to push the passenger seat out of her way. Lacey flexed her toes in her too-large boots. Her feet tingled, heat pulsing through them as if they'd been soaking in a bowl of warm water for the past fifteen minutes, but now the tingles faded, leaving a faint throb in their place.

How's that? Voice asked.

She flexed her toes again, the strapped bandages and socks muffling their movement, but other than a sore pull at the soles of her feet, they *did* feel less tender.

A tinge of awe lifted her words. 'Yeah. Loads better.'

You're welcome, Voice replied, rather smugly. He had, reluctantly, been taking some guidance from Pilgrim's Voice on how to do a little accelerated healing. It blew Lacey's mind when he tried to explain it to her, and she didn't wholly get it (she suspected her Voice didn't, either), but the results spoke volumes.

The material of Tyler's shirt was hot and humid under Lacey's hand as she helped push the woman up and out. She winced only once as she squeezed out after Tyler and her weight settled on her feet, but the pain really wasn't too bad. In the two hours she'd been jammed in the back seat, Voice had worked wonders. She gathered her rifle from the back footwell.

Sweat broke out on Lacey's brow as she straightened away from the car. Without the shade of the interior, she was an ant trapped beneath a water glass. The humidity was bad out here, but it was nice not to have two overheated bodies shoved up against her.

Abernathy was unfolding the map on the hood, spreading it flat, but Lacey didn't spare it more than a glance as she limped by. As she slung the rifle on to her shoulder, her feet instinctively trod the same path Pilgrim's boots had taken. She held her hand open as she entered the field, the paintbrush-like heads of the plants tickling her palm as she walked. Definitely wheat and not dead grass.

By the time she reached the fuel tanker, Pilgrim had finished his climb. She lost sight of him as she stepped into the tanker's shade, but she heard the clanging tolls of his boots up there, moving away from her.

We going up? Voice asked.

Lacey considered it. The ladder was rusted and didn't look too safe. She had a moment to envisage it sheering away from its fittings while she was hanging off it, sending them both crashing to the ground, to broken bones and gushing blood.

You're such a drama-banana.

It *had* held Pilgrim's weight, so hers shouldn't be a problem.

'Screw it,' she muttered, and drew the rifle's strap over her head, out of her way.

A minute later, breathing heavily, she heaved herself on top of the container and brushed flakes of rust off her hands.

Pilgrim was staring out at a view that Lacey didn't dare look at as she gingerly made her way over to him. The tanker had once been painted white but was now a nicotine-fingered yellow where it hadn't been eaten away by rust. Her eyes scanned over the ghostly red wording.

TEX-A-CO, Voice read, enunciating each syllable.

Her boot came down on a large, puckered bubble. The thin, crisping paint disintegrated underfoot, leaving a brownish, flaking pockmark.

She'd intended to do a sweeping scan of the area herself, but her eyes landed on the ocean and didn't get any further. It was the darkest sapphire she had ever seen and it went out so impossibly far that her stomach went hollow and cold at the sight.

Here it was. The end of the world.

'No more east to go,' she murmured.

Not without a big-ass boat, Voice agreed.

This had been her and Alex's goal, to reach the coast, to find people Alex believed could help Addison with the troubling things the girl heard inside her head. Lacey expected to feel some sense of victory for getting here, maybe even a small amount of closure. Instead, all she felt was a deep, abiding sadness, a poisonous growth of weeds in the soil of her gut, green and alive in the darkness down there, and it would only spread the longer she gazed out at the nothingness of that ocean. She felt small and stupid in the face of it.

You okay? Voice asked softly, feeling the sadness along with her.

'It's too quiet,' Pilgrim said, not looking at Lacey.

She could hear the surf and the murmur of Abernathy and Tyler's less than civil conversation back at the car, but she knew that wasn't what he meant.

He's right. I don't hear anything out here.

She followed Pilgrim's gaze and squinted against the sun, lifting a hand to shade her eyes. A mile or so away, the top storey of a white building peeked out from above the treetops. Large, like an antebellum plantation house, it sported dark shutters on the windows and a number of white columns that jutted up to support the roof of its upper-floor balcony.

'Is that it? Ruby and Albus's Inn?' It was a ten-minute drive away, if that.

Pilgrim made a soft affirmative noise.

She dropped her hand from her brow to frown at him. 'I thought you said you hadn't been here before.'

'I haven't.'

'Then how do you know that's it?'

'I just do.'

Well, *that* explained everything.

They listened together for a while longer.

'You think something's happened?' she asked.

Pilgrim looked at her, curiosity in his gaze.

'You said it was too quiet,' she said.

He lifted his shoulder in a shrug. 'I like the quiet. Maybe it's a good thing.'

'You've intentionally surrounded yourself with a group of women. You can't like the quiet *that* much.'

'I didn't intend to. I seem to attract strays.'

She narrowed her eyes on him. 'You're calling me a stray?'

He didn't reply, but he was doing that almost-smile thing he sometimes did these days, a glimmer in his eye that told her a part of him wanted to smile outright but his face was too trapped by habit to let it.

Shaking her head at him, she unslung her rifle, and he lifted his hands in mock surrender. Smirking, amused even when she didn't want to be, she lifted the stock of the gun to her shoulder and pointed it at the Inn, sighting down its scope. It didn't magnify the view by much, but it brought the building a little closer. She surveyed the windows, the trees, everything she could see. Nothing moved. She relayed all this to Pilgrim.

'Let's go take a look,' he said, and stepped around behind her, making his way towards the ladder.

'You should be careful, you know,' she said to his back, slinging her rifle on to her shoulder and following after him; their boots knocked a matching chorus on the metal. 'Strays are way more likely to claw your eyeballs out if you upset them.'

He'd turned to face her as he began his descent. 'Or give me rabies?' he asked, lowering himself. 'Turn me into a mad, slathering fool?' Not waiting for a reply, he disappeared from sight.

'Yes!' she shouted after him. 'If you weren't one already!'

Seeing the long black hearse parked in the Inn's driveway freaked Lacey out. God. Was there a *body* in the back of it? A slumbering corpse ceremonially laid out seemed somehow creepier than a dead body out in the open.

Abernathy seemed excited to see it and openly complained when Pilgrim made her stop their car at the top of the driveway. They piled out. Lacey held the rifle in both hands, finger relaxed but curled ready around the trigger. Tyler held nothing in her hand. Their eyes met and Lacey registered the wariness there, the undercurrent of pure trepidation. She kept forgetting she wasn't the only person worried about a loved one.

'Looks like smashed glass on the ground, by the front tyre,' Pilgrim said.

In their short ride to the Inn, the sun had been lost behind a solid wall of slate-grey clouds. Still, flecks of glass twinkled among the gravel.

'What's that?' Sunny asked, pointing to a heap of clothes on the lawn.

Pilgrim and Abernathy automatically fanned out left and right, moving slowly, guns in their hands and eyes trained on the Inn, the bushes, the hearse, the lump of clothes. Tyler went with them, sticking close to Pilgrim.

Lacey positioned herself so she'd have a clear shot of the building if she needed it. The front door was flung wide open, a splash of colour in the welcome mat (she could make out the dark wooden flooring inside). The house itself felt deserted, its innards purged of everything but dust and cobwebs. The lonely sound of a windchime sang out a greeting.

Her gaze flinched to Abernathy when she shouted, '*Hello?*'

'Come on,' she said to Sunny, and they both crunched along the drive while Pilgrim and Abernathy stalked the grass. Tyler pulled ahead, walking quickly, skirting ever closer to the hearse.

A quiet noise from Voice and his single word directed Lacey's attention to the grass.

Blood.

There were more dried splashes of it on the gravel, and Lacey picked up her pace to catch Tyler up – unarmed, the smaller woman would be unable to defend herself. Lacey couldn't help but notice how Tyler's shoulder-blades had pulled tighter together, how her eyes hopped around.

Pilgrim had stopped next to the bundle of clothes. Stared down at it.

'Voice?' Lacey whispered.

No one's hearing anything. There's absolutely nothing to hear.

Pilgrim went to one knee and flung aside what turned out to be a blanket. A woman lay beneath it. Lacey could see the silver of her hair, a thick, coiled braid, the gold shine of a charm bracelet at the woman's wrist. Only when the scent of old blood and meat on the turn hit Lacey's nose did she realise she'd been breathing in the fresh ocean breeze up until that point. She pressed the back of her wrist to her nose, willing the bad smell not to catch hold.

'No. That's not Clancy,' Tyler whispered. 'That's not her.'

Fleet as a fox, Tyler dashed across the remaining distance, dropping to her knees beside Pilgrim. She didn't do anything at first; she resembled a carved statue, her head bent and unmoving. But then, with great care, she touched the dead woman: on her cheek, her brow, above her heart on her chest. Abernathy gazed over at them for a long moment before moving to the hearse, ducking down to peer inside.

'There's an absolute shitload of blood in here,' she called out to them, straightening up to squint around the property. 'Looks like the windshield got shot out. The dash is partly wrecked.'

'What about Jay? You see him?' Pilgrim asked, and Lacey had never heard him sound so clipped, so utterly cold. His expression was placid, but she recognised it for what it was: a mask. He hadn't touched the dead woman. The hand not holding his gun remained clutched around the corner of the blanket he'd removed.

Abernathy shook her head in a negative. 'No signs in here.'

'Jay!' Tyler rose to her feet in an inelegant lurch, stumbling a bit when she whirled around to shout for him. 'Jay! Jay, can you hear us?'

Sunny swatted a fly away from her face then went straight back to worrying at her thumbnail, chewing it like a chicken wing. 'I don't see anything. Do you?' she asked Lacey.

Lacey shook her head. Nothing. A stronger breeze swept across the lawn, shivering through the grass as if it were the luxurious pelt of an animal. On their left, running alongside the northern perimeter of the property, the dense, impenetrable line of a hedgerow trembled as a gust passed along it.

'Jay!'

Pilgrim's voice boomed so loud Lacey startled, feeling an echo of a flinch at the spot behind her ear.

A small, muffled crack had her gaze skipping back over the

lawn to the scraggly, overgrown hedgerow. It was shoulder-height and dense with a waxy green foliage.

Is that a hand? Disbelief coloured Voice's words.

Bizarrely, what did indeed look like a hand had poked itself out of the bottom of the hedge. Its fingers gave a minute wave. 'Over here.'

It was a gravelly rasp lost in the rustle of grass and leaves, but Lacey heard it and so did the others. Abernathy was marching over from the hearse, her strides long and ground-eating. Tyler was running again, and Pilgrim was almost as quick. Sunny came hard on Lacey's heels as she more cautiously followed the others.

The whole bush shook as an arm emerged, followed by a shoulder and the crown of a head. Black, glossy hair, curls of it as luscious as the vegetation it was breaking out from.

Pilgrim caught hold of the arm, pulling, dragging.

'Wait, wait, wait.' The man's voice was strained and breathless. 'Don't yank on me.'

'You're injured?' Pilgrim's voice was brusque with concern, the coldness from before having vanished.

A rough clearing of a throat. A wince. 'My side's hurt.'

Tyler hovered anxiously, practically dancing around Pilgrim and Abernathy as the two cautiously finished extricating the young man out of his hiding spot. He came bristled with leaves and bits of undergrowth, his brown skin smudged with dirt. He kept one arm clamped around his ribs. The bandages wrapped messily around his midriff were soiled with blood in different stages of drying.

He doesn't look so hot, Voice said.

No, he didn't. Aside from the new blood, the guy was drawn and pallid, his eyes red-rimmed, lips cracked. Tyler had lowered herself behind him and was propping him up in her lap. Lacey didn't miss the tender way she stroked his hair off his forehead.

'Water?' Jay rasped, and Lacey saw how boyish he looked underneath the dirt and grained-in pain; it was there in the hopeful lift of his brows and his soft brown eyes. 'I finished the last of what I had a while ago.'

A fine tremble shook his hand as he accepted the bottle of water from Abernathy. She had to uncap it for him. He fumbled it to his mouth and downed a few sips. Trickles escaped, streaking down his jaw and neck. Tyler dried his chin with her sleeve.

Lacey cast another apprehensive glance at the Inn, scanning its windows, the open front doorway, the shadowed space beneath the raised porch. Sunny was doing the same, dividing her attention between the building and the road they had arrived on. The Uzi Lacey had given her hung from its strap over her shoulder, but her hand was closed over its grips. Unconsciously, Lacey adjusted her hold on her own gun, tucking it more firmly into her shoulder.

Some serious shit went down here, Voice murmured.

Yeah. Yeah, it did.

'Who did this to you?' Pilgrim had his pack off and was bringing out first-aid supplies and another bottle of water. As he reached to unwind Jay's bandages, Lacey backed away a few more yards, the smell of blood and open wounds turning her stomach. She swallowed thickly and turned around, focusing on the hearse. She hadn't quite believed Abernathy when she'd told her they'd escaped in one. But there it was.

With one ear, she listened to Jay's reply as she studied the sun-damaged matte-black of the car's paintwork, the tiny bits of jewelled glass littering the leather upholstery visible through the open driver's door. There was more blood in there, streaked across the dash. Bloody fingerprints smeared on the steering wheel.

'It's was like they thought we were here to hurt them,' Jay was saying. Despite the water he'd downed, he sounded parched and raspy. 'They shot before we even finished pulling up.'

'And Albus?' Pilgrim asked.

'You were right. He was here. He wasn't alone, either. But, Pilgrim, he was so skittish. They all were. Jumping at noises, shooting before asking who we were.' A whimper escaped him as Pilgrim found a sore spot. When he spoke again something had caught in his throat. 'And Clancy. She . . . It all happened so fast. There was so much blood, but – she . . . she didn't suffer, Pilgrim. It was quick.'

A silence, then: 'That's good.'

The hearse's rear compartment was empty of more dead bodies, thank God, but there were a couple of rucksacks back there, as well as a fuel can and what looked like pillows and sleeping bags.

'Where did they go?' Abernathy asked. 'Because this place is a ghost town.'

A rustling of movement and a few soft moans; Lacey assumed Pilgrim was wrapping Jay back up again. The guy was panting for breath when he answered.

'They left not long after they patched me up and bundled me in here. I wouldn't go with them – I know they didn't want to leave me here, but I wouldn't budge. I had to wait for you guys. His friend, this big black dude – shoulders twice as wide as me – he said this place wasn't safe to hang around in. That I needed to hide.'

Pilgrim grunted. 'He was right about that.'

'Pilgrim.' Jay's tone was grave. 'They were leaving to go to Elysian Fields.'

Lacey didn't have first-hand knowledge of what had happened in St Louis, but she'd seen the pictures of what the doctors had done at the hospital there, and she knew what she'd been told about there being more places like that out here on the East Coast, but even if she didn't have that information, she saw how Abernathy stiffened from the corner of her eye and how Pilgrim's jaw set like granite. Even Tyler looked uneasy.

Voice isn't liking this news, either, her Voice said. *Not one bit.*

'Why there?' Pilgrim asked, packing his supplies away with more force than was necessary.

Jay went to shrug but quickly suppressed the motion, his eyes squeezing closed. 'I don't know, but they had a man with them. His hands were tied. They took him when they left. Maybe he was the dude who said they needed to head for the birds? It's all muddled in my head—' His eyes popped open and his gaze swept around those assembled, searching, frantic.

It landed on Lacey and stopped. She nearly took a step back from the intensity of it.

'Lacey,' Jay whispered. 'You're her.'

She forced herself to return his stare. He was looking at her like she was a unicorn or something.

You have yourself a fan, Voice said with his version of a smirk.

Jay had the most luxuriant liquorice-black hair she'd ever seen on a man. Maybe even on a woman. A small green leaf was stuck in it.

'Lacey,' he said again, his voice dissolving into a whisper. 'I'm so sorry.'

She flicked a glance to Pilgrim, unsure of what he meant. She offered Jay a half-smile, stilted and uncertain. 'There's no need to apologise—'

'She was here,' he said, cutting her off, anguish darkening his eyes to black. 'I told her you were coming – she knew – but she left anyway. I think . . . I think maybe she was worried about Albus. She was arguing with' – he waved a hand near his head – 'with something, I don't know. I was pretty confused.'

Her abdominals had clenched, as if bracing for a blow. 'What're you talking about?'

Jay lifted his hand to her, it was closed in a loose fist, but the silver twinkling of a chain dangled from between his fingers.

Oh my God, Voice breathed.

'What is that?' She heard her own voice in her ears but couldn't remember speaking.

'She must've slipped it into my hand when I wasn't paying attention.'

Lacey couldn't bring herself to take it at first. She stared at the chain, an unnameable emotion building inside her as Jay opened his hand to reveal the St Christopher medallion.

'How . . . ?'

Lacey had last seen the necklace when she'd given it to Alex for safe-keeping. It was impossible for it to be here. *Impossible.* Lacey had left Alex in a church too many miles back to count. She was gone and she wasn't coming back. What was Jay *doing* with it?

Her body moved without direction, her fingers closing over the body-warmed metal. She shut her eyes as she rubbed her thumb over the embossed image. She didn't need to see it to know what it depicted: a man with a staff, wading through water as he carried a child on his back.

She felt a tremor in her heart. God, her chest hurt.

'Who gave this to you?' she whispered, unable to hope, because hope was a cruel bastard who liked to hurt you when you were at your lowest ebb.

'I found it after . . . after Addison was gone,' Jay said, faltering. 'Your niece was here with Albus. I talked to her. I didn't see it, but she must've climbed into the library bus before they drove off. She must have, because she was gone when I woke up.'

Everything that came after Addison's name filtered through on delay, dumb sounds floating through the rushing of her head, comprehension coming later. Hot tears pooled in her eyes, fat and unwelcome, and a sob built in her throat. She lifted the St Christopher to her lips, kissing it, crushing it in her hold and pressing her closed fist to her mouth, hiding behind it, not wanting this man, or any of them, to see her cry. She didn't want to have a breakdown *at all*, but the tears came whether she wanted them to or not.

A library bus, Voice said in wonder. *Did you hear that? Exactly like the one we heard about. Addison has been with Albus this whole time . . .*

The necklace Lacey clutched had once belonged to Ruby, Albus's sister, long before Lacey had taken possession of it. And now, without a single doubt, Lacey *knew* it was this medallion, this St Christopher, that had guided Albus to Addison when her niece had needed it the most. Voice had been wrong when he'd once told her it was just a piece of metal and that it held no magical properties. It *was* magic. It was a totem. A thing that protects. And now it had found its way back to her, the same as it had found its way to Albus.

A hand, heavy and warm, came to rest on her head, palm cupped to the curve of her skull. She knew the hand belonged to Pilgrim and the sob she'd been holding back broke free.

'You're sure it was her?' Pilgrim asked Jay.

Tyler was gently hugging Jay as he rested back against her, her arms looped around his shoulders. He shifted in her lap, discomfort plain on his face. Tyler eased up on her hold.

'Seven, eight years old?' he said. 'Skinny, with dark curls. She patted my head like I was her pet and I think . . . I think she sang "Here Comes the Sun" to me.'

That made Lacey laugh through another sob. That kid, man. She missed her so much.

'She showed me a sketchbook, too. You're in it,' Jay said to Pilgrim. 'So is Lacey. She must've took your photo of Lacey with her,' he added with an apologetic grimace. 'I don't have it any more. Sorry.'

'Let's concentrate on what's important.' The warmth of Pilgrim's hand left Lacey's head as he bent to retrieve his heavy pack. He swung it on to his back in one practised move. 'How long ago did they leave?'

Jay frowned around at his surroundings. 'What time is it now?'

'Couple hours shy of midday,' Pilgrim told him.

'OK, so I'd say it was nearing dawn when they left and I passed out. So . . . maybe a few hours?'

With that, Pilgrim set about giving them all instructions – Sunny and Tyler to check for supplies and to clear out the hearse and get it ready to drive. Lacey to go fetch Abernathy while Pilgrim transferred the last of the gas from their small car into the hearse and prepared Jay to move him into it.

Lacey hadn't even realised Abernathy had left.

She left while you were bawling. Voice had, of course, kept tabs on the woman.

Lacey wanted to protest against the use of the word 'bawling', but she'd speed this along if she just ignored it. Besides, she was practically buzzing with joy. Addison was okay and only a few hours ahead of them!

'Where'd she go, Romeo?' she asked.

A wet raspberry sound blew in her ear. *Went to scope out the grounds. Head down the side path there.*

Lacey traipsed her way quickly across the lawn, bypassing the Inn and its porch and the welcoming maw of the open doorway. She started up the side of the Inn, aiming for what looked to be a fenced-in vegetable patch. What she really wanted to be doing was squeezing every last detail out of Jay about her niece, but Pilgrim was right. The faster they left, the faster they would catch up to Addison and Albus. Lacey could get the information out of Jay as they drove.

'Is he gonna be all right, do you think?' she asked as she glanced over the allotment. Lettuces, spinach, beans, trellises with tomatoes climbing through them, more vegetables she didn't have the names for. They had a nice set-up here. As she passed by, she plucked a piece of fruit off a small lemon tree. Brought it to her nose and breathed in the citrus. Saliva flooded her mouth as memories flooded her mind. Of home. Of her grams. Of home-made lemonade and lemonade stands, and meeting Pilgrim for the first time.

It's a gunshot wound in the gut. I doubt it. Voice wasn't one to pull his punches. *The bullet's still in there. It needs to come out, and it's not like any of us are handy with a scalpel. Tommy made a good point, though – there might be doctors at Elysian Fields who can help.*

'Sounds like a long shot.'

It's either that or leave him in the bushes.

Lacey shook her head at him.

They found Abernathy out on the back lawn, calf-deep in overgrown grass. The expanse of ocean that spread out as a backdrop to her made Lacey's mouth fall open. It was . . . Well, words failed her, because 'large', 'big' and 'massive' didn't do the sight justice. This close, the ocean went on *for ever.*

'First time, huh?' Abernathy asked, watching her take it all in.

'Yeah.' Lacey picked her way over, careful of where she placed her feet in the tall grass. Without the Inn to block them, the flurries of wind coming in off the waves were strong enough to buffet her off course a time or two. She wasn't a weather forecaster, but from the darker, heavier clouds hanging ominously over the water it looked like a storm was a-brewing. 'Those rainclouds don't look so good.'

'Sure don't. Storms off the ocean can get rough.'

Lacey stopped dead when she reached Abernathy's side, eyes landing on the mounds of earth the tall grass had been hiding.

Are those what I think they are? Not waiting for an answer, Voice continued: *Why is it everywhere we go there's freshly dug graves in the backyard? Here. Home. Your sister's house. It's becoming a pattern. A real shitty one.*

Lacey counted. Five. Five dead people rested here.

'First time with these, too?' There was a vague smirk on Abernathy's face, but then there *always* seemed to be a smirk waiting on the sidelines of her mouth. The fact that the woman was annoyingly attractive despite her bad attitude made it all the more aggravating.

'No,' Lacey said shortly. 'I've seen home-made graves before. Dug a few myself.'

Abernathy nodded and didn't comment. 'No one was lying when they said this place wasn't safe.' She kicked at the loose soil. 'Wonder what killed them off.'

Lacey shrugged. 'All I know is I wanna get the hell out of here.'

A sharp, strident whistle lifted high over the Inn. Lacey raised her eyebrows at Abernathy.

'I think the master is summoning us,' Abernathy said.

Lacey followed her back along the side of the Inn, stopping for Abernathy to dip inside the vegetable patch and pluck a handful of tomatoes from the vine before they continued on. Lacey accepted the two offered to her, and both of them were munching on the juiciest tomatoes Lacey had ever tasted when they made it back on to the front driveway. In their absence, Pilgrim, Sunny and Tyler had manoeuvred Jay into the rear compartment of the hearse. Tyler was in there with him, covering him up with blankets and fussing over the pillow under his head.

Pilgrim was waiting for them beside the driver's side, his hand on the open door, ready to get in. 'There was a boy with Albus's group,' he told them, and Lacey didn't like the dark look on his face. 'A young teenager. Jay described him, and it sounded too much like Hari for comfort. We need to go. Now.'

The tomato Lacey had just got done swallowing threatened to make its way back up again.

'Hari?' she said, like a stupid, broken toy.

'Hari,' Pilgrim repeated, drawing in a deep inhalation. He looked away from them, his expression as stormy as the distant sky he was gazing sightlessly into. He blew out a tired, mirthless laugh. 'All the stories and all the wondering, and the Flitting Man was here all along.'

And was never a man at all, Voice said.

Chapter 2

Addison

Addison wasn't afraid of the dark. The dark was her friend.

What *wasn't* her friend was the hard jut of metal that was poking itself into the back of her hip and had been for about a bajillion hours. But today she was being a mole – a mole packed in soil, taking a snooze – and a sleeping mole didn't move, and it didn't snuffle around or scratch to get out, no matter how small its burrow.

The metal cubby-hole she'd crawled into (hidden under a swingy-up panel on the outside of the library bus) wasn't a burrow, of course. It was a hard box that bounced sound around inside of it. It was like being in the belly of a great robot, the rumbling of its engine shaking her bones, the hum of the road its whirring circuitry. All the noise would probably swallow any small creak she made but, still, she didn't shift her weight much. Even when her left arm went all tingly and the blood inside it got old and sluggish. Even when knocks and thumps gonged off her robot walls and made her heart jump.

It had been cold at first – there was a cool, constant draught down by her feet – but the metal soon warmed up with her body pressed to it and the heat from the engine's heart and its turning axles, making her small box toasty. It hadn't made it any less hard and uncomfortable, though. She needed more flesh on her hips and butt-bone, that's what Lacey would say and playfully pinch at a non-existent roll of fat at her waist. Lacey knew all her ticklish spots and Addison would laugh and squirm to get away whenever she attacked them, but Lacey'd never let her. She'd lock her in close and wriggle her fingers in her sides, wringing even more giggles out of her.

Addison's stomach twisted like she had a starving animal curled up under her ribs, but it wasn't hungry for food. She frowned, unhappy, because this ache couldn't be petted or soothed or fed a bite to eat. Only Lacey could make it go away.

From the secret place at the back of her head, Fender started a soft hum, a tune that settled the aching twist in her gut. Fender sang it in a way that was both appealing and hopeful at the same time. Whenever Lacey sang it for her, Addison would always smile when she got to the *duh-n-duh-duh* part in the chorus. It was the song that Lacey would always recognise whenever she got close enough to hear it. Her favourite beetle song, and now Addison's favourite beetle song, too. It was *their* song.

Fender was humming it now, mostly to apologise, because Addison was still upset about Fender convincing her to crawl inside this cubby-hole. Chief must have partly agreed with Fender because he'd bounced up and down next to the library bus, directing her attention to this side compartment box. And now she was stuck here for ever. Unless she banged to be let out. Which she couldn't do because Albus would find her stowed away and make her go back to Jay and the Inn (she hoped Jay was okay).

Something else stopped her from knocking to be let out, though. Maybe it was Gwen and her too-quick-to-shoot gun. Maybe it was Jake and his scared, darting looks. Maybe it was Hari and his watchful baby-hawk eyes. She didn't know, but she had to admit that she did feel safer being in the dark and hidden away in here.

Back in the bushes with Jay, Fender had said that what she would have to do would be risky but necessary.

R. I. S. K. Y.

A new word for her. She wasn't sure what it meant, but Fender made it sound not so good. She enjoyed the *isk* sound in it. It would probably be what lizards did when they flicked out their tongues. *Isk*, *isk*, *isk*.

Before slipping into the library bus's compartment, Fender had opened up Addison's own metal box inside of her head and hidden inside it, sweeping Chief in along, too, dropping the lid down on them both. It had flummoxed Addison. Normally, *she'd* be the one to shove them in there to keep them quiet, to hide them away, to pretend like she was normal and nothing weird was going on – no voices in this noggin', no sir, no ma'am. It was rare that Fender ever initiated being locked up. And Chief *never* went in willingly, like he had this time. Maybe that was another reason why Addison didn't bang to be let out.

Addison recalled how Lacey's Voice had made a habit of sniffing around her, a nosy old hound on the scent, but he'd only ever overheard the smallest snippets from Fender, and, even then, Addison suspected it was only because Fender had *wanted* him to hear. She'd long been in the habit of shutting both her head buddies inside their own special box, muted and out of trouble, and she'd gotten good at keeping them hushed up, too. Her mommy had drummed it into her that it would be dangerous if they ever got found out.

Neither one of her head buddies had said a word since Addison had crawled inside the library bus's cubby-hole. Not having Chief or Fender speak to her didn't meant she hadn't felt them back there, though. They were restless, concerned about where they were going and what they would find. And she was lonely. It hadn't taken very long for her to ease back their lid the tiniest bit and seek out their company.

Fender's humming now turned into a medley of her aunt's

favourite beetle songs, songs Addison had learned by heart. Emboldened by Fender's quiet humming, Chief squirmed his way out, too. Addison held in her complaints, wanting to grumble at him but not having the heart to do it; there was barely enough room in here for her, never mind him, but he wriggled his way over her so that they were nose to nose. He didn't smell of mud and grass any more, but of oil and engines, of tyres and the hot metal of working parts. It was a nice smell and Addison breathed him in.

Chief didn't speak. Instead, he patted his hand over her face very gently. The dark shine of his eyes turned upward as thuds sounded over their heads. It wasn't the first time she'd heard them move around up there, and she didn't know what was going on, but the seam of light down by her feet had got brighter and brighter the longer she'd been in here. It had to be full morning by now. Maybe even lunchtime (telling times and stuff was extra hard when you were hiding in a secret box inside the belly of a giant robot-library-bus).

Something jabbed into the side of her box – she felt it like a physical shove – and then it kicked the van's underside. She bonked her head on the box's roof and mouthed an *Ow*. The engine dropped down its growls from a girl-bus to a boy-bus, all deep and grumbly. A loud hiss came through the gap by her feet, a fake whispering, all snake sounds with no words in them. The brakes? But it already felt loose and squirmy down here, the back wheels not gripping like Addison had gotten used to.

The bus skidded sideways, she felt it go, and she jammed her feet and hands against the walls as she slid across the slippery surface along with it. Chief clutched on to her, clamping himself like a limpet to her front.

From above her came shouts. She recognised Bruno's deep call and Gwen's higher, alarmed cry.

There was nothing Addison could do to stop her shoulders, elbows and knees bonging into metal, but it didn't matter so much because she wasn't the only thing making all the noise.

She came to a stop with the most awful squealing-metal sound. Addison gasped as she was thrown against the box's side-lid, her shoulder and hip jolting painfully. She cried out. The panel popped open, but not all the way. A cold gust of air rushed in and a strip of daylight hit her in the eyeballs, making them water after being in the dark for so long.

The panel had jammed partway open. A foot-wide slither showed off the grey-grit of the road, a teeny-tiny green shoot sprouting from a crack in the blacktop and part of what looked like a huge tractor wheel that was as flat and airless as Addison's lungs.

She drew in careful, shallow breaths, waiting for a spike of pain that meant her rib-bones were sprouting out of her side like that teeny-tiny green shoot was sprouting out from the road. Luckily, her rib-bones remained unsprouted. In the back of her head, Fender pressed against the bones of her skull, a firm, silent pressure that reminded her to stay still, stay quiet. Something bad was happening out there. Something Fender didn't like.

Addison couldn't help but startle when the first thump cracked against the library-robot-bus. It wasn't anywhere near her, but it was loud and angry, like whoever threw it wanted to hurt someone. She pressed both hands to the jammed panel and *pushed*, desperately wanting it to budge wider. The gap wasn't big enough for her to fit through and she felt a sudden urgent need to *get out.*

Three thirds of Chief's head and his black, glistening eye appeared in the gap to look sadly up at her. He shook his head as if to say, *It's no good, you stuck, girl.* Addison scowled at him. He was no help.

A series of rapid bangs and cracks attacked the library-robot-bus and Addison cringed into a ball, but only for a second, because she was squirming around and jamming her numb feet through the gap – she could get partway out if she wriggled, she was sure of it. She was being a mole after all, and moles could fit through the smallest of holes. Her legs and numbed feet fizzed with sparks as dead blood fired back to life, and she groaned quietly at the unpleasant tingling.

The back-and-forth shouting started. A man somewhere she couldn't see and who didn't sound close enough to concern her right then, and Gwen, mostly. She heard murmurings above her, too, from inside the robot's belly – Bruno, Hari, maybe even Albus at one point – but she only listened with half an ear (even when the yelling man started counting), because she was too busy shimmying her hips back and forth, her butt wedged fast in the too-tight gap, the edge of metal digging into her flesh hard enough to make her bite her lip against the discomfort.

Chief had grabbed on to her ankles and was doing a poor job of tugging on her, trying to help her through. Thankfully, Fender remained calm, and that prevented Addison from panicking – at least on the outside. On the inside she was a calamitous pumping of blood and panting breaths. She didn't want to get *stuck*. Getting stuck would be awful because living beings weren't meant to be closed up in tight spaces where they couldn't move and couldn't see and all the oxygen they needed to breathe was being sucked out of the world and what was that *wetness* slipping down her back? Was it *blood*? Was she *bleeding*? Oh God, she's bleeding. No, no, wait. Wait, it's okay. Take it easy, Addy. It's only rain. You can hear it if you stop to listen, see? *Plink-plink-plink*.

Water slipped through the panel's hinge and dripped on her. Just rain.

And, actually, despite the chill, the water was helping – the dampness in her shirt, the trickling slickness on her skin. She slid an inch lower, the top of her butt scraping free from its clamped position. Her knees hit concrete. Quickly, she twisted her torso, inching herself into the widest part of the gap, her chest compacting down in size as she breathed out all her air in one long breath and squeezed and pushed and wriggled some more. It hurt. The corner of the panel scraped across her shoulder-blades and she winced through a whimper.

BANG-BANG-BANG-BANG-BANG! So many *BANG*s, although they couldn't really be called *bang*s – it made them sound too flimsy – because they were BIG and filled the space inside her cubby-box and inside her ears like a gigantic, tolling bell. She felt those *BANG*-punches, too, shivering through the metal jammed against her belly and back, punching tiny fists into the solidness of the world around her.

Go! Fender hissed.

She flinched and the corner gouged deeper into her flesh. She shoved and wrenched herself downward and, with a tearing sensation at the back of her shirt, she slipped free.

She dropped flat to her belly (her legs felt as floppy as Alex's noodles when she left them to boil too long), inhaled a quick, deep breath, feeling the compacted version of herself *pop* back into shape, and rapidly squirmed her way under the van and out of sight.

The BANGs had all run out, but the loud noises hadn't. There were chaotic shouts. The *whoosh*ing slide of the library door. Thudding feet on the floor overhead. Snappish demands of *Stay Down* and *Don't Move*. People Addison didn't recognise. At her back, heat toasted her; she pressed her belly tight to the ground, careful not to let her head or shoulders touch the hot metal. It was dry under here, though, and her shivering settled down.

Lying flat, she watched two sets of booted feet shuffle by the door. Biggish in size. Men? One boot had dirty, grey tape wrapped around its toe. The hem of his pants legs had frayed into ragged holes by the heels, as if moths had decided they were lunch.

More boots stomped around above her.

A buzz of worry came from Fender, but she didn't look away

from those boots. As long as they were over there and she was here, she was okay.

There was a thumping scuffle and a protest, then the stomps of descending feet. Gwen's boots and ankles appeared – Addison was familiar with the blue jeans and scuffed brown leather.

'Get your hands *off* me.' An awkward stumble of feet and Gwen yanked herself away from whoever it was that wore the bumble-bee-coloured laces in their shoes. She was now facing back towards the bus. 'Bruno? Bruno, are you okay?'

Addison's belly tightened against hard blacktop. What had happened to Bruno?

There was a low rumble of a reply, but it was churned up and stifled, as if Bruno had stuffed his mouth full of food and was talking through it. Which was Bad Manners, but Addison figured she could forgive him because she was fairly sure he wasn't snacking on anything right now.

'Line up with your back against the van. Do it.'

From her feet's surprised stutter, Gwen had been grabbed again, turned and shoved into place. She ended up with boots pointed away from Addison, so close that if Addison crawled forward a short distance she could reach out and touch her ankle.

Another minute of barked orders all round, some more manhandling, and four pairs of feet were lined up:

Gwen's brown leather boots.

Albus's dusty hiking shoes.

Hari's once-white-now-grey tennis shoes.

And Bruno's massive boats for footwear, which Addison felt sure could fit three of Hari's shoes in each. But he was there and standing, which meant he wasn't hurt. Right?

'Got a half-unconscious one tied up in here,' a voice called from inside and above her.

'Bring 'em out,' ordered the bossy one, Taped-Up Toe, if Addison's hearing was working right. The buffeting of the wind and the creaking of the van's suspension near to her head was making sound bounce around funny under here.

'Who are you people?' Gwen asked.

Taped-Up Toe walked their line, moseying on by like he had all the time in the world. 'We've had eyes on this road for the better part of a month and we've seen nothin' but wild critters 'til you folks came along.' Boots turned, stopped. 'Smarter question is, who're *you* people?'

A heavy weight was being dragged across the floor directly above Addison's head to the far corner, where the library's stairs and exit were located. An uncoordinated clatter of thuds later and the owners of the final two pairs of footwear dropped into view.

Jake's feet were all floppy and useless on the ends of his legs. He got dumped to his knees on the wet road, and that was where he stayed, kneeling and on best behaviour. It was the first time Addison had seen his hands. They rested palms up on his thighs, fingers curled inward like dead spiders laid out on their backs. He wore black gloves.

Strange, Fender whispered from very far down in her ear. *It's not glove weather.*

'We are on our way to Elysian Fields.'

Addison abandoned all thoughts of gloves and weather and frowned at Hari's feet. Should he be telling them stuff like that? They're complete strangers. Didn't seem very smart to her. Chief was already on his way past, belly crawling over to Hari and poking him hard in the back of one heel. Hari didn't react.

Behind her ear, Fender had grown very still, as if listening intently.

After a long pause, Taped-Up Toe said: 'What you know about Elysian Fields?'

A gaggle of words, some from Gwen's mouth, some urgent sounds from Albus, nearly all of which were a forestalling attempt to prevent more information coming out of Hari. But Hari spoke right over them.

'Trinity Hills,' he said, loud and clear. 'It is near here, I believe.'

The wind and rain lashed.

Addison breathed silently through her mouth.

'There ain't nothin' there. We been and looked. Just an empty welcome centre and some museum about energy.'

'And a whole bunch of windmills,' a second fella chimed in. He was wearing a pair of grimy running shoes with stripes down their sides.

'Wind turbines,' a woman's voice corrected. Addison did another feet check. Yes, that one pair on the left, with the yellow-and-black bumble-bee laces, were smaller than the rest. So, there were four of them: three men and a woman. Four against four. Even numbers, if you didn't include Jake.

Or you, Fender whispered, sounding very far away.

Or her.

'Yeah, wind turbines,' Stripes said. 'And a shit-ton of wildlife. It's bird central out here. Freaks me the fuck out.'

Addison couldn't see the birds from under the bus, but she could imagine them: a huge cloud of dark, speckled dots swirling and dipping, so close now that they spread across the sky like a big, billowing blanket, blotting out the sun. Maybe it was the together-flapping of all their wings that was causing the winds. A damp shiver scurried up Addison's back, the warmth of the bus's underbelly fading now that the engine was off.

'Point is,' Taped-Up Toe said, 'we ain't found anything. Not for want of lookin', neither. So you folks are either lyin' or bein' lied to.'

There was some more squaring-off of stances – four against four (not including Jake) – and Addison got the impression that weapons were being levelled at her friends. She held her breath as the silence stretched out.

'What have you been looking for over there exactly?' Bruno's question was cautious, and there remained an element of talking-through-food to his speech.

'Have you been livin' under a rock? Everyone's heard the tales from way back when of some high-end medical set-up out here. Welcoming fools in to get their voices sucked outta their brains – easy as going in for a root canal, they say. All lies, of course. You ask me, they're pumping some subliminal shit into the air around here.'

'Explains the freaky fucking birds,' Stripes threw in.

'Right, the freaky fucking birds,' Taped-Up Toe agreed. 'Can't lay my head down without seeing a bunch of dead people in my dreams. All blackened and stiff-like, just lying under this great red sky that's screaming down at 'em like the worst kind of white noise you ever heard. Merle here wakes up every morning with words in his head, don't you, Merle? Talking about death and slaughter and such. And he's not the only one. Plenty of our camp are getting the same thing. So you can understand how we're all a bit fucking paranoid about new people with wheels driving through these parts.'

'What they're trying to say,' said Bumble-Bee-Lace woman. 'Is that we're not stupid. We have channels up and running now. Monitoring things. We *know* what they do to people like us in that place, and it's nothing so pleasant as a root canal.'

'Look, friends,' Bruno said slowly. 'We don't have anything against voice-hearers, if that's what you are.'

They definitely are, Fender murmured, sounding troubled.

Bruno was also a liar-liar-pants-on-fire. Gwen had some *serious* issues with voice-hearers. They'd been the ones who'd killed her best friend, Rufus.

'We lost some of our own,' Bruno continued. 'And that man right there knows where they are. He brought us out here. We're just out here looking for them. That's all we're doing, nothing more.'

'We ain't trusting no one but *our* own any more. Get it?' Taped-Up Toe said. 'So unless you got something interestin' to tell us, we're about done with this little chit-chat.'

Uh-oh. Addison shifted backwards, soundless, scooting her way out from under the bus. She got to her feet, her legs feeling only a little shaky now, and found herself sandwiched between the library bus and a truck so tall it went up and up and up until her head was craned all the way back before she got to its top. No wonder they got bashed to a stop. It was twice as big as them.

Ignoring Chief's impatient hops and waving arms, she snatched up the first hefty thing she saw: the black plastic lump of a side mirror. She bounced it in her palm, testing its weight.

Losing his nerve, Chief dropped to all fours and scampered under the tall truck and was gone, leaving her there to fend for herself, the traitor.

'Fender, help?' she whispered, and felt the equivalent of a confirming nudge at the back of her skull. The mirror was big and heavier than it looked – and she didn't have as much room as she'd like to manoeuvre – but she cranked back her arm and slung it good and high with a fast burst of energy that shot through her arm. It sailed over the top of the library bus on a near-perfect arc. She didn't wait for it to crash down (although she hoped it hit Taped-Up Toe in his stupid head) but let out a belting war-cry, then ducked low and slid under the truck, following after Chief.

Muck and slime coated her hands and knees as soon as she was under it. Yech. But she went fast, using the years of built-up sludge to slide her way through, slick and slippery like an eel. They would be coming for her – she heard their yells of surprise as the mirror smashed to bits at their feet, heard the confusion that stalled them for a few precious seconds (she whooped a few wild yells of her own to spur them on) before they set out to investigate.

A distraction, that was all Addison could give Albus and the others. She was just an eight-year-old girl, after all, smart and fast, sure, but she didn't stand a chance against *four* grown-ups.

That was crazy thinking. Two, maybe. But not four. And not ones with guns.

Addison finished wriggling out from under the truck, hopped to her feet and shot off in a dead sprint. She got a faceful of sheeting rain as soon as she was out in the open, a blustery squall hitting her and forcing her to lean into it as she powered through.

She was glad for the truck's length; it would take extra time for them to detour around it and spot her. She chugged her arms and her legs only felt bleurgh for the first handful of strides, and then she was sprinting across the gritty shoulder and off the road, fast as a cheetah. A low metal guardrail blocked her way and she vaulted it like a gazelle, feet hitting a steep verge on the other side. She careened down the bank on heels and butt, reaching the bottom in a skidding, arm-wheeling run, and was up and off again. Her feet pounded the pavement of a parking lot with no cars and nowhere to hide.

Her reading was getting good, even better with Fender's input, but she had no time to read the expansive signage plastered to the front of the warehouse-sized building on the lot's far side. She recognised the pictures in the hanging posters, though. Mattresses, beds, comfy sofas, armchairs, desks, wardrobes. A store that sold furniture.

Addison didn't head for it. She had no idea if she could get inside and didn't want to risk getting trapped with her back to its wall and nothing but an expanse of parking lot between her and her pursuers. Because they were back there. She didn't need to look behind her to know they'd given chase. She heard at least one, their shouts lost to the wind, their feet pounding the asphalt as fast as hers. She had a decent head start, but it wouldn't last long: her legs were far shorter than theirs.

A surge of power hit her mid-stride and she burst forward, her lungs opening wider, oxygen sucked greedily down and the world smearing into a blur on either side.

To the north-west, she spied Chief jumping another guardrail and disappearing into the trees. A whole blockade of trees. Shadowy and full of cover.

Addison flew after him.

She was leaping the guardrail in seconds, her back foot clipping the top and almost tripping her. Her chugging arms weighed heavier, her legs were seizing up. Her shoes sunk into soft, mulchy soil, slowing her down further, but she was among the trees and that was enough. Trunks closed around her as she dodged further into their crowd, sacrificing speed for furtiveness. She was good at this. Being sneaky. She didn't need Fender for that. She was the mouse that never got caught.

Thigh muscles on low burn, Mouse-Addison worked her way deeper, keeping one eye on the noisy, stomping figures that followed in her wake. Two had been sent after her – Bumble-Bee-Laces and Stripes – and they crashed about like stampeding goats in their search for her. They argued a lot, too. Maybe they were married, like her mommy and daddy had been. They'd argued a lot, too, the last time he'd come home. Addison had hidden in the attic room until they'd quit and Daddy had gone away again.

She darted her way from tree to tree and from bush to bush, staying out of sight, but one of them was as practised at being a cat as Addison was at being a mouse, because they somehow stayed on her tail no matter how sneaky she was. So she did the only thing she could: she drew Bumble-Bee-Laces and Stripes further into the woods and further away from their friends, in the hope that at least in splitting them up it would help Albus.

Addison couldn't go back now, either way. Albus was on his own, and so was she.

Kinda.

We're lucky there's no sunshine, Fender murmured. *Keep to the shadows*.

Addison and her two new best running buddies were shielded from the worst of the wind and rain, but there was still *a lot* of noise, and the deeper they went, the more it unsettled Addison. Shushing branches, shaking leaves, creaks, cracks and a constant, rhythmic thumping that seemed to surround her. It hid concealed in the canopy of trees, just out of sight, and it kept Addison's nerves frazzled. Chief had chosen to sidle back up to her, pressing in close whenever she paused to scan the way, and for the first time ever Addison waved him off, not wanting or needing his clinginess. Something wasn't right in here, and having Chief's anxiety leach into her wasn't helping.

Don't stop, Fender told her.

Occasionally, she would hear the caws of birds, but they were distant sounds, lonely and far away. Every time she stopped, she would look all around, eyes worrying the gaps and dark spaces in the vegetation.

The incline she had been slogging up in increments was minimal but consistent. Her heart hammered, and not wholly from exertion. Her stomach had cramped tight with hunger and, if she were being honest with herself, dread. She stared through the trees. It was so gloomy in here, the day having died a death somewhere between the falling rain and the shade offered by the covering branches. But the darkness couldn't hide the ghostly white boles glowing from between the shadowy trunks up ahead. Addison frowned, unsure if she were imagining them.

'Do you see?' she whispered.

A corresponding noise came from Fender. Neither of them knew what those glowing white boles were.

Cautiously, Addison moved forward, boots instinctively avoiding fallen twigs and crisp-dried leaves. The wind became a force that pushed back at her. The loose curls of her hair battered at her face and the material of her shirt flapped at her sides; the whipping noise cracked in her ears.

Woodland began to fall away, the trees thinning out, and Addison paused, hidden at their edge, not willing to break cover. The terrain dipped down into a vast stretch of fields, a natural valley surrounded by three sheltering hills. Along the rolling curve of one hill's backbone, a tidy line of white spires stood sentry. They had collected what little daylight was on offer and seemed to shine, white as bone.

Addison had never seen anything like them before. They held her rapt as the blades on each spire rotated in eerie synchronisation. Dozens and dozens of them.

She could hear them now. It was a different kind of sound to the wind. Unnatural. Reproduced. It hit her as a low, animalistic moaning that came in waves.

Down in the valley, more of them – an endless field of spinning that stretched away. They were planted in exact rows even as the land dipped and rose in gentle swells. Her eyes began to blur at the symmetry of them all. Even at a distance, their size was terrifying to Addison; spires as tall as tower blocks, blades as large as airplane wings, each tip reaching impossibly high. She couldn't count that high, but there were more than she had numbers for, scything blades cutting over scything blades, spinning in perfect rotation.

'Are they alive?' she breathed.

I guess they are, Fender said just as quietly. *In their own way.*

Something dark and swift swooped past her head and she flinched, heart catapulting into her mouth, hands swiping off the attack, expecting to connect with arms and shoulders, but instead she caught sight of a bird as it flapped away from her and quickly gained altitude.

Addison's mouth dropped open as the lagging bird joined its brothers and sisters as they washed into view, a tidal wave that flowed out from above the treetops on her left. They blotted out the sky, a swarm of feathery blacks and browns, vast and unstoppable. She let out an involuntary noise and shrank back from them, crouching instinctively: a tiny, dumb creature lost in the shadow of its mass.

Not a single black, glistening eye twitched in her direction, their urgent race to keep pace with their neighbours their only concern. Addison sucked in a dramatic breath as they, as one, arrowed down into the field, a speeding stream aimed for the nearest of those white spires.

Her fists clenched as she waited to hear the violent machine-gun *thump-thump-thump* of bodies colliding with the cutting blades, but at the last second the leaders at the head of the charge suddenly shot upward – the speed of the directional change astounding Addison – and a swirling whirlpool of dark bodies poured after them. At the height of their ascent, the swarm lost coherence and burst outward in a hazy dispersal. The softening in its ranks hung for a moment, and Addison stared in wonder as rogue pilots, lost to the group, tumbled away, turning and flipping through the air, wings messily outstretched but unable to catch. Addison gasped as those small bodies slammed into those ever-rotating blades, their lifeless forms batted away, dropping without struggle. There were no grisly *thud*s as they hit the ground, only the drowning, rhythmic beat of the indifferent wind.

The remaining squad re-formed into a dark, liquid mist that danced as it moved away from her and across the field. Thousands of tiny individual creatures undulating in tandem.

'An animal's instinct is to survive,' she murmured, staring after the birds. Grouped together. Safety in numbers. 'That's what Hari said. That they know something we don't.' She inhaled a shaky breath. 'What's down there?'

Her eyes traced a black ribbon of road that snaked its way in and out of the spinning spires, disappearing in places behind the swells of the land, reappearing once again to weave deeper. It led somewhere. She knew it, as well as the birds.

Her gaze lifted to them as they flowed and twisted in the

strong, buffeting winds. Beautiful and dream-like they were, as hypnotic as all those spinning bone-white blades. So hypnotic, in fact, that she didn't spot the shadow leave the cover of trees behind her, silent and swift, their footsteps quieter than even her own. She didn't suspect a thing, right up until a hand came down and clamped itself over her mouth and stifled her scream.

CHAPTER 3

Albus

'Let's everyone calm down,' Bruno said, his large hands spread wide and open, his stance disarming.

Is this what they meant by a Mexican stand-off, Albus wondered, eyeing the scene before him. The rain was pelting down, the library van doing very little to shield them from the gusting winds blowing in from the east. Albus and Bruno remained locked in against the library van's siding, Albus's knees half bent and his back jammed against its side panel, using it to shore him up. Bruno's jaw was swollen and bruised, his lip cut from where he'd taken a smack to the face with the butt of a gun. But he stood tall, his hands out and his gaze alert as it switched to the two guns currently in play.

A few feet away on Albus's left, Jake was slumped on his knees by the library's rear steps in the exact same spot he'd been dragged to when physically removed from the van a few minutes prior. He hadn't given a single leg twitch or arm spasm since chaos had descended upon them.

The Mexican-stand-off part was really between three people. Gwen, a blond-bearded guy in a baseball cap called Merle and the older guy who'd been doing most of the talking so far (and was likely the self-appointed alpha).

It hadn't only been the exploding dud of a car mirror

smashing into their midst like a grenade that had afforded Gwen the opportunity to overpower Merle. It was also the call of a wild ululation from whoever had slung the side mirror that had helped Gwen along. As two of their hijackers had sprinted away in pursuit of their surprise attacker, Gwen had leapt at the baseball-capped Merle, somehow knocked his gun out of his hand (where it had flown off somewhere Albus hadn't registered), wrenched Tallulah off Merle's shoulder and jammed its barrel into his gut. There she'd paused before blasting his spleen through his spine because that last man – the self-appointed alpha who had enough gaps in his teeth for three people – had jabbed his own handgun at Albus and Bruno and informed her that he'd blow their brains on to the van's lovely decal if she didn't put down her rifle.

Gwen had not put down her rifle, and Gap-tooth hadn't yet discharged his weapon.

So that's where they were right now, and had been for about ninety seconds. It hadn't escaped Albus's notice that his and Bruno's positions uncomfortably resembled a firing squad execution waiting to happen. The only slight relief he felt was that Hari was out in no-man's-land by himself – he'd left the cover of the library van at some point to retreat into the open, past where Gwen was standing with Tallulah's muzzle thrust in to Merle's gut. No guns were currently pointed Hari's way.

The only things that moved were Gap-tooth's and Merle's mouths. Albus watched the shape of their lips closely, filling in any blanks the driving wind, his impaired hearing and his knocking heartbeat dampened.

'They're saying it's a little girl,' Gap-tooth said.

'A *girl* threw that?'

The 'that' the blond-bearded Merle was talking about lay exploded in pieces on the ground, bits of black plastic and broken glass scattered through spreading pools of rainwater.

'Saying she's headed for the trees, and she's *fast*.'

'They're going in after her?'

Albus's heart thumped harder, a solid series of two-punches to the chest that knocked him nauseous. Were they talking about *Addison*? But wasn't that too implausible to believe? How had she got here? Sneaked into some secret part of the van when Albus and the others were too preoccupied to notice? The simple answer to that was yes. Yes, that was *exactly* what she'd done. Within minutes of their first meeting, she'd guided Albus through a backyard wasteland of overgrown grass and fallen fences while the voice-hearers who were hunting her down closed in on all sides. She was more than capable of creeping on board a van without anyone seeing.

But Albus hadn't once felt her presence on the drive out here, and he'd gotten used to being able to pinpoint her location with unnerving accuracy: she was a small piece of iron ore to his natural lodestone. As long as she had his sister's necklace, Albus could find her.

She must have removed it, he thought. That was the only way she could have stowed away undetected. She *knew* he'd have sensed her nearby if she'd kept it on her person so she'd taken it off.

He was oddly proud of her. Tossing the car mirror, and then howling at the top of her lungs like a feral she-cat, had been an impressive distraction.

'You think they'll come back soon?' Merle asked, his eyes rolled in his buddy's direction so he didn't have to move his head. Drips plipped off the ratty bill of his cap. (Albus's long hair had plastered to his skull, its ends dripping cold rivulets down his cheeks and neck, but he dared not move to wipe them away.)

'They come back and someone's getting a lead sandwich for lunch,' Gwen said.

'Gwen,' Bruno warned. 'Don't.'

Albus braced himself as a particularly hard gust rocked him, shuddering through the van behind him. He felt its side panel tilt, taking him with it, and then sway back into place. His thighs trembled, a low burn igniting in the muscles from the bent position of his legs. Still, Albus didn't budge. That muzzle-bore was looking straight at him.

'Hmph.' Gap-tooth rubbed a rough hand over his damp, stringy hair; he could move all he wanted – he had no guns pointed at him. 'Hope they nab her. Bitch almost cleaned my clocks with that damned mirror.'

A wink of sunshine blinked at the corner of Albus's eye.

'You should both put your weapons down.'

Five heads swivelled in Hari's direction.

The boy was wet through and shivering, but he didn't cower in his drenched clothes; he faced Gwen and the two men, guns and all, his shoulders straight, his chin up. It must have cost him – Albus knew how shy the boy could be and how difficult he sometimes found it to maintain eye contact, and this situation was fraught with tension. Another stir of pride nudged its way past his nausea.

'We should, eh?' Gap-tooth asked. He readjusted his grip on the gun, fingers re-clamping and firming up. But now, instead of being aimed steadily over Albus's heart, it began to drift, becoming vague in its direction.

'We can all get what we want from this.' The rolling strands of Hari's sunshine voice reached out not just to Albus, but to everyone, flowing in sinuous, glowing waves that blinked in and out as Albus's faulty hearing stuttered. It danced before the men's faces, its golden light reflected in the shine of their eyes. It seemed to hold them rapt, although Albus was sure he was the only one who could see it.

He didn't miss it when Gwen's posture changed, the stiffness across her shoulders relaxing, the finger around the rifle's trigger loosening a fraction.

'You mentioned a camp before,' Hari was saying. 'Imagine

taking them the news that you have found the *one* place you have all been searching for.'

Albus chanced a glance at Bruno, but his friend was staring at Hari as if he couldn't quite compute what was happening. His hands, held out and open, began to drift down to his sides. He shifted in place, and Albus realised he was slowly transferring his weight on to the balls of his feet. The hand nearest Albus curled into a tight, hard fist, and the big man mumbled something through his split lip that Albus didn't catch. Every line of his friend's face was taut. Albus shot a hand out to press a palm to Bruno's arm, steadying him, asking him to wait and not do anything rash, to give Hari the chance to speak.

Thankfully, no one had seen Albus's swift move and accidentally blown anyone's arm off.

'How?' That came from Merle.

'Come with us to Trinity Hills and we will show you,' Hari said.

'I told you,' Gap-tooth said, slow and simple. 'We checked already. There ain't nothin' there.'

Hari bobbed his head in a single, resolute nod. 'There is. You didn't search it properly.'

Albus noted that Gwen had taken a small step back, her rifle's muzzle pointed down somewhere around Merle's right hipbone. If she fired now, she'd likely chip his pelvis, and that was it. 'Jake was taking us there,' she said. 'He knows where Elysian Fields is.'

As if scripted, Albus, Bruno and Gwen all swivelled their heads the opposite way to Jake, and Merle and Gap-tooth followed their example. Gap-tooth's gun now wavered at knee level on Albus.

Jake looked back at them. He was no longer restrained – he'd been cut loose when he'd been physically dragged out of the van – but it was obvious he was there under duress: the bloodied shirt and head wound attested to that. The downpour seemed to have revived the concussed man somewhat; he sat a little straighter, his head no longer too heavy to hold up. His eyes were narrowed – likely from the rain pelting his face – and most of their bleariness was gone.

'You'll show us?' Gap-tooth asked him, and there was a strange hint of childlike excitement in his tone. It was in stark contrast to his earlier tone, and Albus once again let his eyes travel along that amorphous, staccato funnel of gold all the way back to where Hari was speaking.

'Tell them you will,' the boy said to Jake.

Jake's gaze shifted from Hari to Gwen and then settled with some weight on Albus. It was a penetrating look, as if he were searching for something – a hidden sign or a signal – and Albus stayed very still, not wanting an accidental shift in his expression or movement to influence him in any way. He didn't want that kind of power, not over anybody.

Whatever the meaning behind his behaviour, Jake dropped his gaze to the smashed bits of mirror scattered across the wet ground, choosing not to look at anyone as he answered. 'I'll show you the entrance,' he said to nobody and everybody.

Gap-tooth's face screwed up. He waved his gun about as if it had transformed from a deadly weapon into a harmless prop that could be utilised to get his point across. 'What entrance? We passed right through the main entryway.'

'No. It's a different kind of entrance.' Rainwater dripped from Jake's eyebrows, his nose, his chin, and resignation dripped from him, too. Albus wondered if he should be concerned by how utterly defeated the man looked.

'Fine. We have a deal.' Gap-tooth shrugged as if it was all decided and tucked his gun away, under his waistband.

Hari darted in from the side and Albus choked out a shout, in warning, in shock, a stone dropping into his stomach as the boy dashed right up to Gwen and pushed her rifle away from Merle. The gun swung wide left and exploded, bucking in Gwen's hands, the gunshot slamming into Albus's ear as if it had gone off right next to his head instead of twelve feet away. He jerked backwards, crying out and covering his ear, and banged his shoulder and arm roughly against the van. One knee buckled, his shaking legs giving out, and he landed ass first in a puddle.

Gap-tooth was down, on his back, writhing in his own ass-deep puddle, except his was made up of blood and was filling up faster than the rainwater could keep pace.

Albus yelled, '*Ohhwww!*' because he couldn't form the word 'no', and the sound of it sent a jagged, teeth-ripping yowl down his ear canal. Bruno was no longer beside him, he was charging towards Gwen and Merle, and Hari was dancing out of their way as the two twirled like dancers around the rifle, the gun gripped between them like a top-quality branch being fought over by a pair of possessive dogs.

Bruno didn't even bother with the rifle, he went in hard and brutal, his fist coming over the top of Gwen's shoulder and slamming Merle full in the face. Albus *felt* the crunch, felt the terrible crush of Merle's nose as it flattened against cheekbone. The blond-bearded man's baseball cap flew off as if it had been fired from a cannon, and before Merle could dodge or drop or react to having his face pulverised, Bruno slammed a fist into his head a second time.

Merle dropped like an anchor on dry land. His head bounced off asphalt. He didn't move again.

Albus didn't move, either. He cradled his head in one hand and stayed in his puddle, the rain cool on his hot skin. He and Jake had become twins in their inability do anything more than sit and exist.

Gwen had stumbled back from her final dancer's twirl, Tallulah grasped in her arms like a prize, and looked down at Merle, then over at Gap-tooth, who'd ceased his writhing and was lying still, and she couldn't decide on where to look because she turned away from them both to glance at Albus, and her expression was so lost, so devasted, that he attempted to get up from his puddle to go to her but fell back again when his legs wouldn't work.

'I didn't mean to,' she said, the sounds muted to him. 'I didn't mean to. It was—' She kept on turning and would have said more, Albus was sure of it, but she stopped when she came to face Hari, because Hari had one hand clamped over his mouth and the boy's eyes were filled to the brim with tears.

Albus couldn't hear his sobs – the rain had picked up in intensity with the eruption of gunfire and was drumming down, lashing the road in a continuous, battering susurration – but he could see Hari's shoulders trembling, could see how he tried to stifle his crying. Then Bruno blocked his view and was hugging the boy close, cradling him against his chest and swaying them where he stood.

And muffled in the background, in his one good ear, Albus heard Jake talking to himself, telling nobody and everybody, over and over, that he'd show them the entrance. He'd take them *all* to the entrance, he swore.

Chapter 4

Addison

Addison didn't move from her crouched position. She had frozen stiff when the hand closed over her mouth. She couldn't remember the last time someone had successfully snuck up on her. And no one had *ever* snuck up on Fender.

Don't panic, Fender murmured.

She stayed still, and that was when Addison began to notice details. Like how small the hand was that covered her mouth, and how little the fingers were that curled into her cheek. The body pressed against her back was warm but slight, and strangely bumpy at the gut.

Addison strained her eyes right. Could make out no more than an arm, skinny and covered in a too-big sweater, its cuff hanging loose around a bony forearm. Addison breathed in through her nose and scented the richness of soil and wriggling worms, and beneath that, faintly, the smell of smoke and something else, something more distinct; it reminded her of the bike shop she, Lacey and Alex had visited one time, of cold metal and rubber and slippery lubricating oil.

'*Shhhhhh*,' a voice whispered in her ear.

Addison somehow resisted vigorously rubbing at the mad tickle in her ear.

Without the hold on her mouth being removed, a tap on her

shoulder directed Addison's attention left. A second, equally small, hand pointed, and Addison stiffened at what she saw. No more than a library bus's length away, a man had stepped out from between the trees and was staring, as transfixed as Addison had been, at the mass of birds soaring and swooping above and around the countless spinning blades. A teeming segment had broken free to glide high on invisible updraughts, a vast, wide ribbon that undulated as it rode the wild winds up there.

Addison didn't need to look at the man's feet to know it was Stripes. She'd failed to spot Bumble-Bee-Laces beside him because his body had blocked the woman from view, but when she turned to address him, her gaze slid straight past him to where Addison was crouched with an unknown stranger plastered to her back.

'*Run*,' the voice blurted, and the hand vanished from Addison's face and the pressing warmth disappeared from her back.

'Stop there!'

Addison didn't stop, she was up and chasing after the fleet, running figure before those two words had left Bumble-Bee-Lace's mouth. Setting eyes on her sneaking accoster for the first time was a surprise. They were small. Smaller than Addison. Dressed in soiled clothes: cords, a dark sweater that swamped their frame, filthy trainers with Velcro fasteners. When they threw an alarmed glance over their shoulder, Addison was met with very wide eyes in a dirty face. She couldn't tell if it was a boy or girl – they had longish, rain-dampened hair, which could mean anything.

Within five paces, Addison had caught up, and in five more she had left the kid behind. The child's small feet blurred, working double-time, but Addison knew it wouldn't be enough.

'Come on!' she gasped at them, sprinting down a grassed slope. The trees continued to thin out, but Addison stayed at the boundary, not wanting to run out into the open, and *definitely* not wanting to run towards the looming bone-spires and their whirling blades of death. A blacktop path cut through the grass ahead, shiny and wet. It led down towards a wider road – the same dark ribbon of roadway she'd seen weave its way to smaller and smaller ribbons as it wound around and through the hills and troughs of the land. She didn't know where it led. Maybe nowhere she wanted to go.

Behind her, the kid grunted. There was a thud of bodies hitting the ground, loud even over the *shwoop-shwoop-shwoop* of the thundering wind. Addison kept going. Her feet slapped blacktop, harsh smacks that stung her soles, the unforgiving surface juddering up her legs and rattling her bones, and she wanted to run and run and never look back, but how could she when the kid had tried to help her? How could she leave them to fend for themselves when they had gone out of their way to warn Addison her pursuers were closing in? Had even tried to lead her away from them?

Without stopping to think how silly she was being (and how her aunt Lacey would chew her out for caring about a complete stranger), Addison whirled around and raced back the way she had come. She sprinted straight at the man who was struggling to pin down the wriggling, biting creature who Addison now considered her friend. He had a knee jammed into their chest, against the bulky item that Addison had felt pressed to her back when the kid had plastered themselves to her. It looked like a . . . stuffed raccoon.

With no time to ponder on why the kid was carrying around a stuffed animal, Addison yelled at the top of her lungs as she closed the distance. (Alex had told her that even though wild bears were large and frightening, if she ever came face to face with one, she should be as loud as possible and make herself twice as big as she was, and twice as scary, too.)

Stripes's head snapped up, and Addison could tell he was unprepared for a wailing girl-child to come charging at him, and even from a distance back, Bumble-Bee-Laces's pace faltered and fell into a shambling fast-walk.

It was working!

The kid reared up again, trying to wrench free, and Stripes punched them in the face. The kid slumped to the grass. Stripes planted his foot and was halfway up to meet Addison, his ugly mouth snarling, eyes glaring at her. She felt a tingling awareness expand in the back recesses of her head. A rush of something hot and pure flexing through her skull, the bones creaking. Stripes's hand went to his waist and the gun tucked under his belt. She covered the last two steps in a rush as he pulled the weapon free.

The very first time Addison had ever experienced this surge of power, she had been terrified by the rabid pounding of her heart, the heightened sense of touch and smell and taste, all so acute it was like toppling inside a rainbow. But now she welcomed the violent pummel of sensation. Power coursed through her and she willingly surrendered to it, the same way the paper boat she and Lacey had made had surrendered to the wash of floodwater they'd dropped it into (Addison had gasped as the surging rainwater snatched the boat from her hand and swept it up. She had chased after it, but the boat had been washed away so fast it was impossible to catch.) Now Addison *was* the paper boat, and Fender, Fender was the powerful torrent of water that she yielded to.

Addison easily caught the man's wrist as his gun arm came up. He had a split second to look surprised before Addison twisted sharply. She felt the give, felt the audible snap, his bones as brittle as twigs. The heavy gun landed next to her foot.

He'd have screamed right then, but Addison was already yanking on his broken arm, so much harder than she could have on her own, the limb pulling free from its socket as easily as pulling a cooked bird's wing from its carcass. His scream choked itself into a squeal so high it could have ruptured eardrums. His other hand clamped her arm, hard enough to bruise, hard enough to make her gasp, but her foot shot out, the sole of her boot connecting with his knee. It *crunch*ed in a way that was satisfying and sickening in equal measure.

He made a weird gurgling sound and collapsed, his one good hand cradling his shattered kneecap as he curled himself into a blubbering, incoherent mass.

Addison scooped up his fallen weapon. It was cold and heavy in her hands, and she had to use both to lift it up and point it at Bumble-Bee-Laces. She met the woman's startled eyes. Addison wasn't even out of breath.

Bumble-Bee-Laces didn't raise her own weapon. Her knife hung limply at her side as if she'd forgotten she had it. Even without looking at the towering spires and their whirring blades, Addison felt them. It was like having a second, monstrous heartbeat, big as a dinosaur, beating from behind your shoulder. Its presence was mountainous.

'Go away!' Addison called to the woman. Her arms were beginning to shake under the weight of the handgun. She didn't want to have to shoot. She'd shot somebody before and it had *not been fun*.

Bumble-Bee-Laces sent her companion a quick glance and backed up slowly, and with that first step whatever loyalty that had connected her and the man on the ground was severed. Her eyes didn't leave Addison or the gun again until she was a goodly distance away. Then she spun on her heel and fled and within seconds was lost in the trees.

As swiftly as Fender's help came, it withdrew, leaving Addison standing there, trembling and sick to her stomach. This always happened afterwards. Everything on the inside of her – her lungs, her heart, her muscles, her bones – all somehow felt slack and scooped out, as if someone double her size had tried her on like a shirt and had stretched her out to two sizes too big. It would take a little while for her body to shrink back to normal.

She dropped the gun weakly, the butt banging into her thigh.

She did her own backing up, leaving the man, who was now whining under his breath and hiccupping every now and then into the grass, and moving over to the kid. They were conscious, their head held up so they could see what was happening. They didn't scoot away from Addison, but they did watch her warily. Their nose was bloody, and their eyes were shiny with tears, but they hadn't cried.

'You okay?' Addison asked.

The kid nodded. 'Mr Rocky says thank you.'

Addison frowned and glanced about them, searching. Was there another person out here? How the heck were so many people sneaking up on her and she not noticing?

The kid got up, wincing a bit as they did. They touched their nose gingerly and scrunched it up a bit, whispering a quiet, '*Ow*' as they did. With Stripes making his pitiful, annoying noises, Addison tugged the kid's sleeve and guided them away, not stopping until they were both standing on the blacktop path. The rain misted down more here, but it had already drenched them thoroughly, so what would a little more wet do?

'What's your name?' Addison asked.

They had stopped messing with their nose and were re-arranging the stuffed raccoon at their chest. The raccoon wasn't actually a stuffed toy but a children's backpack, the kind where the straps were made out of the animal's arms and legs so it looked like it was piggy-backing you when you wore it. Except this kid had it on back to front, so the raccoon was chest to chest with them. It was a little worse for wear: one ratty ear was half hanging off and the stitching down its back was coming loose near the butt. Still, it looked pretty cool.

'I'm Lev,' they replied. Their longish hair was slicked back and tucked behind cute little ears. Their eyes were wide and curious. Blue, Addison thought, though the lack of sunlight made them more stormy-ocean than sky. 'What you gonna do with that?' they asked, indicating the gun Addison held.

She cast a quick glance at Stripes, but he was too wrapped up in his own suffering to bother them. Still, Addison would feel better being away from him. She motioned Lev into walking and went to step off the path, but Lev's small hand stopped her.

'This way,' they said, and nodded down the pathway.

Addison almost baulked. She wasn't sure she wanted to go near any of those bone-white spires and their swinging blades, and this path led right to the nearest ones. She wasn't sure she wanted to head back into the woods, either, though. Bumble-Bee-Laces was in there – she might not have retreated as far as Addison hoped. And she didn't think it wise to backtrack all the way to where she'd left Albus and the others. She didn't know what had happened after she'd left them, but, good or bad, she would have to continue onward and believe that she would find Albus later. Which left only one direction.

She sent a nervous glance up to the birds. They were a little further out than before and mid-dance, beautifully poised, on the verge of another hypnotic, suicidal dive, and she looked quickly away before she could be drawn back in, transfixed, to gawp at them again.

We'll be all right if we go with them, Fender said. *Don't worry*. Chief had stayed out of sight since she'd shooed him away earlier, and Addison was weirdly okay with that. She loved him, but he could be such a baby sometimes.

'Me and Mr Rocky know where to go. Just follow us, okay?' Lev's brow hiked up and they stood there, waiting, apparently needing a reply.

Addison nodded at them and resisted another round of checking over her shoulder. 'Er. Who's Mr Rocky?' She dutifully followed after the kid as they moved off. She couldn't work out Lev's age, but she thought they were a little younger than her. Seven at the very most.

Or they're just small for their age, Fender said.

'This is Mr Rocky, silly.' Lev patted the raccoon affectionately on the head. 'You can speak to him, you know. He can hear you.'

'Um. Okay.'

'He says hello.' Lev smiled at her, slowing just enough for Addison to come level with them.

'Hi, Mr Rocky,' Addison said to the raccoon, and Lev beamed wide, the smear of blood under their nose not detracting from the sight one bit.

They followed the pathway all the way to the road, where, curiously, everything became quieter and stiller. Addison stood gaping up at the nearest spire, which was still a whole parking lot away from them. She felt lost in the enormity of the structure. It went up so high she was sure it must touch the stormy grey clouds. The rotator-wings swept around and down, and she felt its movement in her marrow, in her blood, in the same way the ocean's waves flowed and ebbed. She didn't even flinch when a hand closed over hers – she'd expected it somehow, as if the power of this place had conjured a hand up from the earth, made it from mud and moulded it by wind.

Lev's fingers were cold.

'Cool, huh?' they said, smiling.

'Yeah,' she said, because they were, even if they did make her uneasy.

'Let's go inside.' And Lev bounced ahead, practically skipping as they dragged Addison along.

Chapter 5

Addison

Leaves skittered in with them before Lev dragged the fallen branch into the gap, shunting it into place where the broken shutter should have been; the branch's wild, leafy spray plugged the hole up nicely, hiding it from anyone nosing around outside.

Lev and Addison jumped down off the barrels.

They were underneath wind turbine number forty-three. Well, not exactly *under* it, more to one side. Each wind turbine (that's what Lev called the massively high spires with death-blades spinning from their tops) was planted on a huge concrete base, and each base had been built flat by cutting into the uneven, hilly ground, carving out a perfectly rectangular chunk, laying the foundations and filling it in with concrete mix.

Built into the base of this particular turbine was a set of sunken steps leading to a single locked door. She and Lev had entered through one of two windowless, slatted openings situated on either side of this sunken alcove and in the earthen banks, each one dug through at door height. The right windowless opening had been broken long ago and was now plugged closed and camouflaged by the mentioned branch. Getting inside had been a tight fit for Addison – not nearly as tight as squeezing out of the library bus's side-panel box, but close enough to have given Addison cold-sweat flashbacks.

There wasn't much light filtering through the slats of the other unbroken opening, but what little there was showed a basic square room. Concrete walls, concrete floor, concrete ceiling. A section on the right was barriered off by a steel guard-rail that ran around a square opening cut into the floor. A hole full of blackness. A metal ladder hooked over the hole's lip, leading down into the dark. A gap in the guard-rail provided access to the ladder, a loose chain hanging down and not preventing anyone from going up or down it.

A low, creaking groan came from behind Addison, as if a predator outside knew she was in there and was leaning against the locked door. Breaths snorted through the opening's slats. Addison closed her eyes and breathed, imagining she could feel that gargantuan yawning sweep of the turbine's blades passing high over her head. She was a mere ant in its mighty presence. Thinking about being so small and unimportant settled her heart rate.

Through the slats, long, horizontal lines of dim daylight lit the back concrete wall in thin, pale strips. It painted Lev in stripes, as if they wore the hide of some exotic animal.

'We're going down?' Addison whispered. She didn't know why she was whispering.

'Yep,' Lev whispered back, either following Addison's example to be polite or because they liked to whisper.

Addison could feel her tension pull tighter. It vibrated, hot and quick, almost with its own melody. Addison wasn't afraid of the dark, but she wasn't entirely sure about darkness and a deep, endless hole in the ground that might drop down for ever.

'We're going to monkey our way down the ladder?' she asked, eyeing the hole in question. She was glad she didn't have the gun any more – she'd gone to hide it underneath a moss-covered slab of rock she'd found outside, but Lev had offered to let Mr Rocky carry it for her. Addison had gratefully handed it over, and the gun had vanished inside Mr Rocky's zipped-up torso.

‘Yep. The ladder.’ A rattle of chain-links and Lev nimbly dropped over the lip of the hole exactly like a monkey and on to the ladder. They scurried down it and out of sight.

Chief slinked out from behind Addison and sniffed his way over to the hole, crouching on its far side to lean over and peer after Lev. He was wide-eyed. Impressed or scared or both. It must go pretty deep.

‘What’s down there?’ Addison asked him, not liking the tremble in her voice.

Chief shrugged, tentatively reached over to grip the ladder’s rungs, gave them a solid tug and shrugged again. He leaned far out of the way as Lev’s head popped back up.

‘Coming?’ they asked, smiling cheerfully.

‘Sure,’ Addison replied, with as much enthusiasm as she could muster.

The climb down was uneventful. They descended into pitch-blackness, down, down, down, the temperature dropping the further they went. At the bottom, the space was narrow – room enough for both of them to stand side by side, but little more than that. Addison really *was* a mole now, underground and burrowing deep into the earth. She wondered how far she’d have to go to reach the bubbling molten core of its centre, like she’d seen in her junior geography book. She sighed, sad again at the thought of her lost books – the one with the fairy tales in, and her favourite, with all the different animals of the world. She hadn’t had many, but she missed them a lot.

For a time, the wailing moans of the wind echoed down the tunnel; it sounded mournful, as though it was upset that Addison was leaving it behind. The occasional far-distant creak or clatter made one or both of them pause mid-step as they listened to the wind and rain rage from somewhere above them. But unseen sounds or not, Addison felt safer in this tunnel than she had outside. So did Lev, going by how they traipsed along with confident strides despite there being nothing to light their way.

As a guide, Addison walked with her hand on Lev's shoulder. She'd naturally curled her fingers around the soft fur of Mr Rocky's arm-strap. It was strangely comforting. It reminded her of when she and Lacey had climbed up four flights of unlit stairs in an empty office block, corkscrewing their way higher and higher to where Alex waited for them. She distinctly remembered that floating feeling, of being towed along in the darkness, tethered only to Lacey's rucksack and tugged along like a puppy on its leash. She had felt safe in Lacey's care, despite being someplace unknown to her. If she tried real hard, she could even pretend that Lev was Lacey and that the tugging sensation at her hand, gripped around Mr Rocky's fur, was actually Lacey tugging her along. Addison missed her more than she missed all her books combined times a million.

She had been *so* close to seeing Lacey again. So close she couldn't think about it too much because her chest got tight and a lump lodged in her throat that she couldn't swallow past without it hurting. Addison had been alone for a long time before her aunt had shown up at her mommy's house. And that had been okay because she at least had Fender and Chief to keep her company. But having Lacey and Alex in her life had been the same as standing in her backyard in the mornings and having the sun creep into view, slowly lighting you up where you stood – from toes to belly to chest to face – and it was warm and glowing and it made you feel warm and glowing inside and you couldn't help but be happy because you were happy to be found. And now Addison was here, in the dark and cold, so far from any sunlight and from her aunt that she might as well be a mole for ever.

Addison rested a palm flat to the wall at her side, running it along the cool, rough concrete as she and Lev walked. The solidness felt good; her thighs had been trembling since climbing off the ladder. She had pushed herself a lot over the last few hours. Fender had pushed her a lot, too, and her stomach was an emptied-out pumpkin because of it.

We need to eat something.

Addison felt the slight turning of Lev's upper body under her grip. 'Hungry?' Lev whispered back to her, not slowing their pace. 'We got food. Don't worry. Gimme your hand – we'll go faster.'

Addison released her hold on Mr Rocky and they bumped around for a bit before Lev gripped on to her fingers. Lev's hands were cold and a little clammy, but Addison didn't mind. She let Lev pull her into a quicker walk.

'Where're we going?' she asked.

'Almost there.' The grip on Addison's hand tightened and Lev's pace picked up even more.

Addison stumbled a step. '*Hey*,' she complained.

Lev didn't slow down, despite Addison's ongoing grumblings, and for a time Addison could do little more than concentrate on not trampling the back of Lev's heels.

Addison, look. Light up ahead.

She chanced a glance and almost stumbled again.

A dull wash of flickering red light chased back the darkness at the end of their tunnel. It was so dim she wondered if she was hallucinating at first, the closed metal door it spotlighted a figment of her imagination, too. But the dim red flicker continued, and, with it, a very faint *buzz*ing that cut in and out each time the light dropped out.

That one spot of red illumination narrowed the door down to a tiny, shrinking speck. Addison knew it was her eyes and brain being tricksy with her, but she couldn't help losing her breath as the darkness at her back and on each side squeezed inward. She quickly shuttered her eyes closed and then opened them again, needing to reorientate herself or else pitch sideways into a wall.

She hadn't realised she'd pulled Lev to a stop until Chief

materialised out of the darkness and galloped ahead, his nails *click*ing faintly against the concrete. He slowed and entered the red light in cautious steps; the spill of dim light slid over his oil-black skin like spreading blood. Addison shivered at the sight.

'Why's it red?' she whispered, the uneasiness she thought she'd left with the wind turbines raising the hairs on the back of her arms.

'It's mergent sea lighting,' Lev said, and popped a shrug. 'You get used to it.'

'Mergent sea?'

Maybe they mean 'emergency', Fender suggested.

Chief was snuffling along the bottom of the door. Addison was pretty sure he was putting on this show of bravery to make up for being such a scaredy cat earlier when they'd been hiding underneath the library bus.

Abruptly, he stopped his snuffling and his posture became alert. Head held low, he backed up a small step. Then backed up a second step and away from the door.

Addison heard it, too. A drawn-out scraping noise coming from the other side . . .

Chief scrambled in a sudden rush to retreat and tripped over himself. The edge of the door narrowly missed him as it was slammed open in an angry, shunting push.

CHAPTER 6

Amber | Albus

A tinny, electronic-sounding beep woke Amber. Her eyelids flickered open and she sat bolt upright, blinking at her surroundings. It was the same room: the same all-white panelling, the same dark grey carpet, the same overly bright LED spotlights dotting the ceiling. Two narrow beds were separated by a white side-table, on top of which sat their tray of half-eaten food.

The left-side bed was neatly made, its covers iron-smooth. The once-crisp cotton sheets of Amber's bed were wrinkled and mussed. She glanced down at the bundled cradle of pillows she'd set up beside her and against the wall. Where she'd laid Jasper down to sleep once she'd finished feeding him.

Except Jasper was gone.

'No,' she murmured, and scrabbled for the pillows. 'No, no no.' She tore the cushions aside, digging down into the sheets as if she'd find him burrowing under the covers. 'No!' she screamed. '*No!*'

She ripped the sheets away and jumped up from the bed. She knocked into the food tray and it clattered to the floor, spilling bits of fruit and uneaten crackers, upending a half-full jug of water, but she didn't spare it a single glance. She continued to fling the pillows and sheets away until she was staring at a bare plastic-covered mattress.

'Jasper?' She dropped to her knees, bumping them hard despite the thick carpeting, and frantically checked under both beds. 'Jasper?'

The baby was nowhere.

She ran to the only door and jiggled the handle. Knew it wouldn't open – the door had been locked since they'd been left alone in here – but yanked and pulled on it anyway. When that did nothing, she smacked her fists off it.

'Hey! Heyyyyy!'

She drummed on the door until her hands hurt. Then she kicked at its base.

Amber hadn't meant to fall asleep. The *last* thing she'd wanted to do was lower her guard. She'd only laid her head down for a *second*.

The electronic tone sounded again, this time two beeps in sequence, and Amber's gaze slid up the wall. A tinted dome hung in the ceiling's corner. A camera. Next to it, set flush in the panelling, was the black, circular waffle-grid of a speaker. A crackle emitted from it.

They were watching her. Listening, too.

It was probably the same woman with the nose ring who'd wordlessly brought Amber and Jasper food and drink. Amber felt stupid – it had likely been drugged.

Or you were exhausted and passed out, she told herself. They'd made you march for hours and hours while carrying Jasper. She'd barely been able to stand by the time they brought her in here.

Amber wanted to scream and throw things at the domed camera, demand they return Jasper to her or else, but she knew yelling and baseless threats wouldn't get her anywhere. These people would do whatever they wanted; it didn't matter if she shouted, pummelled the door, or stayed mute.

She kicked the door one last time and then pressed her back to it, breathing heavily. She examined the room. She already knew there was nothing in here she could use (she'd already thoroughly checked it over), but she looked again anyway. The cutlery that had arrived with their food was plastic and flimsy. The bedframes were attached to the walls. Everything was blank and white and safeguarded against tampering.

Like a prison.

Neither of the two nameless men who had taken her and Jasper had said more than two dozen words to her since leaving the Inn, and she'd made no attempt to talk to them. She'd barely been able to look at the dark-haired man with the dead, black eyes, because every time she did, she'd flash back to Mica's pleading, terrified expression and the blooming spread of blood staining the front of his T-shirt.

As they'd walked, time had become impossible to measure beyond the rhythmic drum of combined footfalls and the sporadic murmurs of the two men as they spoke to each other. They had watched Amber at all times, but she had received little more than instructions to walk faster, to remind her to take drinks of water, or to keep the child quiet. After countless hours of forced marching, a solitary woman with a nose ring had awaited their arrival. She hadn't said a word to Amber, either, and Amber had nothing to say to her. What would be the point?

The only thing Amber cared about was Jasper. The boy's warmth, his gentle snuffling as he burrowed closer to her, his baby smell. The first time she'd addressed her captors since leaving the Inn was on discovering Jasper missing. Amber didn't even know why they'd chosen to take him away from her *now*. She was thirteen years old; they could have removed him from her safekeeping at any time they'd wanted.

Amber scooted her back along the cool wall until she was directly under the dome. There was a fair chance they couldn't see her from this angle.

A third series of beeps came from the speaker. *Bleep, bleep, bleeeeep*.

The door she'd been banging on unlocked with a *snick*.

Amber tensed, her head swivelling so fast it sent her momentarily dizzy. She closed her cold hands into tight, trembling fists. Pressing her back even harder into the corner, she wished she could disappear into it. A tear trickled from her eye, sliding down to the corner of her mouth. The tip of her tongue poked out to lick it away.

A fresh burst of noise came from the speaker and, when Amber recognised what it was, a low whimper escaped her mouth before she could smother it with a hand. The sound quality was thin and crackly but she would know Jasper's coos anywhere.

Amber blinked more tears from her eyes and the bleary, unlocked door cleared back into focus.

'Jasper,' she whispered.

The baby gurgled louder, his happy burbling filling the room as if someone had lifted him closer to the microphone.

Amber sniffed and sidestepped, once, twice, edging closer to the door. When she was close enough to reach the handle she glanced up at the domed camera's watching eye and felt a scurry of shivers slip down her spine.

She tentatively opened the door, enough to peer around the doorframe.

Sitting in the well-lit corridor, its head cocked and tongue lolling from the side of its mouth, was a large, mostly black-coated dog. It panted a greeting at her, its golden-brown eyes watching keenly as Amber tensely waited to see what it would do.

When it did nothing more than sit and pant, she opened the door a little wider and shuffled partway out from behind the doorjamb.

'Hello,' she murmured.

The dog's ears twitched and the panting stopped long enough for the animal to stretch its neck out and direct a series of inquisitive sniffs at her. Amber gingerly reached out a hand and the dog *whuffed* a loud nostril-clearing snort and shook its head. Its flappy ears and jowls *whap*ped like hanging bedsheets left outside in the wind to dry.

The dog stood and Amber hastily withdrew her hand. Without a backward glance, it trotted off, leaving her in the doorway.

It ambled its way down the white-walled, brightly lit hallway away from her. There were big potted plants arranged at equidistant intervals along the grey carpeting, their leaves waxy and too-green. The dog didn't pause to sniff or cock a leg at any of them. When it reached the end of the hall, it stopped to look back at Amber. Its tail wagged once. It *woof*ed quietly as if to say, *What are you waiting for?*

Amber looked in the opposite direction, searching the entire length of the hallway for anyone spying on her. No one stood watching. It was an empty stretch of corridor, the kind you'd find in any corporate office block of old. She did, however, spot two more black-tinted ceiling domes.

Another *woof*, a little louder.

The dog was waiting.

Trinity Hills was exactly how Jake had described it. A sleek, modern architectural box made of shiny dark grey granite. It reminded Albus of a school trip he had taken to Mount Rushmore. Coldly sterile, impersonal and largely colourless.

Gwen had driven the library bus at a steady 15mph for the final two miles to Trinity Hills, the ruined tyres running flat and the rubber sloughing off to leave a juddering, wheel-rim-screeching ride that rattled the bones of everyone on board. The squeal of metal from the vehicle mingled with Albus's teeth-grinding, ear-dying excavation work so that he couldn't tell where one torment ended and the other began. He sat in the back of the van, alternating between gazing out of the side window at the spinning blades of row upon row of industriously working wind turbines and clasping his face between his hands, doing his best to block everything out.

Following the fateful Mexican stand-off, and after Hari's tears had been calmed, Bruno had checked the two downed hijackers and given Albus a sober shake of his head, confirming that both men were, indeed, deceased. Albus hadn't expected anything different. Neither of them had moved since hitting the ground, not even when blood-mixed rainwater had flooded Gap-tooth's gaping mouth.

Albus hadn't spent more than a handful of seconds looking at the bodies. Instead, he'd felt a driving need to concentrate on the living. Namely, Addison. He'd wanted to go look for her but it had taken a frustrating number of minutes to relay his intentions to the others, searching out a dry piece of paper in the library van to write Addison's name down and then gesturing out to where the other two hijackers had run in pursuit of her. Gwen hadn't believed the girl capable of stowing away with them, but her arguments were without any real vigour and she'd had difficulty holding Albus's eyes while she'd made them. In truth, Albus had had difficulty holding hers, too.

'Can you locate her like we did last time?' Bruno had asked him.

And Albus had been forced to shake his head. No, he couldn't find her like he had last time, and for Gwen and Bruno, that had been another check against the possibility of their surprise distractor being Addison, and Albus hadn't possessed the energy to explain his suspicion that a too-clever-for-her-own-boots Addison had removed the St Christopher necklace to avoid being detected.

'We're just as likely to bump into the two who went sprinting after her than to bump into whoever they're chasing,' Bruno said, with far too much logic for Albus to counter. 'If it is Addison, she knows where we'd be heading, right? Same as she did when we left her with Jay.'

Albus had been forced to admit that, yes, she did know where they'd be heading.

'Okay, then. Because us hanging around here while these fellas lie dead doesn't seem like the smartest game plan to me. It'd be best if we got gone. Agreed?'

Gwen had nodded, while Hari had remained silent, waiting on Albus's response.

Albus had reluctantly conceded.

'Good,' Bruno said. 'I'll get Jake secured and loaded inside and we'll see if this tin can on wheels can get us a little further down the road.'

As Bruno and Hari headed for Jake, who remained slumped on his knees looking bedraggled and lost, Albus had trailed after Gwen. She'd gone to stand over the man she'd shot, gazing down at him while rain pelted her bent head and shoulders. Gap-tooth appeared to be floating in the bloody pool that had formed around his body, his feet, knees and chest a trio of surfacing land masses in an unmapped ocean. Albus had paused beside her, hesitating a moment, wanting to make sure she was aware of his presence before pressing a brief, reassuring touch to her back. Without acknowledging him, Gwen bent her head close – maybe to seek solace, or maybe simply to eliminate the distance so she could be heard over the percussively drumming rainfall.

'I didn't shoot him, Albus,' she said in his good ear. 'Not like you think. Hari pushed my gun up so it was pointed point-blank at him. I don't understand why he'd do that, but it felt . . . it felt like he did it on purpose. I know that doesn't make any sense. I *know*, but I don't know how else to explain it.'

Trauma and shock could skew a person's perspective. It could mess with emotions, too. And Gwen had been through an awful lot. Albus had seen sides of her over the past two days that he'd never seen in her before, but that didn't mean he would discount her claims or dismiss them out of hand, no matter how outrageous they may sound. So he had nodded to her, so she knew he'd heard and was processing what she'd said. And her relief had been palpable.

Albus had also glanced over at Hari, had found the boy hovering beside Bruno and Jake as Bruno half dragged, half lifted the guy to his feet. The boy hadn't been watching the two men nearest him, though; his eyes had been fixed on Albus. Albus had expected the boy to drop his gaze now that he'd been caught staring. But Hari didn't. If anything, a silent recrimination had appeared behind the boy's eyes, as if Albus had somehow betrayed him.

In the end, it was Albus who'd looked away first, unable to hold Hari's gaze any longer, and that had disconcerted him for reasons he didn't want to analyse too closely. Gwen's suspicions had burrowed into his head, was what he'd surmised as he watched Bruno usher Jake up the van's steps and out of the rain. Suspicion could be as contagious as a winter's flu.

You shouldn't hide from the things you're scared to understand, Al, he imagined his sister saying, as she had many times in the past. *You should always try to find the truth.*

Albus had jumped a little when Gwen spoke up from beside him. 'I'll give the van a quick once-over so we can go,' she said, and brushed past him.

He'd been hesitant about her leaving his side, then. Not because he didn't trust her or think her capable of doing her tasks, but because he felt he was somehow abandoning her to the chaos the storm was throwing up around them. What if once he lost sight of her through the rain, he wouldn't be able to find her again? He was being ridiculous, of course, and to prove it to himself, he'd skirted around the front of the library van as he left his companions behind.

He passed by the eighteen-wheeler's chipped chrome grille, and approached the highway's safety barrier. He'd been out in the rain for so long by that point he'd already been soaked through and could barely feel the chill any more.

Stretching out below him, from the bottom of the muddy embankment – where three sets of footprints veered and slid their way down (two sets belonging to adults and one to a smaller child) – to the dark, sheltered treeline, the parking lot was a barren battleground of rain-filled puddles, each a different-shaped mirror reflecting the grey skies overhead.

Of Addison or her two pursuers there were no signs.

She's long gone, Ruby told him, and a part of him had known that already but he'd needed to look for himself.

Above the treeline, Albus had glimpsed a climbing murmuration of birds. It funnelled upwards, a bending, warping hurricane of avian flight that the rains and winds did their utmost to rip apart. The winds at the top of the embankment did their utmost to whip Albus's long hair into his eyes, but he smoothed it back as best he could, tucking it behind his ears.

'I didn't want to be near the dead bodies.'

Albus had regained his equilibrium since jumping at Gwen's words a few minutes ago, so he didn't react when Hari spoke from close behind him and appeared at his side.

For a short while, they'd both stared out into the gathering gloom, the wisping tendrils of what could have been the remnants of the murmuration Albus had seen teasing at the treetops. They wiped moisture from their faces and sniffed from time to time.

'Do you really believe it was her, Albus? Do you think Addison is nearby?'

He'd felt the boy's gaze on him, and it wasn't the words themselves that conveyed Hari's intense curiosity – he had spoken with an innocent enough intent – but the golden flow of his words poured so freely from his mouth, as though they were a slave to their own currents, that Albus couldn't mistake the boy's overeager interest. He doubted the boy was aware of the tell, and Albus wouldn't be the one to reveal it to him.

Albus had shrugged carefully, not yet understanding why his

answer was so keenly awaited. Again, he thought of his sister's advice. About seeking the truth, even when you were afraid of what you'd find.

Albus nodded in reply, because he *did* believe Addison had been the one to help them, and he saw no harm in sharing that belief.

'It was dangerous for her to follow us. I have to wonder why she would throw away the opportunity to see Pilgrim again in favour of aiding us. She has known us for so little time, yet she is willing to draw danger to herself as a madman would waving a metal rod in a lightning storm.'

A poor comparison, and Albus wished he could tell Hari so. A madman didn't choose to be mad or to wave a metal rod around. Addison had understood the risks, and she had taken action anyway. That wasn't madness, it was bravery. Naïve bravery, possibly, but bravery all the same. He didn't think the amount of time Addison knew a person mattered one jot, either. Albus had seen how easily she made connections, how quickly smiles came to her and how naturally she offered a pat or a hug to those she thought needed one. She was a good girl. She hadn't been corrupted by this broken-down world like the rest of them, even though she lived in it the same as they did.

Hari must have picked up on Albus's disapproval, because he didn't linger over the subject. 'I once sat with a man who was very close to death,' the boy said. 'He had only a few breaths left to him and he chose to use them to speak to me.'

Now that Albus had turned a sharper eye to it, and was straining his good ear towards the sound, the treacle slink of Hari's speech seemed less vibrant than before, less dense, as if it had become more persuasive. As if it were feeling its way.

'He told me that from a young age he had heard death calling to him. He had spent a lifetime blocking its siren song from his ears. He said that the song of death dwells in the hearts of all men, even if they cannot understand what they hear, and it is not a matter of how fast you flee from it, but how hard you fight from running *towards* it. That moment when you are high up and you think, "What if I step off this ledge and into thin air?" Or the moment when you stand before a vast ocean and are overcome with the urge to swim out and out and just keep swimming until you can swim no longer. It lives in all of us, this wish for self-destruction. It lives in Addison, too, even if she is not aware of it.'

Albus shivered hard, his shoulders hunching inward as he released an unsteady breath. Whether he believed what Hari was saying or not, the effect of his words hit on a cellular level that Albus couldn't deny. He gazed across that water-riddled parking lot to the swaying treeline and the crowding shadows beneath, leading into the woods, and nothing but dark thoughts waited for him there.

Behind them, the coughing, spurting rumble of the library van firing up signalled their need to return, and Albus was unduly grateful for the interruption. He'd turned away from the sight of the trees where Addison had presumably vanished, and he was turning away from Hari, too, not having any desire to continue their conversation, when he saw Bruno heading their way.

'Is Gwen going to drive us?' Hari asked him, throwing a dark-eyed look towards the van.

'She will,' Bruno had replied.

'Does she still have Tallulah?'

At the top of the embankment, the wind had become a vicious thing; Albus had needed to shield his ear against the worst of its driving gusts. As a result, he missed Bruno's response. However, the subdued sludge of the man's words leaking past Albus's boots and down the muddy hill told Albus that his answer must have been an underwhelmingly short one.

'Maybe she should not,' Hari said, gaze directed somewhere down at Bruno's knees.

When Bruno answered a second time, the wind blew hard, snatching the words out of his mouth and delivering them straight to Albus. 'Those dead men back there caused us to crash our van and fired guns at us. Don't be mistaking who was in the wrong here, Hari.'

The boy had bobbed his head once in acknowledgement and the discussion was over.

Albus's ear had ached worse than ever as the three of them retraced their steps. He'd felt the phantom touch of Hari's hand on his forearm.

'Are you OK, Albus? I'm sorry if I made you worry.'

Albus had stopped walking without realising and was staring down into the dark depths of the boy's eyes. He saw a miniature version of himself reflected back, and he knew if he looked closer still he'd see a tiny version of Hari there, too, in the reflection of his own mirrored pupils. Back and forth they went, an infinity of Haris and Albuses, becoming tinier and tinier, facing off for ever until one of them inevitably blinked out of sight.

Hari's long, almost girlish, eyelashes – spiked to points from the rain – shuttered down, cutting Albus off from himself. He'd instantly lowered his arm when Hari touched him, dropping his hand from his ear, and was now robotically nodding Hari's concern away. He even managed a smile.

The boy had smiled in return – a moderate curve of his lips – and carried on ahead, slipping out of sight around the corner of the van. Albus and Bruno had trailed after him.

The windshield van's wipers beat to and fro, and Albus imagined each sweeping arc clearing his mind, sweeping away the troubling thoughts and lingering doubts. Through the glass, Gwen sat behind the wheel, ready and waiting. Beside her, in the passenger seat, was a sallow-faced Jake, buckled in and all set to go. When Albus climbed aboard, he had been ready to leave that stretch of highway far behind them.

Unfortunately, the parking lot of Trinity Hills instantly reminded him of the parking lot they'd been standing over from their embankment lookout. As Gwen took the turning to enter, Bruno pointed out a spot at the rear that was far away from the main buildings.

'Park so we can drive straight off if we need to,' he suggested, and Gwen did as instructed.

Albus studied the sharp-angled structure made up of sloping lines and tall glass windows. A landscaped lawn of artificial grass, sculptures of dancing women with too-long arms and tapering legs cavorting across it. The lot was empty but for a spreading, lake-sized puddle in its centre. Thankfully, no bodies were jutting up from it like newly arisen land masses.

'See those streetlamp-looking posts with the tinted fishbowls on top?' Jake said, pointing out of the windshield at various spots. 'Up on the side of the building, too. Below the second-storey windows.'

Albus had moved up to join Bruno and Hari behind the front seats. He followed Jake's pointing finger, picking out each post topped by a black sphere roughly the size of a soccer ball.

He'd counted up to seven when Jake said, 'They're surveillance cameras. They'll already know you're here.'

Albus's attention zipped right back to the building's main glass doors. They remained closed. From the corner of his eye, he spotted Gwen's hand slip off her lap and over to her hip. Where her handgun was holstered.

'It's no secret we're coming anyway, right?' Bruno asked Jake, his lidded eyes unpausing in their own surveillance. 'They have Amber and Jasper expressly for that reason. And you radioed in to say we were back.'

Jake glanced over his shoulder at him. The lines on either side of his mouth were white with tension. 'That's right. Though they never replied to me.' He pointed again, this time at Bruno's waist, where the black-and-yellow plastic walkie-talkie was clipped, hidden by his windbreaker.

In all honesty, Albus had forgotten Bruno had it.

Bruno unclipped the radio and Albus jumped when it crackled to life. The LED light on the top lit up red and a woman's tinny-sounding voice emitted from it.

'We see you. Don't be alarmed.' Bruno turned up the volume. 'We're sending someone out to welcome you inside.'

Before she'd finished her sentence, a large traffic barrier began to rise to a tunnelled single-lane roadway on one side of the main building. It had restricted access to what Albus had assumed was a ramp leading down to allocated underground parking for the centre's staff and VIP visitors. Perhaps even a tradesmen's entrance to some kind of secure storage space. Along with its wind farm, Trinity Hills had obviously been an extremely well-funded, cutting-edge research centre for sustainable energy. So far, no expense had been spared in its presentation, underground parking for employees potentially being a small part of it.

'Listen, lady,' Bruno said into the walkie-talkie after some fumbling at its buttons. 'There's no way in hell we're just waltzing in there.'

'We're offering you a show of good faith here, Bruno. Please don't throw it back in our faces.'

'How does she know your name?' Gwen demanded, swivelling in her seat. She hadn't switched off the van's engine. The wipers continued their *swish-thump* rhythm. Without waiting for an answer from him, she shifted the gear into drive. 'We shouldn't have driven in here like this,' she said. 'It was stupid.'

'What else should we have done?' Bruno replied tightly, upset but not the kind of person to take it out on somebody. He was bent low to peer out of the windshield over Gwen's shoulder. A wall of sheeting rain hit the van's siding and a small squall grabbed hold of the vehicle and shook it on its suspension. 'For all we know,' he said loudly, to combat the rise in noise level, 'Bianca or Cloris, or the one of the boys, told them our names.'

The wind suddenly dropped away, and so did the storm's clamour. In the lull that followed, a mad pattering of raindrops hit the roof in a close-to-soothing tempo.

'Albus,' Hari murmured, staring out through the windshield.

Albus followed his line of sight, leaning in so close he could feel the tremendous heat coming off the boy. Making their way up the centre of the ramp, appearing from the tunnel's dimness and emerging into daylight, was the solitary figure of a slim, bony girl. She lifted a shielding hand up, as if surprised to find herself outside in the rain.

'Amber,' Hari whispered, and it echoed in Albus's head like rolling thunder.

The radio clicked to life and the giggling of a baby came through so clearly Jasper might have been inside the van with them. 'As I said before, you're all welcome inside,' the woman told them pleasantly. 'And, I must stress, *all* of you. I know Jasper is as excited to see you as we are. It would be a shame to keep the little sweetheart waiting.'

CHAPTER 7

Addison

The person silhouetted in the doorway didn't move. The dingy emergency lighting threw them into a shadow-play of the blackest of blacks and a blood-lit, horror-filled nightscape. Their expression (angry? Murderous? Pleased? Hate-filled?) was unknown because their head was covered by a jacket's hood.

The person stepped into the tunnel with Addison and Lev, and Lev immediately dropped Addison's hand. Addison poised herself to run, her heart hammering manically, calculating how far it would be to sprint back the way she had come and scurry up the ladder.

Lev ran and threw themselves at the hooded person and Addison almost turned on the spot and fled screaming into the darkness. But Lev didn't attack, they *hugged* the person, arms wrapped around their waist and face buried snug against their chest.

'You went outside again, didn't you?' the stranger accused. A girl. Addison could tell that much at least.

'Don't be maaaad,' Lev's muffles pleaded.

'I *will* be mad. I told you not to go out. It's not safe. Everyone's been worried sick about you.'

'I'm sorry, Riko.'

The girl, Riko, seemed to notice Addison for the first time.

She stiffened and pushed Lev behind her. She produced a long, pipe-shaped baton-thingy from somewhere and brandished it at Addison, even though they were separated by a long tunnel of space and it could in no way reach her.

'Hi.' Addison waved.

'What . . . ? Who're you?' A whole world of confusion coloured Riko's words.

'Addison. I'm Addison. Hi,' she said again.

'I found her outside,' Lev told her proudly. 'She was being chased by some goons, so me and Mr Rocky helped her.'

Addison didn't know what 'goons' meant, but she liked the sound of it. *Goooons*.

'What goons?' Riko asked sharply. She pushed back her hood to scowl down at Lev. What Addison thought must be deep, black hair framed a narrow, pretty face and narrow eyes. Eyes shaped differently from anything Addison had seen before. She stared and couldn't stop. Riko was nearer to Lacey's age than Addison's, so she guessed, maybe, that probably put her around fifteen.

'Just some goons,' Lev said, looking down at their feet. 'Mr Rocky says they weren't too nice.' Another shrug – Lev sure liked to shrug. ''Sides, they're gone now. Well, the one is gone. The other Addison bust up pretty good.'

Those amazing eyes found Addison, and Addison blushed, heat climbing up through her chest and neck and infusing her cheeks.

'How?' Riko demanded. She hadn't lowered her pipe baton-thingy.

'How?' Addison repeated.

'Yes,' Riko said, still not sounding too pleased with everything she was hearing. 'How exactly did you "bust up" somebody?'

Addison glanced at Mr Rocky, currently being hugged by Lev, and took a gamble. 'Well, I had Fender to help me.'

'Fender.' Again, not pleased.

'Yes.' Addison tapped her head. 'Fender. My head buddy.'

Riko was silent for the longest time, her dark, narrow eyes studying Addison until Addison shuffled in place. Standing alone, without Lev nearby, reminded her how cold it was down here and that her clothes and hair were damp from the rain. She shivered and wrapped her arms about herself.

A weighty sigh came from Riko and she lowered her pipe-baton. It disappeared where it came from. 'You alone?' she asked Addison. 'Apart from this Fender, I mean?'

Addison didn't think mentioning Chief would help any (nor would mentioning Albus and the others), so she nodded.

'And no one saw you come in here?' she directed this question at both of them, and it was Lev who quickly answered.

'No one saw. We swear, Riko. You can ask Mr Rocky.'

Another sigh. 'Fine. Come on, then.' Riko gestured with her head to the door behind her, turned and disappeared through it.

Lev grinned and beckoned to Addison, and Addison didn't hesitate at all before hurrying to follow.

A generator room. A power-supply room. An energy-collecting-and-storing room? It was one of these. Addison didn't know which. Whatever it was, and despite the contraptions and machinery packed into it, it felt airy compared to the tunnels and dark spaces she, Fender and Chief had been guided through. It had no windows, of course. Moles living in the ground didn't have windows. That was silly.

Wind-up lanterns provided a warm and inviting yellowish glow as Addison stepped further inside, and she exhaled a huge breath in relief. She hadn't realised how on edge the buzzing, red-lit corridors had made her. The emergency lighting was everywhere down here.

Upon entering the power-supply room, Lev scampered

away, heading for a rag-tag smattering of children cuddled in a nest of blankets and heaped clothing against a back wall. Lev dived on them, and a burst of giggles erupted from the heap as a scrum of play-fighting and hugs were divvied up.

Addison counted heads. Ten children. Twelve, including Lev and Riko. She quickly scanned the rest of room, eyes skipping through a maze of welded pipes, wiring, control boxes, dials, gauges, electrical panels and ventilation fans. Laid lengthways, three huge boxed-in cupboards dominated the room, each sprouting wires and a dead-celled TV. They were as big as four chest freezers stacked together and were bolted to the concrete floor by solid metal legs. Each unit had a face of sorts on its end: two eyes in the form of maker plates and a square LED panel for a mouth. The middle unit had two tall embossed Gs stamped into its metal skin.

'GG,' Addison read aloud. She smiled. It had its own name.

A more human face peered out from behind GG the power unit. That brought Addison's count to thirteen. Some of the children were dirtier than others, but all were dressed in warm clothing. Their hair was oily and longish but combed neatly around ears and collars. They differed in age and size, ranging from what Addison guessed was four up to Riko's fifteen-ish. She had never seen so many kids.

A second door opened and an older boy came in, probably around Riko's age, accompanied by a smaller girl who was much shorter in height. Lev spotted her from all the way across the room and jumped up from their cuddle-fest and hollered a greeting. The younger girl, her sleek dark hair tied back from her face, burst into tears.

Lev ran.

The younger girl ran.

And somewhere in the middle they collided. Locked in a hug, Lev stumbled back a step, laughing. They whispered in the younger girl's ear and Addison saw how the girl's expression changed from upset to delight in two seconds flat. She leaned back to pat Mr Rocky on the head and Lev laughed some more.

They must be close buddies.

Addison wandered a little, then, touching wires here, running her fingers across a dusty control panel there. She went over to the centre unit and patted GG on its sturdy side. It felt warm to the touch. The child hiding behind it scuttled away, reappearing a few seconds later behind the far unit, sidling over to stand with the rest of his or her group (there was too much dirt on this one to tell if it was boy or girl).

'What's this stuff for?' Addison asked Riko, who'd remained beside her, as if not trusting her to investigate by herself. The teenager was taller than Addison had first realised, her hooded jacket hiding a slight, willowy frame.

'They stored power from the turbines, then redistributed it.' Riko had a firm voice, unaccented and no-nonsense. It reminded her of how Alex, Bruno and Gwen spoke. Grown-ups. 'They're used to heat and light this place. Run hot water. Things like that. There are more than one, we think.'

'More GGs?' Addison smiled around the name, enjoying the shape of it in her mouth.

Riko seemed confused by her. 'Yes. We think. In other sections. We don't go exploring that far.'

Addison patted GG the unit on its side again, leaving her hand there to warm her palm. 'How far?'

The girl was regarding her like you would something that had crawled out of a dank, dirty hole. Which wasn't so far from what Addison had done. Riko made no reply.

'Why not explore?' she asked instead.

It was Lev who answered her. They had come back over with the girl they had been hugging in tow. A few other kids had strayed over with them, hanging back, their curiosity over the newcomer outweighing any fear.

''Cause that's where the ghosts are,' Lev said solemnly. 'We don't go where the ghosts live.'

Addison's eyebrows hiked up.

'Ghosts?' she asked. Were they like monsters?

But Riko was already shaking her head. She had an air about her that made Addison suspect she'd been a guard to a princess or a queen before whatever had happened down here turned all the emergency lighting on. She was so take-charge and leaderly. Addison had to fight down the urge to blindly submit to whatever Riko wanted, her resolve dissolving as soon as the older girl opened her mouth.

'We're not talking about them.' Riko's dark eyes were steady. Two of the smaller children had shuffled to hide themselves behind her, scared faces peeking out at Addison. Three of the others had locked hands as they stared at her, not quite sure if she was there to gobble them up or maybe just cut off their toes and force-feed them back to them.

Lev, who'd found a bottle of water from somewhere, paused in their sips to wipe a sleeve across their mouth and say, 'The littlies get frightened if we talk about them.'

The bottle was offered to Addison and she accepted it gratefully, taking a long drink instead of stating the obvious: that Lev was a "littlie", too. Addison quietly inspected the group as she drank. Fear lingered in the air, like the smell of the unwashed children did. But why live here if they were so scared? How far away were these ghost-monsters? In what part of the underground tunnels were they?

Lowering the bottle, Addison stayed clear of the 'Gh' word and said, 'Why stay? You could just leave.'

'And go where?' Riko asked. 'It's as dangerous outside as it is in here now. At least this is home. We have shelter. Warmth. Food and water.'

Addison stared at the bottle of water she held. She squeezed the flimsy plastic and it crumpled slightly in her hand. There was no label to read and the water had tasted a little like sucking on a penny, but it was fresh and clear. They had clean water here. Supplies.

Fender had been quiet since encountering Riko, and Chief was nowhere in sight, but she felt them stirring now, a shifting around, as if unhappy with the direction her thoughts were leading her. Fresh water and supplies. Lots of GGs and power for lighting and heat.

'Does this place have a name?' she asked, being purposely casual, as if she didn't care a spit if Riko answered her or not. She took another sip of water. Being all leisurely-like.

Riko was studying her as closely as Addison had been studying her bottle of water. Addison didn't think she was fooling her for a second.

'The land itself or where we are right now?' the older girl asked carefully.

'Both?' she said.

'Technically, we're on Trinity Hills land. But down here? Down here it's called Elysian Fields.'

Riko's expression warred between politeness and impatience. 'No? We definitely don't have any Ambers or Jaspers here.'

'Are you sure?' Addison was peering about, making a mental list of each child, not that she knew what Amber or Jasper looked like. 'They'd be new. Last couple of days new.'

She had been firing a lot of questions at Riko over the last twenty minutes, and most of the kids had gotten over any lingering fear of her and had grown bored and wandered off: some back to the blankets, others to group together to play quietly or talk between themselves. One kid around five was chewing on what looked like a candy bar, its wrapper reflective silver foil.

Lev had stuck around to listen to Addison, and even they had been looking like they were losing interest in all her questions.

They grinned when they spotted Addison enviously eyeing the kid's snack, told her they'd get her one and skipped away.

'We don't have "new" people,' Riko was saying, sounding as if it was an effort to keep her tone even. 'You're the first person we've seen in weeks. There's no one in this part of Elysian Fields but us.'

That made Addison pause. 'This part' meant other parts, right? *More* than one part.

'What other parts are there?' Addison asked curiously.

Riko sighed. It was becoming a familiar sound to Addison. 'Come with me.'

Addison trailed her past the trio of massive units (which Addison thought of as the three GGs now), heading for the back corner and the second door the older boy and Lev's friend had come through.

As they passed, Riko addressed the older boy; he was sitting beside one of the lanterns and reading to three younger kids. 'Malcolm, keep an eye on everyone, would you?' she asked. 'I won't be gone long.'

Addison tried not to get distracted by the book Malcolm was holding. Its cover was bright with colour and she wanted nothing more than to sit down and listen to the story. With difficulty, Addison dragged her eyes away and stepped into another corridor with Riko when the girl motioned for her to follow.

This corridor resembled all the others: gloomy; red emergency lighting; concrete.

She heaved a Riko-like sigh.

The older girl didn't give Addison's eyes time to adjust but directed her to turn right. Their footsteps echoed.

'So GG stores power . . .' Addison said, mulling it over as she widened her stride to match Riko's. She felt her groin pull uncomfortably. 'And you hand-wind the lanterns. But red lights are always mergent sea lights' – she snorted to herself – '*Emergency* lights. Hm. Emerge. En. See.' A left turn at a branching corridor and on to a much wider passageway. More closed doors. Doors Addison was tempted to open and look through. Though maybe not if there were ghost-monsters living behind them.

How many rooms *were* there altogether? Was this part of Elysian Fields bigger than her mommy's house? The new, wider corridor stretching away from them suggested it was bigger. Way bigger. Addison went back to mulling out loud. 'All these corridors have emergency lights. I actually don't know what "emergency" means,' she admitted, shyly glancing at Riko from the corner of her eye (the girl had moved three steps ahead of her while Addison had been lost in her wonderings).

Riko didn't fill in the missing gap in Addison's knowledge. Addison tried not to feel disappointed.

'But these aren't *proper* lights, right? They're so dark. Real lights are bright. And white. Or maybe yellow. So how come so many red ones everywhere?' Addison asked into the silence of their echoing footsteps. 'Why isn't GG powering the bright lights?'

Riko halted so quickly Addison almost ran into the back of her. She dodged to the side as Riko turned to her.

'What are you doing here?' Riko demanded, staring down at her. 'Who *are* you?'

That confused Addison. She'd told Riko who she was. 'I'm Addison. Or Addy, if you like.' Only Alex or Lacey called her Addy, but she wouldn't mind if Riko called her that, too.

Riko rolled her pretty eyes – their whites were pink in the horrible lighting. '*No*. I know your name. I want to know what you're *doing* here.'

'I . . .' How much should Addison tell her? She had followed Lev down here because she didn't have any other options. She'd been cold and wet and tired, and Albus was somewhere she couldn't get back to, and Lacey wasn't anywhere nearby to look out for her (Addison didn't even *know* where Lacey was and her hope of seeing her aunt again was wilting like a plucked flower left without water in summer heat). On top of that, Alex was gone and never coming back, same as her mommy, and Fender wasn't helping her *at all* right now, same as Chief. And what was up with Chief to keep disappearing on her? He'd done it a few times now, so obviously *he* didn't want to be around her, either.

Tears filled Addison's eyes before she knew what was happening. Her mouth softened on the words she was trying to get out, making them all mushy and wet.

'Don't,' Riko said, looking panicked. 'Don't do that. Don't cry.'

Addison bowed her head, embarrassed. Even as the tears fell, she swallowed back the ache in her throat and rambled out her excuses, not wanting Riko to think of her as a crybaby. 'I lost my friends. They were stopped and got shot at and I ran away – not because I was scared, but because I was trying to help – but I got chased and ended up by the wind turbines that I didn't know the name of, and then Lev turned up. And I didn't know where to go from there, so I followed them down a ladder in a concrete room, but I still need to get to my friends – Albus and Bruno and Gwen and Hari – because we were already headed here, to Trinity Hills, 'cause someone took Amber and Jasper – the two I was asking you about.' That was too many names, Addison knew. Riko would never sort them all out. But Riko had placed a hand on Addison's shoulder and was squeezing gently, and Addison couldn't stop talking. 'They came to Albus's Inn and killed his family – lined 'em up on his porch like . . . like porcupines – and then they brought Amber and Jasper here. To this place. Elysian Fields, that's what Jake called it. And Albus needs to find them, so I need to find them, but first I gotta find Albus because I lost him, like I lost Alex and my aunt and – and . . .' The tears fell in earnest now and she covered her eyes with her arm and just let them come.

'What did you do to her?' That was Lev. They sounded accusatory.

Addison hadn't heard their approach, but she felt Lev's small hand on her back. It rubbed warmth between her shoulder-blades and the kindness in the act made Addison's breath stutter and her breaths gulp noisily, emotion clogging up her throat.

'I didn't do anything!' Riko said quickly. 'I asked what she was doing here and then . . . and then *this*.'

'You must've done something.'

'I was bringing her to show her the map and I asked her a couple questions and now—'

Addison peeked out in time to see Riko wave her hands wildly about to encompass everything that Addison was. Addison sniffed and dropped her arm. Looked up at Riko. 'What map?'

Riko jabbed a thumb behind her up the corridor. Addison lifted the bottom of her shirt and scrubbed her face with it, wiping tears and snot away, and probably dirt, too. Eyes clear, she checked around.

The passageway continued onward, drip-fed in red as emergency lights glowed dully at intervals, all the way to the end and a large metal door. Feeling better, Addison walked on. A spacious area opened up on her right with tables and chairs and black (green?) potted plants. It was hard to tell in the red-tinged dimness. No doorways here, just a wide-open space with counters lining the walls on two sides and cabinets above them. An eating room? Addison spied vending machines on a far wall, six of them, all broken open and their innards emptied. Littered across the tabletops were crumpled-up juice boxes and plastic trays smeared with old, dried-up food. Plastic cutlery lay abandoned next to drinking beakers and tipped-over jugs.

Riko didn't gesture to any of those things. She indicated a large drawing on the last wall. It roughly resembled a huge compass, with each of its four arms pointing north, east, south and west. At its centre was a big, round circle. Addison silently spelled out the letters in her head.

A-T-R-I-U-M.

'Elysian Fields,' Riko said. She tapped a finger on the southern arm, partway up the widest vertical corridor. 'And here we are.'

While Addison listened as Riko explained the layout, Lev unzipped Mr Rocky's spine and pulled out three candy bars wrapped in silver packaging. Addison almost snatched their hands off, accepting them. She mumbled a heartfelt thanks as she ripped the first open with her teeth and bit into it. The texture surprised her. Grainy, like eating bits of dried rice. But sweet, too. It was pretty good. She worked on chewing as her eyes roamed the map. She could read some words; some she couldn't. Most, she didn't recognise or understand even when she pieced the letters together.

'Where's the real way in?' Addison asked, because she might be young and hadn't visited many places yet, but even she knew going through a locked concrete room under a swirling wind turbine and then climbing down a tall ladder into an unlit service tunnel wasn't the best or easiest way to get into somewhere.

'The main entrance is here.' Riko's finger went high, pointing to a blocky portion right at the northernmost tip.

The letters there spelled E-N-T-R-A-N-C-E. And next to it: M-U-S-E-U-M.

'That's how people normally get inside here?' At Riko's nod, Addison said: 'Can you take me there?' This was why she was here. Why she'd stowed away on the library bus in the first place, knowing her aunt Lacey was coming but leaving the Inn anyways because she needed to help Albus. Like he'd appeared out of nowhere to help her when she'd needed it the most.

She could picture him easily, his smile all warm and cosy, like being given an affectionate hair ruffle, and his kind, clear eyes. And then she thought about all the sad things that had happened to him: his poorly hands, his hurting ear, his sister and friends being put in treasure holes. Now two more of his family were lost down here. A girl and a little baby, maybe alone and scared in the dark, the meagre red-lighting hiding things that crept closer and closer to them from the cover of the shadows.

Like ghosts, Fender whispered.

Albus wouldn't be able to find Amber and Jasper on his own. And he didn't know about the ghost-monsters. But Addison could. With the help of Riko and Lev.

'Can you take me?' Addison asked again, because Riko's and Lev's brows had come down in almost identical frowns and neither of them were answering.

Lev sent a nervous glance in the direction of where the big metal door was located at the far end of the hallway. North. 'It's scary that way. Real scary.'

'Ugh,' Addison muttered, tearing into the second candy bar and biting off half in one go. 'Does the map say where these ghosts are?' She had to swallow her mouthful and repeat herself when both Riko and Lev stared uncomprehendingly at her.

Riko gave her about the bajillionth odd look and said, 'Maps don't show that, but we think they're here.' A tap to the centre circle. 'And possibly here.' A second tap to the left-hand arm. Addison did the rhyme in her head that Alex had taught her. Naughty Elephants Squirt Water. It meant it was west.

'What kind of ghosts?' she asked.

Riko and Lev exchanged glances. Lev did their shrug thing. 'Haven't seen 'em. Not exactly.'

'That big door at the end of this wing is locked and blocked from the other side. We don't open it. Wouldn't even if we could. We *can* get through to the main atrium other ways, though, if we had to. But no one is allowed to any more.'

'Not any more?' Addison asked.

Riko's mouth flattened into a thin line. 'One of our kids got sick and I sent—' She paused, her lips disappearing entirely, they were pressed together so tightly. 'We needed asthma medicine from the clinic and Tom said he'd go. Said it wouldn't take long, not if he was quick. Anyway, he went in and . . .' Riko trailed off, shaking her head. Her eyes lowered, her silky hair falling forward to hide her face.

'Bad things happened,' Lev finished for her. 'We heard bad things.'

Lev had curled an arm around Mr Rocky at some point and was absently stroking the raccoon's fur.

'What kind of bad things?' Addison asked.

'Screams,' Riko said, her voice hard, her fine, dark eyebrows crowded in on themselves. 'Great wailing cries that echoed through the vents. And howls, a whole host of them. It went on for so long.'

'They *ate* him,' Lev whispered, stroking away at Mr Rocky's fur.

'W— what could do that?' Addison asked, her pulse pounding heavy and thick in her throat as her eyes returned to the map. The three bars she'd eaten sat leaden in her stomach. She half wished she hadn't wolfed them down so quickly.

'Not what,' Riko said. '*Who*.'

'Would they . . . would they eat babies?' Addison asked, thinking of Jasper.

'They eat *everything*,' Lev said, hugging Mr Rocky tight. 'And they'll eat us, too, if they can.'

Chapter 8

Pilgrim

The storm had hit the coast. It shrieked at the top of its lungs as it stampeded on to land, its howls, wet-throated with rain, chasing after them and leaving the ocean far behind. Driving had become treacherous, made even more so by the hearse's missing windshield. Grit and leaves whipped into the car and winds lashed; they beat at Pilgrim's hands and face. He had to squint his eyes to see.

The portent of birds Jay had pointed them towards, if that's what they were, had vanished from the horizon, lost behind a maelstrom of clouds. The late-morning sunshine had long been snuffed out and the day turned to a false twilight streaked through with orange. The headlights were a poor substitute for the sun. Pilgrim stuck to the centre of the road where he could, power-line poles swaying, trees coming alive to squabble with their neighbours. The hearse rocked and shuddered as the building gale swiped at them; Pilgrim felt it lift under the car and shunt them upwards, wanting to rip them from the road.

His head ached from his prolonged focused attention. He took one hand from the steering wheel to rub at his gritty eyes and a giant, splintering *CRACK* rent the air. His hand flew away from his face, snapping back to the wheel. A warning cry came from the back seat. Voice's joined it.

Tree! Watch the tree!

Pilgrim stomped on the brakes, tyres juddering as a great old oak next to the road, as tall as the three-storey Inn, tore straight down the middle. Pale-wooden meat exploded from the trunk, a detonation that blasted it apart and sheared off one mighty arm at the shoulder. The hearse skidded, fishtailing as it screeched to a halt.

'Back up!' Lacey yelled from the passenger seat. '*Back up, back up!*'

Pilgrim wrenched the hearse into reverse and floored the gas, eyes trained on that gnarled, heavy bough as it sawed towards them; it would crush their car's roof like a soda can. The hearse leapt backwards and he heard gasps and thumps from those in the rear. Something kicked the back of his chair.

The tree crashed down, the whole world leaping up to meet it. Branches squealed on paintwork, glass shattered and the rustle of leaves burst through the windshield as if the storm itself had fallen upon them. Sapling wood whipped at Pilgrim's face, stinging his cheeks and his shielding arm. Shouted curses came from Abernathy. Pilgrim heard Tyler yell Jay's name.

Scorched rubber burned his nostrils and the squeal of the tyres' spinning caterwauled in his ears. He lifted his foot off the gas pedal. The screaming died but the acrid stench remained, as did the smell of freshly cut timber.

Pilgrim heard nothing from the passenger seat. He hadn't wanted Lacey up front with him, not with the danger of grit and flying detritus flying through the space the windshield had once occupied, but she couldn't be dissuaded. He shoved at branches, pushing his hands through a prickly wall of leaves and twigs, uncaring that they drew blood, and found Lacey's shoulder, her neck, cupped his palm to its warmth, felt the curve of her jaw and the beat of her pulse. He released his breath as her hand came up to grip his wrist, holding it tightly.

'I'm okay,' she said, breathless, and he felt the vibration of her words in his palm. 'I'm okay.'

'Can you get out your side?' he asked.

'I think so, yeah.'

Her door clicked open and the interior light came on.

'Get *off* me.'

Pilgrim twisted in his seat to find Abernathy balled down in the foot-space behind the passenger seat, trapped there with Sunny sprawled on top of her. In the rear compartment, Tyler leaned over Jay, shielding him as best she could where he lay stretched out in a cocoon of blankets.

'Everyone all right?' Pilgrim had to yell to be heard over the storm. 'Tyler, you good back there?'

Tyler briefly glanced up to give him a brief wave and a nod.

Pilgrim reached over his seat and gripped Sunny's elbow, pulling at her, helping her up, but it was a muddle of limbs and too-tight spaces, and Sunny wasn't moving fast enough for Abernathy's liking so she shoved an elbow into her. Sunny yelped in pain.

Pilgrim frowned. 'Take it easy.'

'*You* take it easy,' Abernathy snapped, grunting with effort. 'You just drove us into a fucking tree.'

That's not fair, Voice said. *You attempted to get out of its way. You failed, of course, but you did try.*

The rear door swung open and Lacey came in with the wind. Leaves kicked up around her head as she leaned inside, bracing her knee on the seat and jamming her arms underneath Abernathy's, looping them about her chest.

'Come on,' Lacey muttered.

Surprisingly, Abernathy didn't complain as Lacey muscled her out of her wedged position. 'I told you we shouldn't be driving in this,' Abernathy said, but most of the heat had drained from her.

Pilgrim had to agree. The winds were probably topping out

at 50mph right now and, by all indicators, would be getting worse. But they'd had no choice. There wasn't the option of sitting tight and waiting for the storm to pass over. Albus was out there with Hari, and Lacey wasn't about to wait on *anything* before getting to Addison.

Something slinked by outside Pilgrim's window and his head snapped left. Off the road, in the cover of trees, three sets of luminous eyes stared back at him. Wild dogs? Wolves? Coyotes? Whatever they were, they didn't move. Their ears were laid flat, their heads lowered, but, as one, their ears pricked up and all three turned, their snouts pointing in the direction the hearse had been headed.

'Pilgrim?' Lacey said, pulling his attention back into the car. 'Can you get it started again?' The engine had cut out.

When he looked back to the spot where the three wild animals had been, they were gone.

Gone to find shelter, no doubt.

After three key-twists and an extended sputtering, Pilgrim fired the hearse back to life and got an unhealthy whirring squeal for his trouble.

Sounds like some creature is trapped in there and is getting crushed to death, Voice said.

Jesus. Nice visual.

Making sure the hearse was in reverse, Pilgrim pressed his foot lightly to the gas. The whole car juddered, the squeal hitting ear-splitting levels before he eased off the pedal. They were stuck.

As Pilgrim kicked his door wide enough to get out, Voice said, *How are we going to get anywhere in this storm, least of all find a pack of flying birds?*

Pilgrim had no answer and stared at the downed tree lying across the front of the car. The hood was partially caved in and a hubcap was missing. Carried off to Oz, as far as Pilgrim knew. The light from one unbroken headlight bled through leaves and branches, the tree's insides glowing red, russet and gold, as if a fire had been set within its heart.

'What're you hearing out here?' he asked Voice.

Everything. Nothing. It's not only out here that a storm's raging. I can hear a gaggle of voices, too. Angry, upset, confused, eager, curious. A bunch of them, and not that far away. Tommy says it could *be Elysian Fields but it's probably not enough voices for that. More likely a camp. Maybe even some random group. It's impossible to tell.*

A camp. Perfect. Pilgrim had heard about them. Recently formed encampments where people struggling with accepting their voice were either encouraged to go (read: forced to), or presented themselves voluntarily in order to learn how to live more harmoniously with them. The camps were a direct result of the pervading stories surrounding the Flitting Man – an unseen man made of shadow who entered your home at night and stole you away, leaving nothing behind but the burnt husks of his enemies. He was gathering an army of voice-hearers, they said.

These stories sprinkled water on the growing ideology that being vilified and hunted for the best part of a decade for the past crimes of your brethren wasn't any way to live, and it was time to fight back. Strength in numbers and banding together had been one of the easiest solutions for some voice-hearers – a feat in itself when survivors were so scattered and so many fostered a severe case of paranoia when it came to the voices. Pairing that with close to eight years' worth of simmering resentments and fear-mongering, and a number of messed-up, violent gangs had inevitably popped up. Pilgrim had run afoul of a couple himself.

Of course, all this was a simplified explanation of what was a complicated series of developments, but the burgeoning violence Pilgrim had sensed in many a face-to-face interaction and the righteous anger that drove these people were more than enough to incite a fight with anyone they believed hated them for who they were. And each of these smaller skirmishes would inevitably throw fuel on to an already wild, ever-expanding fire.

Voice-hearers are not all *fire-wielding maniacs*, Voice argued.

Of course not. Just like non-voice-hearers didn't all want to murder anyone who heard a voice. People were complicated creatures. They were also often illogical and prone to react violently when they felt threatened.

The winds were an animal, teeth snapping closed on sleeves and cuffs as Pilgrim tromped to the back of the car and unlatched the rear compartment, lifting it up. It provided some shelter, but Pilgrim still had to hold his hair out of his face as he hunted around for what he needed. Sunny, Lacey and Abernathy joined him in the limited space, huddling as far out of the rain as they could get.

Tyler kept her gaze down as she rearranged Jay's blanket around his shoulders.

'Are we stuck?' she asked, without looking at him.

'Not yet,' Pilgrim replied.

'He can't walk.'

'I can,' Jay said stubbornly. 'I'm not an invalid. The pain is actually better. I don't feel it so much.'

Pilgrim wasn't sure that was a good thing.

'I'll get us moving,' he said. He felt Lacey's eyes on him, but she didn't say anything. He found the tyre iron under Abernathy's pack and pulled it free.

'What's the plan?' Abernathy said, stepping closer, crowding Lacey so much the girl threw an irritable scowl at the taller woman. Abernathy ignored it and pulled her pack nearer and rooted inside it. She pulled out a pair of gloves.

'We lift the tree while Lacey reverses the car,' Pilgrim said.

'Sure. Sounds like a piece of cake.'

'How far away do you think we are, Pilgrim?' The lines at the corners of Jay's mouth and between his brows were deeply etched, and darkness had gathered under his eyes. His searching gaze skipped from Pilgrim to Tyler to Lacey, the only three who had any inkling of an answer. His face was shiny with sweat, his hair damp and curling more than usual. As soon as Tyler got done tucking in his blankets, he restlessly pushed them aside.

Lacey was the one to answer. 'We must be close. One way or another, we keep heading for where Addison told you to head.' She was grave-faced, not meeting Jay's eyes as she pulled on a woollen hat and tucked her hair in. 'To the birds.'

'But we can't see them any more,' he pointed out.

'We head in that direction,' Pilgrim said. 'I'm sure we'll get our bearings when we get closer. Come on.' He left them and headed for the front of the car.

Trees barricaded them in on either side. They'd chosen to take minor roads, not wanting to chance running into anyone on the main highway. Unfortunately, that also meant they hadn't seen a house or a building for quite a few miles. Only the woods and the wide expanses of fields and fallow farmland. If they had to leave the hearse here, that meant leaving Jay in the middle of nowhere.

What about this camp? We could take him there. It came out hesitant, Voice feeling his way into the subject. Which was wise, because it was a crazy fucking idea.

Like I said, Tommy doesn't think they're very far, Voice added. *And at least it's something we can track . . .*

'Shut up,' Pilgrim muttered, because he knew the suggestion wouldn't be limited to the confines of his head for long. Within seconds, Lacey was beside him.

'No. No way. You *know* we don't have time to divert anywhere else. We're already how far behind Albus and Addison? We need to keep going.'

'It's a non-issue. Don't pay him any mind.' He wrenched open the driver's door, gripping it hard as the wind tried to rip it from his hold. 'Get in.'

Lacey didn't climb behind the wheel. She stood toe to toe with him, her head tilted back, the hair not held in place by her hat whipping about her face. She met his eyes dead on and he felt an insufferable stirring of affection at how she stood up to him. Her chin had jutted out with a hint of the mulishness that ran in her family, but now it was tempered with steel, hard and inflexible. He wanted to tell her that he'd lost people, too. That the last thing he wanted was to lose more. The heaviness of Clancy's body as he'd carried her into the Inn and laid her out on the parlour floor was fresh in his mind. He could still feel the terrible, limp weight of her in his arms, the way her head rested heavy on his shoulder.

Lacey's eyes lasered into his, but Pilgrim stared back, unfazed.

'Get in the car,' he told her.

Sunny and Abernathy were waiting at the head of the hearse and Pilgrim could feel their eyes on them, watching their stand-off.

The wind and rain buffeted him, but it was a particularly hard flurry that pushed Lacey up on to her tiptoes and finally got her moving. She slammed down into the seat and wrenched the door shut – Pilgrim came close to losing a couple of fingers.

With a horrendous, ear-grating squeal, Lacey fired up the engine.

'Fuck!' Abernathy yelled over the noise, wincing. 'Sounds like a spin drier full of cutlery!'

The splinted bough was large. Pilgrim waved Abernathy to follow him and found a position that worked on the passenger side. He jammed the tyre iron between wood and metalwork and levered the rod back and forth as he worked to shunt the limb off the hood. Abernathy got in beside him, turning her face away from the scratchy branches, reaching in with gloved hands, searching for a decent hold. She pushed upwards, straining against the weight. He couldn't hear a thing over the wind and the squealing engine, but he felt a shift, the subtle lifting of the hearse's front suspension. He leaned so hard into his tyre iron he worried it might snap.

'Back it up!' Sunny yelled from the front of the hood, and Lacey cranked the engine.

The squealing ramped up and the hearse's flank, pressed against Pilgrim's thigh, shuddered and groaned. The stench of melting rubber made his eyes sting.

'Lift!' he yelled at Abernathy.

Sunny was yanking and pulling from her side, the whole canopy of foliage shaking as if alive with a family of hyperactive squirrels, and with a horrendous screeching wrench the hearse shot backwards, tyres skidding on wet asphalt. Pilgrim stumbled away, yanked off centre, his tyre iron clanging to the road. Abernathy ended up on one knee and Sunny twirled in a half-circle before regaining her balance. But the car was free.

The hearse's hood looked as if it had lost a fight against the Hulk's fist; the engine hissed and clanked, audible even over the howling rain. But it *was* running.

Pilgrim helped Abernathy to her feet and picked up his tyre iron. He paused, half bent, his attention caught by something sitting in the middle of the road, way past the fallen tree branch. One of the wild dogs was watching him. Neither the storm nor the people and their beaten-up car seemed to be bothering it. Its red-grey fur was matted down, its ears flicking every now and then as raindrops pelted it. It remained seated on its haunches as Pilgrim finished straightening up.

Is that normal wolf behaviour? Voice asked.

The wolf's mouth opened in a panting, teeth-flashing grin, then it got to its feet and shook itself vigorously, flecks of water spraying in every direction. Done, it took two very deliberate steps towards Pilgrim and the fallen bough, stopped with one paw raised off the ground, head cocking as it lowered it on a final purposeful step, then spun a one-eighty and trotted away. And not into the cover of the trees, as Pilgrim thought it would, but choosing instead to follow the road's centre line, not deviating from it as it shifted from a trot into a full-out, loping run.

No, Voice answered himself. *That was most definitely not normal.*

Pilgrim glanced over at Abernathy, wanting to see if she was witnessing the same thing he was, but she was busy brushing dirty water and leaves off her jeans. Sunny was already heading back to the car, a slight limp in her gait.

'Let's go,' he told Abernathy, glancing back up the road. The wolf had vanished again.

Sliding into the passenger seat, Pilgrim wiped his face dry with his arm and sniffed back a sneeze. He stared ahead. The tree blocked most of the road, but he stared anyway. It took him a moment to realise Lacey wasn't driving away. She sat, her hands on the wheel, staring out of the side window and into the trees.

'What's the hold-up?' Abernathy said, thumping a hand on Lacey's seat back. 'Let's roll.'

'I need to go.'

Pilgrim had to lean in to hear.

Lacey turned towards him. She had a bizarre look on her face, one he was having trouble reading. 'I need to go,' she told him.

'We all need to go,' Abernathy said. 'Now floor it before this baby croaks.'

The intensity in Lacey's eyes held Pilgrim still. 'Addison's here,' she said. 'My Voice can hear her. Out there.' She pointed.

Pilgrim's gaze went past her to the woods. Dark and full of shadows, the storm having snuffed out the sunlight. It led to someplace he didn't want her to go.

'We can drive—'

'No,' she said. 'The road doesn't lead through there. I need to cut through.'

Voice was silent as he concentrated on listening. *There is something out there, but I can't . . . I can't quite catch it. A melody of some kind?* He sounded frustrated with himself.

Tyler's eyes were waiting for him when Pilgrim twisted around to look in the back. She didn't have to say anything for him to understand; her hand went to Jay's head and gently stroked his hair. Pilgrim couldn't see much beside the crown of his head and his thick, dark curls. Despite Jay's assurance that he could walk, Pilgrim knew he wouldn't make it more than ten minutes before collapsing.

Sunny and Abernathy were both watching him, their wet hair dripping, their noses red from cold. Lacey was watching him, too, her eyes steady on the side of his face. The bruises and cuts that marred her skin reminded him of how easily she'd been hurt, of how vulnerable she was when he wasn't there to protect her. And of how little time had passed between him finding her again and this moment. He was being torn in so many different directions he had to grip hard to his thighs, needing something to hold on to.

'I *need* to go to her, Pilgrim,' Lacey said, seeming to understand his inability to vocalise his thoughts. 'Me and Alex, we promised each other we would keep her safe – a pinkie promise – and I haven't been doing a very good job of keeping my end of the deal.' Her mouth tipped up in the saddest smile Pilgrim had ever seen on her, and he felt it crack open a fissure inside him, a crevice that went so deep it swallowed every argument he was preparing to make. Lacey wasn't the same gullible teenager he'd found selling lemonade outside her grammy's house. She was a survivor. Always had been, right from the moment he'd made that ill-fated decision to stop at a sleepy-looking motel, to the moment he found her in the middle of a burning cornfield. He had to believe she would survive this, too. Lacey loved her family. More than anything else in the world. It was the sole reason she had placed herself in his path to begin with. He couldn't stop her from going after the last remaining member of it.

'Okay,' he said quietly.

Her eyes shone and her bottom lip trembled. 'Okay?' she asked.

'Yes, okay,' he said. 'You have your rifle?'

'Tucked down there.' She indicated the side of the passenger seat he was in, and Pilgrim slid the weapon free and passed it over to her. She held it sideways in her lap, muzzle pointed downwards and away from him. 'I'll leave my pack with you,' she told him.

Pilgrim nodded. He doubted she would need it where she was going, and it would only get in her way. Lacey stared at Pilgrim and he counted off the seconds, a slow count of five that felt like fifty. She was biting at the inside of her mouth, a hollow cutting a divot into her cheek. He pressed a gentle fingertip to it.

'Someday, you'll eat a hole straight through your face, doing that.'

Her cheek went back to normal. 'It's a better habit than chewing my nails.'

He grunted in agreement. 'I heard that's worse than licking a toilet seat.'

She broke into a smile and it warmed him all the way through to a place that no wind or rain could ever touch. He adjusted her woollen hat where it had rucked up a little on one side and, when he was done, she leaned across the seats to briefly rest her brow against his shoulder. It was all Pilgrim could do to not grab hold of her and refuse to let go.

She's not a child any more, Voice said quietly. *You can't protect her from everything.*

He would always try, whether she needed him to or not.

'Elysian Fields,' he said, and Lacey lifted her head. 'I was told to watch out for a forest of white and wind when we got near to it.' He glanced back at Abernathy, because she'd been there when their friend Jackson had said it. Jackson was one of the people Pilgrim had lost along the way, his final words used to warn Pilgrim and which Pilgrim now used to arm Lacey. 'He was talking about wind turbines.'

The furrow in Lacey's brow deepened. Her throat rippled when she swallowed. 'They have no idea what they're getting themselves into, do they?' The storming winds shivered across the car, blowing in through the missing windshield and sending her words up into the air, where they whirled around Pilgrim like so many scattered leaves.

'No. They don't.' None of them did. Not Addison, not Albus. Only Hari. Pilgrim would bet Hari knew exactly where he was going.

'I'll watch out for them,' she promised.

'Good. We'll find another way around to you. Be careful.'

'You, too.' She turned away from him, turned away from them all, but not before Pilgrim saw her jaw work, saw how her lips twisted to the side as she bit down on the inside of her cheek again, hard enough to draw blood. 'See you soon,' she said, and shunted open the driver's door, battling against the wind as she got out.

She seemed to pause for a second in the door's gap, her back to them, and Pilgrim waited for her to say something more. But she didn't. She let the door slam shut and started away, slinging her rifle over her shoulder. She walked quickly and he watched her go, right up until she hit the treeline and entered the woods and was lost amidst the trunks. She kept her head down the entire time and didn't look back.

No one moved or spoke. The storm raged around them, every now and then taking side-swipes at the hearse and rocking it on its suspension.

A whole minute ticked by before Abernathy threw up her hands. 'What the fuck are you doing?' Her glare was so fierce Pilgrim felt the physical prodding of it at the back of his head. 'You're really letting her go like that?'

Rather than reply, he clenched his jaw and busied himself with scooting into the driver's seat, awkwardly manoeuvring his long legs over the centre console and sliding into the spot that Lacey had vacated. It was still warm from her. He had nothing to say to

Abernathy. What else had he been supposed to do? He could accompany Lacey, sure, but it would have meant leaving the hearse behind, leaving Jay and inevitably Tyler, leaving the *road*. Which didn't feel right. It felt like something was trying to drag him off a catwalk hanging over a chasm and into a dark abyss.

That damn wolf. It was surely a common wild dog, regularly seen in these parts and nothing more, but another part of him was screaming at him to trust his instincts, and his instincts were pointing him forward, straight as the proverbial arrow – as straight as the white line down the centre of this road. He had been told once, by an old woman with an X-ACTO knife who liked to call him *Sonnenblume*, that he was someone who set people on their rightful paths. That was his role, even if he aspired to nothing else. And if he was to believe that, he had to believe that his choices meant something. Maybe he *was* helping Lacey on her path. And now he had to stand fast and follow his, regardless of the painful knot in his stomach or the constant pull at his neck that made him long to look in the direction she had disappeared in.

You always find your way back to her, Voice said softly.

Yes. He always did.

'I swear you're such an idiot sometimes.' A scuff of movement from the back, and he watched through the rear-view mirror as Abernathy ungracefully climbed over the back seat and into the rear compartment. Tyler complained loudly as Abernathy came very close to landing on top of Jay.

'Oh, shush, woman,' Abernathy snapped, and crawled by them on her way to her pack. She muttered to herself as she ripped the top open and dug around inside. She came out holding a paperback. Pilgrim didn't need to read its title to know it was his copy of *Slaughterhouse Five* that he'd lent to her what felt like an age ago. She thrust it up in the air, as if daring Pilgrim to come and confiscate it from her. 'I'm taking this with me. I haven't finished it yet.'

She shoved the slim paperback into her jacket pocket, shaking her head in disgust, going back to muttering to herself as she double-checked the gun holstered at her hip. 'I can't believe you turned me into a reader, you fucker.'

'You're leaving, too?' Jay asked her. The thought seemed to upset him.

'Well, I'm not staying here with you losers. You're all set up in here anyways – a fitting place, considering you're half dead already.' She smirked at him as she knocked her knuckles off the hearse's wood panelling.

'That's not funny, Abernathy,' Tyler said.

Abernathy ignored her, speaking to Jay. 'You can do way better than this treacherous little rabbit, by the way.' She lifted a nod at Tyler. 'Just so you know.'

'Why would you say that?' Jay said, and Pilgrim heard the confusion there. 'We're fine.'

Abernathy spent a drawn-out moment locking eyes with Tyler from across Jay's prone body. Nothing was said between the two women, but Pilgrim got the feeling plenty was communicated. Abernathy released Tyler from her stare and turned it on Pilgrim, their eyes meeting in the mirror. He thought she was about to say something to him, felt it in the drawing of her breath, in the parting of her lips, but all she did was smile faintly. He thought he would say something, too, but it seemed they didn't need to share words to communicate, either. Abernathy knew what Lacey meant to Pilgrim and, for maybe the first time in a long time, she was choosing to do something for someone other than herself.

She offered an offhand wave to the car in general as she climbed out the back hatch. 'Try not to die,' she said, and swung it shut with more force than necessary. She ducked into the wind and hurried away.

And then we were four, Voice said gloomily.

Chapter 9

Lacey

Between the wind and the roar of the shaking trees, the tread of Lacey's boots walked alone. She fought the need to keep checking over her shoulder, paranoia already setting in. Instead, she pulled her hood up over her hat and kept her head down, her hands shoved deep in her jacket pockets. The weight of her rifle strapped over her shoulder felt good and reassuring.

Cracks and pops ricocheted as branches were snapped free. Lacey's eyes darted to each sound, but no more tree limbs dropped out of the skies or threatened to cave in her skull. Something other than the storm seemed to stalk her through those woods, and Lacey welcomed an end to her cross-terrain hike. She didn't, however, welcome the sight that greeted her when, twenty minutes later, Voice warned her to slow down and take cover.

She pressed up against the trunk of a cedar, her fingernails digging into its craggy, rain-softened bark as her eyes passed over the trio of people, two tending to a downed figure. The man was obviously injured – he was laid out on his back and his two companions knelt, bracketing his lower body. It looked like they were attempting to splint his leg. Lacey winced as the man's cries echoed above the creaking and whipping of the storm-lashed trees.

'How many?' Lacey whispered.

Three here. Voice kept his voice so low it was a whisper of air inside her ear. *But at least two more ranging ahead. They're voice-hearers*, he added, which she had already guessed.

'Should we go around?'

These, maybe. But the other two are where we need to go. Voice hadn't said too much about what he'd been hearing, except there was singing and it was her all-time favourite Beatles tune. He had taken to humming the tune over and over while they'd traipsed through these woods, the same one she would sing whenever Addison was upset or feeling down, or simply to put a smile on her girl's face. It was *their* song, really, and knowing her niece was out there, close enough for Voice to hear her, made Lacey want to sprint full pelt past these three people in her way and not stop until Addison was by her side.

We need to play it smart, Voice said, as if concerned she might jump up and start making helicopter noises while waving her arms about like a loon. *But she's definitely been through here. Sounds like she's the one who did all the damage to that guy.*

A bolt of emotion speared Lacey right through her middle. She had to rest her head against the trunk for a second, her fingernails digging deeper into the tree's soft bark to get a hold of herself. If Addison had had to fight to get away from these people, then Lacey wasn't going to lose any sleep over hurting any of them if she needed to. She drew in a long, fortifying breath, swung the rifle off her shoulder into her hands and checked it was loaded and ready to go. She kept low as she broke cover and circled back, using the vegetation to hide, not taking any chances as she put more distance between her and the injured man's exhausted whimpers – he sounded as though he'd been in pain for a while. Lacey didn't feel sorry for him.

Look up, Voice whispered.

Far above her head, through the swaying tops of the cedar trees, the sky was a funnel of dark, swirling movement. She closed her eyes briefly, thinking her vision was glitching out, but when she looked again the sky continued to roil and turn over itself. It took her two deep breaths to realise it was birds. They were directly beneath the flying flock.

Head for the birds, Addison had said.

Lacey had arrived.

She grew more nervous as she continued on, the tree density gradually thinning and the cloaking gloom of shading boughs lifting as gaps widened between tree trunks and the cover offered by the undergrowth. She was soaked to the bone, the rains finding her from all directions, but she became less and less concerned about the three people she was skirting around *and* the storm. She knew the noise of so many thousands of birds must be tremendous, but she could *feel* the thunderous beating of wings, too. Felt it everywhere – in the ground under her boots, in her head, in her chest, in the air all around her, throbbing into her skin. Even her eyeballs pulsed in time, a tribal drumming that was too controlled to be alarming, yet she felt fear beat its tattoo into her anyway.

She wasn't expecting her foot to land on firm, smooth ground, and she glanced down to find blacktop beneath her boot. The strip was featureless, no markings, no signs of where it went or where it came from. A single-lane track. She followed it. Voice would tell her if she needed to find cover.

The blacktop sloped down, the trees falling away, and mammoth blades rotated into view, long and spinning – as big as aviator fins – sweeping the horizon. Then came the towering pillars, wider than any tree trunk, and finally a never-ending field of fan-topped spires, row after row after row of turning wind turbines. Hundreds of tapered blades revolving in unison, and they had been revolving for an eternity and would continue to turn long after Lacey and everyone she loved was gone. She stared, open-mouthed, as a streaming train of birds elegantly swooped its way through the obstacle course of fast-turning blades. The dizzying movements pulled at Lacey's eyes, dragging her in until she unconsciously raised up on to tiptoes, felt a vertiginous tilt of a banking glide and the sudden accelerating lift as a powerful updraught pushed her skyward. She vaguely wondered if this was a hallucination, but the pounding in her body, her drumming pulse at neck and wrist, matched the spinning blades' rhythm, each spin drumming their reality into her—

whump-whump-whump—

WHUMP-WHUMP-WHUMP—

—a giant heartbeat, the *universe's* heartbeat, powering everything in sight: the land, the skies, the birds and the winds they rode. Voice said something, but Lacey couldn't hear him, could only stare at how stark the whites of the turbine's towers and blades were against the black bodies of the swarming birds and the dark grey backdrop of the storming skies. A hand dropped on her shoulder and Lacey gasped, violently wrenched from her inertia, and whirled around. Her fist flew out and she smacked Abernathy square in the face.

'What the *fuck*?' Abernathy had grabbed her nose and was hopping backwards, out of range.

Lacey grimaced and held her hands up. 'I'm sorry, I'm sorry. I didn't hear you.'

'I've being hissing your name for, like, half a minute already. You'd be deader than shit if I'd been one of those people back there.'

Lacey did a quick, belated scan of their surroundings. She felt like an idiot. What had gotten into her? Standing here and staring off into a space like some braindead robot. *She* was the one who deserved to get punched in the face.

'I'm sorry,' Lacey said again. 'I got . . . I got distracted. What're you doing here?' She looked past Abernathy again, hastily checking the roadway, the trees, eyes flicking to every shaking section of foliage or twitching branch. But Abernathy was alone. Lacey didn't know if she felt disappointed or not.

Abernathy gave an offhand shrug. 'Seemed stupid, you coming out here on your own, so we all pulled straws.' It came out sounding overly nasal, which Lacey suspected was a deliberate exaggeration.

This is great, Voice said, still at quarter of his usual volume. *We're probably going to need her for what I'm gonna do.*

Lacey frowned. 'What're you gonna do?'

Ask for directions. As soon as I'm done, you should move, and move quick. If I'm overheard by anyone out here, they could be on us pretty fast. Head down this roadway and keep going until I tell you different.

'Um, okay . . .'

Abernathy was watching her. 'You're not talking to me, are you?'

'No. You should get ready to run.'

Abernathy's expression turned quizzical, but Lacey didn't concern herself with explaining.

Here we go . . .

Even prepared for it, Lacey flinched at the loudness of Voice's call.

ADDISON. HOW DO WE GET TO YOU?

Lacey didn't hang around to listen to anything else, she took off, hitting a run within three strides. The blacktop felt good and sturdy under her boots. Her hood flew off and the wind slapped her extra-hard in the face.

Her speed started to get away from her on the downward slope. The land wasn't flat here, and despite dropping down into what felt like a sunken-in bowl, the roadway dipped and rose beneath her, winding around and between hillocks and sloping gradients. It was like dashing into an immense maze, not knowing which turn would take her where. Titans soared above her at every crossroad, each turbine rising out of the earth, up, up into the sky, their heads ornamented by bladed coronets, their dark, billowing hair made up of an ever-moving undulation of birds.

The audial and visual commotion played on a loop – rain, rhythmic winds, spinning blades, pounding feet, panting inhalations – a disorienting miasma that pummelled Lacey's senses. She threw glances left and right, on the lookout for anybody they didn't want to meet, but her eyes stuttered out of focus, unable to settle on any one thing.

You keep saying 'four, three, four, three', but what's 'four, three, four, three' over and over again? Voice asked, his frustration a tense band around the back of Lacey's skull.

'Four thousand three hundred and forty-three?' Lacey panted out.

I don't know! All I'm getting is 'four three, four three'. And something about a branch.

'Hey. Look.'

Abernathy was pointing over at a wind turbine on their right. It was so huge Lacey didn't know what the woman was pointing to exactly, so she slowed her run to a jog and then to a raggedy walk, sucking in breaths as she scanned the concrete platform.

'How about a four and a two?' Abernathy called breathlessly. 'Close enough?'

The turbine's base itself was so large in circumference, Lacey doubted she, Pilgrim, Abernathy and Sunny would reach even halfway around it while linking hands. Her gaze slid higher and she finally saw what Abernathy was pointing at. Two black numerals, the height of an average-sized adult, were stencilled to its side. Forty-two.

Lacey's head panned left. Stopped. And there they were: a four and a three. Wind turbine number forty-three.

Jackpot, Voice said.

'*Hey!*'

Abernathy wasn't doing the yelling this time. Dulled by rain and tossed around by the wind, the two figures were closer than their shout conveyed – less than half a football field away, if Lacey had to guess. They had appeared from between two long lines of reflective panels, all set at ground level and tilted at a forty-five-degree angle. They kind of looked like a giant's scaled-up version of her grammy's Scrabble tiles stacked in their racks, except these were reflective and a purplish-blue colour where they weren't smeared with moss and dirt and decomposing plant-life.

Forget about the solar panels, Voice said impatiently.

Lacey, Abernathy and the two men did that thing where no one reacted for several long seconds, as if each were waiting for the other to make the first move. Lacey could shoot them. The wind might interfere with her aim, but she was a crack shot with a rifle and they weren't *impossibly* far away. But the sound could alert others in the area, and Lacey didn't know these people. Look at what had happened to Jay and Clancy. Shooting first perhaps wasn't always the right decision.

Abernathy broke the stalemate. She snatched Lacey's elbow and dragged her into a run, yanking her along as she set off for wind turbine number forty-three. The woman was *fast*. It was all Lacey could do not to get tangled up in her own feet.

'There better be something there,' Abernathy ground out as they closed in on the turbine. This near to it, they had to dodge around the fallen carcasses of birds littering the ground, skipping around them in some macabre game of hopscotch. Lacey accidentally punted one, the feathery body flying away like a kicked football.

Field goal!

Far above their heads, the blades *whoosh*ed down and Lacey instinctively ducked, bracing herself for the hurricane blast. But it never came. The winds dropped out and her hearing cleared, as if popping after a blockage.

Look!

Lacey followed Voice's nudge at the backs of her eyeballs. She took over the yanking, grabbing on to Abernathy and taking the woman with her as she scrambled up a grassy knoll and past the jutting edge of the turbine's concrete platform. Around the corner, a sunken concrete alcove was hidden between two slopes in the land and a set of sunken steps led down to a door.

'There's no fucking handle!'

The door was a smooth, featureless panel of metal. That didn't stop Lacey. She hustled Abernathy past the steps, completely ignoring them, and let her go to clamber up the neighbouring slope to a narrow slot cut in the wall. It had been stuffed with the leafy head of a broken-off branch. Lacey hauled the sizeable branch out to reveal a windowless gap of eight inches by sixteen.

'In!' Abernathy hissed. 'Get in!'

Lacey wasn't convinced she would fit, but she dived for it anyway, shoving her rifle through first, hearing it clatter off something hollow and metallic, and squirmed through after it head first. She gasped out a '*Shit!*' as she fell, twisting to the side in an attempt to save her face and neck. Her shoulder slammed into something hard and unforgiving and she cried out as she rolled off it. She hit the floor in a breathless heap and lay there gasping for three full seconds before scrambling up, groaning through the pain in her shoulder, and raised her hands, grabbing on to the opening's lip, ready to help Abernathy through.

Abernathy wasn't coming through, though, she was shoving the branch back into place, forcing Lacey to back up or else get a mouthful of foliage. Her call came from the other side. 'I'm gonna run interference. If I'm not back in five, or if you hear gunshots, name your firstborn after me.'

Abernathy left no time to argue. With a flurry of running footsteps, she was gone, and Lacey was left alone.

Voice was silent as he listened with her, neither of them daring to speak. After long, tense minutes, Lacey left her post and went to collect her rifle from where it had clattered to the floor. She quickly investigated the area she was in and discovered that the thing she had fallen on was a metal drum barrel – the kind that had once housed crude oil or gasoline. It had been pushed under the windowless opening. Presumably to let people climb on top of it and out into the open.

She checked this side of the door, smoothing both hands down its sides, finding a handle but unable to depress it. Locked. Rubbing at her sore shoulder (it would bruise bone-deep judging by the pain level – a solid seven), Lacey turned a slow circle and zeroed in on the chained-off section in the corner.

'Addison was in here,' she murmured, going over to inspect the workman's ladder and the shaft it descended into. 'She came through here and went down.'

The crinkle and rustle of leaves brought Lacey's attention back to ceiling height and the gap she'd fallen through. She brought her rifle up and aimed, sidestepping deeper into the shadows.

The leafy camouflage was pushed aside. A grey section of sky was revealed. Lacey could see sheeting rain, falling at a slant, and nothing more.

'Abernathy?' she whisper-called.

Nothing.

She curled her finger around the trigger and, tucking in her chin, lowered her eye to the rifle's sights.

A dark-haired head appeared, the matted, windswept crown of it turned away as they checked for something over their shoulder. Lacey almost shot a hole straight through it before a breathless Abernathy turned to her and said, 'Help me through or shoot me, but be quick about it. They're on their way back already.'

Lacey almost advised that Abernathy come in feet first, but there wasn't time for messing around. She hopped up on to the barrel and gripped on to Abernathy's wrists, getting uncomfortably close to the woman's face as she drew her in close enough to hug her under her arms.

Abernathy's words came out strained. 'How the fuck did you fit through here?'

'Breathe in,' Lacey told her as she leaned back, putting some real weight behind her pull. Abernathy's arms had wrapped around her shoulders, her breaths hot in her ear.

'I *am* breathing in. *God.*' She twisted and squirmed, and Voice suddenly whispered a low *Hurry it up!* And Lacey heaved backwards, hard enough to worry she might seriously injure the woman.

Groaning, Abernathy slid further through and Lacey hitched her higher, finding herself hefting most of Abernathy's upper-body, her butt and hips now wedged. Lacey experienced a moment of pure panic as she imagined the two men coming upon Abernathy, trapped from the waist up, legs poking out of an opening the size of a dog flap, and she gave a huge, adrenaline-fuelled yank. With a sharp, tearing sound – and the momentum of their combined weight – Abernathy shot through.

Lacey did her best to jump clear, pulling Abernathy with her and away from the metal barrel, but she only partially succeeded. She landed feet first, but Abernathy's weight slammed into her and shoved her back. They landed in a heap, Lacey on the bottom, all her breath knocked out. She wheezed and shoved ineffectually at the bulk pinning her, desperate to breathe. Abernathy rolled away, hissing through her teeth.

Lacey couldn't move. She tried. Gave up. Lay where she was, willing her lungs to work as she watched Abernathy get up and go about hiding their entrance all over again. Somehow, with gargantuan effort, she flopped over and managed to get hands and knees beneath her and pushed herself up on to all fours. There, she stalled, flashing hot with pain. Man, she was so done with this place.

'Thanks for cushioning my fall,' Abernathy said in a low voice, leaning down to grip Lacey's bicep. She helped her the rest of the way up.

Lacey tried for a smirk, but it came out as a grimace as her shoulder twinged. 'Yeah, well, next time you can be the mattress.'

'Fair deal. Shall we?' Abernathy performed a half-bow, gesturing over to the ladder, offering the lead to Lacey. It might have been mildly amusing if she hadn't stiffened halfway through it, her hand clutching at her back, her face contorted.

'Getting old, huh?' Lacey said to her.

Abernathy gave her a *go fuck yourself* look, shifting her hand away from what was obviously a pretty bad sore spot.

'I get it,' Abernathy said, limping her way past. 'You're scared to go first. It's OK.'

Lacey flipped her the bird, even if it was to the woman's back and she couldn't see it.

Let's go, Voice whispered, urging Lacey on. *Addison is inside.*

Lacey pushed through a heavy fire door, the red bulb housed in its wire cage above it casting an angry glow over the sign marked 'Maintenance 2'. On their way to this room, they had met only empty corridors and sparsely furnished rooms. If this was Elysian Fields, no painted walls or mood lighting softened the industrial setting to make Lacey think it was anything more than a storage bunker of some kind.

She wasn't sure what she'd been expecting, but grey concrete walls, drab white panelling and cement-poured floors wasn't it. Its bare-boned factory aesthetic was sharp-edged and cold, and the Maintenance room wasn't any different.

Huge behemoths of machinery filled the space. Workmen's walkways ran on two levels, connected by ladders leading up and down. It was a world of perfect scaffolding and shiny railings, iron girders, brackets, ventilation shafts, tubes and miles of multicoloured wiring in organised bunches. Lacey had an excellent view of it all because she and Abernathy had stepped out on to an observation gantry overlooking the work floor below. Everything smelled of motor oil and greased lubricant.

There was more red lighting here, caged bulbs in brackets screwed to bare walls and attached to support pillars. There was no machinery noise of any kind – these behemoths of industry were dead lumps of metal and cable. Yet some kind of power hummed through the grating beneath Lacey's feet.

She's gotta be in here somewhere, Voice said. *We were told 'Maintenance'*.

'Addison!'

I didn't mean yell her name, he complained.

Lacey had been feeling nauseous since climbing down that shaft ladder – dread of what she might find and fear that, once she found it, it would be bad – and now it returned tenfold. She tasted acid in the back of her throat but couldn't swallow it away. Her throat had locked up.

'Addison!'

A sense of movement at the far end of the room, a blink of a shadow, and a head popped out from behind a cylindrical drum and waved. In the dim red-lit light, Lacey couldn't recognise specifics, but they were small and Addison-sized, and that's all that mattered.

'Addy,' she whispered, her voice breaking.

Lacey didn't remember her mad clamber down the metal steps or hear Abernathy's hissed warning to be careful. She didn't remember anything but, first, being on the gantry beside Abernathy and, next, being on the workshop floor and running for the cylindrical drum where Addison hid.

The one solitary kid that waited for her had a stuffed raccoon strapped to their front.

'Hello,' they said, and Lacey could tell the kid was nervous by how they couldn't stand in place without hopping from foot to foot. The sleeves of their too-long sweater hung over their hands and they were twisting the ends round and round like sweet wrappers.

'You're not Addison,' Lacey said stupidly.

The kid grinned and patted the top of their head. 'Nope. I'm smaller. But I can take you to her. We gotta hurry, though. We were someplace bad when Fender heard you. Addy sent me back to get you.'

Her stomach cramped so hard she almost hunched over. 'What do you mean "someplace bad"?'

'Someplace the ghosts could get her.' Grin gone, the kid's eyes were wide and sincere. The sleeve-twisting cranked up a gear as their gaze shifted over Lacey's shoulder.

Did she just say 'ghosts'? Voice asked.

Before Lacey could shoot off more questions, a huffing-and-puffing Abernathy came up from behind. 'Addison?' she asked the kid.

'No. Hi. I'm Lev.' A finger-point to the raccoon. 'This is Mr Rocky.'

'The raccoon has a name?' Abernathy said.

Lacey wanted to scream at her to shut up. 'Lev, *where's Addison*?'

'It's okay. She's in the vents.'

A beat of silence while that sank in.

'What's she doing in the vents, Lev?' Lacey had to fight to stay calm and not to shout it. She didn't want to scare him away (Lev was a boy's name, so she was sticking with 'him' for now).

Lev cocked his head at her. 'Hiding. From the ghosts.' He said it like it was the most obvious answer in the world.

'Of course, she is,' Abernathy said, totally dead-pan. 'I heard ghosts don't like vents. Too blowy.'

Lacey clenched her fists, her patience hanging by a very thin, very frayed thread.

She's just trying to lighten the mood, Voice reasoned. *Everyone's so tense.*

Lev gave a sombre shake of his head. 'I hear 'em through the vents sometimes, too. They might crawl up into 'em like we did with Addy. Which is why we gotta hurry. What's your name?' he asked Abernathy.

Abernathy told him and Lev made three attempts at it before he got it halfway right.

'Call me Abbie,' Abernathy told him.

'Now we're all acquainted, can we *go*?' Lacey waved the kid to come out.

With a short nod, Lev and Mr Rocky slipped from behind the drum and dodged past her. He dashed across the workshop floor, disappearing into the array of machinery. Lacey had to hustle to keep up. He zipped behind a line of sarcophagus-sized cast-iron vats, and Lacey followed, turning the corner to find an empty gangway.

'Lev?' She turned a full circle.

The kid was gone.

'Lev!'

A scuffle of feet. Two small hands appeared over the top of chest-high aluminium tubing on Lacey's right. The hands hopped up and down as if the kid was bouncing. 'Over here,' he hissed. He must have dipped down and skidded right under it.

Abernathy snorted breathlessly. 'Parkour's still popular with the kids, then.'

'You can go "round".' One hand pointed back the way they'd come. A gap where the silver tubing bent upward at ninety degrees, arcing high overhead, offered them an alternative route, and Lacey and Abernathy backtracked through it, meeting up with Lev on the other side.

'Sorry. Forgot you're so big,' he said, and quite deliberately sized them up and down.

Abernathy snorted again.

He took off, tracking a bundle of ankle-level pipes to a four-foot-high unlit passage passing through the wall. He went in without hesitation.

Lacey bent her head and neck and scraped her rifle's barrel on the roof as she slipped in after him. At her back, Abernathy made more noise than was necessary as she brought up the rear.

The brief glimpse Lacey had of her when she checked was of Abernathy folded over like a fortune cookie.

Lev was a dark, indistinct outline ahead, and Lacey sped up a little to stay close. 'This'll take us to Gym,' he said, hushed. 'We can cut through Plants.'

The toe of Lacey's boot *clang*ed off some unseen pipework and she winced at the noise.

'Lev? Tell me about the ghosts.' She didn't want to give credence to what Lev had said, but she also wanted information. She turned sideways to squeeze through a section where the passageway narrowed. More complaints came from Abernathy behind her, interspersed with some well-placed cuss words as the woman banged herself off the breezeblocks; it was difficult to keep low and side-walk at the same time – human bodies simply weren't made to bend that way.

Lev's whisper sounded closer than Lacey had been expecting, as though the kid was afraid to speak too loudly in case something heard. 'They hunt people and eat 'em. Burn them, too. Sometimes. Well, not really. That was before.'

'Before what?' Lacey found herself whispering, too.

'Before the mergent sea lights floated on.'

It's like learning a different language, Voice whispered, catching his own dose of the Whispers.

When Lacey had first found Addison, her niece had had similar habits with her speech. She'd been living alone for a while, just her, herself, and whatever voice she heard in her head. She would talk in overly literal references or mix words up. Her world had been so limited up to that point that she'd only had so many points of references at her disposal when trying to communicate. From day one, Alex had tasked herself with expanding the girl's vocabulary, and Addison had been a fast learner.

'Addison asked us for help,' Lev explained with a little more volume. ''Cause she explained about the baby. And about

Amber. So we're helping her get to them. But helping means taking her through the vents.'

It was *dark*, but as the walls widened back out, a faint reddish smudge beckoned at the end of their passage.

I'm so confused right now, Voice admitted.

'Need to go quicker,' Lev said, and moved off, leaving no space for more questions as Lacey shuffled as fast as she could, not wanting to lose the kid again.

They came out in a red-lit bare concrete stairwell. Rather than take them through one of the two doors, one marked 'Heating 3' the other 'Water 3', Lev went up. A flight of clanging metal stairs later, a push through a self-closing door, and Lacey and Abernathy came out into a large basketball court.

It smelled of well-used tennis shoes and rubber mats and brought memories rushing back of classes spent shimmying up ropes and hanging upside down off monkey bars. In the gym's opposite corner, a low-lit enclave marked an exit, the glossy floor a dark ocean streaked in claret lying between them. Benched seating, three tiers high, extended the length of the two longest walls.

Nothing moved. Everything was silent.

I really wasn't expecting to see one of these down here, Voice said.

Lacey hadn't, either. Their three sets of shoes squeaked on the gleaming floorboards. Lacey found herself examining the bleachers, scanning along them for solitary figures sitting in the dark, their heads slowly panning to watch as Lacey, Abernathy and Lev made their way across.

Pushing through a set of double doors and they were in another corridor, except this one wasn't industrial factory, it was windowless elementary school (albeit a chilly, vermillion version of it). Two dozen metal lockers ran along either wall. Message boards hung with a confetti of posters and notices pinned to their cork surfaces. The smell here reminded Lacey of her grams's pantry in the winter, of its cold tiles and hard brick, the whiff of cardboard boxes that held packets of oats and seeds and cereals.

There was no time to investigate what was inside the lockers or read the noticeboard's messages. Less than twenty seconds later they were leaving the hallway and entering a classroom.

An island of joined tables with small stools stood in silent attendance, trays of bedded plants laid out down their centre. About half of the plants were dead or dying, drooping like weary pilgrims. The rest were alive. Pipettes and measuring jugs and other strange-looking apparatus littered the rest of the counter space. On the back wall, a large white eraser board dominated the room. Faint marker pen listed a number of plants: cat-tail, chicory, clover, dandelion, plantain, purslane, wild asparagus. A solitary desk chair sat in front of the whiteboard and four dust trails evidenced where the teacher's desk had been dragged away.

Lacey found the desk pushed into the corner, shoved flush against the wall. On top of it, someone had precisely positioned a compact metal filing cabinet, and on top of *that* was one of the children's stools. Together, they resembled a rudimentary set of building block steps, all leading up to a square opening set a little below ceiling level.

Oh no, Voice said.

The grated ventilation shaft was roughly the same dimensions as a van's side window, maybe a little wider. Big enough to slide and wriggle through on your belly, but not for crawling.

'I liked Miss Mendoza's class best. She let us draw pictures,' Lev said mournfully, climbing atop the desk and making his careful way up on to the filing cabinet.

'Is this the only way to get to Addison?' Lacey asked uncertainly.

'Nope,' Lev said. 'But it's the quickest and safest. Right, Mr Rocky?'

Abernathy had given no outward sign that something had

caught her attention, but Lacey suddenly sensed the unnatural stillness in her. Glancing over, she saw the woman had sharp eyes on Lev.

'Miss Mendoza?'

Lev paused, one knee on the stool and one knee off. Lacey took a quick step forward, concerned the kid might fall.

'Did this Miss Mendoza have a first name?' Abernathy asked.

Lev gave her a little shrug and, hanging from his shoulders, Mr Rocky seemed to shrug along with him.

'No?' he said. His nose scrunched up in thought. 'I mean, she let some of the littlies call her Nessa – 'cause Mendoza is kinda hard to say. But Nessa isn't a *real* name.'

Abernathy closed her eyes and seemed to count to five. She rubbed a weary hand through her hair, all intensity in her demeanour fading to a grudging kind of acceptance. 'It's short for Vanessa,' she murmured.

Lacey considered her reaction. 'You know her?' she asked.

Abernathy gave her own small shrug. 'Not so much. Just someone I met in St Louis. I suspected she'd maybe come from another facility, but I didn't expect it to be this one.'

'She was a teacher there?' There hadn't been much talk of St Louis outside of its hospital and the experiments conducted by the doctors. Lacey was having difficulty connecting something as mundane as a person teaching class with the appalling things that had occurred within its walls.

'Not really. But she was interested in the kids. Asked them a lot of questions. Was real curious over them in general.'

'You saw Miss Mendoza?' Lev asked excitedly. 'Is she all right?'

'Er, yeah. Sure, kid, she's peachy.'

Lacey might not have known Abernathy for long, but she recognised when she was being flippant. Lacey wouldn't be surprised if Miss Mendoza was *not* peachy, at all, and that Abernathy was likely the reason for it.

Lev smiled happily. 'I'm so glad! It was Miss Mendoza who showed us how to get to Forty-three, you know.' He chatted away as he crawled up on to the stool and began messing with the grate's fastenings. 'Said in a mergent sea, or if we ever got scared, we should leave through there. It was a secret, though.' He made a soft *shhhh*ing noise, lips pursed. 'Only us big kids were allowed to know, and we couldn't tell. Not even to a grown-up.'

Forty-three. The number on the wind turbine, Voice said.

Without realising it, Lacey had moved even closer, and Abernathy joined her, both standing guard and ready to catch the kid if he came tumbling down. He gave a quiet grunt and one side of the grate popped free. The vent seemed to have shrunk since the last time Lacey looked at it.

It hasn't shrunk. You're just realising you're gonna have to fit through there and you're starting to freak out about it.

Lacey had a flashback to when she'd found her grammy crammed inside the understairs closet at their farmhouse, a space so cramped the old woman had contorted herself into weird, uncomfortable angles to fit.

Despite the chill, sweat broke out on Lacey's brow.

'Miss Mendoza told us there were other children who needed her. Mr Rocky cried when she left. *I* didn't, though,' Lev added quickly, glancing down at them to make sure they believed him. 'Not me. Nope. But Mr Rocky cried *a lot.* He was real sad.'

One final tug and the grate came off. Lev passed it down and Lacey set it aside. By the time she looked back up, the kid was inside the air duct, the soft bumps of elbows and knees thumping as he shuffled further in, his feet wiggling out of sight. 'Come on,' he said, the call faint and contained. 'It gets bigger soon, I promise.'

'You've got to be fucking kidding me,' Abernathy muttered, eyeing the vent.

Lacey's palms were damp and she felt light-headed, but Addison was waiting for them on the other side of that shaft and that was all the incentive she needed, right?

If Abernathy can fit, we can, too. But Lacey detected the hint of doubt beneath Voice's words and that sped Lacey's already pounding pulse into an even faster beat.

She turned to Abernathy. 'Age before beauty?' she asked, and she heard how weak and desperate she sounded. She tried working up some saliva in her mouth, but it didn't want to cooperate. Her throat ticked dryly.

Judging by Abernathy's frown, she'd been ready to argue, but one look at Lacey's face and she said, 'You're freaking out, aren't you?'

'No . . .'

Abernathy heaved a sigh. 'Fine. But this'll be *two* you owe me. Don't think I'm not counting.'

She hopped up on to the desk and Voice gave a low, appreciative whistle.

Look how agile she is, he said.

The filing cabinet *bong*ed as Abernathy's weight depressed the metal inward, and she sent Lacey a warning glance. 'Not one word about me being fat.'

She's perfect, Voice breathed.

Abernathy handed off the stool to Lacey, neither of them needing the extra height, and hiked herself up and over the vent's lip, squirming her way inside. It took some manoeuvring to wriggle herself fully in, her lower legs kicking for momentum, but she fitted. Within seconds, she'd slid out of view.

'It's honestly not so bad in here!'

Yeah, right.

Our turn! Voice said, gung-ho and chipper.

Lacey wasn't fooled. She had to wipe her damp hands on her pants before heading up.

Entering the shaft was like sliding into a coffin head first.

Dark, confined, cold. As she slid herself along, pulling with her elbows and knees and shimmying with her hips, she kept her ears trained on the soft, squeaky, scuffling noises coming from ahead. Sweat moistened the collar of her shirt and trickled from under her arms. Tight spaces had never really bothered her before, but since she and Abernathy had squeezed through the concrete window of turbine number forty-three and descended the ladder into the utter pitch-black of the unknown, the abiding darkness of this place was starting to mess with her head.

The air duct was too small for her to easily twist around and check over her shoulder. She felt terribly exposed. Anyone could sneak up behind her and Lacey wouldn't know it until a hand clamped around her ankle and dragged her backwards, fighting and screaming into the dark.

Her lungs felt as cramped as her body. Her harsh pants bounced and echoed around her head. She knew Abernathy could hear her – it would be impossible not to – and twice the woman asked if she was all right, and twice Lacey lied and told her she was fine.

A low, fearful moan stopped Lacey dead. 'What? What is it?'

'Nothing,' Abernathy said shakily. 'I just got a faceful of cobwebs.'

The woman's obvious fear conversely eased some of Lacey's own. 'Are you afraid of spiders, Abernathy?' she asked.

'No.'

They got moving again.

'Because you sounded kind of scared.'

'Shut up.'

Lev's whisper came from very far away. 'Almost there.'

Lacey didn't inhale a full, deep breath until she followed Abernathy out of the narrow duct and emerged into something that felt more like a crawl space.

She got on to her hands and knees.

A sudden flash of luminance hit Lacey square in the face. She twisted her head away, squinting her eyes closed.

'Sorry,' Lev murmured, and directed the flashlight's beam away from her.

'You had a light *this whole time*?' Abernathy asked, pissed.

'Yeah?' the kid said slowly.

'Why is it only making an appearance now?'

'We didn't need it until now . . .'

Now that Lacey could make out her surroundings again, she saw Abernathy was stretched out on her side, reclining on one elbow. Lev sat about ten feet away, knees tucked up against the stuffed raccoon cradled against his chest. He had a slim penlight in one hand.

'Well, *next* time, why don't you damn well—'

Lacey touched Abernathy's ankle, silencing her before she could let her annoyance get the better of her. She fell into a surly silence.

'Why get the light out now, Lev?' Lacey asked.

''Cause from now 'til we get to Addy, *no* talking. Not whispers, not nothing. I won't be able to say which way to go, so you'll have to watch me and Mr Rocky, 'kay?' Lev gave the penlight a little wave. It made the shadows jump around them and the shaft twist in on itself.

Lacey's stomach rolled sickly.

'And if the light goes out,' Lev said, soft and serious, 'you stop and be still. Be very, *very* still.'

Great, Voice whispered. *That's just freaking great.*

CHAPTER 10

Albus | Pilgrim

The woman on Bruno's radio directed them faultlessly. They saw no one else as they walked from the underground parking tunnel, through two solid steel doors to a concrete stairwell, and down, down, to an echoing lobby that matched the granite-grey exterior of the welcome centre above ground. Albus tried not to think about the distant, solid, ratcheting sound he'd heard as the steel door had clunked shut from somewhere above them.

'What *is* this place?' Bruno asked, his words reverberating back to him off the cold granite plinths and miniature walled channels that held artful beds of white-grey pebbles, all low-lit to perfection.

On one wall, engraved in gilt and spotlighted, a list of names ran in two columns headed by the grandiose title FOUNDERS OF ELYSIAN FIELDS. Amber stuck close to Albus's side as he tilted his head to read them. The girl had filled them in on what she could, which hadn't been much. She'd seen only four people, three of whom had been at the Inn (one of them Jake), the fourth the woman she believed was speaking to them on the radio and who'd been waiting for her when she'd originally arrived. Albus would consider it extremely suspicious if the *whole* thing wasn't already crazy. They were *underneath* a working wind farm in some secret commemorative galleria.

'Originally a bunker for the elite.' Jake shrugged with a wince. He noticed that Albus was perusing the names. 'Those are financial backers, mostly. Bunch of rich folk who got to bring their families down here when the shit hit the fan. Then, over the years, it changed into a sort of research facility. It's kitted out with not only a top-of-the-range radio-communications centre but a high-tech medical suite, designed to handle any and all surgical emergencies. And it never runs out of power. Not with the wind farm feeding everything.'

'What are you researching, exactly?' Gwen asked. Tallulah was slung over her shoulder, but her firearm was in her hand, muzzle pointed at the floor, the gun's safety on. They had been allowed to keep their weapons, which had allayed some of their fears.

'The voices, mostly,' Jake said. 'There's been a lot of work done on them here, unsurprisingly.'

While they'd wandered through the galleria, Albus had kept an eye on Hari, but the boy remained an unassuming presence, silent and watchful, as was his way. Albus noted the physical distance between Hari and Gwen, though, and didn't think he was imagining the frostiness that had settled between the two.

'How long have you been here?' Bruno asked, his head craned back to appreciate the square-cut ceilings and their fancy recessed lighting.

'Me, personally?' Jake asked, something close to alarm flashing across his face. Albus wasn't sure if anyone spotted it other than him and Hari. 'I'm pretty new, actually. So, not long,' he said.

The radio interrupted further conversation. 'Enough chit-chat, Jake. You're not a tour guide. Go ahead and take them to the Meeting Rooms.'

'This way,' Jake said, nodding his head for them to follow. They'd made the decision to tie Jake's hands again, and he hadn't fought it. As they each filed after him, passing through a double-wide set of heavy, elaborately tall doors that appeared to be constructed from dark-grained wood, Jake walked with both his wrists bound behind his back by duct tape. The richly furnished hall he led them along – more granite walls, a plush carpet runner laid down its centre and spindly, black-limbed, leafless trees in planters made of the same dark-grained wood as the double doors – boasted a number of paintings on either side, nearly all of them of important-looking men in suits and polo shirts.

'More rich investors?' Gwen asked, her head panning left to right as she took them all in.

Jake offered another awkward shrug. 'I'm guessing so. I haven't cross-referenced the name plaques with the list in the lobby.'

The granite surfaces and high, echoing ceilings were replaced with clean white panelling and charcoal-grey carpeting. Industrial-style steel doors cropped up more and more and the ceiling height had reverted back to a normal range. Amber gripped on to Albus's arm and leaned in to whisper, 'I think this is one of the corridors I came down.'

'When will Albus meet the person in charge?' Hari asked. He'd been quiet since they'd entered the stairwell that led them down into Elysian Field's cold bowels.

Jake made a soft, humming noise, considering. 'When they're ready to meet him.' His demeanour had changed significantly since they'd stepped inside the lobby. He seemed more relaxed, his gait loosening up as he'd wandered, his eyes no longer darting in nervous little tics.

He's on home turf now, Albus, Ruby said, as if reading his thoughts and reciting them back to him. *You're exactly where they want you.*

They. He pressed the flat of his palms to the sides of his legs, stilling their fine trembling. His throat was dry and in dire need of a drink, but he could hold on to his nerve for as long as it took to get Jasper back. Then they could worry about getting out of this place.

He turned and found Bruno's eyes waiting for him. His friend looked as uneasy as Albus felt, but he gave Albus a nod all the same and Albus could read his intended message without any words being spoken: *I got your back, brother. We're in this together.*

'What about the dude who shot our friends full of arrows?' Gwen asked Jake. 'When do we get to meet him?'

Jake had no need to reply, because just then Amber's grip on Albus's arm released and she gasped. At the same moment, Albus spotted it: the thinnest thread of sound wavering and bobbing its way towards them. It was the purest, happiest blood-orange Albus had ever had the pleasure of seeing.

'Jasper!' Amber cried, and took off so quickly it came close to making Albus's head spin.

'Hold it!' Gwen snapped, and lunged after her, snagging hold of the girl's wrist. 'We stick together. No exceptions. No running off.'

But, already, Albus and Bruno had picked up their pace, walks turning into fast jogs. Hari came close on their heels. As they converged on the Meeting Rooms, Albus made sure to hold the two teenagers back, allowing Gwen and Bruno through first, their weapons ready. At the sight of Jasper, sitting on the floor, a plastic toy doggy being enthusiastically chewed in one spit-covered fist and his chubby legs spread for an assortment of alphabet blocks scattered around him, Bruno, Albus and Hari halted dead. Amber and Gwen, however, kept right on going, and Albus let the girl go. Gwen and Amber dropped to their knees in front of the boy, both her and the girl sing-songing their hellos. Amber carefully picked Jasper up and he came to her willingly, gummy smile stretching his cheeks, his toy doggy dropped in favour of gripping hold of Amber's dark blonde locks.

'Hey, baby,' Gwen cooed, her gun stuffed, forgotten, into its holster. 'Hey, how you doing? Are you doing okay?'

Jasper gurgled at her, waving his sturdy arms at her as if to say, *Yes, ma'am. Me and my toy doggy are doing just dandy, thank you for asking.*

The rest of the sizeable room, dominated by a long conference table and a full complement of chairs, was empty of people. A number of areas branched off from the main one, each with a glassed-off partition and its own smaller-scale arrangement of conference table and seats. Albus spied projectors and presentation equipment in a number of them.

Bruno slowly lowered his gun, his look of confoundedness so great a bust could have been made of his head and face to forever demonstrate the definition of deepest confusion. 'What in the world is going on, Albus?' he asked, doing a slow circle of the Meeting Rooms and shaking his head at their apparent innocuousness.

Albus wished he knew. None of this made any sense, any more. If they had wanted only Albus, which is what Jake had initially said back at the Inn, why had the woman on the radio insisted they *all* come down here? A creeping, awful panic was building inside him, because Albus *knew* the one thing that linked them all; the one thing that made Bruno and Gwen, Hari, Amber and Jasper so special. And *no one* outside a chosen few should know what it was. No one.

He was beginning to think that entering this place had been the biggest mistake they could have made. One he wouldn't be able to take back. It wouldn't matter that Jasper and Amber had been safely returned to them if they were stuck down here, in a strange, unfamiliar and dangerous place, with little idea of how to get out again.

Hari was standing in one corner, underneath the solitary, black plastic domed security camera. He stared up at it as if trying to divine the meaning behind its existence.

'It is different here,' Hari said. The subdued quality of his voice was evidenced by the thinness of the honied strands sinking low to the floor, as if too wary to rise high enough and be noticed. 'Different to what I had expected.'

'What were you expecting?' Jake asked. He hadn't moved further inside with the rest of them but remained stationed at the Meeting Rooms' entryway. With his hands tied back and chest thrust out, he looked to be standing at attention, like a guard.

When Hari transferred his thoughtful inspection of the camera to Jake, his brow held the smallest of troubled frowns. 'Less silence.'

Trinity Hills' lot was empty but for a pond-like body of water in its centre and one other vehicle: a thirty-five-foot-long library bus. On its bullet-riddled livery, the slogan *Feed the Mind, Free the Imagination* arced over a line of cavorting books with legs and arms and googly eyes. Not one seemed to care that they'd been shot full of holes.

One man waited with the vehicle, lounging on the bottom step at the rear, where a sliding door was currently open. He was huddled up in a rain-soaked jacket and black leather gloves, looking drenched yet unaffected. His slicked-back hair was dark, almost black.

Whatever conversation the man had been having on the radio in his hand ended when the hearse showed up. Pilgrim made sure to pull up a good ten parking bays away from him. The hearse rattled and whined, sounding as if it were dying a slow and pain-riddled death, but Pilgrim didn't switch off the engine and he didn't put it into Park. Not yet.

'You should talk to them,' he said, leaning against the steering wheel as he watched the man watch him.

A pause. *Who, me?* Voice asked.

'Yes, you.'

Why me?

'Because if neither you nor Tommy can't get this gentleman to be friendly, I'll have to shoot him.'

'What's going on out there?' Jay's voice was dopey, his speech a little dulled. He'd been asleep for the last part of the drive.

'The library bus you told us about is parked up here,' Pilgrim told him.

'It's looking worse for wear, too,' Sunny added. She'd scooted over to the near-side window to get a better look at the man casually lounging on his step. 'He looks like the kind of clientele I'd keep a close eye on if he waltzed into my bar.'

Pilgrim grunted. She wasn't wrong. He looked like trouble.

Jay made a sleepy noise of interest. 'Albus or Addison?'

'No,' Pilgrim replied. 'Just Mr Slick here. Voice?'

All right, all right, I'm going.

'Tommy will try,' Tyler said, before Voice could get started.

Voice didn't seem to mind losing his chance at making a new friend, even though he must have sensed Pilgrim's annoyance with him. At least if Voice had reached out, Pilgrim would've been able to hear his side of the conversation. Now he'd have to trust that Tyler and Tommy would represent their interests in a way that wouldn't land them all in hot, skin-melting water.

Pain pelted the hearse's roof and the engine's whine competed with the watery gusts that swept across the open expanse of the lot, but all went quiet inside the car as Tommy attempted to open up a line of communication. Pilgrim studied Mr Slick closely, alert to any minute change in his expression, but he might as well have been looking at an oil painting. The man sat up straighter by the minutest degree, his gaze intensifying as his head turned the slightest amount, angling his ear a few degrees towards the hearse and its occupants. And that was all.

'He can hear something, all right,' Pilgrim murmured.

I'm not surprised, Voice said with a wince in his tone. *Tommy is being* really *loud.*

Without taking his eyes off the hearse, the seated man relayed a few words into his walkie-talkie. Then he put it away in a pocket. He lifted a hand and waved Pilgrim over, then relaxed back in a show of insouciance Pilgrim didn't buy for a second. But he put the hearse in Park and left the engine running anyway.

'Sunny,' he said, without turning around. 'Get behind the wheel. If anything happens, drive out of here. Tyler, you're coming with me.' He didn't need to look at Tyler to know she was about to protest. 'Tyler,' he said again. 'You're with me.' He opened the driver's door and got out. He pulled his collar up high around his face, though it did little to protect him from the storm's onslaught. He was already soaked through – being precious about getting wetter was pointless.

When he heard the shuffling of Sunny's movements, and the rocking of the car at his back as she climbed between the front seats, Pilgrim quietly closed the door. He waited for the *click* and *thunk* of the rear hatch to sound before stepping to the front of the hearse. A second later, Tyler joined him there in a slicker with its hood up.

'He's welcoming of voice-hearers,' Tyler said to him over the downpour. 'He called me and Tommy "sister".'

'You remember the last place we came across a guy wearing gloves like that?' Pilgrim asked.

Tyler nodded.

Two guys had chased Pilgrim and Abernathy out of that hospital basement in St Louis, bullets whizzing past their heads and chipping at the masonry all around them. Abernathy had claimed that the one guy who'd been wearing gloves had been hiding a tattoo on his hand. The spiral design of a voice-hearer. What a voice-hearer had been doing in a facility concerned with eradicating voices was anyone's guess. Pilgrim had never got to question him or his boss – a lady by the name of Vanessa Mendoza – like he'd wanted to.

'Let's be cautious and see what he has to say.' Pilgrim kept his hand away from the gun tucked under his belt, and he didn't miss the sheathed knife this fella had stowed in the top of his boot, or the fancy bow and quiver of yellow-flighted arrows he'd leaned against the side of the library bus.

The seated man smiled a welcome. He had the darkest eyes Pilgrim had ever seen, so dark you couldn't tell where his iris ended and the black of his pupil began, but they creased in a way that told Pilgrim he spent a fair bit of time smiling. That could mean he was a happy-go-lucky kind of guy, or it could mean he liked to smile while he cut the fingers and toes off people who looked at him wrong. Hard to tell quite so early in a first meeting.

'Hi there,' Mr Slick said. 'What can I help you folks with?'

'This bus,' Pilgrim said, loud enough to be heard. 'Where are the people who were travelling in it?'

Mr Slick nodded his head behind him at the Trinity Hills building. 'Inside.'

'And who did all the shooting?' Pilgrim asked, doing his own head-nod at the side of the library bus's bullet-riddled livery.

'Don't know. All I know is those on board survived.'

'And how'd you figure that?'

'I saw them leave it not too long ago. Heard a few of them talking, too. The one fella, though – he was a little "tongue tied", if you get my meaning.' He winked at them and grinned at his joke.

So Albus was alive and well? That's good, at least.

'There was a boy with them? Around fourteen? Spoke with an accent?' Pilgrim asked.

The humour died from Mr Slick's mouth and the fine lines around his eyes disappeared. 'Yeah, seemed to be. You know him?'

'No,' Pilgrim said, calm and even. 'Don't know him at all.'

The man was completely expressionless now. It was like

trying to read a rock. 'He seemed to be liked by the others well enough.'

Pilgrim bet he was. Tyler had been silent up to this point, but now she spoke.

'Did you get the impression he was a voice-hearer?' she asked.

The man opened his mouth to answer, but then his expression closed down even further. 'I don't know.' Water dripped from his nose, dripped from his chin. He seemed to suddenly realise that he was the one doing all the answering. 'What do you guys want anyway? Why are you here? And in a hearse, to boot? That's pretty wild.'

'It's reliable,' Pilgrim said, and had to wait while the man gave the battered hearse a long, considering look.

'Whatever you say, man. Whatever you say. So why the visit?'

'I'm here for my friend. The tongue-tied one.'

'Ah,' Mr Slick said, nodding in understanding. He stuck a thumbnail between his top front teeth and picked at something stuck there. 'Well, a girl came out and got him. They all seemed to know one other, so I wouldn't worry any.'

This is getting weirder and weirder, Voice said.

Yeah. Pilgrim was done talking to this yahoo. 'I'm heading inside. Unless you have any objections?'

The man spread his arms out wide. 'By all means, be my guest.'

'You don't have to check with whoever is on the other end of that walkie-talkie first?'

The man gave him a sly smile but said nothing.

'I'm leaving my two friends in the hearse over there,' Pilgrim continued. 'That's Sunny in the driver's seat.' He pointed her out to make sure the man didn't mistake her for some other woman in another hearse somewhere. 'She has a voice called Beck. She's one of us, so you don't need to worry any about her, either.'

'Gotcha, gotcha.' Mr Slick nodded. 'We're all one big happy family, right?'

'Sure,' Pilgrim said, without inflection. 'She also has an Uzi, in case you were wondering.'

'Noted,' Mr Slick said, and smiled.

Pilgrim looked at Tyler. She was staring at the guy as if she'd never seen this form of human before. Pilgrim wasn't sure if he had, either. He left him sitting where he was, not offering a single word of farewell, mostly because he disliked the man intensely but also because he had nothing else to say.

He returned to the hearse and leaned down to talk to Sunny through the driver's window.

'Stay here. Keep on eye on Jay while Tyler and I go in. If there are any medical folk inside, I'll send one out. I'm not sure if our resident library-user over there intends to hassle you,' he said, sending a look over his shoulder (Mr Slick was scratching his jaw as he watched Pilgrim and Sunny's exchange), 'but I'd keep your Uzi handy, just in case. I'm sure the bus won't mind catching a few more bullets if you think it's needed.'

Sunny turned off the hearse's engine and it was a relief to have the rattling whine die out. 'Did he say anything about Lacey or Addison?' Sunny asked.

I don't hear her over this way, Voice chimed in.

'No,' Pilgrim replied. 'I don't think she's on this side of the wind farm. Besides, the less he knows about our business the better.'

The tenseness around Sunny's eyes didn't ease, but she nodded to him and refrained from asking more questions that he likely didn't have the answer to. He was beginning to think he liked Sunny. Maybe not Beck, but Sunny was all right.

He left her there and went to the back of the hearse. The hatch was up. Tyler was inside, kneeling next to Jay and holding his hand. She was bent low over his head, whispering to him. Jay looked up at her with an expression that Pilgrim hadn't gotten to see too often over the last seven years. It felt almost voyeuristic to be witness to it.

'Tyler,' Pilgrim said, loath to break up their moment but fighting the need for them to get moving. He'd expected a battle with Tyler, an unwillingness to leave Jay, but she awkwardly crawled back towards Pilgrim and hopped out.

'Look after her,' Jay said to him. He still sounded too drowsy for someone who'd woken up more than ten minutes ago. Pilgrim reached in and rested a hand on his ankle, and even through the layers of Jay's pants and two blankets, he felt the heat pouring off him. Jay's face had been slick with sweat the last time Pilgrim had looked at him closely, but now it was bone-dry.

'I will,' Pilgrim promised, wanting to set Jay's mind at ease. 'Drink some water and rest up. We'll be back.'

Once the rear hatch was closed, Tyler was off and walking, marching her way across the flooded lot, leaving Pilgrim to catch up. He was starting to understand why she hadn't argued about staying with Jay – they were heading into Elysian Fields. A sister facility to St Louis Hospital, itself a scientific and medical installation, with doctors and nursing staff and supplies. A facility Tyler had blown to smithereens while the entirety of its population, women and children alike, were still inside.

He'd drawn level with her as they were circumventing the large pond-like puddle.

'No explosions today,' he told her. 'Got it?'

She passed a brief look his way. 'I'm not here for that. I'm here to help you, and Lacey, and Abernathy. Tommy and I swear.'

Pilgrim couldn't ask for more than that. He looked back over his shoulder at the man lounging on the library van's steps. Pilgrim cupped his hands around his mouth and yelled over the wind. 'Which way did they go?'

'Stick to the ramp!' Mr Slick called back cheerfully. 'They went in the tradesmen's entrance!'

They passed under the raised traffic barrier and started down the sloping ramp and into the cover of an underpass – a square-shaped tunnel that was large enough to accommodate a full eighteen-wheeler with its trailer attached. The incline wasn't insignificant, and Pilgrim had to wonder how deep it went. He could only see as far as the reinforced steel roller-shutter door that was currently down.

Neither Pilgrim nor Tyler spoke as they drew nearer to this dead end. There was a single door to their left which read 'Main Reception'. Pilgrim tried it. It was locked.

'Now what?' he asked, looking around the space. There was absolutely nothing here. A low metal guardrail ran along both sides of the sloped roadway (to prevent any collision damage to the concrete walls in case of driver error), a slatted roller-shutter, the locked Main Reception door, a security camera bolted in a metal safety shroud high up near the ceiling, and the two of them. That was it.

'Should we be doing something?' Tyler asked.

A red light blinked on and the security camera swivelled ten degrees to the left. Pilgrim stared into its lens, feeling a chill raise the hairs on the nape of his neck as the dark lens stared back at him.

An echoing, mechanical *clank* and the roller-shutter door shivered in place, rattling. With a motorised *whir*, it began to rise.

That's not ominous at all, Voice said.

Pilgrim waited for the shutter to clear his head and walked beneath it. Tyler was a step behind. As soon as they cleared the door, it stopped with another loud rattle and reversed direction, lowering to a close at their heels.

For an unnerving count of five, Pilgrim couldn't orientate himself. They stood in a lit section of the roadway, but the concrete ramp disappeared into blackness. No more lights illuminated their way. They could have been in a never-ending service tunnel on some colossal spaceship carrier for all Pilgrim knew.

Another distant section of the underpass flared into brightness, and seventy feet away sat a wild dog on its haunches. It had planted itself exactly centred in the roadway, its fur a shiny black in the harsh, artificial lighting.

Actually, I think it's a normal, domesticated dog, Voice murmured, and Pilgrim experienced a sense of déjà vu so profound he wanted to pinch himself to make sure what he was seeing was real.

The sections between where Pilgrim and Tyler stood and the dog sat lived in darkness, cut off and left to drift in the nothingness of space.

'Motion-activated,' Tyler said.

She moved forward and the next section flickered to life. And that's how they proceeded – hopscotching from dark to light, leaving the darkness in their wake even as they stepped into blocks of white illumination. The dog waited patiently for them, sitting at attention, its soft brown eyes curiously watching the two humans approach. It waited until they stepped into its section, stood, turned left and padded away, slipping through a propped-open doorway.

Pilgrim and Tyler shared a look and then followed.

Three minutes and thirty-two seconds passed as the dog led them deeper. Pilgrim knew this because he counted the seconds, as well as the number of footsteps it had taken, noting each turn at the intersections of every corridor, which he would need to reverse when coming back the same way. They crossed a cavernous airplane-hangar-sized storage area, an impressive sight and a highlight of their tour. No planes were stored in the vastness of its space. Instead, it was occupied by row upon row of warehouse-sized storage racks. Shelves thirty feet tall stacked with an array of boxes, containers, tubs, cans, bottles, crates. Each bay numbered and meticulously organised. Pilgrim had glanced along each row as he silently counted off the seconds in the *click*ing and skittering of dog claws. There were tools, engine parts, piles of clothing in different sizes. Household products, learning materials, food. The list went on and on. Everything an underground facility would need to survive.

One more thing caught his attention as they followed their furry guide. There were no people. Not a single soul had crossed their path.

Where is everybody? Voice whispered.

They walked a final, long corridor, glass walls taking the place of industrial concrete. Floor-to-ceiling sheets of glass, some blackly opaque, others frosted but transparent, the insides of which revealed ghost-like desks and chairs and blurry-edged whiteboards. The place was permeated with the freshly-laid carpet smell of new offices, sharp and manufactured, yet the hint of something astringent and foul lurked beneath.

The dog trotted past all of these without deviating once to investigate an enticing scent or mark a bit of territory. It went to an unremarkable-looking red door. Behind the black-tinted fish-tank glass of this room, there were so many twinkling lights and glowing screens swimming around inside that Pilgrim couldn't decide where to focus first.

The dog whined and scratched to be let in and a murky shadow detached itself from a desk and crossed the room. The door opened to a plump, mousy-haired woman with a nose piercing. She was a stranger to Pilgrim. It wasn't this woman who the dog went to – nor was it any of the small team of people who manned the computer monitors and tech arrays. The dog quickly scooted around the plump woman's legs and padded straight over to an old woman sitting in a comfy office chair.

'Hello, *Sonnenblume*,' Matilde said, smiling a welcome at Pilgrim. 'I didn't know if you would make it.'

Chapter 11

Addison | Lacey

A whole lot of time had passed since Addison had been left alone with Riko in Lev's nest. Every few seconds, Addison would glance at the shaft Lev had scampered into and her foot would jiggle with impatience and nerves and something else that made her pulse throb too fast in her neck. How long was it going to take to get Lacey and bring her back here?

Not that *here* was a good place to be. Lev's nest was better than being left in a single airduct tube with limited routes of escape, but Lev still hadn't been pleased about leaving them *anywhere* in these tunnel systems. And Lev had passed on their anxiety as if handing over a buzzing hive of bees for Addison to hold on to.

'Nest' was really the only word Addison had to describe the service cubby Lev had left them in. It was a recessed, low-ceilinged ventilation snug – and when she said 'low-ceilinged', she meant she could reach up and easily touch it, even with her butt sitting on the floor. And when she said 'floor', she meant a grated platform with a single hatch that opened to reveal a ladder that went down, down into the darkness. The grates were covered in snuggly bedsheets and blankets and a pillow, which Riko had put dibs on.

Lev had told them that this was their secret store. In case

anything Worse happened than Bad. At some point in the past, they had snuck a box of supplies up here, which included food packs, bottled water, a trove of silver-wrapped candy bars, two flashlights, warm clothing and a partridge in a pear tree. Okay, not the partridge-and-tree bit. Addison didn't even know what a partridge in a pear tree looked like, it was just something Lacey liked to say whenever Alex listed stuff. It had always made Alex roll her eyes and pull a face, which made Addison laugh.

It was impressive, the amount of stuff Lev had carted up here. They'd had to push or drag everything through yards and yards of ventilation ducts.

In addition to the more essential supplies, a stack of books leaned precariously in one corner and a naked plastic doll with no head lay butt-up next to a crayon drawing of Mr Rocky. The raccoon was standing on a beach, facing the ocean, the sun a bright, waxy yellow in a fluffy-clouded, blue-scrubbed sky. It was very pretty and Addison didn't mind admitting she was a little jealous of how good it was.

The nest felt pretty cosy with everything packed into it. When Lev had been in there with them, "cosy" had become more "too close to not be kinda awkward".

'It's been five minutes,' Riko whispered from her pillow-seat across from Addison. Her whisper was more breath than sound (Lev had told them to *be quiet* and *not move*). 'I'm going to click the flashlight off for a while.'

Five minutes? Was that all it had been? Addison really needed to get this time-clock thing learned. It was getting embarrassing.

A *click* sounded and the nest went so velvety dark Addison could have reached out and stroked its soft, black pelt.

For every second her foot jiggled (she could count those), a rustle of sheets and clothing sounded from across from her. A few foot-jiggles later and Riko shifted again. Maybe Riko wasn't as comfortable with the dark as Addison was. Addison scooched over, inch by inch, moving across the space to Riko's side.

'What're you doing?'

Addison didn't answer but settled down, the body-heat emanating off the girl warming Addison's whole right side. It felt nice in the chill. A cool draught had been passing through the nest since they'd got there. Addison could understand why Lev had brought so many coverings and an extra layer of warm clothing.

As more time and foot-jiggles passed, Addison became aware of a vague red glow under their butts, seeping through the gaps where the blankets hadn't fully covered the grates. When she peered downward, the emptiness of the drop falling away made something flip upside down in her stomach, and she looked away quick.

A duller, even fainter glow came from deep inside one of the two ducts that fed into their cubby. The duct Addison hadn't ventured down yet.

'It's like we've been gobbled up,' she murmured, mostly to herself, but also partly to Riko and Fender.

She could just make out the angle of Riko's head as it turned towards her.

'We've been swallowed down into the biggest of bellies. Inside a beast *so big* it can eat an entire building if it wanted. And it's all glowy red down here because it's all blood and flesh and insides – like when you open your mouth and look right in. And these ducts must be its veins. We're crawling round the veins, trying to get to the heart. What does that make me and you, do you think?' she asked Riko.

The older girl stared at her, the pinkish shine of her lovely-shaped eyes unblinking.

Addison waited for her answer.

'Blood clots?' Riko finally said.

Addison frowned. 'Is that bad?'

'I don't think it's good.'

They fell silent for a while. Surprisingly, it was Riko who broke it.

'Why doesn't your voice speak much?'

Addison's eyebrows hiked up in surprise. 'Fender speaks. We wouldn't know Lacey was even here if Fender hadn't been singing.' Her eyebrows reversed course and came firmly back down again, because everything had happened so fast – Fender hearing Lacey, and Lev being sent to fetch her. Addison hadn't really thought about how it had all been communicated so quickly between Lacey, Lev and Riko, all with very few words being spoken aloud. 'You hear a voice, too?' she asked, although it wasn't really a question. She already knew the answer.

Riko studied Addison – as best as she could in the dimness anyway. 'Yes, I hear one.'

'What's its name?'

Another pause. 'Riko the Second.'

Addison grinned. 'That's so perfect.' Her smile faltered, dropping off one side, then the other. 'I kinda have two, but I think Chief is angry with me. He's been going missing a lot.'

'Hm. You're likely growing out of him.'

'Huh?'

'It happens.' Addison felt the brush of Riko's shrug against her shoulder. 'A lot of the littlies go through a similar stage. You're kind of old for it, to be honest. What are you? Seven?'

Addison's spine snapped straight. 'I'm *eight*,' she corrected, slightly above a whisper, and Riko shushed her with a stern look. They paused to listen, ears cocked towards the ducts.

A distant whistling howl trembled as it rose and fell, threading through the tunnels as if seeking out their hiding spot. It came from very far away – Addison wasn't sure if her ears were playing tricks or not. Neither she nor Riko moved until it slowly faded away and Addison didn't take a full, deep breath until she felt Riko take hers first.

Probably just the wind, she thought.

After a slow minute (maybe?), and when the whistling howl didn't take up again, Addison and Riko went back to their hushed conversation, heads bent towards each other.

'Miss Mendoza said it's a pre-language thing,' Riko whisper-said. 'Before children develop speech, they use other senses to understand the world. So images, feelings – sometimes just a presence or sense of touch – work better for them. It's easier to communicate that way, so that's how a child's early voice manifests.'

Addison didn't know what 'manifests' meant or who Miss Mendoza was, but she didn't want to interrupt to ask.

'Most of the littlies don't even call their voice a "voice". Seb's three and his doesn't have a name yet, it's just pretty lights and *boop*ing sounds. Sometimes he says it floats around like sparkling bubbles. Laura's is a warm tingle that lives under her tongue. You said this second voice of yours is called Chief?'

Addison scrambled to keep up, her brain shooting off fireworks, crackling with too much information. She nodded mutely.

'Do you see him more than he speaks? Does he appear to you as if he's real?'

'Um, yeah. But only I can see him. I know he's not *real*-real.'

'You do *now*. Which is probably why he's been going missing. Your other voice – Fender? – are they the talker? Fender's probably taking on the main role now. No one really ever has more than one voice, Addison. They're just different versions of the same thing – as the littlies get older they'll eventually outgrow the more childish ones, too.'

Addison looked around for Chief, a low-lying panic fizzing up through her chest. She didn't want him to be *entirely* gone. He could be silly and overly sensitive and she had to send him to Time Out sometimes, but he was *hers*.

She'd never really thought about any of this stuff before. Chief had always been there, since before she could remember. Snuggling down with her at night, crooning softly in her ear if she'd had a bad dream and woke up sweaty and whimpering.

She remembered him running around a lot when she was little. He'd loved it when she chased after him, and she'd cackled with glee when he chased her back. Her mom had always said she was full of mischief when they got like that. Fender, though, Fender came later. When she'd started running her finger along the lines her mommy had read in her storybooks. And when her mommy had left and Addison had been all alone in that big, creaky house, Fender had come with words and grown-up advice. When she'd needed them the most.

Fender was quiet, but she felt a solid presence back there, behind her ear. Fender was around. Fender wouldn't leave her. Addison mentally prodded for a reaction, zeroed all her attention on that one spot where Fender lived, waited, chewed on a knuckle (because her foot was sick of jiggling), until she couldn't bare the silence a second longer.

'Fender, why aren't you saying stuff to me?'

She felt the unfurling, the gentle expanding outward, until Fender was keenly aware and tuned into her.

I'm very sorry, Addison. It's just so distracting here.

Addison looked around the nest. There was *nothing* going on right now, apart from sitting and waiting and a preoccupied Fender not talking to her. It was turning her buzzing hive of nerves into grumpiness.

I mean distracted by the littlies, Fender explained. *They're so noisy, and I can't help but listen. Even now, I hear them. I know who's hungry, who's sleepy, who's giggling at a story they're being told. I hear them all.*

Addison strained her ears. Heard a faint ticking sound, which could have been the *click* of too-long nails on metal. The *click* of something slinking closer on all fours, saliva dripping from a snout. Addison froze, gaze locked on the two shaft openings, eyes flicking from one to the other. The *click*ing slowed, slowed, and ceased altogether. Then, nothing.

She licked her dry lips.

They're like you and Lev, Fender was saying. *They* all *are.*

'But Lacey said kids shouldn't be able to hear anything,' Addison said, feeling argumentative for some reason. 'It's impossible, that's what she said. Alex, too. You gotta be a teenager to even *maybe* get to hear one. And even then, not for sure.'

How could Lacey know? She only knows you. Does she have more nieces we don't know about?

'No,' Addison muttered.

'It's not impossible,' Riko murmured quietly. 'Miss Mendoza has worked with every prepubescent child in Elysian Fields. She told me she believed *all* new children born will eventually hear a voice in one form or another. And it scared her, because it meant that every doctor and scientist out there who was working to stop the voices would never succeed. Not as long as babies are being born. The voices are never going away. And anyone who doesn't or can't hear one will eventually become obsolete.'

'Obsolete?'

'Won't have a place in this world any more.'

'Wow,' Addison breathed. 'Is that really true? Wait, wait.' She pressed her palms flat to her knees, struggling to keep her excitement in check. 'Is Miss Mendoza *here*? Can I take Lacey to speak to her?' She looked around as if the woman in question might pop into existence if she knew Addison was looking for her.

Riko's head lowered, shaking slowly, her sleek, black hair shimmering with faint burgundy highlights. 'No. She told the Board what she thought was happening and, well, they didn't take it very well.' She looked up to meet Addison's eyes, her face a grave slash of shadows and slanted, disapproving brows. 'They sent her away. They claimed she couldn't make such sweeping statements without *real* evidence to back it up. A couple of dozen children here didn't mean *all* children *everywhere* were the same. She left. And now I'm glad she did. She wasn't here for what happened.'

'You mean with the emergency lights and' – the last word was let out in a breathy, non-existent whisper, because saying it aloud was like letting a poisonous snake out of her mouth, all ready to strike – 'the *ghosts*?'

The *ess* of *ghosts* was a fading hiss between her teeth when a streaking shadow burst from the shaft on the left. Addison gasped, flinching back into Riko's shoulder, almost knocking the older girl over, stifling a yell as Chief leapt at her legs and wound his arms around her knees, big black eyes gazing up at her, limpid and moist. She received a quick, fleeting image from him of a glistening, slug-like creature with blank, cloudy eyes and a pointed mole-rat face, its teeth bristling and incisor-sharp. She shoved it away with a reproving smack to his shoulder.

'You scared me!'

'*Quiet.*' Riko raised herself to a crouch, her eyes so intense on the shaft Chief had flown out of that the initial jump of fear Addison had experienced at his appearance surged back full force.

Addison grabbed up the flashlight Riko had dropped. Got her feet beneath her. Held the heavy tube ready to strike. The howling whistle from earlier blew a colder, stronger draught through their nest and tendrils of Addison's hair tickled her nose. She shivered a full-bodied shiver, her teeth grinding closed, and Chief pressed tighter against her thigh, his clawed hand grasping on to her knee in a death-grip.

From inside the shaft came a gliding thump. Scrapes. Harsh, raspy breathing.

The slithering scrapes slid so close Addison felt their vibrations in the grates beneath her. She lifted the flashlight higher, muscles powering up for a skull-cracking blow. A shadow rose up, dark and lumbering, its head emerging from the duct, and Addison brought the flashlight down with all her might.

Riko gasped out her name and Fender yelled, *No!*, and Addison didn't know if Fender diverted the downward swing, or if her own reactions were so fine-tuned she did it herself, but the flashlight missed Lacey's skull by less than an inch. And then none of it mattered any more, because Lacey had collapsed half out of the shaft, gasping for breath, and rolled on to her back, her arms opening to Addison, her eyes shining unshed tears as she said her name with so much love and relief that Addison's eyes blurred with tears, too.

She threw herself at her aunt and the pained grunt that came out of her was the most wonderful sound Addison had ever heard.

The girl clamped on to Lacey like a koala, arms and legs wrapping around her at neck and waist, her weight on top of her close to squashing all the remaining oxygen out of Lacey's lungs. The position hurt her bruised shoulder from her earlier fall, but Lacey laughed and hugged Addison so fiercely she felt every breath her niece took, every rise and fall of the delicate birdcage of her ribs, and every thud of her rapidly beating heart. She was *so* alive that Lacey's laugh became a sob, and she stifled it by pressing her mouth hard against Addison's shoulder.

'I'm digging the reunion,' Abernathy whispered from somewhere down by Lacey's feet. 'But could you move your asses so me and the kid can come in?'

With some manoeuvring, and a helpful shove or two from Abernathy, Lacey scooted herself and Addison further into the little den of space she'd fallen into. Another girl, older than either Addison or Lev – just a few years Lacey's junior – had lit a larger flashlight and was motioning for everyone to keep the noise down while simultaneously ushering everyone inside. Addison ended sitting askew in Lacey's lap, hand braced on her shoulder, grinning down into Lacey's face so widely Lacey could see her back molars. She couldn't help but grin back.

'Hey,' Lacey said.

'Hi,' Addison said, giggling under her breath, and it was such a wonderful sound that Lacey impulsively gathered her close again. She felt the girl's arms fasten around her in a ferocious squeeze, and it was painful and good and Lacey didn't want it to end. She kissed the side of Addison's head.

Finally, when the girl's embrace didn't let up, Lacey gently wiggled her fingers into her side, above her waist, where she knew the girl was ticklish, and got the desired result. Addison squirmed and snorted a louder giggle, pushing away from Lacey and sitting up.

Lacey took the opportunity to give her a thorough once-over. 'You okay? Are you hurt anywhere?' She passed her hands down her arms and over her legs, checking her from head to toe. She appeared fine, if dishevelled and in need of a good wash and hair-brush. Lacey gently pushed the girl's curls back from her face and stroked her thumb over her forehead. 'Tell me you're okay,' she pleaded.

'I'm okay. I pinkie promise.'

I'm getting an all-okay from her voice, too, Voice threw in, and Lacey felt the glow of pleasure coming from him.

She bit her lip, her smile turning tremulous. 'Good. That's real good.'

'I knew you'd come,' Addison whispered, smiling all over again.

'Always,' Lacey agreed, and tilted the girl's head to press a tender kiss to her cheek. 'I'd always come for you.'

In the only space left available – the rest taken up by a cardboard box stuffed with what looked like microwave dinners and plastic bottles, along with a stacked collection of children's books – Abernathy and the two kids were conversing in low tones.

'Who's your other friend?' Lacey asked Addison, nodding to the teenaged girl.

Introductions were hastily and quietly given. Lacey had to bite back a smirk when Addison asked if Abernathy was Lacey's sidekick.

'At this point I'm starting to feel more like a babysitter,' Abernathy said dryly, casting a glance around at their company.

Riko was a solemn-faced East Asian girl who paid close attention to everything Lacey and Abernathy did and said – she didn't appreciate the babysitting comment, Lacey could tell that much. Lacey hadn't been faced with this level of suspicion from Lev, so assumed it must be Riko's default setting and not to be taken personally.

'You got here just in time,' Addison told her. 'A bit longer and Lev or me might not've been able to come back for you.'

Lacey would have to circle back to that. First, she had important questions that needed answering. 'You were with Albus,' she said to her. 'That's what Jay told us. On a library bus.'

Addison's eyes lit up. 'Is Jay still awake?'

'Awake?'

I think she means alive, Voice said.

'Oh. Yes, he's awake. He's with Pilgrim and our other friends.'

Addison gasped. 'So Pilgrim really *isn't* in my backyard any more?'

Lacey smiled. It was a lot to take in, she knew. 'No. Pilgrim is awake, too. There's a lot of stuff we need to catch up on, but first, tell me where Albus is.'

And Hari, Voice said grimly.

'I *was* with Albus on the library bus. But then we got split away.' Addison made a dividing motion with her hands: palms together, then spreading apart. 'That's why we gotta go. He doesn't know about the ghosts here.' She said this last part with a grave expression that Lacey knew her niece reserved for times when she was being 'very serious'.

'Lev already mentioned these ghosts . . .' Lacey said slowly.

'I know what you're thinking. Both of you,' Riko said, dark eyes assessing Lacey and Abernathy in turn. 'You think we're a bunch of kids with overactive imaginations. But they're real.'

'Aren't ghosts by their very nature *not* real?' Abernathy said, because of course, she would. 'What I don't get is what's a bunch of kids even doing down here? By all accounts, it's not a very kid-friendly place.'

'We live here,' Riko said.

'I got brought here,' Lev piped up. 'By my daddy.'

'Some of us came here with family members. Others were left here. Some of the littlies – the youngest – have always been here.'

'So it *is* a facility?' Lacey asked.

Riko frowned slightly. 'No. It's home.'

'So where are the adults?' Abernathy asked.

Riko glanced at Lev. He turned his head from her and rested his cheek against the top of the raccoon's head. Riko placed a hand on the back of the kid's neck, her slim fingers stroking through his hair. 'They're all dead,' Riko said quietly.

CHAPTER 12

Pilgrim

'You're dead,' Pilgrim said, rather stupidly.

Matilde looked down at herself and patted her chest and belly as if to make sure she was, in fact, alive. 'No, my dear. Not quite yet. You of all people should know how tricksome death can be.' She fussed the dog sitting adoringly at her feet, rubbing its ears and scratching beneath its chin with her arthritic hands.

Matilde wasn't dressed as Pilgrim had last seen her, in bundled layers of clothing topped off with a thick terrycloth bathrobe. She was in high-waisted jeans, hiking boots and a turtleneck knitted sweater. She was also a thousand miles away from the snowbound cabin where he, Ruby and Albus had left her with the Flitting Man's people closing in and an X-ACTO knife in her hand, ready to end her life before the Flitting Man caught up to her.

'Did Ruby know you were still alive?' Pilgrim asked, the question coming out harshly. He felt horribly betrayed, and he wasn't sure why. He had met Matilde once, had spent little more than an evening with her, and yet she was one of the few people in his life who had been honest and real with him. And here she was, having made him believe she was dead and gone for *four years.*

'She did and she didn't,' Matilde said, quite straight-faced.

'Still speaking in riddles, I see.'

She broke out in cackles, the worn lines of her face wrinkling charmingly. 'Jonah would have known, yes, but dear Ruby would have had her doubts, I think.'

'She must have known,' Pilgrim argued. 'Jonah wouldn't have been able to keep such a secret from her. Voice can't keep anything to himself – that's not how this thing works with them.' He waved an agitated hand next to his head, and by the sheer animation of it he knew he was letting his anger get the better of him.

Tyler was a silent presence by his side, observing everything in minute detail, he was sure.

'I haven't spoken to my voice since the night you left my cabin,' Matilde said. 'And it hasn't spoken a word to me.'

That shut Pilgrim up.

She gave him a sad smile. 'Can you imagine yours doing such a thing?'

No, he could not. Voice wouldn't last a day before caving.

Voice didn't comment, but Pilgrim felt him listening intently.

'We couldn't take the risk,' Matilde said. 'If the Flitting Man heard us, if he suspected we had tricked him this whole time, then this whole terrible charade would not have worked. We had our parts to play, too – Ruby, Jonah and I.'

Pilgrim's heart beat its mad *thump-thump-thump* in secret. Questions wanted to burst out of him, a thousand-a-minute, but he stamped them down because this woman had deceived him and he wouldn't play this game with her. It was far too weighted in her favour for it to be fair.

Matilde settled back in her chair, getting herself comfy. The dog, a male opposed to the female bitch Pilgrim had met on a cold wintery night, laid its head on Matilde's lap and submitted to her petting. The name of the breed came back to him in a single lightning-strike of remembrance.

Doberman! Voice crowed, and would have snapped Pilgrim's fingers if Pilgrim had let him.

The steady stroke of Matilde's hand on the Doberman's head became meditative, rhythmic, and Pilgrim felt the slowing in his chest, a soothing calm seeping through him.

'First, you must understand how the Flitting Man works,' Matilde explained, her hand never ceasing its long, smooth pets. 'He is not brash and bold. He is a coward, plain and simple. He is the snake in the garden, tempting you away from all that is honest and good. He is the worst of everything inside us: he is vindictiveness and spite, greed and jealousy, and he can sow those seeds with a mere word or thought, because he *knows* us. Better than we even know ourselves. He has had centuries of practice. Centuries of refining and tweaking. And if introduced in the right environment, at the exact right time, what he sows has the capability of spreading like a poisonous weed. This crossroads we find ourselves at?' she said, and tapped her toe off the floor, a quiet *click* that marked her point. 'This divergence in our paths? It has been a most fertile ground for the Flitting Man to plant his hateful seeds, and they have been *flourishing*. You have seen it first hand, have you not?'

Pilgrim thought back to his run-ins with Charles Dumont and his gang, with Posey and the half-mad Gunnar in Memphis. Not to mention the doctors and medical staff at St Louis Hospital who had ramped up their inhumane experiments in response to their fears over the Flitting Man's encroaching influence. Yes, he had seen it first hand.

'That doesn't explain this charade you mentioned,' Pilgrim said.

'As he is an insidious creature that slithers his way around without being noticed' – she weaved her hand through the air, her cadence rising and falling like the slinking of a snake – 'he also hides like one. He has always been difficult to find. The only way to lure out such a creature is to make it feel so safe and so confident that it no longer fears to show itself. And so, we first started by removing one of his biggest opponents. Me. Charade number one.'

'You died.'

Matilde smiled at him. 'I died. I vanished. *Poof*' – she clapped her hands together – 'I was gone. Jonah and I only really had one night to settle our plans. Back during that dark winter's evening when you came to visit.'

'I remember.'

'Our plan had many threads, all of which could have become tangled or severed at any moment, but it was a plan that we hoped could work, with a little help. And so, we began sowing our own seeds. My dearest Ruby wrote her letters and corralled support wherever she could while evading his attention. All the time waiting for him to make his first moves. We were the first to name him the Flitting Man. Did you know that? It was Ruby who came up with it. She was a writer at heart and excellent at using words – she knew how to make them powerful, yes? She knew how to make the heart sing and emotions swell. When rumours of this *Flitting Man* began gaining traction, she and Jonah knew his arrogance would begin to grow as his followers grew. After my "death", I even admit to feeding into the unrest a little myself. I helped spread my own tales of this Flitting Man and his desire to unite voice-hearers. It's an ethos that I share, in as much as, yes, those with voices had to find a way to come together if there was ever to be a future for us.'

Pilgrim felt the need to sit down. 'The way you say it makes him sound like it isn't all bad, the things he's done. The things people have done and *are* doing in his name.'

Matilde gave him the kind of look reserved for a favourite nephew who'd just dropped the Thanksgiving turkey on the floor. 'No one is *all* bad. You should know this by now, *Sonnenblume*. Good things spring from bad situations *und umgekehrt*. Same with the voices. Are you next going to tell me you think the Flitting Man is somehow responsible for the voices being here? I've already told you why, if you recall.'

'You told me we needed them.'

'*Ja*, it is as simple and straightforward an answer as I can give. I know you do not like it, but there it is. Everything that happened, we did to ourselves. We died in droves so that many more things could *live*. The earth, the plants and the creatures that crawl and swim and fly upon it, and, yes, that even includes *you*.' Matilde crooked a swollen-jointed finger to Pilgrim, to Tyler, and around to each person working at their tech stations. 'This new world will belong to the likes of you and your children and the voices they will hear, because we cannot go back to our old, selfish world where we each lived in our own separate spaces, alone and afraid, turning our face from every atrocity. Do you understand that there can be no more "Us" and "Them"? No more, I say! Not in *any* capacity.' She said it sternly, the creak of her aged voice rising to an uncharacteristic bark. 'And if we let the likes of *him* begin this new period of human history with *more* death and destruction? With more slaughter and the burning down of people's homes and families? Then we will live in the ashes of those deeds and we will never escape them. Not ever. We must do better. We must *be* better. For each other. We will all be deserving of it this time, yes?' Her words rang with authority.

The tapping of keyboards and the soft beep of computer inputs had ceased, and the room was silent as Matilde slowly, tiredly, settled back in her chair. The bright passion in her rheumy eyes dimmed to a mild, twinkling ember. She went back to gently rolling the Doberman's soft ears between her fingertips.

Pilgrim needed that moment of stillness to gather his thoughts, to circle back to something she'd said to him right at the start of their conversation. 'Feeding into the unrest,' he said. 'When you first saw me, you said you didn't know if I'd make it. You've been here in Elysian Fields for how long?'

'Ach. I am terrible with timeframes. Bonnie?' She said to the plump young woman with the nose piercing. 'How long since we arrived?'

'We've been in the general area a while now, but here, specifically, it's been . . .' She did some quick calculations. 'Four weeks and two days.'

'Thank you, dear. We've been here for four weeks and two days,' Matilde said to Pilgrim. 'I am useless with all these doo-dahs and doo-hickeys' – she flapped a hand towards the electrical equipment, more specifically the radio and telecommunication tech – 'but we've been monitoring the channels. Fed titbits of anonymous intel to people in the voice-hearing camps that have sprung up. I would have liked every research facility shut down and the suffering inside them stopped, but that will be an ongoing mission for somebody else.' She gave him a shrewd look, her thin lips pursing in a puckered starburst. 'Oh, do not think I don't know what you did at that hospital in St Louis—' She stopped and quirked an eyebrow at him. 'Is Hoyt still your name? Or are you insisting on being mysterious and answer to something else now?'

Pilgrim's cheeks warmed a little in embarrassment, which only ignited his ire all over again, because he couldn't remember the last time he'd been made to blush. 'I go by Pilgrim.'

She considered it, mouthing his name silently, her lips smacking as if she were taste-testing it. '*Ja*, I like that much better, I think. Much better. Well – Pilgrim – I am aware of what happened in St Louis. Of what went on *here* a short time before I arrived and the firm suspicion that *he* was here not long before that . . . I, myself, have travelled many miles and done many things – not all good – in order to get to this place, and I did it all because there was no one else who could but me. *Me*, do you hear?' She made a point of meeting the gaze of everyone in that room (with Matilde, her people numbered six strong, dog not included). 'There are no riddles here now. I state merely the obvious when I say that what we hear is only a voice. And they may push and coax and bully us, but they cannot *do*. Not without our permission. What the Flitting Man does, or tries to do, is blasphemous. Neither God nor snake, nor anything in between, should be allowed to take away free will.'

It began to dawn on Pilgrim how ruthlessly single-minded this old woman was. How dented and repaired and tarnished her moral compass had become in order to get to this point. She had admitted to playing a part, however small, in fabricating, bolstering and spreading rumours of the Flitting Man. On top of that, she claimed she hadn't been alone in her actions.

'And Ruby?' he asked, his jaw tense and tone tight. His stomach hurt, right in the middle, as if someone were slowly pushing a long, wickedly sharp knife into him. 'What was her part in this?'

Here, Matilde's countenance softened. 'Why, Ruby had the biggest charade to perform of us all. She allowed herself to be captured. She knew the Flitting Man would come for her, same as he had for me. That he would be unable to stay away. She was a brave girl to do that alone,' she said quietly and with such aching fondness. 'To face him and not break. She gave the ultimate sacrifice to him, offered it of her own free will. You remember what I told you about that? That it will only be through the greatest of sacrifices that all will be saved? Well, that girl offered hers up, and it hurt her far worse than any injury inflicted upon her body. Far worse even than her own death.'

Pilgrim didn't want to ask, didn't want to hear about Ruby's suffering in any form. Hearing of it pained him. It would always pain him. 'What did she sacrifice?' he whispered.

Matilde smiled sadly. 'Her brother.'

Pilgrim was reeling. As shocked as he'd been to see Matilde, and disconcerted to hear of the machinations the old woman had been a part of all these years, he couldn't believe that Ruby would betray her own brother. She wasn't capable of it.

'No, she wouldn't do that. She loved Albus more than anything.'

'Of course she did, *Sonnemblume*.' Matilde said it with so much compassion that Pilgrim found himself relaxing, the tense muscles in his neck easing a notch. 'She also wanted a future for him. Wanted all of you to have a future. Albus's gift is so incredibly rare, you see; an absolute empath who can see when true death has touched a person and left them forever changed. They have passed to the other side, you see – however briefly – and they know what awaits them there. Even if they do not recall. They leave a part of themselves behind – it is impossible not to. But that, in turn, leaves an emptiness inside them. Ruby was one such person, and Jonah would come to fill that emptiness within her. She always understood that Albus could be the one thing that would attract the Flitting Man's attention above all else. Someone who was able to find others like her, someone who could ensure the longevity of his existence in such a sparsely populated world.

'So she sent Albus away. Told him to gather these special people to him like a shepherd herding his flock, and he did it willingly because Ruby had told him to. Albus loves and trusts his sister – why would he question her motives? But the whole time, Jonah knew these people would be the nectar to the Flitting Man's bee. He would fly to them and surround himself with them as a king surrounds himself with an honour guard. The ultimate protection. The perfect safety net. And when he was fat and ripe with his own hubris, his arrogance would make him do the one thing I've been waiting all these silent years for. The snake would finally, finally reveal itself.'

'He has,' Pilgrim told her. He couldn't quite read the small smile playing around her lips – it was part self-satisfaction and part sorrow. 'He has revealed himself. The Flitting Man is here.'

'I know. This entire section of the facility is locked down now. There is no way out unless we open the doors. Which isn't going to happen.'

Pilgrim's stomach muscles tightened, that invisible knife sliding ever deeper. 'You're going to kill everyone?'

Matilde's eyebrows shot up. 'What? My, no, dear. I was rather hoping you could tell me who he is.'

CHAPTER 13

Addison

Elysian Fields' main northern entrance – both supply and worker access – were through the wind farm's visitor and welcome centre: the area comprised a state-of-the-art, pre-cast concrete-and-glass building clad in highest-grade granite, with two-storey reception foyer, a compact sustainable-energy museum, meeting rooms and offices, and a bespoke road system, parking lot and sculpted landscaping. Earlier, Addison had seen the brochure and made Riko read parts of it out to her.

That was the way Albus, Bruno, Gwen and Hari would have entered by. And where Pilgrim would have headed, too, after Lacey had left him.

All five of them were tucked inside Lev's nest, their legs pulled up and backs flat to the metal walls. It was a tight fit. Elbows prodded elbows and knees were pushed up against knees. Lacey and Addison sat side by side, and Riko, Abernathy and Lev sat opposite them – although Lev mostly crouched in the mouth of the shaft they'd entered through.

'Lev's tunnels lead to the atrium,' Addison was whispering (everyone had been warned again by Riko to keep as quiet as possible). 'That's where we need to pass through to reach the others. So we'll be mouses, like I'm a mouse sometimes. Fender will help me. Chief, too, I guess,' she added. She was finding that Chief had been more a hindrance than a help recently – he'd almost made her cave Lacey's skull in with his latest antics. 'Voice can help Lacey, Mr Rocky can help Lev, Riko the Second can help Riko, and whatever yours is can help you,' Addison said to Abernathy.

Abernathy pulled a face. 'None for me. I'm all on my lonesome.'

'Oh. Then *we'll* look out for you, 'kay?'

One side of Abernathy's mouth smiled at her. 'Sure, kid. Why not?'

'There's no need for you to go at all,' Lacey said to Addison, and Addison rolled her eyes because she knew Lacey would suggest going on ahead without her. She could be very predictable sometimes.

Addison patted her aunt's raised knee. 'Albus and Bruno are my friends, Lacey. Gwen and I suppose Hari, too. They saved my life and you should be grateful because I'm your only niece.'

'I *am* grateful. I just—'

'And I can take care of myself,' Addison went on. 'I was on my own for a long time after Mommy left, and I did fine.' She only ever brought up Mommy as a last resort.

'She did fuck up that dude outside,' Abernathy said to Lacey, and Addison wanted to hug her for being on her side but didn't because Abernathy was kind of scary.

'I *did* fuck him up,' Addison agreed. 'Does that mean I stomped his knee? Because I did. I stomped his knee good.'

Pinkish-tinted teeth flashed at her as Abernathy grinned. 'It most definitely does mean that.'

Beside her, Lacey sighed.

'Bad things always happen when we split up,' Addison said to her aunt quietly. 'Like with Alex. We shouldn't split up no more.'

Lacey heaved a bigger sigh, so big Addison imagined all the air being sucked from the ventilation systems in one massive vacuum-suction. 'Okay. Fine. But you stick next to me like *glue*. Got it?'

'Got it, loud and clear. Copy and ten-four. So we're mouses. Small and fast. *You're* a mouse,' she said to Lacey. 'And *you're* a mouse,' she said to Abernathy. 'You're both sneaky and smart. Be not there.' And because Riko seemed the most nervous, Addison leaned over and grabbed her hand and squeezed it in both of hers. 'We can do it, Mouse-Riko. I know we can.'

Riko gave her a little frowning smile. 'You're such a weird girl.' But she squeezed Addison's hands in return, her fingers strong and cool.

'And we run and hide if we hear the ghosts?' Lev asked in a whisper, their eyes big and round as they looked at each person stuffed into their overly crowded nest.

'Are you sure it's not the wind you're hearing?' Abernathy asked. 'There's a storm raging outside, if you hadn't noticed.'

'We're not stupid. It's not the wind,' Riko said, meeting Abernathy's gaze head on, and Addison got nervous because Abernathy stared straight back at her, something dangerous settling in her expression.

Lacey murmured Abernathy's name and whatever made her look so dangerous was gone, like a switch had been flipped, and she lifted a hand in conciliation. 'Fine. Not the wind, then. We'll take your lead on it.' She gestured with the same hand for Riko to go on ahead of them.

Everyone tucked their legs in close as Riko bumped and squeezed her way past to the open shaft. 'Lights out,' she told them, and clicked her flashlight off, stowing it away in a back pocket.

While Lev had led Addison through the early sections of tunnelling – because they were an adventuring space pirate (their words, not Addison's) and had it all mapped out – Riko would take over the next part until their shaft hit the outer corridor of the atrium, and then through to when they found the next set of ventilation shafts entering the northern arm of the facility. Lev and Riko said they'd never known the ghosts to physically enter the vents leading into their southern arm of Elysian Fields, but that didn't mean they weren't in the vents elsewhere. It was best they were extra-double-careful from here on out.

Abernathy went in after Riko, Addison third, then Lacey. Lev brought up the rear.

This air vent wasn't such a tight squeeze, but it was awkward. They had to crawl, and Addison's neck ached from holding her head angled up. They had three flashlights between them but Lev and Riko kept theirs off. Riko said she could see by using the faint wash of reddish lighting that filtered through at intervals from the access grates.

Abernathy's head turned back Addison's way and she whispered, 'Riko says we've passed the barricaded doors.' Addison nodded and checked behind to see if the message had been relayed to Voice and Mr Rocky. From the very back, Lev lifted a thumbs-up. Lacey, though, made no response. Addison could hear her breathing; she sounded winded.

Addison twisted further around. 'You okay?' she whispered.

'Yes. Yeah. Don't stop.' A rapid tap to her shoe urged her onward. 'I'd really like to get out of this coffin sometime today. Keep moving.'

Addison moved it. They reached a vertical section of venting and, in turn, each of them descended it, using the inset foot- and hand-holds. The next part was narrower again and they had to lie on their stomachs to belly-crawl through. It wasn't tight exactly, but it felt a whole lot snugger. Lacey's sucking, wheezing breaths got worse. Addison tried to hurry, but she could only go so fast with Abernathy blocking her way.

A few minutes later, Abernathy stopped. Addison heard a faint scratching noise from up ahead and lifted up as far as she could to see. Riko was doing some torso-twisting and bent-arm manoeuvring.

She's unlatching the vent cover, Fender told her.

The darkness lifted and the vent's walls gained a new paint of rouge as Riko opened the hatch and pulled herself through. Pushing hands encouraged Addison to scoot after Abernathy and she squirmed and belly-crawled a little faster. As she emerged from the vent, arms waited to lift her out. Behind her, Lacey practically slithered limp-noodled on to the floor. One look at her aunt's sweaty face and heaving chest and Addison winced in sympathy.

The hands steadying Addison (Riko's, she now saw) released her and the older girl went to help Lev. They set about replacing the grate.

Addison glanced down at her feet, surprised. She hadn't been prepared for carpet. It was thick and spongey under her soles. The walls were no longer concrete grey but were smoothly finished and painted in . . . some other colour – it was hard to tell what because the red emergency lights were doing their job over in this area, too. Maybe they were mating and giving birth to litters of lightbulbs, like bunnies do.

A skitter of what sounded like loose gravel reached their ears. They all froze, heads turned. Addison put her back to the wall, her eyes flicking left and right. Nothing but carpeted corridor. The loose gravel settled and everything was tomb-silent. Riko stepped forward to be in everyone's eye-line and pressed a finger over her lips to silence any talk, then tapped her temple. From here on out, they were to converse solely through Mr Rocky, Fender, Riko the Second and Voice.

Riko pulled out her flashlight and cut through the red-washed gloom with a powerful white beam. She swung it every which way as she led them right, and everyone filed after her. She left the hall and hugged the curving wall of a spacious communal TV room with the biggest screen Addison had ever seen mounted above a decked-out entertainment centre with tech she couldn't name. A set of plush sofas was arranged at optimal viewing angles around it. Next, a games room, and it took all of Addison's restraint to not touch the scattered balls on top of a soft-fuzzy-felt table, though she did stroke the table. The further they went, the more the stench of cold ashes filled Addison's nose. Burnt plastics, burnt metal, burnt fabrics and fibres.

They left the rooms and came out on to a wide boardwalk and an immense open space. Neither Riko nor Lev had prepared her for the sight, and Addison's feet stopped working as her shoes moved from cushioned carpet to cool, hard paving stone.

A full-scale town square opened up before her. A mini-village, with buildings – *real* buildings – made of brick and stucco. There were trees, too, lots of funny-looking knobbly trees with huge, blade-like fronds sticking out of their tops.

'Jesus Christ,' Abernathy muttered, forgetting about the Stay Silent rule.

A nearby trickling of running water had Addison turning in a half-circle, and she found a burbling stream six yards to her left. It ran along a narrow gully beside the boardwalk until it met a miniature pond. It was scummed over with blackish algae and moss, but it was beautiful in its own way.

Dead streetlamps marked walkways and bridges. A clock tower and a *park* with real swings and slides and a monkey bar. Picnic tables and paths, a bandstand and a snack stand. There were food wrappers and drinking cups left on tables and littering the ground. An overturned trashcan had belched up its garbage-innards, as if Mr Rocky the raccoon had rooted through it. A baseball cap lay flattened on another pathway. Someone had laid out a plaid blanket on a patch of fake grass, a book spread open and face down, as if waiting for its reader to return and pick up where they'd left off. On a paved pathway, Addison spotted a bicycle tumbled on its side.

And, of course, there were all the bodies. So many they took up most of the space. A mass of burnt, blackened people, their limbs poking out like insect legs, piled three or four deep and heaped up in the centre of this pretty, small-scale town. Addison couldn't count high enough to cover them all, and maybe that was a good thing.

The smell was much worse here. So strong Addison could taste burnt ashes in her mouth, flaky and dry. Now she understood where it came from.

A cold hand closed around hers and squeezed so tightly it hurt. When Addison looked to her right, Lacey was staring dumbly at the grave (was it still called a grave when you couldn't dig a big enough treasure hole to fit everyone?), and even in the ghastly red emergency lighting she could see how pale her aunt was, how dark and horrified her eyes.

Riko was holding Lev's hand as she walked cautiously out on to the stone boardwalk, stepping off on to the fake grass to skirt along the edge of the picnic-benched park. Their heads were scanning, their postures tense and alert. Both had taken out the sharp paring knives they'd picked up from the break room before they and Addison had first entered the ventilation system.

There must be a lot of ghosts here with so many dead, Fender murmured.

Lacey and Abernathy shared a look over Addison's head, and her aunt dropped Addison's hand to pull her rifle off her shoulder as Abernathy unholstered her gun. They bracketed Addison front and back as they moved after Riko and Lev.

There's no other way through but forward, Fender said.

Which meant skirting the heaped corpses as best they could. Which Addison didn't think was possible. They stretched right across the centre boardwalk, some piling into a second ornamental pond to the west (this one much larger than the first she'd seen), and to the east stacked three deep against the soot-blackened clocktower.

With a sick, sinking feeling, Addison realised there was no going around. They were going to have to climb over.

Chapter 14

Lacey

Lacey looked at the interlocked, melted quagmire of human flesh and bone blocking their way. It had been possible to progress a short distance by stepping-stone hopping between corpses, enough room between each one not to have to touch any of them. But that wasn't going to fly any more. Jammed together, the bodies had created an unavoidable dam. Up and over was their only route.

We've seen some messed-up shit together, Lacey, but this might take the biscuit.

It was the stuff of nightmares. Lacey checked on Addison, but the girl was being surprisingly resolute. Her mouth and nose were screwed up in disgust and a small crease furrowed her brows, but she was dogged in her determination to navigate this hellscape without any help from Lacey or Abernathy. And, honestly, Lacey couldn't have been prouder of her.

I bet she's seen some messed-up shit, too, Voice said.

They'd come across a number of bodies that had been dragged off the pile and eaten. Missing hands, half-eaten limbs, a human foot that no longer looked like a foot but rather a regurgitated hunk of offal. No one commented on their findings and they'd moved quickly on.

Lev wasn't doing so hot. He had thrown up once already.

It had been a surreal moment, watching the kid heave his way through the purging process but trying to be as silent as possible while he did. The rest of them had stood guard around him, weapons ready, until he'd finished. Nothing had appeared. No sounds, other than Lev's muted gagging.

So far, these ghosts were a no-show.

Let's hope it stays that way.

Lev sniffed and wiped his sleeve across his streaming nose. He didn't make a whimper, but, jeez, he must have known some of these people, had lived with them and eaten meals together. Likely Riko had, too.

And they're doing it to help us.

They both must be protected at all costs.

Bodies rose in steepness until they were heaped to a little over waist height. On Lev, they were heaped as high as his chest. Abernathy tapped the kid on his shoulder and pointed to her back, leaning in to whisper: 'I'll carry you.'

He nodded his thanks, but Riko stepped in and pointed at herself. She'd do it. Lev sent Abernathy a smile anyway and shrugged, then went to the other girl as Riko squatted down for Lev to hop aboard. Riko straightened and hitched Lev higher. She may have been slight of build, but Lev's extra weight didn't seem to faze her.

Don't think of them as the bodies of people who'd once been alive, Voice advised. *Think of them as stacked sandbags in a bunker.*

Lacey's first step broke through a solid crust and sank into something softer, wetter. She covered her mouth as her nostrils flared wide, the overwhelming stench of sweet, spoiled meat and open bowels making her gorge rise. She swallowed thickly and placed another foot. The *crunch* it made was awful.

More *crunch*es came from the others as they waded in, arms out. Lev clung to Riko's shoulders, doing a backwards version of Mr Rocky hanging off his front.

Down by Lacey's feet, a woman's black, calcified face had

been pushed into the ground. Her open mouth was packed with sludge and her one visible eye-socket stared at nothing, its missing eyeball roasted until it popped.

Lacey moaned.

Don't look, Lacey. Keep your eyes on where we need to go.

She trod on a thigh, used it as a step, and bit back a scream. Some of the husks still wore clothes, though the material had scorched and melted into flesh. There were a number of doctor's lab coats. A few were wearing medical scrubs. Lacey grabbed hold of sleeves, shoulders, anything to pull herself up and scramble to the top. She had to shut herself off from the noises as her boots landed on backs, on overripened stomachs, probably on faces. It was like trampling over a horde of scarab beetles, their hard carapaces cracking open with each stamp.

Don't think about it, Voice said tightly, and she didn't know if it was revulsion or nausea that clipped his words. *Just keep going. Don't stop.*

Abernathy had moved ahead of her, stance wide, arms out for balance, wading through them like she was navigating boggy swamp-water. Her feet sunk between bodies, but she wrenched them free, as if from a mudbank and nothing more. Addison was close behind Abernathy. Being light and compact was probably an advantage.

Lacey managed six steps before something caught her ankle. She desperately tried to stay upright but teetered too far off-balance and had to drop to one knee. She put a hand out to stop a full-face fall and felt it sink into something slimy and cold.

A miserable groan escaped her.

Lacey squeezed her eyes shut and jerked her ankle free. When she looked back, she saw two unattached blackened fingers had come along with it. A second stiff-fingered hand snagged her calf, and she jerked away from that, too. She lurched upward, made it to her feet, shambled three more sinking steps and dropped again, this time landing on both hands. She tried to push out of the fall as soon as she hit but something shot up her wrist and scurried up her body.

She shrieked. She couldn't help it.

Rat! Rat rat rat!

With one came more, and a stream of vermin swarmed out of their carcass homes. Lacey lurched back and sprang to her feet, her balance miraculously regained. Up until this moment she had been happy that the only light had come from a series of low-wattage, crimson-bulbed emergency beacons dotted around the central atrium. But now the dimness was her worst enemy, and every darting shadow became a rabid rat coming at her, needle-sharp teeth snapping, red-gleaming eyes hungry. She shambled into an ungainly half-run, which lasted all of four steps before she was down again. Her face *smoosh*ed against something so disgustingly wet her gag reflex triggered and she heaved noisily.

She felt a number of hands pulling at her.

Abernathy's voice panted in her ear, 'Come *on*, for fuck's sake! Get up!' and she grunted as she heaved Lacey backwards, physically sliding her bulk across the bumpy, scratching, death-juice-soaked remainders of roasted corpses. A rat scurried up Lacey's leg and she back-handed it away so hard it was catapulted into the dark. She tried to help Abernathy by pushing with her feet, but she was mostly too panicked to do much more than flail.

They both tumbled back, airborne for a second, Abernathy's hand buried in Lacey's shirt, and landed in a gasping, breathless muddle, the other woman cushioning Lacey's fall.

Lacey almost burst out in hysterical laughter, thinking back to Abernathy's promise that she'd be the human mattress the next time it was needed. As far as Lacey was concerned, the debt had been paid in full.

Abernathy squirmed out from underneath her and pulled herself over the last layer of dead bodies, a soldier belly-crawling through no-man's-land, desperate to be out of it, and Lacey scrabbled after her, all attempts at being quiet clean gone from her head.

It was only when she was panting for breath, sprawled out on her back on a corpse-free piece of boardwalk, with Abernathy doing the same not five feet away, that she heard the howling. In a clear, bright moment of clarity, she relaxed, because she knew it was surely the storm finding its way inside somehow, the gale-force winds hurtling down the empty corridors to create such a haunting ululation.

But then another howl joined the first, and then another, and another, until there were seven, eight, nine, even more of them, all howling together, all getting louder, coming closer, and terror tore through her because Voice whispered—

Ghosts . . .

and Lacey thought, no. Ghosts didn't exist. But wolves did.

CHAPTER 15

Pilgrim

Pilgrim stared at Matilde, speechless for perhaps the first time in his adult life. 'What do you mean, tell you who the Flitting Man is? Don't you know?'

Matilde favoured him with a bemused smile and gently pushed her Doberman's head off her lap. The animal immediately lowered itself to the floor and curled up. Matilde brushed non-existent dog hair off her jeans and brushed her hands together. 'How would I know?' she answered simply. 'I've never seen or spoken directly to him. And my voice hasn't seen him since, oh, long, long, long before anyone in this room was an amorous gleam in their parents' eyes.'

'So what were you planning on doing?' Pilgrim asked, feeling at such a loss his words came out short and sharp. 'Pull the fingernails out of any and all of Albus's friends until they confess?'

'I am sure I would have worked it out eventually,' Matilde said. 'And I have one of my own watching them closely. Jacob knows what signs to look for. And, if all else fails, I have no doubt that confronting him in person would make him break character.' She lowered her voice to a mock stage whisper and gave Pilgrim a wink. Her eye disappeared into a fold of winkles. 'He's yet to learn I'm here.'

'It's the boy,' Tyler said. 'Hari.'

Matilde's attention swivelled to her.

'Hari is the Flitting Man.'

Matilde's damp, rheumy eyes studied Tyler. 'Are you sure? And I mean one hundred per cent sure. Because if you aren't, this could get tricky.'

Tyler's eyes flicked to Pilgrim and the edge of doubt in them made him pause. *Wasn't* she sure?

'I mean, it *was* Hari,' Tyler said. 'When I met him.'

'And when was that, dear?'

'A – a few months ago.'

'Hm. And what about you?' Matilde asked Pilgrim, and he again became aware of the keen intelligence in her eyes, rheumy or not. 'When did *you* meet him?' she asked.

He breathed in and out slowly, because he knew his answer wasn't without its own holes. 'It's been a few weeks, I'm not sure how many. And only briefly. At the time, I had no idea who he was.'

'So, we are *not* one hundred per cent sure. Bonnie, show me video feeds again, please.'

Matilde rose from her seat and went to stand behind the nose-pierced woman's computer. A bank of monitors was arranged on the desk before her. With a quick flurry of keyboard presses, the main monitor changed to an enlarged live feed of Albus, Hari, a young teenager holding a baby and bopping him up and down on her hip, and three other adults, one of whom appeared to have his hands tied. They were in what appeared to be a conference room, some of them sitting in the comfy chairs at the long, executive table. A big black man was pacing back and forth behind the teenager with the baby. They all seemed to be deep in animated conversation. The man with the tied hands appeared to be at the centre of it.

'If that's your man in there, he's taking some heat,' Pilgrim said.

'Jacob will be fine. I've known him since he was a teenager. He is very loyal.'

Looking at the feed, Pilgrim had a sudden idea. 'Do these security cameras run throughout the entire facility?'

'Bonnie?' Matilde asked.

Bonnie swivelled her chair to face them. 'Yes. I mean, technically. But the other parts are all offline and shut down. We don't run main power through there.'

'Could you?' Pilgrim asked.

'It is a tomb in there, *Sonnenblume*.' Matilde's tone was sombre. 'It is a place for the dead now.'

'*Can* you get them running? Lacey's in there.' At Matilde's questioning look, Pilgrim said, 'The girl you carved for me.'

We don't know for sure she's in there, Voice said, but he didn't say it with much conviction. If that was where Addison was, Lacey was in there, all right.

'Ah,' Matilde said, with a slow, knowing nod. 'Yes. Bonnie, get the cameras online, please. See what you can do.'

Bonnie shot Matilde a surprised look, but she recovered quickly. 'Um, sure. Give me a sec.'

It actually took Bonnie forty-six seconds, but whatever magic she weaved with her tapping fingers, the screens of all four monitors began lighting up with static shots. She cycled through them, and Pilgrim found himself leaning so far over her that he could smell the soap in her hair.

'Stop there. What's that?' The top-right panel was showing a vast open space that had picnic areas and a bandstand. It caught his attention because he'd first mistaken it for a static shot of somewhere outside. But no. It was definitely an interior.

They built a village park underground? Voice said incredulously. *Was this whole place built for YouTube celebs and Facebook millionaires in case of a nuclear fallout or something? Wait, what's that? Something's moving in there.*

Pilgrim peered closer at the image, and Voice was right. It wasn't a static image. There were figures moving around. 'Can you get closer?' he asked.

Bonnie clicked her mouse and the camera zoomed in.

'There,' Pilgrim murmured, relief coursing through him. 'There she is. Abernathy, too.'

And she found Addison. Look!

Pilgrim's relief was short-lived. He frowned and leaned in even nearer, his nose in danger of bumping the screen. 'Something isn't right. Why are they backing up like that?' He straightened abruptly when the tiny figures began pulling out weapons. He jabbed a finger at the monitor. 'Where is this? How do I get there?'

Bonnie checked the feed information. 'It's at the very centre of EF, south of where we are right now. But you can't get in. It's all sealed off.'

'Unseal it.'

Bonnie threw a nervous glance at Matilde, and Pilgrim spun to face the old woman.

'Unseal it.' It wasn't a request.

'It's not that simple,' Bonnie was trying to explain. 'It's not something we can just open remotely. We disabled the doors so they couldn't be tampered with.'

'Can you get them working again?'

'I . . .' Another quick glance at Matilde, but Matilde was being unusually quiet. 'Maybe?' Bonnie offered tentatively.

'You're coming with me. Let's go.' Pilgrim rolled Bonnie's office chair back and pulled her out of it. The empty swivel chair rattled away on its casters.

She grabbed for a small canvas kitbag, roughly the size of a hardback book, and muttered defensively, 'Wait, wait. I need my tools.'

He marched her across the room, the steel band of his hand wrapped implacably around her arm, and yanked open the door. He didn't tell Tyler to follow – right then he didn't care what she did.

'Pilgrim.'

The power in Matilde's voice stopped him dead, snapped his head in her direction.

The Doberman was on its feet and standing alert at her hip. 'If you choose Lacey, you will have to deal with the consequences, *mein Sonnenblume.* There is no way out of this place for the Flitting Man. Know that. *Believe* it. This is where the old world ends. It *must* end.' She looked every one of her advanced years, as if she had lived three lifetimes over without any rest. Fatigue hung off her, marked off her years in every line of her bent body and crooked, weathered hands. The dog pressed its flank against her leg, and she seemed to draw strength from it. 'Good luck,' she told him. 'I hope you aren't going to need it.'

He ran, his grip a manacle tethering Bonnie to his side, and she had no option but to run with him.

CHAPTER 16

Lacey

Wolves hunted in packs. And that was all Lacey knew about them. Alex had once advised her and Addison to yell and wave your arms at a bear if you ever met one in the wild, but she had never covered wolves in her impromptu wilderness lessons. So Lacey fell back on what she knew.

She unslung the rifle from her back and expertly slid the bolt back just far enough to glimpse the chambered round. She flicked the safety mechanism over and brought the rifle up, tucking the stock into her shoulder, locking it in tight.

The lighting would be a major handicap.

She glanced around, looking for a vantage spot, somewhere with height, but there was nowhere suitable nearby and nowhere she had time to get to. She started to back up instead, her plan to hopefully make it all the way to the north wall before they were flanked.

Do wolves flank? Was that a thing they did? Oh, Alex, I really wish you'd covered wolves in your Wild Animal Rescue 101.

She called Addison over to her, needing her niece to stay close, and Riko and Lev came with her. The puny kitchen knives the two of them clutched seemed ridiculous now that she could see them properly. This whole rescue mission seemed ridiculous in hindsight. Pilgrim and Albus were doing just fine while Lacey and her group were in deep fucking shit.

The wolves' wild howls were like a dirge, a rampant call to arms. They were getting so close it was difficult to determine which direction they were coming from.

Maybe we should run? Voice said, his fear racing like a hot current through Lacey's veins.

'Lev?' Lacey called over. 'Where's the vent at?'

'Back there,' he said, pointing. It was all the way over by the north atrium door, past the sizeable dry fountain in the shape of a ballerina. Not close. But getting closer if they kept backing up.

On her other side, Abernathy had pulled her gun from its holster. Her eyes worried the shadows, straining to pick out movement. 'Is this a bad time to tell you I only have four bullets left?'

'They're called rounds or cartridges. Not bullets. They're not bullets until after they've been fired.'

'Well, fuck me. I stand corrected.'

'Here they come,' Addison called, dropping into a defensive crouch.

It was the shine of their eyes that Lacey saw first, and that was good enough. She breathed out slowly and set her eye to the rifle's sights. A shine of eyes on her right, launching high as it leapt up the pile of corpses.

She pulled the trigger, smooth and firm. The stock kicked back into her shoulder, and she relished its solid, connective punch. She might not understand the nature of wolves, or what had happened to these poor, burnt bastards, but she understood how primer ignited the gunpowder in a cartridge, how the effect of the propulsion shot the bullet down the rifle's bore at immense speed. She understood the trajectories and speeds a bullet travelled and its singular, destructive power. A moving target complicated things, but the rest was simple physics. And Lacey was precise. A splash of water as another wolf came at them through the ornamental pond, and she waited a split second for it to turn just so, for its torso to open up to her. The bullet slammed the animal in the chest, flinging it back as if punched by a fifty-pound mallet. Lacey worked the bolt-action and it slid like glass, chambering the next round. She swung it left, panned quickly to her next target – they were coming fast now, closing in. She fired again, watched a third wolf jerk backwards and go down. Re-chambered. Shifted target.

Pandemonium had broken out. Abernathy was yelling and firing her gun. On her other side, Riko and Lev had abandoned their knives for now and were throwing whatever came to their hands at a wolf that was attempting to flank them. God, the beasts were *huge*. She'd assumed they would be average dog-sized, but these creatures were mastiff-big.

Lacey!

Lacey shrank lower behind her rifle, getting down and compacting herself in, just an eye and a gun and a trigger-finger. It was hard to tell friend from foe now that the fighting was moving to close quarters, but Lacey trusted her instincts.

She lost all sense of time as she targeted, aimed, fired. Targeted, aimed, fired. Two more wolves. One tried to crawl closer. She shot it in the head.

That was five. She thought she'd got five. How many *were* there?

She panned back around, wanting Addison in her periphery where she could see her, and that second of distraction was all it needed. The wolf landed before her and its jaws snapped closed. Her arm would have been bonemeal if she hadn't got her rifle in the way, teeth clashing on metal in its place. Lacey was almost jerked off her feet as the beast viciously shook its head, the rifle's barrel clamped in its teeth.

Let it go, Lacey! Let it go!

It went against every one of her instincts, but she released her rifle and she tumbled backwards as the wolf pulled in the opposite direction, its hind legs skidding out from under it. The animal dropped the gun, its snout wrinkling back as it snarled.

Its eyes seemed to follow her hand as she inched it to the top of her boot and the flip knife she kept there. Her fingertips brushed its handle. The wolf leapt and the red emergency lights shut off and total darkness descended.

Tracking the wolf's leap in her mind, Lacey ducked aside, the bulk of the wolf colliding with her shoulder instead of her chest. Teeth snapped at the side of her head, gnashing at nothing as she thrust herself backwards and away. The beast's weight crushed down on top of her, slamming her to the floor. A flood-lit stadium level of wattage switched on, bank after bank, filling the atrium with dazzling bright lights, and the wolf cringed away, whining deep in its throat as it squeezed its eyes shut.

The animal was so crushingly heavy that Lacey couldn't free her pinned arm, couldn't shunt it off her, and no amount of blazing lights, or Voice yelling at her to move, were going to stop it ripping her face off when—

It opened its eyes.

It was so close Lacey could see the tiny pin-pricks of its pupils, could feel its hot, fetid breath baste her face. With bared fangs it lunged for her throat, teeth snapping on air as Addison grabbed its tail from behind and *heaved* the two-hundred-pound creature off her in one go. An impossible move for a girl her size. *Impossible.*

Unless she'd had help.

Pilgrim! Voice had never sounded so happy.

Pilgrim appeared over her, his shadow blessedly shielding her smarting eyes from the glaring light-source, and fired his gun at the wolf as it turned on Addison and leapt at her. It collapsed in a whining heap at Addison's feet and Pilgrim stepped clear of Lacey to unload a final shot into the creature's skull.

That was closer than close, Voice breathed. *Oh my God, my blood pressure.*

'*My* blood pressure,' she corrected breathlessly, and sat up.

Lev was collapsed on his butt not far away, his shoulders

heaving with his fast, gulping breaths, but he was whole and unharmed. Riko was hunched over next to him, looking dazed as she looked around at the new people. Pilgrim hadn't come alone. A face she didn't recognise was doing something over by the open atrium doors – she was a harried-looking, heavy-set woman with the most striking green eyes Lacey had ever seen.

And a nose ring, Voice added.

Tyler was there, too, and she was being tended to by a furious Abernathy.

'What the fuck was *that*?' Abernathy was practically shouting as she whipped off her jacket and wrapped it haphazardly around Tyler's blood-drenched arm. Lacey only caught a brief glimpse of it, but Tyler's hand looked partly mangled and pretty torn up. A dead wolf lay six feet from them, the hilt of what appeared to be a screwdriver driven into one of its eye-sockets.

Tyler winced bravely through Abernathy's ministrations, her face so pale as to be almost translucent. The red splash of blood on one cheek was garish in comparison. 'It would've ripped you in half, Abernathy. I didn't have much of a choice.'

'Yeah, well . . .' Abernathy fell into silence as she finished tying the impromptu bandage, fashioning the jacket's sleeves into a makeshift sling. 'Just don't think this makes us friends,' she muttered.

'I know.'

'Because it doesn't.'

'I know. *Ouch*.'

'Sorry.' Abernathy carefully readjusted the sling.

Shaking her head in amusement, Lacey turned back to Pilgrim and Addison and found them eyeing each other. She couldn't help but laugh at the sight. It was so priceless! The child who shot the man, and the man who came back from the dead. That had to be a Western ballad, right? If not, she should write it immediately.

Voice laughed, too. *You've gone loopy*.

'I'm alive. We're *all* alive,' she said, and laughed again, positively giddy with the feeling. 'It's a damn miracle!' One she *must* thank God for the next time she said her nightly prayers. Please remind me to do that, she thought to Voice, who snorted, because he knew as well as she did that there was no God.

Pilgrim smiled down at Lacey and offered his hand, and she took it. He pulled her effortlessly to her feet and she hugged him out of sheer gladness – a good, hard squeeze – and let go of him to pull Addison into a hug, next. The girl happily returned it.

'Me and you are gonna have a talk about that wolf-yanking stunt you pulled.'

Her niece hid her face in Lacey's chest and mumbled, 'A good or bad talk?'

'Both.'

Lacey felt the nudge of Addison's nod. 'It was Fender's fault, then,' she said.

A noise of utter surprise pulled Lacey's attention to the newly opened north atrium door. Even more people were coming in – a whole host of them, none of whom Lacey recognised.

This is turning into a real party.

'Albus!' Addison shouted in delight, and pulled out of Lacey's embrace to go to him. She didn't make it more than two steps before Pilgrim clamped a hand on her shoulder and stopped her.

He was staring towards the newcomers. Not at the long-haired man who had uttered the sound of surprise, but at the teenage boy standing at his side. He wasn't very old, but something about his boyish mop of hair and soft brown eyes reminded Lacey of Jay.

'Hello, Pilgrim,' he said quietly, in such a lovely-accented voice that Lacey was instantly charmed by it. The boy smiled a slow smile of recognition.

And Pilgrim lifted his gun and shot the boy dead-centre in the chest.

CHAPTER 17

Pilgrim

Pilgrim immediately squeezed off a second shot, needing to be sure, watching it slam Hari backwards, knocking him off his feet.

'Get away from him, Albus!' Pilgrim yelled, advancing in long strides, his gun trained on the downed Hari.

'Albus, *back away*.' It felt so strange to address the man after so many years. So strange to *see* him. He didn't look any different: his hair was a little longer, maybe, but that was all.

And he's missing some fingers, Voice said, dazed. *Pilgrim, what are you* doing?

But Pilgrim's attention was already elsewhere, his gaze dropping to his old friend's hands, saddened beyond measure by what he saw. Albus had had so much taken from him, and now Pilgrim was going to take more.

Albus hadn't moved. He stood frozen in place, staring in shock at the boy, who was bleeding out at his feet. Reaching him, Pilgrim took hold of his friend's hand, pulling him away, not thinking twice about gripping on, not even when he felt the missing digits.

'Watch out!' Abernathy yelled.

Pilgrim dodged the punch, the big black man's fist sailing over his head as Pilgrim stumbled back. He dropped Albus's hand, but already the big man was staggering and blinking, looking around as if not knowing how he'd got there.

'What the . . . ?'

Pilgrim had no time to deal with him because a pretty blonde-haired woman, probably around Albus's age, was swinging a deadly-looking rifle round to bear on him.

'Stop,' Pilgrim told her.

She didn't stop. Her movements were jerky and unco-ordinated and her mouth lifted into the ugliest slash of a smile Pilgrim had ever seen, one he knew this woman had never worn before today.

He shot her in the throat. She gurgled, blood spurting from her mouth, but there was no reaction to what must have been agonising pain – her eyes were dull and emotionless. Despite the mortal wound, her rifle continued to rise and Pilgrim shot her twice more – once in the shoulder and once in the heart. She fell backwards, crumpling on to her back, and didn't get back up.

Albus was moaning, a dreadful, grief-stricken sound that Pilgrim wished he could block out and never, ever hear again.

'Pilgrim, what are you *doing*?' And he felt Lacey clutch at the back of his arm.

'Get away!' he screamed at her. 'Get out of here!'

He's in here, Lacey! he heard Voice shout at her. *The Flitting Man's in here!*

She couldn't be present for this. She couldn't. This was the price he had to pay, wasn't it? The consequences that Matilde had mentioned. To save Lacey, to save Addison, he had unmasked the Flitting Man. They had seen each other, had looked in each other's eyes and, in that moment, they had known each other as perfectly as two souls could. Pilgrim had recognised it in the boy's smile. Hari had known what was coming. The boy was dead, but the Flitting Man was not. Not yet.

Consequences, consequences, consequences.

'GET OUT!' Pilgrim roared, swinging an arm at Lacey, at Addison, too, as she cowered close to her aunt.

'Abernathy, take them!' It was the last thing he would ever ask her to do, and she seemed to know it. Tyler was there with her, and her eyes met his as she gathered Lacey close, drawing her away. Abernathy lifted Addison into her arms. And whether Lacey was in too much shock to fight it, she let herself and her niece be dragged away.

Pilgrim was lifted bodily into the air and slammed down to the ground. He grunted as his clavicle snapped and his head bounced off stonework. He rolled dizzily on to his back as the big black man reached down for him and dragged him up again, as easily as if Pilgrim were a child. He held Pilgrim aloft, boots dangling a full foot off the floor, and there was that slow, knowing smile. Oh, how he hated this fucker.

'I have killed you,' the black man whispered, and the accent was fainter, a mere trace of the boy's lilt, but it remained. 'I have crushed you under my boot-heel a thousand times and smiled as you died. *Worm*,' he breathed, bulbous eyes unblinking. '*Cockroach*.'

The hands at Pilgrim's throat tightened on each word.

'*Maggot. Dog*.'

The blood thickened in his temples. His eyesight dimmed. He struck at his assailant with his one good hand, and that was like a child hitting an adult, too. It had no effect.

Something jolted them in place and Pilgrim heard a grunting, urgent shout, and rolled his eyes into focus.

Albus hung off the black man's back. The big guy now held the weight of two full-grown men and didn't falter at all. Albus couldn't speak but Pilgrim heard the desperate plea in his yell, could read the tormented anguish written across his old friend's face. And the black man simply reached one large hand back, grabbed Albus by his mane of hair, ripped him off and flung him aside. Twenty feet away, Albus smashed through the bandstand's wooden balustrades and crashed on to its platform.

Choking out a growl, Pilgrim writhed at the end of his attacker's one-handed grip, frantically twisting to free himself. The toe of his right boot scraped across the ground and a thrill rushed through his body – *almost!* – and two hands re-clamped his throat and *squeezed*.

No!

Hazily, Pilgrim thought: Voice. Help me.

And as if waiting on the sidelines for this exact opening, Voice bulldozed his way in. Pilgrim's left hand jerked into life and his arm came up, his broken clavicle screaming its protest as he jammed his thumb knuckle-deep into one bulging eye. There was no gradual increase in pressure, no leeway given for the black man to surrender – only a straight-through thrust that ruptured the eyeball and rained hot liquid down the back of Pilgrim's hand. The big man didn't make a peep.

Oxygen-deprived, feet kicking spasmodically, Pilgrim's eyelids fluttered. His thumb hooked itself in the ruined eye-socket and yanked so hard to the left that the black man's head snapped halfway round his neck. The man's grip loosened from around Pilgrim's throat and his arms gave out. Pilgrim dropped. His feet hit the floor and his knees folded under him.

But the black man's clawed fingers didn't fully let go of their grasp as Pilgrim's weight pulled the man down with him. Groggily, Pilgrim raised himself up, hooked his working right arm under the big man's chin and yanked upward sharply. The man's upper vertebrae separated from the rest of his spine with an audible *crack*.

Pilgrim slumped back on his knees, gulping great lungfuls of air. His throat felt swollen shut. He touched it gingerly.

'Thanks,' he croaked to Voice.

You're welcome, compadr—

The slim, sharp point of a stiletto blade slid into Pilgrim's back, precisely between two ribs, to find his heart. He felt nothing but a brief pinch of cold, as if a winter chill had passed through him. He twisted his head and found a young girl, dark blonde, a happy, burbling baby on her hip.

'I want you to watch this before you go,' she told him, and the voice lilted and sang, her tongue dipped in gold, as if it had been gilded.

Already, Voice was frantically setting to work: slowing down Pilgrim's heart rate, the blood pumping from the wound on his back becoming sluggish, the flesh painfully knitting back together tiny thread by tiny thread. Feeling faint, Pilgrim lowered himself, a slow descent made in careful degrees, until he lay curled up on his side.

It's okay, Pilgrim. I got this. I can fix it. There was a tremble in Voice's delivery, though, that made Pilgrim wonder. *Just hold on.*

The world was now tilted at a ninety-degree angle and he watched the young girl with the baby walk downwind from him and towards the dancing ballerina in her fountain, and he could have cried – maybe he even did – because Lacey hadn't listened to him. Always so stubborn. Always so brave. Always loving hard on those she considered her family, even when it put her in harm's way. One day it was going to get her killed.

She must have broken away from Tyler and was running back to him, eyes so angry and scared, searching for him, finding him where he lay and her entire face falling in disbelief. It was like it was all happening in slow motion, her mouth softening on a cry, Lacey not even paying attention to the girl who was innocently approaching her. He tried to call out. Couldn't.

— Voice, help her.

I can't, Pilgrim. I can't do both. I can't help you and *help her.*

— Leave me.

Don't ask me to do that, Voice moaned miserably. *Please don't.*

Pilgrim was getting weaker as Voice directed all of his body's processes to the damage caused by the knife. Pilgrim's breathing was dropping out. He could barely feel his chest rise.

I can't lose concentration. I can't . . .

— I'm asking you to save her. This one last time. Please, my friend. Save her for us.

He took them back to a snowy cabin in the mountains, and the cold, winter's evening when they had first met Matilde. There had been such conviction in the old woman that night, such belief that Pilgrim had a greater purpose than the one he'd assigned himself: to drift, to survive, to aspire to nothing more than living through one day, then the next, and the next. She believed that, by the end, he would play his part and lead all the players to where they needed to be. And wasn't he here with Lacey and Albus, with Abernathy and Tyler and all the others, in the one place the Flitting Man had come to of his own free will? Where he'd been forced to unmask himself? And if that had been true, couldn't the other things Matilde told him be true, as well?

'*A girl. One you will go back to time and again,*' she had said, and her words had crystallised in her mouth, a blue-haze frost that shimmered in the lantern's firelight. '*And you* must *go back. She is your centre – all your roads lead to her.*'

And their roads *had* led to her, hadn't they? Against all the odds, they had found Lacey time and time again.

It was all true. Every last bit of it.

And, now, they had to finish it.

Pilgrim drew in as much breath as Voice would allow: a single, painful, hitching sip, enough for two final words. Words he had used before. Words that had been used *on* him, yet he'd never fully understood their meaning until now.

'*Defend her.*'

Voice made no response, but Pilgrim felt the sudden release, felt the blood begin to pour freely from the wound in his back in heavy, pumping flows. His lungs started to stutter, searching for oxygen that was no longer there. His heart missed a beat, then two. And he heard Voice, distant but clear, calling to

Lacey, warning her, pouring strength into his own final words.

It was enough. It had to be enough. Because nothing remained but the creeping cold and the far-away murmurs of Voice speaking, and that was okay. In fact, it was just fine.

Together, as they had done all things for as long as Pilgrim could remember, he and Voice closed their eyes and, as one, they died.

CHAPTER 18

Lacey

As the cracking retort of the second gunshot ricocheted and the teen boy was being struck by bullets, Lacey's mind kicked into high gear, any shock she felt overridden by the stark, terrifying need to protect those she loved.

Hari, Voice said, breathless with awe. *He just shot Hari.*

And Hari was the Flitting Man. Did that mean Pilgrim had killed *him*, too? Would it really be that easy? Somehow, Lacey didn't think so.

She registered multiple things in quick succession: Pilgrim halting her niece in her tracks as Addison called out Albus's name; Pilgrim's gun-arm remaining outstretched as he strode past, eliminating the distance between him and the threat in Albus's group; a young, skinny girl, a few years younger than Lacey, whirling away from the three adults beside her, her hand protectively cradling the head of the child she was carrying; Addison, already recovered from her stall, making as if to follow after Pilgrim, her second shout drowned out by Pilgrim's thundered roar for Albus to move away from the fallen boy; Jay's descriptions of Bruno and Gwen matching the tall, muscled black man and the white lady with light-blonde hair who were at Albus's side, their alarmed shouts mingling with everybody else's; and how woefully, upsettingly lacking in arms Lacey was for this situation, having only her flip knife to hand.

Addison didn't make it to her third step before Lacey snatched a handful of her niece's shirt and yanked her back, uncaring as the girl squawked and flailed about, battering into Lacey's legs as she went down. Lacey didn't quit pulling until Addison was dragged behind her and dumped on the floor.

'Stay there,' she snapped at her.

'Watch out!' Abernathy yelled, and Lacey turned in time to see Pilgrim narrowly duck Bruno's brutal roundhouse punch. Her stomach dropped completely out from under her as Gwen swung her rifle round, slotting a pretty walnut stock against her shoulder.

'Stop,' Pilgrim ordered.

Stop, Lacey, Voice said, in a shockingly similar tone, and it cut through the chaos for one split second – one brief moment when everything seemed to hang still, hovering in anticipation: the poised, electrified energy that preceded the first thundering crash of a lightning storm.

Everything became a mish-mash of sounds and images, forever muddled in Lacey's brain. The fireworks of gunshots, the spilled blood, the beautiful strands of Gwen's hair dipped red with gore. Pilgrim screaming down into Lacey's face, his expression one that Lacey never dreamed she'd see: a sheer, unadulterated fear. Voice's yells for Lacey to get away, to run, the Flitting Man was coming, that he hadn't died with Pilgrim's first bullets. The rough beam of Pilgrim's arm connecting with Lacey's chest, sweeping her back as if she were made of nothing but paper and twine.

Another arm found her – this one slimmer, weaker – wrapping Lacey's waist and pulling her away.

She caught up with herself, then, aligned all the madness into a neat little line, sequencing it with the deaths and the horrors she'd seen, and she almost twisted her head off, craning to see where Addison was. But she was there. Unharmed. Abernathy was picking her up, hefting the girl's weight as if she'd done it every day of her life. She carried her at a dead run across the expanse of the town square, Addison clinging to her like a spider monkey to its mom, heading for where Riko and Lev were waving them to the cover of a curving partitioned wall. Presumably that way led deeper into another wing of the facility.

Though not as fast, Tyler hustled Lacey along, too – an impressive feat for a woman her size, and with her arm strapped to her chest, to boot. But Lacey's gaze snagged on something half-buried beneath a heaped mound of ash and charcoaled bones. It made her slow down.

Her fallen hunting rifle.

This couldn't be the spot where the weapon had been torn from her grip. Indeed, nearly all of the wolves' carcasses were a little ways east of them. Yet, here her rifle lay. Waiting for her.

'No, no.' Tyler panted, tugging at Lacey to get her moving again. 'Keep going.'

'I can't,' Lacey said, staring, mesmerised by the long, elegant sweep of the gun's barrel and its not so pretty laminated wood stock (it was now smeared with the greasy remains of whoever had once lived here).

Lacey, don't do this. Voice was using his stern, grown-up voice, laying down the law, but Lacey ignored him. He couldn't stop her.

'Please,' Tyler pleaded. 'Come with me.' A firmer nudge from the arm around Lacey's waist. 'He'd want you to come with me.'

Lacey patted over the tops of her thighs, smoothed down her rear pockets, shoved her hands deep into her jacket pockets, riffling hurriedly inside as she checked over her shoulder. She couldn't see Pilgrim from here, he was hidden behind the large dried-up fountain, the stature of the ballerina mocking them in her joyous pirouette. It made it much worse not knowing what was happening to him. She could hear the scuffles, the grunts of effort and pain, and the meaty thuds of strikes, but she didn't know who was hurting who.

In her left jacket pocket, she found it.

A single, solitary brass cartridge.

'Lacey, *please* . . .' Tyler tried one last time.

You can't shoot everyone with one bullet, Lacey.

She didn't need to shoot everyone.

The next thing she knew she had the rifle in her hands. The bolt caught slightly as she worked the mechanism, dented teeth-marks marring the dirty metal. But the cartridge loaded into the breech nice and smooth, despite her shaking fingers. She chambered the round, locking it in tight.

She shrugged free of Tyler – the woman had been trying to hook and hold on to her while Lacey was loading the gun – a difficult task when you had no hands to grip with.

'I'm going back,' Lacey told her. 'He's my family. I'm not leaving him again.'

Abernathy was impatiently waiting for them, both arms clamped around Addison's shoulders, preventing the girl from breaking free and running back.

'Get them out of here, Abernathy!' Lacey yelled at her. 'I mean it! *Go!*'

She left Tyler standing there and ignored Abernathy's and Addison's shouts. She ran on legs made of jelly, her breaths coming too fast, her mouth as dry as an old boot. She headed for the fountain, dashing across a stretch of dirty, fake grass, skirting around the fountain's southern edge. Clearing it, she made it to the cobbled pathway leading north to the main atrium doors and was thankful to have solid ground underfoot.

She spotted Bruno first. He was bigger, more noticeable, his body slumped unnaturally at the edge of the path. Lacey's eyes skimmed over him – she didn't care about cataloguing his injuries or determining how he'd died. Six feet from him, Pilgrim lay curled on his side. Lacey's steps faltered, slowed. Her rifle nearly slipped from her numb fingers.

The floodlights hid nothing.

Pilgrim looked as though a giant had thrown him down in a tantrum. His left arm lay at a grotesque angle from his shoulder. Blood had darkened his hair to the blackest of blacks, his cheek and neck stained with it. Worse was all the blood that was pooling beneath him.

She tried to hold back a cry of dismay and couldn't.

So much blood, Voice murmured.

'His Voice can mend it. He's done it before. *You've* done it before.'

Maybe, he said doubtfully.

A girl stepped on to the cobblestones with her, shoes *click*ing. Lacey hadn't seen where she'd come from. It was the same young girl who'd ducked away when Pilgrim had started shooting. She still held on to the small child: he was propped on her hip. It couldn't have been a comfortable perch for him – the girl didn't have an ounce of flesh on her. She was all acute angles and knobbly bones.

The baby's face was flushed, his eyes bright, as if he'd been crying.

'Are you hurt?' Lacey asked her.

The girl shook her head.

Don't get near her, Lacey! Voice yelled in a frantic rush. *Voice says it's him! She's the Flitting Man!*

Terror burst over Lacey like a rainstorm, drenching her in its icy downpour. Her heart accelerated so fast her entire body *hummed*. Her rifle shot up and the girl swung the baby off her hip and up in front of her, blocking Lacey's shot. If Lacey had been having trouble believing such an innocent-looking girl could be something other than what she appeared, this use of a small infant as a human shield laid all of Lacey's doubts to rest.

Lacey, take the shot! Voice was shrill in her ear. *Take the shot! Don't let him escape!*

She tucked her cheek down, aiming along the sights, the gun trembling along the entire length of the barrel. 'Put the baby down,' Lacey ordered, and she hated that her words trembled as much as her rifle.

The girl tilted a quick peek around the baby's head and began sidestepping, circling Lacey where she stood.

Do it! Voice's cry rang in her ears.

I can't! I can't! How can I shoot when there's a *baby* in the way?

The girl was speeding up, not looking where she was going, feet seemingly knowing precisely where to place themselves.

'You don't want to hurt him,' the Flitting Man said in the girl's voice, tone pleasant, friendly even. There was a slight accent, a sing-song quality to the syllables that Lacey instantly disliked. 'His name is Jasper. He's a good boy. Say hello, Jasper.' The girl gave the baby a small jiggle. The sudden movement made the baby gasp, his lower lip jibbing out.

A sudden calmness opened in Lacey's chest, like a break in the storm clouds and a beautiful streak of sunlight cresting into view. She breathed easily, her lungs unlocking and her inhales deepening. Tingles rushed across the back of her neck and shoulders. Her pulse levelled out, heart kicking hard, once, twice, and then settling. The tremble in her hands stilled.

Wait, Voice whispered.

The girl's feet passed from cobblestones to grass and the slightest of dips in gradient had the baby bob slightly in her grip. It wasn't enough. But the noise that came from their right, a soft, mournful call, all sound and no words, pulled the girl's attention that way. The tiniest of spaces appeared above Jasper's right shoulder and under the curve of his ear. It was the size of a dollar coin.

Lacey's heartbeat stopped, as did her breathing. Her body

was filled to the brim with immoveable ballast, heavy and still. She squeezed the trigger in one smooth, progressive pull, exactly how her grammy had taught her, and the rifle kicked, but the muzzle did not move. Lacey was immoveable.

The shot zipped through Jasper's baby-fine curls, the passage of it blowing his hair in a puff of wind – a friendly ghost blowing him a kiss. The bullet hit just behind the girl's ear, splintering bone, sending fragments into her brain. The metal slug continued its journey through soft tissue until it hit the curving cranium on the other side and exited the head at an angle that lodged the bullet into the top of the shoulder, where it stayed. The girl was dead before Jasper dropped from her hold, fell the five feet to the ground and bumped down in the grass.

Lacey thought the baby would bawl and howl his little heart out, the shock of the fall, never mind the hard knock to his legs and butt, enough to make even the most stalwart child wail. But Jasper didn't utter a sound. He flipped over on to his belly and looked the dead girl in the face. She lay on her back, one arm flung above her head, the other folded neatly over her body. She could have been peacefully sleeping, if you didn't look too closely.

Lacey bent over, making sure she would safely miss the cobblestones, and vomited up the contents of her stomach. The acidic gush lit lighter fuel up her throat, the wrenching heaves cramped her abdominals, but she welcomed the discomfort. Tears streamed down her face as she spat, and spat again, and she welcomed them, too. She dropped the rifle beside her vomit and scrubbed her hands on her pants. The greasy ash wouldn't come off. She wiped her face on her sleeve.

When she looked up, Albus was carefully walking over the grass, his left leg held stiff and one of his stumped hands cupped around his ribs. Lacey didn't stare. Didn't think it would be polite.

'Is he gone?' she asked, and didn't know who she was addressing: Voice or Albus.

I don't know. Voice isn't answering me any more.

Albus didn't respond. His nose was swollen and bloodied, and both his eyes were already starting to bruise. He'd stopped next to the baby, the curtains of his long, flowing hair falling to obscure his face as he looked down at the toddler. He didn't attempt to pick Jasper up.

'I'm sorry,' Lacey mumbled, and stumbled past them.

She wanted to run, but her legs wouldn't obey. With ten feet left to go, she dropped to all fours and crawled the rest of the way. By five feet, she knew he was dead.

Pilgrim didn't move as Lacey reached for his hand and drew it into her lap. She clasped it between both of hers. It was limp and warm.

This isn't like last time, Lacey, her Voice said gently. *He's not coming back from this.*

'I know.'

Pilgrim hadn't died easy. But, then, were there any easy ways left to die? She didn't think so.

Maybe that can change now.

She knew Voice said it to be hopeful, but she couldn't muster the energy to care. She wondered about how she should be feeling. The only things filtering through were the aches and pains of her many, many knocks and grazes. She wished she had a drink of water. Her mouth tasted foul. Did that count as a feeling? While thinking about it, she reached out her free hand and smoothed a lock of Pilgrim's hair from his brow.

She felt him at her back, then, and twisted round to look up.

Albus was staring at Pilgrim. The burble of the baby sounded from beyond him, where he'd left him on the grass, but Albus didn't react. Lacey didn't say anything about it, either. As Albus gazed at Pilgrim, she wanted to say his expression was sad or grief-stricken but, in reality, his face was unreadable. His eyes might have seemed wounded, but it was just as likely an effect caused by the bruising.

'Addison's been looking for you. Pilgrim, too.'

Albus glanced at her, then went back to gazing at Pilgrim. She thought that maybe he nodded, but more likely it was a slight rocking of his body, a natural sway that gave the illusion of him bobbing his head. Lacey was aware he couldn't talk.

She stilled her thumbs after noticing she'd been tracing the calluses on Pilgrim's palm. 'I met your sister once,' she told Albus. 'You know, right before she . . .' She bit her lip and squeezed her eyes shut, kicking herself. What the fuck was wrong with her? Why had she brought that up? 'I'm sorry,' she whispered, angry with herself.

Opening her eyes, she watched a tear spill from Albus's eye and run down his cheek. He made no sound, and no more tears followed, but Lacey noticed the direction of his gaze briefly fall to where the St Christopher rested beneath her shirt collar. With a small shake of his head – and finished with whatever contemplation he'd been in the middle of – Albus limped his stiff-legged way past her.

Lacey gently, and with great care, laid Pilgrim's hand back down and got up.

'You're leaving?' she called after him, pulling Albus up short.

He painfully hobbled in a half-circle. Regarded her. Then nodded once. Yes, he was leaving.

'Didn't you hear me just now? Addison's been looking for you. Don't you want to see her?'

Something broke in him, then, and his mouth trembled. Albus dropped his chin down and shook his head. No, he didn't want to see her.

'All right,' Lacey said, softly. 'But will you come back? When you're ready? She'll be so happy to see you. I would, too. I never got chance to thank you for helping her. She means the absolute world to me.'

Albus looked at her, then. Really looked at her for the first time, and the man wasn't unreadable or unresponsive. He was barely holding it together, his seams ripping apart, stitch by agonising stitch. He nodded. Yes, he would come back. Some day. The second nod he gave her was one of farewell, and Lacey returned it.

'Bye, Albus,' she whispered, and watched him make his slow, painful, broken way across what remained of Elysian Fields, leaving everyone he knew behind.

Chapter 19

Addison

Addison had to hold herself back from bounding up the slope, choosing instead to walk beside Matilde's dog. Every once in a while, she'd give its head a rub, right between the silky ears, steadfastly not peeking up at the lines and crinkles on Matilde's face. Addison had never seen so many. It was as though someone had taken her skin, scrunched it up like a piece of paper, and then made a poor attempt at smoothing it out before handing it back over.

She's really old, Fender whispered, a hint of reverence in the words.

Addison felt older than an old, buried bone that had recently been dug up. It was so good to be out in the fresh air. Breathing it in, feeling the gentle breeze on her skin, the warmth of the setting sun. The rains and smudge-grey skies of earlier were gone. The sky was as clear as clear could be.

'Huh,' Addison muttered, squinting upwards. The busy clouds of swooping birds had lost their frenetic, destructive dives and loops. Now, they seemed to wheel and float in joyous blooms of life, high and safe from harm. A handful had broken away to track Addison and Matilde as they steadily trudged on, cawing cheerfully overhead.

The only thing that broke the tranquillity was the crying of the baby. Lacey trailed a dozen steps behind them, jiggling the baby, talking to the baby, patting the baby's back. Doing everything in her power to stop the tears. Addison had offered to carry Jasper – she reckoned she could get him to giggle if she tried hard enough – but Lacey had twisted away as soon as Addison had reached for him, snapping out a firm, uncompromising 'No.'

The old lady didn't seem out of breath as she joined Addison and the dog at the top of the hill and, oh my, the climb had been worth it. The view was *awesome*. The wind turbines didn't seem so scary in the early-evening light, either. The glint of sunshine made them glow a soft, burnished yellow. The languid spinning blades reflected the sun back to her on every rotation and even the oppressive, crowding trees she'd ran through yesterday were rich in colours of browns, russets and golds. If Addison looked real hard, down between the humps and bumps of the land, following the black ribbon of the pathway to one particular wind turbine, she thought she could see a black-haired Riko and a much shorter Lev (with Mr Rocky strapped to their chest), emerging from the concrete bunker beneath number forty-three; a raggedy line of littlies followed them out. They were all so teeny and distant. Addison waved to them anyway, even though she was too far away for them to see.

Matilde had insisted that Riko and Lev alone lead them out of Elysian Fields via the secret service tunnel. She hadn't wanted to cross paths with anyone. Addison secretly hoped that they might bump into Albus on the way, but he'd vanished along with the storm.

At the thought of him, an invisible hand pressed down on the back of Addison's head, her chin dipping down. The sudden sadness weighed so heavily she felt the presence of it all around, inside and out, as if it lived in the world now and she was feeding it with every breath she took and with each beat her heart made.

Beside her, the dog leaned warm and firm against her hip. Addison patted its head in thanks.

'I think this is the perfect spot.'

Addison smiled at Matilde. Or, at least, tried to smile. Her face felt wrong, as if it had forgotten the mechanics of it.

'You mustn't be sad, my darling,' Matilde told her, but her own eyes held a sheen of sadness, too. 'You have much to do. The children here will be wonderful new friends for you. You'll see.'

'But what about Albus?' Addison said quietly. 'He left without any of his friends.'

The dog shifted out from under Addison's petting and padded over to Matilde, pressing in close. The old lady's swollen-knuckled fingers absently stroked along the animal's sleek neck, seeming to gain strength from the dog's presence.

'For now, Albus's heart is pierced and full of pain. Understandably so. He must pull out such a large, tender thorn, yes? Let himself heal. But it will take time. Quite some time, I fear. In the meanwhile, you and your friends will be here. The red skies are passing, and more and more people will be drawn to you and this place. Sunny and Jacob will go to Memphis and bring back friends who understand what this world needs to be now. If we can get Tyler and Tommy to leave Jay's side for more than a minute, maybe she can be convinced to help, too.'

Addison was still getting caught up on all the new faces and names. After such a long period of sneaking and silence, it would take some time for Fender to adjust to how noisy everything had become. Fender had told Addison that the voice inside Matilde was especially loud. Louder than any they had ever come across. So loud it was like listening to a stadium full of people all speaking as one.

With so much communication shooting back and forth, Fender hadn't been able to keep up, or even relay half of it, but already there had been news of a convoy of vehicles arriving at

Trinity Hills. Riko and Lev had whooped with joy at hearing that Vanessa Mendoza was leading these newcomers. Taking a slower route east than Lacey and Pilgrim, Vanessa Mendoza had made it to Elysian Fields just in time to administer emergency medical aid to those who needed it – Jay being the first in line. Addison had whooped her own cry of joy when Fender had whittled down all the flying bits of incoming information to learn that Jay was expected to make a full recovery. He would need to have the bullet removed from his side, and Tyler had already been directed to the medical bays where special ant-bee-oh-ticks pills were stored, but he would be A-OK.

Tyler's long-term prognosis, on the other hand, was less certain, according to Tommy (who'd spoken to Fender after a halting, awkward introduction). The damage caused to the muscle structure and nerves of Tyler's hand was extensive. Tommy was unsure if they would ever regain the full use of it.

Matilde was watching her.

Addison didn't know how long for.

'You are not alone any more, Addison. Not in grief or sorrow, not in times of happiness and celebration. You will all have each other, and no one will ever be forgotten.'

Addison felt tears burn at the backs of her eyes because she had spent so much of her life alone, save for Fender and Chief, that the ache of it had sunk so deep she had feared it would never fully go away. Not even when Lacey and Alex had found her.

'You promise?' she whispered.

'I promise, my darling. We have always lived our lives behind one set of eyes, haven't we? But now you will see through many, and any pain or joy you feel will be shared.'

Addison let the words soak in. Maybe she would even ask Lacey to write them down for her later. She glanced over at her aunt. Lacey had stayed a few yards back with Jasper, as if wanting to give Addison and Matilde space to talk. Since Addison had found her aunt standing over a forever-sleeping Pilgrim, Lacey hadn't spoken much. She *had* embraced Addison tightly, though, which was sometimes the only communication you needed. Even Abernathy had gotten a big hug from Lacey when the taller woman had turned away from Pilgrim, roughly wiping at her eyes in an attempt to hide her crying.

Matilde was no longer looking at Addison; she was tilting her head back to the sky, contemplating its blue depths. 'You know, long ago, as the very first thoughts sprang into being, and the human mind was flowering in its youth, we were given a similar opportunity. To have a voice who heard us and for us to hear a voice. A universal understanding, if you will. One that could be experienced, by all people, together. But the fear of the unknown, and a lack of belief in ourselves, made us think we did not need to be anything more than we already were. No doubt a smattering of arrogance played its part, too. And so we were left alone. Singular. I think that's a sad, lonely way to live, don't you?'

Addison gave a solemn nod. Being sad and lonely was the worst.

Lacey approached with the baby. Jasper had finally stopped his tears, but his cheeks were mottled red from all the effort, and his baby blues swam with dampness.

'Here, pass him to me,' Matilde said. She took the baby from Lacey and held him securely in the crook of one arm, patting his back with her free hand. 'We are going to be quite fine together, aren't we, little man?'

The baby stared sombrely up at her.

'Take Hoyt down with you when you go, please. He can't go where I am going.' The dog – a *boy* dog – looked up at his name, breaking into a huge yawn that showed off his chewing teeth. He huffed and energetically shook his head. Addison found it funny he was called the same as Pilgrim's old name. The dog was so well behaved Addison was beginning to suspect he'd forgotten how to bark. She supposed that made him an ideal pet. Lacey would let her keep him, for sure.

'OK, off with you both. I shall see you in another time, in another life.'

'You sure you don't wanna stay?' Addison asked, frowning up at the old lady. Now that they were all together: Riko, Lev and the littlies, Vanessa Mendoza, Tyler, Jay and Sunny, Lacey and Abernathy, and someday, hopefully, Albus, then it made sense that Matilde should stay with them, too.

'Thank you, but it is past time I leave. *Du biste meine Sonnenblume, ja*?' She tweaked Addison's nose.

Addison giggled and scrubbed the tickle away.

'Now, off with you. Shoo.' Matilde flapped a hand at her and Addison backed up, grinning. The old lady met Lacey's eyes, and some kind of understanding passed between the two. Lacey nodded to her and passed over a small cloth-covered bundle no bigger than a hardback book.

What was *that* about? Addison wondered, eyeing the package as Matilde magicked it away into a jacket pocket.

Grown-up stuff, Fender replied.

On the way back down the hill, Addison took hold of Lacey's hand. Her aunt's fingers were cold but warmed up the longer Addison held them. Their pace remained unhurried. The dog stayed close by their sides. Addison looked over her shoulder a time or two, but already Matilde and Jasper were lost to the trees.

'What did she want with Pilgrim's gun?' Addison asked, swinging their arms a bit as they walked.

Lacey didn't reply straight away, and Addison waited patiently for her aunt to put her words into a nice, neat order. Maybe she hadn't thought Addison would have guessed what was hidden under the cloth.

'A souvenir, I think,' Lacey said at last. 'She and Pilgrim were old friends, you know. It's nice to have keepsakes sometimes.'

'Like Ruby's necklace?' Addison asked.

'Exactly like Ruby's necklace,' Lacey said softly, and smiled down at her. It was a crack of a smile, small and broken, but it was one hundred per cent real, the warm fondness of it prompting Addison to squeeze Lacey's hand good and hard.

Before their trek up the hill, Lacey had returned Ruby's necklace to Addison, and now Addison touched delicate fingers to the St Christopher hanging at her throat, letting her fingertips trace the engraving on the medallion.

'Albus gave this to her, you know,' Addison told her.

'He did?'

'Yep.'

'You know what the engraving on it is?' Lacey asked, and Addison shook her head. She did know, she just wanted her aunt to explain it to her.

'It's of a man called Christopher. He crossed the most treacherous of waters, carrying those he loved upon his back, so he could lead them to a safer place. He protects people. That was his job.'

They were closer to the wind farm now, descending down to join the path. A few of the littlies had spotted them. A small girl tugged on Mr Rocky's foot, and Lev turned to look to where she was pointing. Addison's friend broke out in a huge smile upon seeing her and waved enthusiastically. Addison smiled, too, and lifted both hers and Lacey's clasped hands to waggle a wave in return.

Acknowledgements

This book was hard to write. And by 'hard', I mean nightmarish. Torturous. Soul-destroying. It's made me say, multiple times to multiple people, that I'm never gonna write a series again. 'It's standalone books for me from here on out!' I've cried, while stuffing my face full of comfort food. Maybe a duology at the most. If I'm feeling brave. Series are hard, man. My hat goes off to every author who can produce so many follow-on books and then write a perfect finale that satisfies in all areas. So, because this book was like giving birth to a fourteen-pound baby Pinhead from *Hellraiser*, there have been a number of people who've helped me along the way . . .

Camilla Bolton for being such a lovely person and an agent who's always on the other end of a phone or email if I've needed her. Frankie Edwards at Headline for being so amazingly patient and generous with her time while I've been writing and rewriting and editing and sending last-minute emails with amendments and new chapters attached. I couldn't have done this without you two, so a massive, heartfelt thank you to you both.

My gratitude also goes to everyone behind the scenes at Darley Anderson Literary Agency and at Headline for their support and hard work over the past few years, including but not limited to: Jade, Mary, Kristina, Sheila and Rosanna, and Katie, Caitlin and Jo. And, lastly, my forever thanks to Mari Evans for taking these books and putting them on bookshelves for readers all around the world to find. It's been a dream fulfilled, and not many people can say that.

There are a lot of people, online and in real life, who have offered kind words and invaluable advice over the last two years, and to name them all would easily add another hundred words to this book. You know who you are, and I appreciate you and everything you do, so cheers.

Finally (we're on the home straight now!), thank you to you, the reader. Especially the readers who've tweeted or messaged or emailed me, or taken a few minutes out of their day to write and post a review of my books: thank you, thank you, thank you. You're the best.

Oh, and thanks to you, too, Mom. You're the absolute best, as well.

Resources

This book is a work of fiction, but suicidal thoughts and auditory hallucinations are very, very real. I spent a lot of time researching and reading in these areas, so if you'd like more information, or need help and support for yourself or a loved one, please take a look at the following websites.

Mentalhealth.org.uk
Papyrus.org.uk
Rethink.org
Mind.org.uk
Samaritans.org (their helpline is free and available 24/7
on 116 123)